Consider Me

Consider Me

BECKA MACK

**SIMON &
SCHUSTER**

London · New York · Sydney · Toronto · New Delhi

CONSIDER ME
First published in Australia in 2023 by
Simon & Schuster (Australia) Pty Limited
Suite 19A, Level 1, Building C, 450 Miller Street, Cammeray, NSW 2062
Previously published in 2022 by Streamside Literary INC.

10 9 8 7 6 5 4 3 2 1

Sydney New York London Toronto New Delhi
Visit our website at www.simonandschuster.com.au

A catalogue record for this
book is available from the
National Library of Australia

ISBN: 9781761425820

Cover design: J.L. Boudreau
Cover images: Meadow, ArtMari; Mountain, UliyaGrish;
Background, Unchalee Khun (all via Shutterstock)
Typesetting: Midland Typesetters, Australia
Printing and binding: CPI Group ((UK) Ltd, Croydon CR0 4YY

MIX
Paper | Supporting
responsible forestry
FSC® C171272

To my baby boy,

You are the exclamation mark at the end of the happiest sentence.
Thank you for being my miracle and my dream come true.

1

UNLUCKY #13

Carter

"Fuck."

Rolling onto my back, I take a moment to catch my breath, pulling the condom off my quickly deflating cock. My tongue swipes at a bead of sweat that clings to my top lip, and I plow my fingers through my hair. I'm fucking spent.

"No," Laura whines, nearly launching herself across the bed when I stand. "Don't get up yet, Carter."

I hold up the condom. That should be explanation enough, no? "Just throwing out the condom, Laura."

Her brows pinch. "Lacey."

I stifle a laugh. *Oops.* "Right. Sorry. Lacey."

Lacey the blonde bombshell who was on the cover of *Maxim* last August. I remember that much because she told me thirteen times at the bar tonight. I started counting when it left her mouth the third time.

"We could go again," she calls while I toss the condom in the bathroom trash.

I lean my forearm on the wall, taking a leak as she prattles on about spending the whole night together. We absolutely could, but I'd rather she leave. Contrary to popular belief, I value my alone time, even if it could be better spent with body parts buried in pretty girls.

Don't get me wrong; Lacey's the kind of girl you don't think twice about getting into bed with. That's why we fucked like rabbits for the last thirty minutes without pause, after I got her off in the elevator on the way up here, because Christ, I just wanted her to stop talking. I got it the first twelve times—she was on the cover of a magazine.

I thought thirteen was supposed to be a lucky number, not a bad omen.

"Can't," I finally answer, washing my hands while checking myself out in the mirror. I've got a nasty split down the center of my swollen lower lip. I got off easy tonight; the other guy didn't. "Got an early flight."

Our flight isn't until noon; I simply don't want her to stay.

Crossing my arms over my chest, I lean against the door frame and watch her snuggle beneath the blankets. Yeah, definitely not happening. "You should probably head out."

I yank my boxer briefs on and plant my hands on my hips, waiting. She's not doing a damn thing, just staring up at me with wide, blue eyes. She seems to be under the impression the larger she makes those things, the easier I'll sway. I can't even begin to tell her how wrong she is.

I scratch my scalp. Rocking back on my heels, I clap my fist into my palm a couple times, click a beat out with my tongue, and wait for her to fucking *do* something.

"Can I stay here tonight?" she finally asks.

Ah, fuck. This question again. I get it every time. Is it because she genuinely wants to stay, or because she's secretly holding out hope she'll be the one to change Carter Beckett's ways, to make him want to settle down? Sometimes I think there's a pool going with a prize for whoever the winning girl is.

Oh, wait; there is. The prize is the captain of the Vancouver Vipers' eight-figure salary.

My answer is the same every time: "I don't do sleepovers."

"But I . . ." Her chin quivers, watery gaze trembling. For fuck's sake. We met all of two hours ago; what's she crying over? "I thought we got along well. I thought maybe . . . I thought you liked me."

"I liked hanging out with you tonight," I manage. The sex was a solid seven out of ten. "We had lots of fun."

The past tense is meant to emphasize that this is where we part ways and likely never see each other ever again, but instead, it has the opposite effect.

A broad beam spreads across her face. "Maybe we could go on a date."

I try to resist the urge to clap a hand to my face. Really, I do. Instead, I drag that shit down my face in slow motion before scrubbing it back up, all while suppressing a groan. Points for that.

"We live in different countries."

"Maybe I could come to Van—"

"I don't date." Finding the pants I discarded by the hotel room door, I fish my phone out and open the Uber app. "It's not personal. I'm not looking for anything serious right now."

I honestly don't understand how this is a conversation I still need to have. I'm not shy about my personal life.

No, that's bullshit. Nobody knows shit about my personal life, except my teammates and family. But those hours in between games and passing out alone in my bed? I'm not shy about *those* hours. I'm photographed with different women every weekend. Girls know what they're getting into with me. There's even forums. Ones where they bitch about me treating them like a one-night stand all while hoping for a second ride on my stick.

But that's what they are, all of them. One-night stands. They know that going into it yet consistently leave disappointed when that's *exactly* how it plays out.

I stuff my phone away, returning my focus to the woman on my bed. She's fingering the silky red fabric in her hands, eyes on me.

"I ordered you an Uber. He'll be downstairs in five."

"But—"

"Look, Lauren—"

"*Lacey.*"

"Lacey, right, sorry. Look, Lacey, I had a great time with you tonight, but I travel way too much to maintain anything serious."

"Is that the only reason, then?" She slips her hand in mine, letting me tug her from the bed. "Because you don't have time with your hockey schedule?"

"Yes," I lie. "I don't have time." I could make time, I suppose. If I was interested. But I'm never interested.

"Oh." At the very least, it seems to appease her. Maybe it makes her feel less self-conscious. I don't know, and don't particularly care. "Well, can I get your number?"

Fuck no. "I don't share my number." *Ever.*

Before she can reply, the door to my suite beeps twice and swings open.

"You still up, Beckett? Wanna grab a quick game before—*aw, for fuck's sake.*" My teammate and best bud Emmett Brodie pauses at the edge of the room, eyes bouncing between me and Laaa . . . Lacey. He holds a hand up, shielding himself from her. I guess he thinks Cara might castrate him if he even looks at another woman. In all fairness, she might. She's one fierce chick. "This is why I room with Lockwood."

Yeah, he's been doing that for about a year now, since he met Cara. Guess he doesn't like to chance having random naked girls in his room while we're on the road. I get that. I think. I mean, I don't know a thing about relationships, serious or otherwise.

"She's leaving," I say, peeking around him to look at Lacey. She's still naked. She also doesn't seem to give a shit Emmett is standing here. In fact, her gaze drags down his body and then back up.

That's the thing with most of the girls I meet. They don't give a shit who they sleep with so long as he's on the roster and making millions. That's why they're called puck bunnies; they hop from one player to the next.

"Your ride's here," I tell her. "Might wanna get dressed, sweetheart."

"Well, I—"

"He's got a girlfriend and I'm not interested." My jaw tics with annoyance. I just wanna play *COD* with my friend, eat an entire sleeve of Oreos, and pass out face-first in my pillow. Is that too much to ask?

Finally, Lacey tugs her dress over her head, red silk draping perfectly over her hips. Fuck, she's hot. I may not remember her name when she walks out this door, but I will remember that.

"Can I give you my number? That way you can call next time you're in town, or if you change your mind and want me to fly—"

"Sure." I gesture to the pad of hotel paper and pen sitting on the bedside table. "Write it down."

Emmett's eyes widen, the corner of his mouth curving as he moves past me, into the bathroom.

Lacey follows me to the door, looking up at me like a lost puppy. She can pout all she wants; I'm not taking her home with me.

"Well, thanks . . . for tonight. Hopefully I'll see you again."

Her smile is so bright I almost feel bad. But then she leans in to kiss me on the lips and I turn my head at the last moment. She gets my jaw.

"Bye, Lauren." The door slams, and I flip the lock.

"*Lacey!*" she yells from the hallway.

Emmett strolls in, shaking with laughter. "You're an asshole, Carter."

I flop down on the couch while he queues up the Xbox. "They don't get it. I'm not looking for a relationship." I snag the half-empty box of Oreos off the coffee table and twist one apart, licking the icing. "It's a one-night stand, not a marriage proposal."

"So you're shitting on their hopes and dreams at a happy life with a man who loves them?"

Hopes and dreams? What the fuck? "Cara's turning you into a marshmallow. They can hope and dream all they want, just not with me."

"Because you'll never settle down?"

I shrug. "I dunno. Maybe, maybe not. Not any time soon."

He chuckles, tossing a controller into my lap. "One day, some girl is gonna walk into your life and flip your whole world upside down and you're not gonna know what the fuck to do with yourself except drop to your knees and beg her to never leave."

My head bobs as I throw another cookie in my mouth. "And that'll be the day I settle down."

2

BED > SEX

Carter

THE DOWNSIDE OF INTERNATIONAL TRAVEL is the brutal shock to your system when you return home to British Columbia in the middle of December after coasting through Florida and North Carolina for a couple of days.

We're bordering on the edge of a deep freeze, and despite it being highly unusual for the west coast, it's also technically not even winter yet. I live in North Vancouver where it tends to be *just slightly* more reminiscent of a typical Canadian winter, but nothing like this. It feels like a bad omen, but I typically choose to ignore obvious signs.

Still, it's cold as balls, I'm recovering from a hangover, I spent five and a half hours on a plane today playing euchre with my teammates, and I lost every goddamn game except one. Today's one of those rare Saturdays where hockey doesn't exist for our team, and instead of spending it at home in my sweats while I deep dive into a Disney marathon and an XL pizza, I'm walking through a blustery night, heading to a surprise birthday party.

"I'm fucking pooched, man." I stuff my hands into the pockets of my wool coat and tug my scarf up to my chin with my teeth.

"Fuckin' same," Garrett Andersen, my right-winger drawls, east coast twang slipping in like it does when he's tired or drunk. Right now, it's the former. "Nearly bailed but thought better of it. I like my balls right where they are, thank you very much."

His worry isn't lost on me. The birthday girl has threatened to castrate us on several occasions for much tamer offenses. On her bad side is the last place I want to be on Cara's twenty-fifth birthday. She's scary enough as it is, and now we've missed that part where you jump out and yell *"Surprise!"* I'm banking on her already being three drinks deep and happy enough with the glittery pink gift bag hanging off my forearm to forget she's mad at us.

"I'm bailing early," I tell him.

He rolls his eyes. "Yeah, okay."

"What? I am. I miss my bed."

"Uh-huh."

"I can keep it in my pants for one night."

He jogs across the street, dashing ahead toward the bar where he sneaks in ahead of me. "Doubt it!"

The bar looks as I expected it to: a fuckton pink and a shitload packed. I usually thrive on chaos, but tonight I just want to post up in the corner with my teammates and sip a cold beer or two.

In addition to the pink, there's a whole lot of gold and floral. Thank fuck for Cara's best friend, because we were nearly on décor duty until Emmett told us she had it handled. I haven't met her, but she's gotta be brave to willingly take on party décor when the birthday girl runs her own event planning business. Disappointing Cara is never something I want to be responsible for; see the afore-mentioned castrating.

"Gare-Bear! Carter!" A body hurls itself into my arms, knocking the air from my lungs as long limbs wrap around me.

"Happy birthday, Care," I singsong as the birthday girl slithers down my body before crushing Garrett in a hug.

Cara eyes the little pink bag in my hands, bouncing on her toes in her sky-high heels. "Oooh, gimme-gimme!"

"Ah-ah," I tsk, holding the bag away from her. "Where are your manners?"

Her blue eyes roll as she pops a hip. "Gimme my fucking present, *please*."

I snort a laugh as she tears it from my hands, wasting no time tearing the bag apart. Opening the small velvet box inside, she squeals. She pulls out the platinum chain, the diamond-encrusted letter *C* hanging from it, and shakes it in my face. "Put it on, put it on!"

I watch her twirl, sweeping her silky waist-length golden locks over her shoulder, my eyes following the curve of her spine down to her round ass. *Backless dress. Nice.*

Look, she's one of my best friend's girls. I'd never, *ever* touch her, but I'm a man with two eyes on my face. I can appreciate a good-looking woman without a desire to act on it.

Garrett lands an elbow in my rib cage, making me keel over with an *oof*. He snatches the necklace from Cara's outstretched hand, fastening it around her neck. She bounces forward with a peck on the cheek for both of us before guiding us into the bar.

"You guys are gonna have the best time. My friends are amazeballs, 'specially my bestie. I can't wait for you to meet her!" She levels me with a look that tells me to cut the shit before I've even started. "I need you on your best behavior tonight."

I throw my hands in the air. "What the fuck does that mean?"

"You know what it means. Don't try any funny business with Liv."

"Who's Liv?"

She scoffs. "Olivia! My best friend!"

"Ohhh, right, right. Her." I've somehow managed to avoid meeting her for a year, which is probably for the best and definitely at the hands of Emmett. He's mentioned something along the lines of me fucking her once and breaking her heart, which somehow ultimately winds up with Cara dumping him and it being all my fault. So I guess I'm not allowed to touch her or whatever.

Fine by me. I've got a handful of message requests on Instagram from Lacey reminding me exactly why I should take a week or two off from women. Hard to forget her name when she sends thirteen messages in a single hour, the exact amount of times she mentioned being on the cover of *Maxim*. Coincidence? I think the fuck not.

Cara leaves us with the promise of catching up later, and Garrett and I find the rest of our unruly teammates huddled in the corner. By the looks of it, they're at least halfway in the bag already. There's nothing like a Saturday off for my boys.

"How did you two manage to miss the surprise?" Adam Lockwood, our goalie, claps my hand before handing me a beer. "Lucky bastards."

"Got stuck at my mom's." Almost always a mistake. My mom's one of those people that suddenly remembers everything she forgot to say when it's time for me to leave, and it can *never* wait until later. She never stops talking, a trait she denies both owning and passing down to me. It was seven when I finally left, and I still had to go home and shower.

"Eh, Woody." I nudge Adam's arm, noticing he's missing the redhead who's normally hanging off his arm. "Where's your girl?"

He runs a hand through his dark curls, shifting uncomfortably. "Court had other plans."

"Ah." Seems it's becoming a regular thing with her. Come to think of it, I can't remember the last time I've seen her. Before I can comment further, a heavy hand claps my shoulder, sending beer sloshing over my hand.

I know it's Emmett the moment he wraps me in one of his suffocating bear hugs. And I know he's drunk the moment his slurred words fan across my cheek. "You're late."

"Sorry, dude." I give his hair a quick ruffle, mostly because it's fun to rile up such a big, burly guy. "Little drunk, big guy?"

He slaps my hand away. "You're not allowed to sleep with any of Cara's friends, FYI."

A groan rumbles in my chest as my head rolls backward. "*Yes*, father." My gaze roams the expansive bar, through the sea of people moving together on the dance floor. "Doesn't matter anyway. I'm not feeling . . . uh, I'm not . . ." The words die on the tip of my tongue when my eyes settle on *her*. "Uh, not, um . . . tonight." I gesture haphazardly with my beer, because that's about all I can manage.

"Pardon?"

I look to Emmett, then back to her. I forget what we're talking about, but nothing can be as important as the petite, drop-dead gorgeous brunette dancing with Cara.

If I'm being honest, *dancing* is entirely too loose a definition to describe the way those two are moving together. I don't know what to call it but, *fuck me*.

Something inside me sparks as I drink in this stranger, the stunning little thing tossing her dark hair over her shoulder, dragging her tongue over her top lip. She throws her arms in the air, head tipping to hear whatever Cara's whispering in her ear. I watch with rapt attention as her head lolls backward, her face erupting with laughter.

I'm entranced, fixated, obsessed. I can't look away, and when Cara's hands grip her friend's waist, slipping in slow motion down to her hips, I fight a groan, 'cause I kinda think I wanna do that.

"Don't even think about it, Carter."

I manage to drag my gaze to Emmett. "What?"

He shakes his head. "No. Not her."

Not her? Who is she? My eyes find her again as a man tugs her into his chest.

Boyfriend? Fuck.

A triumphant noise vibrates in the back of my throat when she gives him a sheepish grin, shaking her head, her mouth telling him *No thank you* before turning her back on him, and me.

And sweet, holy hell, that backside. Creamy shoulders guiding the way down a milky spine beneath the strobe of the lights above. The dip of her waist softens into the sweet curve of her wide hips, her black leather skirt hugging her like a second skin. How the fuck did she get it on? How the hell will I peel it off later? Serious questions I need immediate answers to.

Scissors, I decide. I'll cut it off her and send her a new one.

Garrett touches his fingers to my chin, closing my mouth. "Christ, Beckett. You good?"

I gesture in her direction. "*Dude.*" That's all I've got. *Aren't they seeing this?*

Garrett follows my gaze and hums appreciatively, but Emmett ruins it with an eye roll that's, somehow, audible.

"I'm serious, Carter. Cara will feed you your balls if you touch her."

"I can handle Cara."

Emmett snorts, Garrett chuckles, and Adam hammers a fist into his chest as he chokes out a cough. Nobody can handle Cara. Not even Emmett. *Cara* can't even handle Cara half the time.

"What's her name?"

Emmett's still shaking his head like a jackass. "No. Not telling you."

I watch as she sweeps her dark curls over her shoulder, pressing up on her toes to whisper in Cara's ear before strolling across the floor, hips bouncing back and forth as she goes. She hoists herself up on a bar stool and grins at the bartender. When he slides a beer over to her with a wink, she blushes, averting her eyes. Cute.

I'm oddly captivated by the way she slings one leg over the other and lifts her glass to her mouth, draining half of it in one long pull like it's her day job, and when her gaze scans the room, I'm already planning my opening line. She skims over me, then past me.

Then bounces back to me.

Crimson heat creeps up her neck and pools in her cheeks, so I flash her my signature grin, pulling my dimples all the way in, and laugh when her head whips around. She glues her gaze to the TV screen overhead and promptly begins to pretend like she hasn't seen me.

"I'll get her name myself." I clap my friend on the back and wink at my teammates. "Excuse me, boys."

"Good luck, Beckett." Emmett drowns his exasperated laugh in his drink. "I guarantee she won't buy what you're selling. You'll never land her."

Never land her? Unlikely. I'm the captain of our hockey team and one of the highest paid players in all of NHL history. I can't go to the grocery store without getting a phone number or a proposition, so I use a grocery delivery service now.

But then, I've never been one to turn down a challenge.

3

FIRST TIMES SUCK

Carter

OOOH, THE HEAT ROLLING OFF my new favorite brunette when I sidle up next to her is *sizzling*.

She can't *not* know, but she sure as shit does a good job of acting like she has no clue I'm standing here, pretending to be interested in the commercial on TV. It's one of those SPCA ads with Sarah McLachlan and a fuckton of cute puppies, and I can tell it's killing her to keep watching. One look at her has me pinning her as the type that cries when she watches this.

I sink down to the stool beside her, my thigh brushing against hers when I do that man-spread thing my sister hates. Her gaze slowly falls to the connection, and I think it's incredible she can blush more still, ruby-red heat spreading as she returns her gaze to the TV.

I don't know what game she's playing, but I'm in. I can stare at her all damn day.

I drop my elbow to the bar and my chin to my fist, intent on studying her gorgeous face longer than I've ever studied anything.

Long, thick lashes frame pretty brown eyes, warm and wide, like a cup of espresso. A faint dusting of freckles spatter across her cheekbones and down her nose, just as dainty as the rest of her, and her bowed lips, painted cherry red and turned down around the edges, showcase the perfect scowl. It's a shame; they'd look incredible wrapped around my—

"*What?*"

My brows quirk at her biting tone, the sharp slant of her eyes as she glares at me.

Her eyes fall shut, and she pushes a quiet sigh past her lips like she needs a second to get a handle on herself. "I'm sorry. I didn't mean to be rude. Is there something I can help you with?"

I lift my drink to my lips. "Nope."

She twists in my direction, shoving my knees aside with her own. "No? You came over here to stare at me?"

"Pretty much." I can't be faulted for that, can I? Plus, she can't seem to take her eyes off me either, letting them fall down my body, which my ego thoroughly enjoys. "Can I buy you a drink?"

Her eyes snap to mine, like she forgot I was a living, breathing person. "No thanks." She gulps at her beer, tongue peeking out to flick over the drop of amber liquid that clings to her top lip. "Already got one."

"Once you're done, then." Which'll be in approximately ten seconds the way she's been pounding that thing back.

"I can buy my own drinks," she snaps before tacking on a quiet, "but thank you." Her gaze drifts around the bar like I might disappear if she doesn't look at me.

"I wasn't insinuating that you couldn't. I simply meant I'd like to buy you one and sit here next to you while you drink it."

"Right, but you're already doing that." Her head tilts as she inspects me with such a healthy dose of suspicion I'm ready to admit to a crime I didn't even commit.

"How do you know Cara?"

"She's my best friend," she replies coolly, like she'd rather be anywhere else instead of sitting here talking to me.

Ah, the elusive bestie. Now I know why Emmett told me to stay away.

"Shame we haven't met before now, huh? Cara's been keeping you all to herself." I hold up two fingers for the bartender, then point at my new friend's glass. "What's your name?" I know Cara told me, but I didn't care then. I care now.

She huffs as her new beer appears in front of her. I know she likes beer, so she must really not wanna give me the time of day. Only makes me want it more.

I'm still waiting for her name, so I sit silently, sipping on my beer, because I'm bound to fuck it up if I open my mouth right now. I've been told I lack a filter, something most ordinary people have. But I'm not ordinary; I'm Carter Beckett.

Another sigh, this one resigned. "Olivia."

The name drifts softly across the space between us, and I hum quietly as I roll it around in my head, trying it out there first.

"Nice to meet you, Olivia. You can thank me for that beer later if you'd like." I wink, and she fucking *snorts*. Worse, I fucking *like it*.

"I'd rather bury my entire face in a mountain of snow out front." She lifts her glass. "I'm going to keep my drink, simply because I know better than to waste good beer, and you're going to accept the verbal thanks I gave you a minute ago."

Oooh, I think I like her. Fuck knows it's been a while since I've had to work to get anyone into bed. I'd hate to let all my talents go to waste, and I can't imagine someone more worthy of the effort than the saucy brunette who's still scowling at me.

"You don't know who I am, do you?"

Olivia's dark eyes scan my face over the rim of her glass. "Trust me, I know exactly who you are."

"And who's that, sweetheart?"

"Carter Beckett." I'm not sure I've ever heard the two names spoken so plainly, and I don't know whether to pout or laugh at the way she twists back to the TV, as if she doesn't give a single shit who I am. "Captain of the Vancouver Vipers. And you can take that 'sweetheart' and stuff it up your ass."

Beer slides down the wrong tube and I cough, slamming my fist against my chest. "Not a hockey fan, huh?"

I see it right there in the corner of her mouth, the hint of a smile. "Love it. Played for fifteen years."

My brows skyrocket. "No shit." My thumb skates across my jaw at the idea of messing around with a girl who has a decent grasp on the concept of hockey, let alone one who played the game. "House league?"

She snorts again. It's fucking adorable.

"All right. I'll take that as a *hell no*." My gaze skims her curves, the length of her toned calves, her strappy black heels. "You're a tiny little thing. You must have gotten rocked out there."

"Don't you worry, Mr. Beckett. I can hold my own."

"Spent some time in the penalty box, did you?"

"Almost as much time as you do," she replies, those chocolate eyes gleaming as they flick to the split in my lip from the fight I got into at last night's game.

My grin cracks my face in two. Bullshit she's not at least *a little bit* interested in me.

I draw closer, her magnetism irresistible. "My condo's right down the street."

"How very convenient for you."

"It's only a ten-minute walk."

Olivia lifts her beer to those kissable lips. "So close."

"I can get us an Uber if you prefer."

She chokes out a laugh, slapping a hand over her mouth to stop the onslaught of beer rushing out of it. I'm riveted, watching as she dabs at the corner of her mouth and wipes the bar around her. The amusement dancing in her eyes has me feeling pretty confident about the direction we're heading tonight—right down the street to my condo.

"Oh, Mr. Beckett. You are as naïve as you are pretty." She gives my chest a patronizing pat. "The very last place I'm going is home with you."

"Why?" My face dips closer, and I notice the exact moment her breath catches in her throat. Her tongue peeks out, wetting her bottom lip, spurring on my next whisper. "I wanna fuck you silly. Maybe put *you* in the penalty box."

Olivia's face breaks with a snicker, and it's as cute as the snort. "You can't seriously tell me you pick up women with lines like that?"

"No, of course not."

"Thought so."

I grin. "Normally my name and pretty face are more than enough."

She rolls her eyes, and I snag a curl, twisting that lock of dark brown, the little bit of caramel winding through it, and twirl it around my finger. She's got pretty hair. And pretty eyes. Pretty lips. Pretty thighs. Fuck, she's just *pretty*.

With a gentle tug, I urge her forward, and smile at the way she comes, like she doesn't realize she's giving in to the pull.

"We can be there in eight if you're game for a piggyback ride," I whisper. "Wrap those pretty little legs around my waist before I wrap them around my face."

Heat radiates off her, her lips parting on a staggered inhale before she suddenly shifts back. Clearing her throat, she pulls out her phone and starts flipping aimlessly through Instagram, like she's bored out of her fucking mind. "What a terrible idea that sounds like."

"I beg to differ."

Her eyes sparkle with mischief as she meets my stare. "You're right. My feet are sore from all this dancing. The piggyback sounds wonderful." She smiles when I chuckle, and then tacks on in a more sincere tone, "I don't do one-night stands, Carter."

Well, *shit*.

I skim my lower lip with my teeth, eyeing the way her fingers drum her glass, the way she peeks at me every few seconds to see if I'm still watching her, the flush that creeps into her cheeks when she realizes I am. Her body language, the nerves that make her fidget under the heat of my stare, it doesn't match her snarky comebacks, and somehow it only makes her more intriguing.

"All right," I say, before I've even really agreed to it in my head. Fuck it, why the hell not? If there's a woman I'd ever want to see again, it might be Olivia. "Why stop at just one night? I've got a feeling you're the type of song I'd play on repeat." I might even consider waiving my no-sleepover rule. We can go all day long tomorrow before I send her on her way. I slap a palm to the wood and jerk my head in the direction of the door. "Let's go, beautiful."

Her jaw unhinges. "You're joking."

"I'll even take you for breakfast in the morning." I flash her what I've been told is a particularly charming grin.

She mutters something that sounds a lot like *cocky fucking asshole* in the hands she drags over her face. "You seem to be misunderstanding me." She drains the remainder of her beer before hopping off her stool, stepping in close, getting right up in my face. She smells good, like freshly baked banana bread. Is that weird? All I know is I want to taste her.

"I have absolutely no desire," she starts slowly, enunciating every word, for my benefit I'd guess, "to be another notch in your bedpost. I'm sure this whole messy hair, pretty green eyes, crooked smile bullshit you've got going on melts many panties, but not mine."

I dip my head, smiling. "So you admit it. You think I'm pretty."

Olivia rolls her eyes. "There's not a bit of me that's surprised that that's your takeaway." She gestures over her shoulder. "You can have any girl you want. Go find someone else to take for breakfast."

Well, that won't do. The breakfast offer was exclusive to her.

"But I want you," I whine playfully, catching her hand in mine. It's soft and warm, tiny, mine swallowing hers right up. "I can't take my eyes off you, you're hockey-literate, you've told me to go fuck myself in at least three roundabout ways, and I can't remember the last time I've been this attracted to someone."

She steps closer, and my pulse spikes. Her fingertips dance up my arm, brush across my jaw. Her face lifts at the same time mine drops, and the fire in her gaze holds all the promise of one hell of an unforgettable night.

"Has anyone ever been able to tell you no?" she asks on a whisper.

My chest puffs with pride. "Never."

She grins, and Christ, it's a glorious sight. "Well, I guess there's a first time for everything."

My forehead crumples as she steps out of reach. "What?"

"Enjoy the rest of your night," she calls over her shoulder before she squeezes through the crowd, disappearing, and Jesus Christ, I'm actually gonna have to go home and do what she told me to: fuck myself.

Well, *fuck*. I don't like this.

4

GONNA BE A NO FROM ME

Olivia

Sundays and hangovers are made for two things: junk food and naps.

All I want is a greasy cheeseburger the size of my head and super-sized fries. Instead, I'm sitting in a Starbucks, guzzling an iced latte in the middle of December like I might perish without it, while eating one of those ridiculous *healthy macros* boxes, all because McDonald's isn't serving lunch for another fifteen minutes.

Cara arches one perfectly shaped brow at my drink. "It's cold as fuckballs, Liv."

I hum around my straw and tuck my hands into the sleeves of my sweater. "Winter is coming."

"Winter is *here*," she replies, the *Game of Thrones* reference going where I thought it would—clear over her head. "And you're drinking a fucking iced coffee."

"Iced latte," I correct, picking at my cheese-and-fruit protein box. I poke the hardboiled egg. Seriously, what is this? I'm not into it. This is what I eat Monday to Friday, not Sunday morning after drinking half my body weight in beer the night before. Sighing, I snap the lid in place. I'll make Cara take me through the McDonald's drive-thru on our way back to her place.

"I don't care what's in your drink, Ollie, just that it's *frozen*."

I'm a tea drinker, decaffeinated. Cara says I'm a psychopath, but caffeine makes my stomach hurt and gives me the jitters. This morning though, I need it. I'm sure I'm not functioning all that properly. But I also hate hot coffee so my options were limited when we ordered ten minutes ago. The barista looked at me like I had five heads and asked me to repeat my order.

"My head hurts." I pout, giving her the puppy dog eyes.

"Aw, muffin. You partied too hard."

"My feet are killing me." I'm in major need of a foot soak, or a rub. In fact, I hook one leg around Cara's ankle and scrub myself up and down her long calf.

She shakes me off. "I'm not rubbing your feet. Maybe Em will when we get back."

I make a face. "I'm not asking your boyfriend to rub my feet."

"Why?" She pops a grape in her mouth. "He's got nice hands. Big. Strong." She pumps her brows. "*Magic*."

"Things I don't need to know." I flick my straw wrapper at her.

Cara slings one leg over the other, gaze narrowing as she studies me. "Can we talk about the elephant in the room?"

I sip my drink. My God, it's spectacular. I may not sleep for days. "What elephant?"

"Elephant might be the wrong word. How about six-foot-four wall of sexed-up muscle, reminiscent of a Marvel superhero, or a Grecian god?"

My gaze glides over the café. "Not seeing that either."

She pokes the inside of her cheek with her tongue, the corners of her mouth lifting. "Carter Beckett is the damn elephant, Liv."

"Ah. That elephant." I check the polish on my nails. "We already talked about him." In fact, I just managed to get his irritating, narcissistic face off my mind.

"I was three mojitos and five tequila shots deep. I don't remember a single word of that conversation."

The conversation was mostly Cara putting me in a headlock and towing me as far away as possible from Carter Beckett: captain of the Vancouver Vipers, multimillionaire, and playboy extraordinaire. To her credit, she did attempt to lay out a handful of reasons I should absolutely stay away from him, but it was difficult to understand her through the slurring and the hors d'oeuvres she kept shoving in her mouth every time a server walked by.

"You told me to keep my distance, and I told you I'd already put it between us." There was a moment, a very brief one with my hand in his, his piercing emerald eyes holding mine, that I might have . . . *considered* it. *Maybe*. To be determined. Blame the alcohol for mistakes nearly made.

Carter Beckett is the definition of sexy. He's arrogance dressed in expensive clothing, smooth, corded muscles, and a charming smile, and quite possibly the face of chlamydia; I can't be certain. I'm sure he takes precautions, but the man gets around like a globetrotter.

Cara props her chin on her fist. "I should've guessed he'd like you."

"Like me? He doesn't *like* me. He wants to sleep with me. And how could you guess he'd want to? I'm not his type."

"You are too."

"Am not."

Cara plays with her phone before showing me a photo of Carter and a leggy brunette, his arm around her waist while she sucks on his neck. Bonus points for somehow managing to walk down the street and avoid tumbling into traffic.

"See? You both have brown hair!"

I roll my eyes, ignoring that she's at least a foot taller. I tap on the attached Instagram page and level Cara with an unimpressed look. "She's a Dallas Cowboys cheerleader."

Look, I hate playing the *I'm different* card as much as any other woman, but the truth is exactly that: I'm nothing like the women this man is usually pictured with.

If what I see in the media is any indication, Carter prefers women who look like Cara: legs that go straight to heaven, long, lean torsos, silky straight hair. In fact, I'm still convinced the only reason those two aren't dating is because they're too much alike—mouthy, ostentatious, and proud. Sounds like a good way to detonate a room.

"So you're petite." She swipes a hand through the air, dismissing my unimpressed face. "And okay, you're not a model. But you're a phys-ed teacher, so that's kinda the same—"

"It is not remotely *close* to the same thing."

"But you're as gorgeous as they are." The way she says it is convincing, but then she's always been my biggest cheerleader.

I reach across the table, booping her nose. "Thanks, but you're bound by best-friend rules. You have to say that."

Heaving a tired sigh, I stare out at all the people strolling through the mall with bags looped over their arms. I need to stop sleeping at Cara's after I've been drinking. She pounced on me before I could remember my name, let alone where my backbone is located, and that's how I wound up right here—shopping at the mall on a Sunday morning, and worst of all, without my hangover McDonald's.

See: bad decisions fueled by alcohol.

"I'm hungry," I grumble as Cara's thumbs fly across her phone screen. "For real food."

"Perfect timing, babe." She tucks her phone away and stands. "Emmett's up and he's ordering pizza for lunch."

Something inside me lights up like a slot machine. It might be my stomach. "With bacon?"

"*Extra* bacon."

CARA ANNOUNCES OUR ARRIVAL HOME the same way she announces her arrival anywhere: *with flair.*

She sweeps her arms out wide the moment we step inside, flinging all six of her shopping bags to the floor as she twirls. "We're home, babe! Liv needs her feet rubbed!"

"I really don't," I call back, kicking my boots off. I love Emmett but I draw the line at having my best friend's boyfriend give me a foot massage. As it is, I can't manage to get my fucking sock on properly. It's dangling off my toes, and I'm hopping down the hallway on one foot toward the smell of pepperoni and bacon, trying to fix it.

I hate socks. I hate boots. I hate winter.

My face lifts, nose in the air as I inhale and rub my belly with my free hand. "Smells so good, Em. Come to mama."

I manage to hook a finger in my sock, pulling it over my heel with an *a-ha*, but my landing is all wrong, soft wool on slippery, shiny marble sending me tumbling backward with a few choice curse words, arms flailing in search of anything within reach.

Which happen to be a strong pair of arms. Extra muscly. Corded. Oooh, these forearms are fine as hell. They wrap around my waist, catching me before my ass can hit the ground, and warmth spreads outward from my belly as they right me on my feet. I stare down at the exceptionally large hand covering my torso, keeping me steady, and a shiver dances down my spine at the whispered words pressed to my ear.

"Hi, mama."

My hand slides slowly down his forearm, noting the stark contrast where my fingers curl around. Where I'm milky and soft, he's exceptionally golden and firm.

Hot breath rolls down my neck, and I close my eyes as an enticing aroma swirls around me, hints of citrus mixed with the outdoors, like lime and musky cedarwood.

I know exactly whose arms are around me, whose hands hold me close, whose lips linger by my jaw. I know, but it doesn't stop me from what I do next.

With my body still locked in his arms, my head swivels in slow motion. Super slow. Exorcist style, even. I'm not sure my jaw has ever dangled so low. I could probably fit my whole fist in my mouth if I were inclined to try. My brother dared me to when I was nine, and I did it just to prove him wrong.

When I spy those deep green eyes, that messy mop of chestnut waves, that infuriating, sexy, lopsided grin, I do the only logical thing: I shriek.

I shove Carter Beckett off me and rocket so fast across the kitchen that my legs split. Emmett darts forward, hoisting me up via an arm around my waist while he howls with laughter, and my groin hurts so badly I just want to sink to the floor and cry into a plate of pizza.

"I wish I'd recorded that," Cara wheezes, swiping at the tears freefalling down her cheeks. "Carter, I bet that's the first time you've sent a girl running for the hills like that. Holy fuck." She gestures between me and Carter with a slice of pizza. "That was the best."

My skin crawls as I take a plate and go about my business, trying—*and miserably failing*—to pretend Carter Beckett isn't hanging over my shoulder, watching me choose my slice.

His palms land on the counter on either side of me, bracketing me in. "You gonna hurry up and pick, pip-squeak? Big man's hungry."

"I'm determining which slice is the most bacon-y. Don't rush me, *big man*."

His mouth dips, and goose bumps erupt on the exposed skin where my shoulder meets my neck as he murmurs, "I wouldn't dream of rushing you. All I wanna do is take my time with you, Olivia."

"Oh for God's sake." I twist toward Cara and Emmett, propping a fist on my hip. "Which one of you neglected to tell me he was coming for lunch?"

Cara throws her hands up. "I had no idea."

Emmett guffaws. "Like fuck you didn't. I texted y—" His words die behind the palm Cara slaps over his mouth.

The woman is a sucker for drama. I can assume that's the only reason she's knowingly put me and Carter in a room together again. That or she just really wants to see me knock him down a peg or two. Give the people what they want, I guess.

Carter's watching me, waiting for me to react, so I take the biggest bite I can muster while staring him dead in the eye before I strut by him and sink down to the couch. As luck would have it, he flops down beside me a whole fifteen seconds later, flashing me a grin.

His deep dimples are absolutely adorable. I fucking hate them.

He nudges my shoulder with his. "I got more bacon."

"You did not." I lean into him, examining his piece, on the off chance my hangover impeded my pizza-picking abilities. "Damn it."

He chuckles quietly, placing his slice on my plate, replacing it with one of my less bacon-y ones. It's a sweet gesture, which is why I'm suspicious. He bought me a beer last night, and it sounded a whole lot like he was hoping that would equate to my mouth on one of his body parts later.

"It's just a piece of pizza, Olivia. If you want, I'll eat it."

I tug my slice into my chest. "Back off, Beckett."

Cara tosses a container of dipping sauce on my plate as she strolls by. I dump the entire contents on top of my two slices. Carter watches every second of it, the side of my face heating under his stare.

"Can I help you?" I finally ask.

A smile tips his mouth. "Nah. I'm good."

He finishes four slices of pizza, walks back to the kitchen, grabs two more, and finishes both before I finish my two.

"You're a slow eater," he remarks, setting his plate on the coffee table. I try not to notice the way the muscles in his broad back ripple under his shirt, but damn it, I notice.

I'm about to tell him I'm not a slow eater, he's just a garbage disposal, but the words get lost in my throat when he lifts my feet into his lap and pulls my socks off. His thumbs dig into my arch, and I'm eternally grateful Cara and I spent yesterday morning at the spa.

Carter taps the crimson polish on my toes. "Pretty."

"What are you doing?" I finally ask, then moan when he works a particularly sore spot.

"Cara said you needed a foot rub. So I'm giving you a foot rub."

Should my response be *No thank you*? Probably. But here's the thing: he's got big hands, broad fingertips, a powerful touch, and I drank too much last night, which means I subsequently danced too much. *And he feels so damn good.* "Jesus Christ," I accidentally whimper, folding toward him. "Thank you."

"Don't mention it. If you're a fan of rubs, we can go back to my pl—"

"And you ruined it." I rip my feet from his magical hands and curl them under my butt. "Why'd you have to ruin something so good?"

His gaze locks on mine. "I've been dying to ruin you, and trust me, it'd be so good." At my stunned expression, he laughs, catching the Xbox controller Emmett throws at him. "You blush a lot, Olivia."

Cara snorts. "I'm sure it's difficult for you to wrap your head around, but she's not interested, Carter."

"Doubt it, but okay."

He and Emmett settle into a game of NHL, because apparently when they aren't actually playing hockey, they need to do so virtually. Regardless of the laser focus Carter seems to have, he never lets up with the chitchat.

"Do you like the snow, pip-squeak?"

"Not really."

"Why?"

"Because I have to wear socks."

"Spring or summer?"

"Summer."

"Sweet or salty?"

"Sweet."

"How'd you get home last night?"

"I slept here."

A hum vibrates in his throat, and I have an urge to feel it. "If I'd known you slept over, I would've come back here rather than going home. We could've talked some more."

Is he for real? Does he not remember the girl he had glued to his side a half hour after I walked away from him? He can't have forgotten the smirk he threw me with a wink and the tilt of his head. *Coulda been you*, that's what that look said; I'm sure of it.

"Yeah, well, you had your hands full with a pretty little blonde."

His attention leaves the game for the first time to focus on me. "Not as pretty as you."

Is that supposed to be a compliment? *The girl I hooked up with last night after you turned me down didn't quite stack up to you, but I fucked her anyway?* He's such a manwhore and I'm not interested in being another puck bunny he fucks and chucks, so I roll my eyes in revulsion.

"She didn't come home with me, Olivia."

I snort in disbelief. And, also, I don't give a shit. "Doubt it, but whatever."

"You sound jealous."

"Trust me, I'm not."

"Couldn't bring myself to do it, not when I was looking at you all night." He scores a goal and mutters out a *fuck yes* under his breath while Emmett prattles off a string of curses before declaring he needs more pizza.

"Don't care."

Carter sets his controller down and twists, his expression unreadable, vacant almost, as he watches me. I don't like it. If I can't read him, I don't want him to read me.

"I think you do," he finally replies on a gruff whisper.

His fingers skim the edge of my thigh, over the ripped slit at my knee, his touch gliding so gently across my skin I'm not certain he's actually touching me. For a moment, I revel in the feel of his warm, calloused hands. For a moment, I want more.

For a moment. And then I use my brain.

What the hell am I doing here? Why am I entertaining this egotistical jackass? I could be at home, braless and taking a nap.

"I gotta head out," I call over my shoulder as I leap from the couch. "Thanks for lunch."

"What? Already?" In the reflection of the patio door, Cara points an angry finger at Carter.

"Gotta go to Jeremy's." Not a lie, but I have hours before I need to be there.

I kiss Cara's cheek and hug Emmett, avoiding Carter. Of course, he follows me down the hallway, watching me tug on my knee-high boots.

"Who's Jeremy? Your boyfriend?"

I hesitate. Then lie. "Yes."

"You goin' to your brother's?" Emmett shouts down the hall. "Tell Jer I'll be online at ten tonight if he wants to play!"

Ah, crap.

Carter crosses his arms over his broad chest and arches a brow. "You dirty little liar."

Yeah, well, them's the breaks. I lift an innocent shoulder and let it fall as I slip my coat on. Carter grabs the lapels and hauls me into him. I'm momentarily terrified he's going to try to kiss me, and more so that I won't stop him, but instead he works the buttons of my wool peacoat.

Carter Beckett is doing up my coat.

"Can I have your number?"

I blink up at him. "Uh . . ." I mean to say no. I'm not sure why it's not coming out.

He sees my hesitation as an opportunity, and the man starts prowling toward me, backing me up until I'm against the front door and Carter's chest touches mine. Dear Lord, he feels amazing. Warm and firm, broad and strong. And tall. Shit, he's so freaking tall. My vagina starts doing this little dance, like she thinks she's about to get some. She's not.

His palm skates up my side and my heart thuds a little bit faster when he untucks my hair from my coat and lays it over my shoulder.

"Tell you what, pip-squeak. I'll give you *my* number. I never give it out to girls. You'd be the first." There's an air about him, a smugness shining in his eyes telling me he thinks this is it. This will be what reels me in. "Because you're special, Olivia."

There it is. Is that really the best he's got? How the hell does this man get so many women to sleep with him?

With a hand on his chest, I ease him back a step. I smile at him—extra syrupy—and his own grin grows, all dimples.

He's feeling pretty confident right now.

I can't wait to tear him down.

My fingertip skims the neck of his T-shirt, my palm curving over the nape of his neck as I guide his face down to mine. He grips my hips as my lips graze his ear, and I hate how good he smells. There's an irrational part of me that wants to lick him like a freaking ice cream cone.

"It's gonna be a no from me."

I watch that smug smile melt right off his handsome face before it disappears behind the door I slam.

Damn, that felt good.

5

IS THAT MY FACE?

Olivia

I NORMALLY MANAGE MY LACK of height well. I keep a stool in my office for whenever I need it, and I climb a mean kitchen counter-top to reach the high things I don't use all that frequently. The problem is after all these years, I still forget sometimes. I've pulled countless muscles trying to crawl up walls toward shelves, standing on tiptoes and reaching *just a little bit higher*, attempting to turn into Spider-Man and scale the volleyball net to disassemble it.

Today is one of those days where it's me versus the volleyball net. The noises I'm making are bordering on the edge of sounds I reserve for when I'm alone in my bedroom with my vibrating pocket boyfriend, and I keep glancing over my shoulder toward my office at one end of the gym. I can see the damn step stool right there, holding the freaking door open so I wouldn't forget it.

Sue me for getting a little wrapped up in the last day of school before Christmas break. I'm about to have two weeks off with very little reason to wear a bra.

"*Miss Parkerrr*." Amusement drips from one of the senior boys I can never seem to get rid of. "Wanna come to a party this weekend?"

I barely spare the sandy blond leaning in the doorway of the boy's change room a glance. "Stop inviting me to your parties, Brad. I'm your teacher."

"Yeah, the *best* teacher." Brad saunters my way with the swagger of a man with all the confidence in the world. It's oddly reminiscent of Carter Beckett, and I shudder to think there might be another in the future as arrogant as him. "We'd love to party with you."

I've got a strange urge to knee him where it hurts, but I resist, focusing on the task ahead: trying to get the stupid string out of the stupid loop so I can put this stupid volleyball net away until next year. Brad's behind me a moment later, his chest brushing my back while I try not to choke on his cologne. One spritz is fine; seven brings me back to the Spring Fling in eighth grade where I had my first kiss. It was intoxicating, and not because the kiss was great, but because he wore so much cheap cologne I felt woozy.

Brad puts me out of my misery, pulling the top string, and one side of the net floats to the ground.

"Thanks," I mutter, folding the net into small sections as I move across the width of the gym. Brad strolls past me and leans against the pole that's still attached to the remainder of the net. "Take it down, Brad, please."

"Aren't you at least gonna try first?"

"No, I'm not, because that would be pointless, wouldn't it?" I pin my arms across my chest and lift a brow. I'm a bit of an Attitudy Judy, which, admittedly, makes me a good fit for the role of a high school phys-ed teacher. My teens can handle my sass, and I can handle theirs. "Take it down."

"Geez. Testy." He follows me to the storage room, propping himself up beside the garage-style door while I pack the net away. "You know, my birthday's January third. When we get back from Christmas vacation, I'll be eighteen."

And I'll still be twenty-five, his teacher, and super uninterested. "Good for you." I slam the door down, slide the lock in place, and stalk off toward my office, tossing "Merry Christmas, Brad" over my shoulder.

But Brad doesn't take the hint—he rarely does—and follows behind me like a lost puppy. "Will you ever stop playing hard to get?"

"Are you my student?"

"Yes."

"Then no."

"Fine. But in six and a half months, I won't be your student anymore!"

For fuck's sake. I'm so tired of these ballsy little piglets. Always thinking with the head in their pants, rather than the one on their shoulders. Then they grow up to be men who continue to do the *exact* same thing.

"*Go!*" I shoo him out the door. "Come back in January without this whole flirting-with-my-gym-teacher crap. It's annoying, uncomfortable, and highly inappropriate."

He dashes down the hall like his ass is on fire, and I head back to my office to pack up. On my way out, I flip through my text messages. One from my mom, wishing me a happy last day of school. Another from my brother, begging me to make his favorite blueberry pie for dessert on Christmas, a series of prayer emojis trailing the question. The one from my niece Alannah is a crapload of silly emojis and an *I love you, Auntie Ollie.* She's only seven but Grandma and Grandpa spoil her to hell and back—likely because they go several months without seeing her—so she got an iPad for her birthday and she texts me every day without fail. I don't mind; those *I love you* texts make my heart swell.

I don't have time to even start on a string of messages from Cara before my phone rings.

"How do you do that?" I ask, sandwiching my phone between my ear and my shoulder as I dig my car keys out of my bag. "How do you know the moment I have my phone in my hand?"

"Call it a twin thing," Cara replies simply.

"We're not twins. We're not even related."

"We're soul sisters, Liv, and you know it."

I climb into my car, turn the ignition, and listen to the engine struggle before it shuts itself off. "Fuck me," I groan, giving it another go.

"You need a new car."

"No I don't. Red Rhonda works just fine, don't you, girl?" I pat the dashboard, say a prayer, and crank the ignition once more. The engine roars to life and I sink back in my seat with a sigh, waiting for the car to warm up.

"You are gonna run old Rhonda straight into the ground." Cara laughs. "Anyway, I've got an extra ticket to the game tonight. Wanna come? We're going out for drinks after."

Hockey game? Drinks?

Tell me it's a dangerous idea without telling me it's a dangerous idea. I'll go first: I'll have to spend the entire evening pretending I don't notice Carter, which is hard, captain of the team and all that. He's bound to have a girl or two hanging off him later and that'll irritate me even though I already know he's a manwhore. He's not likely to remember my name, which is likely to piss me off, and truly, I can only keep my knee out of the groin of conceited men for so long.

"I'm pretty tired" is the response I give Cara.

Not really, but I never turn down the opportunity to take off my bra, throw on my grubbiest sweats, and curl up on my couch with a good smut book or four hours straight of Netflix.

"Ah, c'mon, Ol. Don't you remember how much fun we had last weekend? You're on vacation! Let's party!"

Do I remember how much fun I had? Which part? Grinding all over Cara because being a respectable human five days a week is exhausting and I desperately needed to let loose? Or Carter Beckett telling me he wanted to fuck me silly and buy me breakfast? Maybe it was the two-hour post-pizza-and-Carter nap, followed by three hours of *Brooklyn 99* reruns after I got home from my brother's house Sunday night.

I guess it was kinda fun.

"Livvie? Please, babe. For me." The pout she's definitely wearing is audible. "I'll be your best friend."

"You already are my best friend," I point out, but when she whimpers, I sigh. "You're utterly ridiculous."

"And you're soft as fuck. You should learn to say no to me every once in a while." Her shrill squeal rings in my ear before she prattles off details for tonight, then promptly hangs up on me before I can change my mind.

"I DON'T UNDERSTAND WHY THE floors are already so sticky when the game hasn't even started yet." My nose scrunches as I listen to my Chucks peel off the floor with each step. "And especially all the way down here."

I scan the arena as we move down the row and take our seats. We're sitting directly behind the bench—perks of dating one of the assistant captains, I guess—so it's not as if five hundred people have walked down the row before finding their own seats. Which begs the question: Why in the hell are my shoes sticking to everything?

"The floors are always disgusting." Cara pops the top off a king can of beer, depositing it into my waiting hands. "That's why I don't bother with heels anymore."

"That must have been such a tough decision for you to make, what with heels being such appropriate attire for hockey games."

She flicks me in the temple and I snicker, stealing a handful of popcorn from the giant bucket in her lap.

"Carter was asking Em about you this week."

I hammer a fist against my chest as a popcorn kernel lodges itself in my throat. "Pardon?"

"Carter," she repeats, tearing open a bag of Skittles. She dumps at least a third of it into her mouth and gestures at the ice with the flick of her wrist. "Beckett."

I follow her gaze, watching as the Vipers take their home ice for their pregame warm-up, and it takes me no time at all to locate the impossibly large frame of Mr. Beckett himself. He leaps onto Emmett's back, wrapping his arms around him, their raucous laughter bouncing across the ice before Emmett shakes him to the ground. It's an interesting sight, because Google may or may not have told me Carter has an inch on Emmett in the height department.

"No, I know who you meant." I tear my gaze away before he can see me. "I must have heard you incorrectly, though. I thought you said he was asking about me."

"That's exactly what I said. Asked a couple times, actually." She rips open a bag of licorice and gnaws on a piece before whipping it around. I'm fairly certain she's got the entire snack bar in her lap. "Singing some song about you apparently."

I stop twisting the lock of hair that's currently cutting off circulation to my finger, and promptly bury my quickly heating face behind the cool lick of my beer can. "What?"

"My girl made quite the impression on him last weekend."

I snort a laugh. "You mean because he's never been turned down before?" And two days in a row, to boot. Seeing the stunned expression on Carter's face when he doesn't get what he wants is my single greatest achievement.

"Something like that."

"Please, that man had a girl on his hip twenty minutes later."

"He didn't hook up with her though, which is weird. Left alone, right after Emmett put us in an Uber."

I flick a dismissive hand through the air. Did Carter tell me the same thing the next day? Yes. Did I believe him? No. Do I now?

Still no. Regardless, it doesn't matter. He's Carter Beckett, millionaire hockey captain. I'm Olivia Parker, broke high school teacher. We're worlds apart. Hell, we're not even in the same orbit.

Even if we were, one-night stands and polygamy aren't my thing, and neither is the high risk of catching a venereal disease if we get too close and accidentally do the no-pants dance. I've already mentioned I sometimes don't make the best decisions under the influence of alcohol.

I'm not really into the whole dating scene. Cara's been relentlessly trying to set me up with Emmett's *nicer* teammates, her words, and I recently caught her making me an online dating profile. I guess I don't have much time to meet someone, and I keep thinking it'll happen when it's meant to. I'm in no rush, and I'm okay with being by myself for now. I'd rather wait for someone whose priorities align with my own. I'm not interested in dating for the sake of not being alone, and I'm not interested in fucking just for the sake of feeling good.

That's what battery-powered boyfriends are for, and I keep mine in a drawer at home. In fact, I pulled it out as soon as I got home Sunday afternoon after leaving Carter with his jaw dangling. And yes, I thought of his stupid, hot face while I used it. I'm not ashamed.

I'll never tell anyone.

Rather than trying to sort through my thoughts on Carter Beckett, I focus on the moment before me. Despite the warmth in the arena, a cool chill nips at the air as the players float around, stretching out, firing off shots on their goalie. Everything is amplified here, the sharp zip of the blades skating across the ice, the slap of composite sticks against rubber pucks before they whizz through the air, the smell of buttery popcorn, the flashing of lights, and the chatter you can't quite make out, despite it being all around us.

It makes me miss playing hockey. There's something about skating on freshly Zambonied ice, the frigid air whipping at your cheeks, the adrenaline rush when you head for the net with a puck at the tip of your stick. I get out on the ice every week with my niece's hockey team but it's not the same, especially considering the eighteen-year age gap and that I'm mostly trying to wrangle in a bunch of seven-year-olds.

Cara draws my attention with a deep sigh. "Well, he had eyes on *you* the entire time."

"Did not," I murmur, propping my feet up on the glass so I can stare at my shoes rather than search the ice for the man in question.

"Did too, you brat. I may have been birthday-girl wasted but it's pretty hard to miss who the most famous guy in the room has his eyes glued to all night."

Heat rushes to my face, and I hate it. The last thing I want to do is blush over a man who probably calls out the wrong name when he comes. I want to feel like I mean something to someone, not like he's made it a challenge to get in my pants because I'm the first woman who didn't fall at his feet.

Look, I'd be lying if I said there hadn't been a minuscule part of me that was tempted to take Carter up on his offer last weekend. It's been a while, and it's always nice to get politely drilled into the ground. According to Cara, these hockey men have amazing stamina and can go all night. And one as experienced as him must be absolutely mind-blowing in bed. Put me in a coma for a day or two, you know? I could use the chance to catch up on my sleep.

I'll never find out though. I shouldn't, at least.

Right?

No. No, Olivia, damn it.

"I'm sure he'll move on quickly if he hasn't already," is the lame response I finally give Cara.

A body collides with the plexiglass in front of me, and I clamp a hand on Cara's thigh as I yelp.

"Jesus," I mutter, one hand over my racing heart.

Cara snorts a laugh. "Uh-huh. Move on quickly. Right." She nudges me with her elbow before wiggling her fingers at the person tapping the glass. "Think you've got yourself a visitor."

I know who it is. I can feel him there. My stomach twirls and my heartbeat settles between my thighs. Why? I really don't fucking know, other than this guy is sex on a pair of skates, and now I'm pissed off because I'm going to have to go home and give myself another underwhelming orgasm while I flick it to the mental image of this infuriatingly sexy man vying for my attention.

Cara's mouth tilts with amusement. "You're not looking, huh?"

I shake my head, frowning. "Nope. Can't."

"*Olivia!*" Carter Beckett yells. It's unnecessary, really. For God's sake, I'm right here.

There's that damn tapping again. The longer I ignore him, the louder he taps. It's incessant and irritating, and everyone around me buzzes with excitement, wondering why he wants my attention, and more than that, why the hell I'm not giving it to him.

They don't understand. I may be entirely turned off by the way he carelessly collects women, but I'm only so strong. I'm afraid it might be possible to charm the pants right off me. If anyone can do it, it's him.

"Liv, Liv, Liv, Liv, Liv," Carter chants, punctuating each call of my name with a tap on the glass.

"*What?*" I whisper-yell, finally spinning his way, throwing my hands overhead.

His grin is explosive, handsome, sexy, infuriating. Leaning over the boards, he stares down the length of his stick at me, the tip resting on top of the glass. "Hi."

Good Lord, I can't. *What is happening?*

Carter watches as heat floods my cheeks just for him. I can pretend to be aloof all I want, but the man's far more perceptive than he seems. He knows I like what I see, and what I see is him, a man entirely comfortable and confident in his skin, grinning in this goofy, irritatingly endearing way, those striking emerald eyes sparkling with mirth and too much arrogance.

Carter knows what he does to me, and that right there will be my downfall.

He leans closer and I hate myself for inching forward, like he's got a secret just for me.

The corner of Carter's mouth lifts, revealing a panty-dropping grin as he props his chin on his gloved hand. "I'm gonna score a goal for you." There's a sureness in his deep timbre, an arrogance that makes my stomach tighten with anticipation. With a wink and the shimmy of his hips, he skates backward and drops to his knees, spreading his legs as he stretches his groin and blows a big, pink bubble, all without taking his eyes off me.

"You look like you're wavering," Cara mumbles around a handful of M&M's.

I manage to tear my gaze away from Carter. An impressive feat, because he's still staring at me and I'm silently undressing him with my eyes, wondering how big the stick in his pants is. Bet it's huge, like the rest of him. "Huh?"

"I said you look like you're thinking about giving in to his mission to fuck you."

Any hint of desire turns sour in my mouth, and my nose wrinkles as I cross my arms. "I'm not a mission, nor am I looking to be the next girl pictured in the news getting down and dirty with Captain Syphilis over there."

Half of Cara's popcorn goes spilling to the floor as she bends forward with a bark of laughter. "You know, he's actually a total dork and really sweet when he's not trying to get into your pants."

"Right, well, I guess I wouldn't know." I plant my feet back on the glass until they're perfectly positioned over Carter's face. He leans to his left, still smiling like a jackass. "And what happened to all your warnings? You spent the better half of your birthday party reiterating him being bad news and telling me not to fall for it. You're sending me mixed messages."

"Oh, he's definitely bad news. I love him to bits, but if I were a single female, I'd probably want to rip his dick off and ram it down his own throat." She motions at her crotch before pretending to stab an imaginary dick into her mouth. "But then he does stuff like this." She tosses a piece of popcorn over the glass, and Carter catches it on his tongue, pink glob of bubblegum nowhere to be found before he singsongs his thank-you, then promptly collides with Emmett in some sort of bear hug. The two of them go tumbling to the ice together, and when they finally make it to their feet, Carter whacks him on the butt with his stick. "I swear, sometimes I feel like I have children."

A giggle slips free without permission, and I'm thankful to leave the conversation behind when the game finally starts. It's easy enough because Cara's sitting beside me screeching at every play. She didn't know a thing about hockey before she met Emmett, and now she never stops berating the refs.

"Oh come on, ref!" She bangs the glass with her fist. "Don't you have a wife to go home and screw? Quit screwing my boys!"

Carter hops over the boards, smiling at me before he turns and plops down on the bench.

Two minutes later, he lines up for a face-off, bending over, stick across his knees, perfect hockey butt in the air. And he smiles at me.

He skates by the bench. Smiling at me.

Squirts water into his mouth. Smiling at me.

All I can focus on is his tall, broad body moving fluidly, the quick, effortless cross of his feet as he tears down the ice, puck on the tip of his stick. He's constantly yelling, commanding attention, leading his team, cracking jokes with players on both sides.

And when he's not doing that, he's looking at me.

Halfway through the second period, Carter calls for the puck at the red line, hammering the blade of his stick on the ice. He takes off like lightning, twirls around a defenseman, leans forward on one foot as he winds up, and lets that puck fly. My mouth hangs as the puck whizzes by the goalie's head, his catcher coming up a split second too late. The buzzer's already blaring and the warm spot between my thighs is already wet.

I mean—what? No. The ice. The ice is wet. I'm not . . . no. That's . . . that's ridiculous.

I squeeze my thighs together, watching Carter throw his hands in the air with a scream that echoes through the arena as his teammates smoosh him against the boards. He skates by the bench, knocking gloves with every player, spraying ice in the air when he comes to a full stop.

And his electric gaze locks with mine.

His stick lifts in slow motion, pointing. At me. Carter Beckett points his damn stick right at me.

And he winks. *He fucking winks.*

For you, his perfect lips mouth to me.

Oh. No.

The cameras pan my way, my vision bursting with flashing white lights. I sink as deep into my seat as possible, fingers creeping up my face, burying it in my hands.

But Carter's not done. Oh no, of course not. He wouldn't be Carter Beckett if he simply ended it there.

He jumps onto the bench, gloves pressed to the glass, grinning down at me. "You like that, Olivia?" he hollers. "That was for you!"

By far the worst part, though?

My crimson face all over the motherfucking jumbotron.

6

INFLATE MY EGO

Carter

I'M ON THAT POST WIN high, floating on air and feeling invincible. It's a heady, addicting feeling, a hunger I want to feed, and Christ, do I ever know exactly how I want to feed it.

Apparently, though, Emmett's hopes aren't as high as mine.

"Liv's gonna hollow your eyes out with a spork," he says, toweling off in the change room.

Seems like something she would do. But still, I ask, "Why?"

"Why do you think?"

It could be a plethora of reasons. Everything I do seems to piss her off. But if I had to take a wild guess . . . "Because I landed her on the jumbotron?"

"Bingo."

I sweep my arms out. "I only showed the world how beautiful she is."

Adam snorts. "That's good. Save it for when she's jabbing your eyes out with that spork. Might be your saving grace."

Emmett shakes his head but laughs. "You also told the entire world her name."

"Oh come on." I plant my hands on my hips, because really, if I can't name her in the postgame interview when one reporter asked who she was, then what the fuck is this all about? "What girl wouldn't love that?"

I'm trying to win points here, and personally, I think I'm off to a good start. I could read her fury from a mile away. Why was she furious? Because I'm relentless and I drive her nuts? *Possibly*. But I think it's mostly because she wants me and she fucking *hates* that she does.

"This is the girl that turned you down last weekend?" Garrett asks.

Emmett grins. "Twice."

"She didn't turn me down." I ruffle my wet hair with my towel before shoving a toque over it.

"*Twice*." The two fingers he shoves in my face are unnecessary.

"We're just getting to know each other." I shrug. "So she's a little hesitant."

"*Dude*. When you offered her your number, she said 'that's gonna be a no from me' and slammed the door in your face."

Garrett guffaws. "*No*. She Randy Jackson'd you? That's hilarious. Must've kept you up all night."

Okay, so it was funny. Once I got through a moment of stunned silence, I couldn't wipe the grin off my face. There's something about Olivia that's piqued my interest. It's not just her sass or sarcasm, but her softness, lurking just beneath the surface. I'd bet she spits all that fire to keep her resolve from crumbling around her like a sandcastle. She strikes me as an all-or-nothing kinda girl, which is probably why one-night stands aren't her thing.

I don't care. I'm just trying to make *me* her thing.

Maybe that's why the first place my gaze goes when we reach the bar is that wild mane of dark chocolate curls, the caramel bits weaving throughout. She looks like an ice cream fucking sundae, and all I wanna do is taste her.

I slip through the crowed, ignoring the people who want to chat, following the sound of Cara and Olivia's bickering.

"Just pretend it didn't happen."

"*Oooh*. Pretend it never happened. Cool. Cool, cool, cool. Yeah, great advice, Care." Olivia shimmies out of the booth. "I'll *pretend* Carter Beckett didn't name me on TV. I'll *pretend* he didn't dedicate a goal to me in front of all of North America."

Cara lifts a brow, a smile that says she's as much a fan of Olivia's attitude as I am. "All right, tiger. Where are you going?"

Olivia tosses a hand up over her shoulder as she stalks off. "Need another drink."

Shit, I like her. Like to watch her go . . .

Literally, I lean to the right, watching those hips bounce as she moves across the bar. She's got killer curves and a fantastic, round ass. Those jeans she's wearing like a second skin paint a pretty picture of what's hopefully in store for me one of these nights.

Emmett elbows my side before I take off after her. "Behave."

I definitely could, but it's not in my nature.

The sight of her, elbows on the bar, ass swaying gently back and forth as she hums along to the music, is a sight I could drink in all night. But I'm intent on putting a crack in that facade she likes so much, so I close the distance between us, smiling at the way Olivia stills, as if she senses me here.

I dip my mouth to her ear, reveling in the way she shivers. "Cold?"

She spins so quickly she stumbles over a stool as our gazes collide. She reaches out to me to steady herself, and I happily oblige, circling an arm around her waist. Wide eyes stare up at me, her chest heaving against me. I'm not ready to have my ass handed to me just yet, so I keep my observations on her reactions to me to myself.

I do enjoy the show though.

And by show, I mean the way those deep brown eyes blaze a heated path over my face, dipping down my body, before slowly— *so damn slowly*—making their way back up, her teeth grazing her bottom lip, fingertips biting into my forearm.

"Are you done?"

She looks up at me, eyes bouncing between mine, brows knitted in confusion.

"Are you done, Olivia?" I repeat, releasing her waist before prying her fingers off my forearm. She's left marks, but I don't mind. I'll let her carve her name into my skin if it gets me what I want, and what I want is her. "Checking me out?"

Her lips part, head wagging. "I—I . . . what? I wasn't . . . checking you . . . what?"

Well, fuck me sideways and call me Sally. This is a first. She sure knows how to pump my ego when it doesn't need pumping.

Her gaze settles on my self-assured smile, and the moment ends sooner than I'd like when she rips herself free and spins around to the bar, back to ignoring me like it's her job.

Obviously, I take the spot next to her, 'cause getting a reaction outta her is fun. Also, I like being near her. She smells good and she's warm. Plus, I love when she rewards my bad behavior with one of her signature eyerolls. I've never felt more deserving of anything.

She steps away, propping her cheek in her hand so she can glare at me, and I use the opportunity to check out her outfit for the umpteenth time tonight.

She's kicking ass in this outfit, all tight tee, a flash of creamy skin peeking out above the waistband of her ripped jeans, a plaid shirt wrapped low around her hips, the Chuck Taylors on her feet the finishing touch.

I follow the swing of her hips when she juts one out, and my eyes fall to her stellar tits when she pins her arms there. I wouldn't mind fucking those tonight.

When she arches one perfectly shaped brow, I smile.

"What? You can look but I can't?" I prop my chin up on my fist. "Those are called double standards, Olivia. Gender equality and all that."

Her lips purse like she's trying her damnedest not to smile. I wish she would. I caught her doing it with Cara during the game and it lit up the whole place. Wouldn't mind being the reason for one of them.

Taking hold of the soft plaid sleeves tied around her waist, I haul her toward me. She comes willingly, fingers gliding up my forearms.

"How is it that as incredible as your outfit was last weekend, you look even better in this? I mean, plaid shirt, ripped jeans, and a pair of Chucks? *Come on*," I groan, dropping my head back. "You're a goddamn masterpiece. I could just take you home and cuddle you all night long on my couch. What's that term—Netflix and chill?" I wind the sleeves around my fists and bend my neck, the tips of our noses grazing when she tilts her face up. "Come on, Olivia. Let's do it."

I tap the corner of her mouth, right where it's quirking.

"If I didn't know any better, I'd think the way you're gnawing on your lip right now is your desperate attempt at biting back that smile of yours. Come on, Liv. Let it out. Let that bad boy shine."

She does, letting it explode across her face. She lets out the sweetest giggle, too, before slapping a palm across her traitorous mouth. "Oh fuck," she whispers, twisting away.

I intercept the bartender before she can see him. Unfortunately, she turns just in time to catch me paying for the drinks he's placed on the bar, and the smile drops from her beautiful face.

"Hey! Those are for me and Cara."

"And you can have them back when you give me the time of day."

"I don't need to give you anything and I certainly don't need you to keep paying for my drinks." Fists: meet hips. Those whiskey eyes narrow dangerously. Olivia packs a surprisingly ferocious punch. "I have a job, you know."

"Does your job pay thirteen million a year?"

"I'm not impressed by how much money you make."

She truly looks like she couldn't give less of a shit. She does, however, reach for the drinks, hopping up and down, rubbing against me as I hold them above her head.

"What is it that you do, anyway?"

Olivia grumbles something I can't quite make out, except for *God*, *asshole*, and *sexy*. Wish I caught the whole thing.

"Just forget it. I'll get drinks back at the table." She throws her hands in the air above her head like she's done with me.

Thing is, though, I'm so far from being done with that woman. That's why I'm only one step behind her as she stalks back to the booth.

"Did you call me a manwhore?" I ask as I slide in beside her, catching the tail end of her conversation with Cara.

"I would never call you something like that," she insists, swiping her beer from my hand.

"Yeah." Cara accepts her own drink with a smile. "She called you *Mr.* Manwhore."

Olivia hides her guilty grin behind the rim of her glass. "It's much more distinguished."

I give her elbow a gentle pinch. "You're a little shit, aren't you?"

"*Me?* You literally never stop."

"I'm like a puppy," I tell her.

"Annoying, untrained, and requires a lot of work?"

I lean into her, dropping my voice. "I'm exceptionally cute and I thrive on attention."

Another giggle, genuine, sweet, and light, making me smile.

"That's two," I point out.

"Two what?"

"Two laughs I've gotten out of you tonight."

Her brows rise as she sips her drink. "Mmm. Are we keeping score?"

"We are. I'm aiming for ten."

"Well, good luck, buddy. That's the last one I'm giving you."

"We'll see," I murmur, eyes on Emmett as he comes bounding over.

"Ollie! Two weeks in a row!" He scoops her up, yanking her right from the booth, and wraps her in a hug I kinda wish I was on the giving end of. I wouldn't mind seeing how she feels in my arms. When he stuffs her back into her seat, she topples sideways, gripping my thigh to catch herself.

It takes everything in me to gently guide her upright with my hand on her lower back, rather than suggesting we go fuck out this tension that's been vibrating between us for a week now.

"Ollie?" I muse, and Cara starts tapping off nicknames on her fingers.

"Yeah, you know, Liv, Livvie, Ol, Ollie, Ollie Wallie. And of course, my personal favorite." She tosses her head back and moans. "*Oh, Miss Parkerrr.*"

Heat radiates off the petite woman beside me as she buries her face behind her hands.

I skim my bottom lip with my thumb as I watch her. "Are you a teacher, Miss Parker?"

Her hands bracket her face as she stares down at the table. "No?"

"High school," Cara clarifies. "All those senior boys wanna get between her luscious thighs."

"No students are ever getting between—ugh." There go her hands again, raking up and down her face.

Christ, she's exactly the type of teacher I would've died to have in high school. Gorgeous, with a perfect, full ass and a snarky, sarcastic personality.

"I agree, Ollie. Besides the obvious, what you need is a man who knows how to take care of you." My fingers walk up her thigh, and hers curl around my bicep, gripping it to stay upright as the magnetism instinctively draws us closer. "Someone who knows how to hit all the right . . . *spots*."

A beat of silence stretches between us as I hold her gaze, the intrigue that dances in it, even if she doesn't want to admit it does.

"Okay . . ." Out of the corner of my eye, Emmett waggles his finger between us. "What's going on here?"

Olivia blinks, spell broken as she shifts back, taking her warmth with her.

"Nothing," she insists at the same time I declare, "Ollie's playing hard to get."

Cara swipes a loaded nacho chip through a cup of sour cream and points it at me. "She's not playing. She *is* hard to get."

Olivia jabs my shoulder. "And don't call me Ollie. We barely know each other."

"Right. Okay." I slide out of the booth and tug on the tie around my neck, pulling it loose and ditching it in the booth. Olivia's jaw drops when I spin away, and I grin, because she's a damn liar, and I'm gonna prove it.

"You taking requests tonight?" I ask the DJ in the corner. "I've got some work to do."

Back at the booth, Olivia watches with confusion as I roll my sleeves up to my elbows, unbutton my collar.

I hold my hand out to her. "Well, let's go."

"Pardon?"

I curl my fingers into my hand. "Come on. Let's go."

Angry heat pools in her cheeks. "I've already told you I'm not going home with you. You are unbelievable."

Clapping my hands on the table, I groan, head dipping to catch her eyes. "Yes, you've made that abundantly clear. We barely know each other, as you've said, so we're going to start. Dance with me."

"But I . . . I . . ." She looks to Cara for help, and when offered none, blurts, "I don't dance."

"Untrue. I watched you dance all night long last weekend. Trust me." I rub my tired eyes, half burying my next words. "Couldn't take my goddamn eyes off you."

"She prefers to be halfway in the bag before she starts wiggling that ass of hers," Cara chimes. "She's only on her second beer."

"Okay, so you don't dance." I wind her hanging plaid sleeve around my fist, giving it a gentle tug. *C'mon, Liv.* "Do you turn down challenges, as well?"

There it is, the bite of her teeth into her tempting bottom lip, that quirk in the corner of her mouth that gives way to a slow explosion, the grin that ignites her entire face.

She slips her hand into mine, and I know.

I've got her.

7

SO EASILY GOADED

Olivia

OF COURSE IT FEELS GOOD, my hand in his. Long, broad fingers thread through mine, tugging me out of my seat, through the crowded dance floor. The size difference in our hands alone is staggering, and I find myself thinking of all the ways he could put that hand to good use.

The thought itself sends a shiver of pleasure down my spine, which is why I didn't want to do this in the first place. I don't know why it feels nice when he touches me, why I'm drawn to his goofy grin, the way he carries himself in such a carefree manner, so confident and in control. If he gets me alone for too long, I'm afraid I'll let him come knocking on the walls that are definitely not sturdy enough to keep him out.

He belongs here, on the other side, no emotional attachments. Because that's the last thing anyone wants to do with a man who has no inclination to settle down: get emotionally attached.

"Madam." With a charming, dimpled smile, he takes a small bow before hauling me into him. His warm palm presses against my lower back, and I have to remind myself to breathe when his whisper glides over my neck. "Is this okay?"

My throat squeezes, and all that comes out is, "Mhmm."

"What did you think of my goal tonight?"

"It was a beautiful goal," I admit on a sigh. He was a first-round draft pick at the age of eighteen, and cinched the title of captain at only twenty-two. Today, he's one of the highest paid players ever. Carter is truly a phenomenon in the hockey world.

His face beams with pride. "And the celebration? I dedicated it to you."

Apprehension knots in my belly, the same way it did when I saw my face all over the big screen. "You mean when you landed my face on the jumbotron? When everybody around me started wondering who I was and if you'd finally decided to settle down? Or when Sportsnet said I was pretty enough but not the typical swimsuit models you fuck?"

His eyes hood. "You could be a swimsuit model if you wanted to."

He's just not getting it.

"I know that's meant to be a compliment, but it only irritates me further. This is clearly just a fun game to you because I turned you down last weekend. I'm a human being with feelings who has zero desire to be objectified on national television." Ignoring the embarrassment prickling my ears, I step out of his stunned grasp. "Not all of us thrive on attention, Carter. Some of us actively avoid it."

Another step back, and I'm about to thank him for the dance and excuse myself when his hand catches mine.

"Hey. I'm sorry, Olivia. I didn't mean to embarrass you. Guess I was excited to see you again and wanted to let you know. Extreme gestures are kinda my thing, and, uh . . ." He slips his fingers below his toque, scratching his head. "I don't have a fucking clue what I'm doing here."

I don't either. I don't have to wonder if this is his usual MO; if it were, he'd probably be better at it.

Carter's throat works as he looks down at our joined hands, then back up, a silent question: *Will I keep dancing with him?* At my cautious step forward, a grin detonates his face, and he yanks me into him. When the music shifts, the familiar mellow strum of a guitar drifting around us, my body stills.

And I bark a laugh as John Mayer starts singing about a woman named Olivia.

"Did you request this song?"

His answer is a grin, equal parts proud and guilty as our bodies meld together. My eyes flutter closed when his mouth dips to my ear, lighting every one of my nerve endings on fire when he drapes my arms around his neck and buries the lyrics in my shoulder, singing softly and so, *so* deep.

"Fuck, I've had this song stuck on repeat for the last week. Do you like John Mayer?"

My hands skim his broad shoulders, grazing the knotted muscles that ripple beneath the surface. Curving my palm over his neck, I fight the desire to twine my fingers in the chestnut waves peeking out from his toque. "I love him."

"What's your favorite song?"

"I've got two."

"Gimme your most favorite first."

"'Slow Dancing in a Burning Room.'" A slow, sad song, about two people who are destined to fail together, kind of like whatever the hell it is we're doing right now. There's no way this ends well. It's bound to go up in flames; we're just denying the inevitable.

I'm not sure Carter sees it the way I do, because he simply makes a pleased sound and murmurs, "Second favorite?"

"'Bigger Than My Body.'"

He does an absolutely piss-poor job of smothering that damn snicker-snort of his as his exceptionally large body shakes beneath my hands.

My eyes narrow. "Shut up."

"I can't"—*snicker*—"help it!" He bursts with laughter, forehead falling to my shoulder as his arms circle me entirely, clinging to me while he vibrates. He pulls back, wiping at his eyes, and a weird sense of pride rushes through me. Does he laugh like this with other women? "You walked yourself right into that one. You know you're tiny, Ollie, right?"

"I'm not—" I stick my nose in the air. "What I lack in height I make up for in attitude." That's what my dad says, anyway, and I tend to agree with him.

"You don't fucking say," Carter muses sarcastically. "How tall are you?"

"Five three," I lie.

"Bull-fucking-shit." He chuckles, pulling back to take me in. "I'm giving you five one."

A growl rumbles in my throat. "Damn it."

There's that laugh again, and I'm not sure why I like it so much, or the sparkle in his eye as he spins me out before tugging me back against his hard chest.

"So . . ." The hesitation in his voice reminds me he's not used to making small talk. "You're a high school teacher."

"I am."

"How old are you?"

"I turned twenty-five in October." Cara whisked me away to Palm Springs for four days, courtesy of Emmett's credit card. It was difficult to explain the tan when I returned to work on Monday after a long weekend that started on Thursday with a sick day.

"Twenty-five? You're a baby!"

"I am not. Your birthday's in February, so you're not even three—" I squeeze my lips together as the implication behind my words sinks in. Carter grins triumphantly. "Oh shit."

"You Googled the fuck out of me, Miss Parker."

"No." *Obviously*. Call it morbid curiosity.

"What else did you find?"

Other than confirmation that his smile is permanently dazzling and dimple-popping? "That you really like women."

He laughs softly. "What do you teach?"

That he's content in not responding to my findings reminds me why I've told myself to stay away. When you start giving pieces of yourself to people who only want to hold on to them until the next person comes along is when treading the water becomes danger-ous. But when I try put a tiny bit of space between us, Carter pulls me back, bends his neck, and . . . presses a fleeting kiss to the crown of my head.

"Olivia?" He touches two fingers to my chin, closing my gaping mouth. "What subject do you teach?"

"Don't make fun of me," I warn. "I teach health and fitness."

"Why would I make fun of that? That's so cool."

"Yeah? My brother always says it's not a real subject."

"Your brother sounds like an asshole."

I laugh, because yeah, sometimes. Jeremy's four years older than me, and the thing we do best is bicker. He'd lose his mind if he could see me right now, but I'm not going to tell him, and that he hasn't yet texted about Carter's goal dedication means, somehow, he missed it. I'm calling it a blessing. Jeremy's a huge fan, but he would absolutely not be a fan of me being one of the girls pictured going home with Carter.

Ironically, Jeremy got a stranger pregnant after a one-night stand at twenty-two. It turned out to be one of those fate scenarios. You know the type, real fairy-tale, romance novel style. They fell in love, got married, and had their second baby earlier this year. Real life doesn't work like that 99 percent of the time.

I smile at Carter, playing with the hair at the nape of his neck. "He's not all that bad. Jeremy just likes to tease me."

There's something in his stare, a tenderness I don't recognize, one that has butterflies erupting in my stomach at the vulnerability that comes with the way he watches me. He slips his hand up my side, gently placing it over my jaw. His thumb grazes my lower lip, and my knees wobble.

"I like it when you smile," he murmurs. "It makes me want to smile too."

I don't know what to say to that. He's not at all being the man he lets the media paint him to be, or even the one he was last weekend. He's throwing me off my axis, and I'm not used to the instability; my world is already so delicately balanced.

"Okay, so you're twenty-five, five foot one, have a brother, played hockey for fifteen years, teach health and fitness, thrive on sarcasm and sass . . ." He pauses to grin when I bark a laugh. "What else? Did you play any other sports?"

"Oh, everything." I had a privileged upbringing in that my parents had enough money to put us into the extracurricular activities of our choosing. My dad still tells people I took acting classes and that's how I got to be so dramatic, but really, I spent all my time playing sports, and hockey was by far my favorite. Funny, when you consider that my love for the sport started with my brother strapping oversized goalie equipment to me and stuffing me in the hockey net in our driveway at four years old, where he proceeded to fire shot after shot at me until my mom ran out of the house, shrieking. "Softball, soccer, volleyball—"

A howl of laughter sends Carter's head rolling backward, and when the giant man drops his forehead to my shoulder, I frown.

"*Volleyball,*" he gasps. "You played *volleyball*?"

"Volleyball's an incredible sport. I coach the senior girls' team."

"That's amazing." *Is he crying again?* "So cool, Ol." He swipes beneath his eyes. *He's fucking crying again.* "I guess I'm just . . . you know . . ."

I step out of his hold so I can cross my arms. "No, I don't know. Enlighten me."

Laughter bubbles again, and he lays a hand over his belly, his entire body shaking as he fails miserably to get a handle on himself.

"Can you even reach the net?" he chokes out.

"Oh, you're hilarious." Two hands on his firm chest, I give him a shove, and he catches my wrists. "I've got powerful legs. I did just fine; don't worry."

He hauls me into him, fingers sifting through my hair at the exact moment mine run through the silky curls at the nape of his neck. "Mhmm. Powerful *little* legs."

"You're incredibly annoying."

Carter cups my jaw, his thumb sweeping over my cheekbone as his half-lidded gaze drops to my lips. "And yet I think I'm winning you over anyway."

My breath comes in a shallow burst as he palms my hip, nudging the tip of my nose with his. "I don't like you," I barely manage, and my heart gallops at his answering smile.

"You may not like me, but your body sure as hell does. The way your fingers are holding on to my hair for dear life right now tells me so."

The reality of our position sinks in, the intimacy, the two of us tangled together, his mouth an inch from mine. What's worse, we're still slow dancing to a song that's ended who knows how long ago, while the rest of the dance floor is covered with people gyrating.

"Oh." I pull my hands from him, stepping back. "Oh."

"Hey." He chuckles softly. "Come here." He laces his fingers through mine, towing me over to the bar where he sets me on a stool before sitting beside me. "You're about to spiral."

"I'm not about to spiral." *I might be about to spiral.*

"You're about to spiral, Ollie. I don't have to know everything about you to see that you're the type of person whose brain is always racing, overthinking."

I tuck my hair behind my ear, avoiding his eyes. "It feels like a lot of pressure."

"What does?"

Everything. Pressure to give in, pressure to *not* give in. Pressure to fit the mold of all the women who've come before me, the ones that will come after me. Pressure to be different and unique while also fitting in.

With Carter next to me, everybody's watching. The fans at the arena, the sportscasters, his teammates here at the bar. Everywhere I look eyes are on us, watching to see what we'll do next. I don't know how to put it into words.

My gaze rises slowly to meet his, and somehow, he knows.

He tips his head toward the door. "Wanna get outta here?" He slaps a palm across my mouth the second it opens. "Not back to my place. Let's go get something to eat."

"I ate at the game," I blurt.

"You did not, liar. Cara stuffed her face with half the snack bar, and you had one handful of popcorn. I had my eyes on you the entire time and I got shit for it after the game." He chuckles, tracing the shape of my hand with his finger. "Coach said *we don't pay you thirteen mill to make googly eyes at pretty brunettes.*" He pulls my hands to his chest, so much hope swimming in his eyes. "C'mon. Get something to eat with me, please. It doesn't have to be anything crazy. We can get fucking street meat for all I care. It's loud in here and I like talking to you."

Um.

"Please, Ollie. Please, please, please, please." One gentle cheek poke for every *please*. He grips my chin, giving it a little shake. "Pleeease."

"So annoying," I grumble, swatting his hand away.

He props his chin on his fist and wags his brows. "Annoying or endearing?"

"Annoying, definitely." My shoulders sag with a sigh, and as if he senses my defeat, Carter leaps off his stool, punching a fist through the air.

"*A-ha!* I've fucking cracked her!" He grips my waist, spins me in the air, drops me to my feet, and . . . peppers my entire face in kisses. His fingers lace through mine, tugging, before I have time to comprehend what's happened. "I promise, Ollie, you won't regret it."

I have a serious love/hate relationship with the giggle bubbling from my chest, and I need to get a handle on it before I go anywhere alone with this man.

"I'm not going home with you."

He holds up two fingers in a promise. "I won't even ask."

"Okay, well, I have to use the bathroom first."

He pops a kiss on my cheek. "I'll go get our coats."

I pat my red cheeks with some cool water over the bathroom sink, trying to bring the stoking fire down to a simmer. It doesn't work. I feel hot all over. My lady bits are excited, my vagina rubbing her metaphorical hands together because she thinks she's getting some tonight. It's highly probable at this point. Carter got this far; he can definitely get further. The thought is both terrifying and thrilling all at once.

It takes me no time at all to spot Carter when I exit the bathroom, given his size and massive personality. He doesn't have our coats yet.

He does, however, have a strawberry blonde with legs that go straight to heaven glued to his side, her glossy black nails raking slowly down his back. He leans his ear toward her mouth as she presses up on her high heels, whispering to him, and my stomach involuntarily sinks at the smile he flashes her.

My near-mistake and flawed judgment sting like a slap to the face, and by the time I'm climbing into the back of a cab, he's bursting through the door of the bar, hollering my name.

It's too late. I sure as hell have enough self-respect to not subject myself to that playboy bullshit I definitely didn't sign up for. He may not be going home with me tonight, but he's going home with someone.

And quite frankly, who Carter Beckett sleeps with is of no importance to me. He can go fuck himself for all I care.

8

COCK SOCKS & CINNAMON BUNS

Carter

IT'S COLD AS BALLS AGAIN.

"What the fuck is going on this winter?" Adam stuffs his hands into his coat pockets, burying his face up to his nose behind his scarf.

"This is some east coast shit," Garrett grumbles. "I didn't leave Nova Scotia for this. West coast winters are supposed to be mild." A tiny hand tugs on his coat, and Garrett grins, crouching in front of the little boy. "Hey, buddy! Do you like hockey?"

This is one of my favorite events of the year, but the guys are right—it's not normally this cold. The air is frigid, and we've wandered away from the heat lamps for a break. Well, sort of a break. My gaze slides to Garrett as he signs a jersey with his name on the back. It's hard to take a real break here, and none of us are turning away kids.

"Eh, Woody." I nudge Adam in the arm. "Next year maybe think about hosting this in the summer so we're not at risk of losing our balls."

He laughs, surveying the packed park. "This is when they need the money the most. Put a sock on your cock if you're that worried."

I snicker. "Sock on your cock."

Every year, we hold a tree lighting fundraising event on the first day of our Christmas break. This year, it's on the twenty-third.

The Family Project is Adam's pride and joy, an event our team has hosted thanks to him for the last four years, and all the proceeds go to Second Chance Home, a home for kids who are waiting to be adopted. There's tons of cool shit that goes on each year, like mini-stick tournaments, skill competitions, skating, photos with the players, and more. My favorite is the gingerbread house competition. I always "lose" because I eat as I build, but I'm pretty sure eating cookies *is* winning.

"Heads up." Emmett nods toward the cameraman and reporter heading our way. "Tuck your cock sock away for a few minutes and behave."

"Aw, man. I hate behaving." I flash them a grin when they stop in front of us. "Do you want my good side, or my better side?"

Adam rolls his eyes. "Nobody cares about your face, Carter."

"Well, I beg to differ."

"That's because your ego's the size of North America and you like to argue." He swings his arms around me and Emmett, tugging us close, and gestures Garrett over with the flick of his head. With a smile for the camera, he asks, "What would you like to know?"

We stand there for the next several minutes while Adam details the reasoning behind the Family Project, the parents that chose to open their arms to him and love him, gave him a second chance at life and a family, and how his brief time in the foster system led him to this.

"And Carter," Tracy, the reporter, says. "It looks we're only fifteen hundred dollars away from the twenty-thousand-dollar goal here today. Reaching that goal comes with a price to pay for you, doesn't it?"

I lay a hand on my chest. "A pie in the face is a price I'm always willing to pay."

A flash of dark chocolate and caramel over the shoulder of the cameraman catches my eye, and I lean to the left, trailing the dark-haired beauty as she strolls down the sidewalk.

"Well, I'll be fucking damned."

Tracy frowns. "Pardon?"

"Oh, nothing. I just . . ." I watch Olivia disappear into a small bakery, and I disengage from the tangled arms of my teammates. "I've got to handle something. The boys will finish up."

With a quick look in both directions, I jog across the street. The bell over the door jingles when I burst through it, but Olivia doesn't look up to see who's joined her. She's too busy gazing longingly at the treat display, one hand pressed to the glass, the other clutching her wallet.

"Anything else for you today?" the man behind the counter asks as he places an item in a white box.

"Um . . ." Her fingers drum against her brown leather wallet and she shakes her head. "No, I—"

"Oh shit. Is that Oreo cheesecake? I could fuck with that. We'll take two pieces, please."

Olivia whirls around, bouncing off my chest with a gasp. "Jesus Christ, Carter." She whacks my shoulder. "You scared me. What are you doing here?" She smiles at the baker and pulls a five-dollar bill from her wallet. "No cheesecake, please."

I slide my credit card on the counter. "Yes cheesecake, please."

"Carter—"

"How come you only got one cinnamon bun?" I ask, peeking into the box on the counter as the man slices into the cheesecake.

Man, Olivia blushes a lot. I don't know why, but I do know it's cute as fuck, especially when she pairs it with twirling a stray curl around her finger.

"My mom always made them on Christmas morning. I don't know how to make them, so I buy one every year."

"You're gonna last two whole days without eating that? How?"

"Because I have "—she pauses to frown at me when I rip off a chunk and pop it in my mouth—"self-control."

"Oh, not me," I mumble, then swallow. "Holy fuck, that's good." I grab another chunk, and the man behind the counter laughs. "We'll take half a dozen, please." I smile down at Olivia's irritated—*but oddly unsurprised*—face. "You look nice."

She looks down at her outfit, her leggings and chunky leather ankle boots, the oversized hoodie beneath her open wool coat, and—you guessed it—she blushes.

I give her hair a gentle tug. "My favorite part is the toque." I chuckle as a mitten goes tumbling from her pocket, and I pick it up by one of the floppy ears. "And the puppy mitts."

She takes the boxes from the man, thanks him profusely for putting up with me, then follows me outside.

"Does your mom not make cinnamon buns on Christmas morning anymore?" I ask as I offer her half of the one I'm currently eating. When she shakes her head, I shove the rest in my mouth, licking the gooey cream cheese frosting off my fingers.

"My parents live in Ontario, so I don't see them for Christmas."

"Can't you visit?"

"I could, but they're semiretired and travel all winter. My brother lives here, so I have dinner with his family."

"You spend Christmas morning alone? Isn't that kinda lonely?"

"I'm used to it." She eyes me curiously. "What are you doing here, Carter?"

I tip my head across the street. "Fundraiser."

"And what are you doing *here*?"

"Well, I saw you walking and, I mean . . ." I scratch my temple. "Why did you bail on me on Friday night?" Something uncomfortable and foreign twists in my stomach. "I thought we were gonna go get something to eat."

Olivia stares at me for a long, silent moment. "Are you serious? *You* bailed on *me*."

"What do you mean? You left without saying anything."

She rolls her eyes. "Because I came back from the bathroom to you with another woman all over you, Carter!"

"What?" My forehead wrinkles and smooths out just as quickly as my mind drifts back to Breanna. Or maybe it was Brenda. Brynn? Shit, I can't remember, but I know she had red hair. "Oh, Old Red. You're upset about that?"

"You seriously can't understand why seeing another woman all over you might be a turn-off after I'd just agreed to spend time with you one on one?"

"Well, I guess I can, but . . ." I rub the back of my neck. Is she mad at me? I don't want her to be mad at me. "I didn't do anything. That kinda stuff happens wherever I go." I'm not sure that was the right thing to say, even if it is the truth. If anything, she looks kind of scared now. "Are you jealous?"

Her gaze dips to the ground. "No."

"I think you are." I tug on the strings of her hoodie. "And I think I like it."

Olivia swats my hand away. "I don't need to be comparing myself to other women and reminding myself of all the ways I don't stack up, okay?"

Don't stack up? What the fuck? "It wouldn't be fair to compare you to them. You're on an entirely different level."

"I'm aware," she mumbles at the ground.

"Yeah, they're, like, here." I chop a hand across Olivia's torso, then raise my hand as far above her head as I can reach. "And you're way up here."

A sweet, timid smile tugs at the corner of her mouth. "You know, for someone who puts his foot in his mouth more often than not, you sure know how to be sweet sometimes."

"Just another one of my God-given talents." I glance at the busy park. "Hey, wanna come hang out for a bit?"

"Oh, no, I . . ." She shifts her coat sleeve up to check her . . . bare wrist. "Shit. I don't wear a watch."

I throw an arm around her shoulder, burying her in my side, and start towing her across the street. "You're a bit of a mess sometimes, huh? C'mon. It'll be fun."

"Define fun."

"I'm getting a pie to the face if we raise twenty thousand dollars, and I know Adam Lockwood is looking forward to delivering said pie."

Olivia snickers. "What if you don't raise it all?"

"Then I donate the rest of the money *and* get a pie to the face."

"How much do you think I'd have to pay Adam to let me do the honors?"

I grin down at her, tugging her closer. "C'mon, pip-squeak."

Olivia

I'M USED TO BEING THE shortest person in the room. Ninety-nine percent of my high school students are taller than me, even the freshmen.

But *this* is terrifying.

"Am I exceptionally small or are your friends exceptionally tall?" I whisper to Carter as we approach a group of his teammates. He's currently digging into his second cinnamon bun, his fingers covered in frosting, but he does spare me an amused and lingering glance.

"Both. Don't worry. They won't bite." He winks. "I might, though."

I don't know how I wound up here. I was pretty set on not seeing Carter again, or at least not interacting with him. Friday had been a crude but necessary reminder of who he was, because

I'd accidentally let him peek over a couple of my walls and momentarily forgotten.

But now I'm not so sure.

Don't get me wrong: the man is without a doubt as arrogant as the media makes him out to be. He has no qualms about saying whatever's on his mind, which makes him remarkably honest but it's also a little jarring.

For example, I—as someone whose pants he's actively trying to get into—don't need to or want to know that women attach themselves to his body wherever he goes. I certainly appreciate the clarification that what I saw Friday wasn't as it seemed, but the truth was somehow as intimidating as the belief had been nauseating.

The tallest man in the group turns around, and I recognize him immediately as Adam Lockwood, Vancouver's superstar goalie. He spreads his arms wide, stepping in our direction.

"Where'd you go? I thought maybe you went to buy a cock . . ." His eyes slide my way, and his cheeks flush. "Sock . . ." He clears his throat and gives me a shy wave. "Hi. Me Adam. No. Fuck." He claps a hand to his face before offering it to me. "Adam. I'm Adam. I'm sorry. I'm just embarrassed because I don't know you but I said *cock sock* in front of you."

Oh my God, he's adorable. And wildly beautiful, bright blue eyes and dark, tousled curls begging to be touched.

I slip my hand into his. "You can say cock sock in front of me all you want."

Carter's mouth dips to my shoulder. "Can I—"

"No."

"Damn it." He gestures to me. "This is Olivia."

Adam's eyes brighten. "Oh! Cara's friend!" His eyes darken as he looks at Carter. "Oh. Cara's friend."

Carter rolls his eyes. "It's fine. Olivia wanted to hang out with me."

"Uh, that's not how it happened. You dragged me—"

He wraps his arm around my head and yanks me into him, burying my words. "Shhh."

Adam grins, his gaze bouncing between Carter and me. Before I can panic about our intimate position, Emmett appears.

"*Ollie!*" He yanks me out of Carter's hold and wraps me in one of his burly hugs. They're my favorite kind, bearish and bordering on the edge of suffocating. "Care didn't say you were coming. She's at a meeting with some clients."

"I wasn't. I was doing some last-minute Christmas shopping and got dragged here against my will."

A handsome blond appears at Emmett's side, giving me a sheepish smile. "Carter doesn't like to take no for an answer."

"I can tell it's a very difficult concept for him to grasp."

His turquoise eyes flash with mirth, and he takes my hand, introducing himself even though I already know who he is. "Garrett. I bet you'd like me better."

"I bet I would too."

"Can't blame ya." He gestures lazily at his face. "It's the east coast twang."

"Back off." Carter huffs, tugging me away. "She's *my* date."

Um. "This is not a date."

"Pretty sure it's a date, Ollie."

I cross my arms. "Pretty sure you have to ask someone on a date, *Carter.*"

"Eh, whatever. Ask, drag; it's all the same." He threads his fingers through mine and hauls me forward. "C'mon, pip-squeak. Let's go get our faces painted."

"I'm twenty-five. I'm not getting my face painted."

I GOT MY FACE PAINTED.

Honestly, I don't want to talk about it.

"You look so pretty."

"I have your damn jersey number on my cheek, Carter!"

He folds his lips into his mouth in an attempt to hide his guilty smile. "*So* pretty."

Just trust me, he'd said. Well, it'll be the last time I do. I'd sat down with a clear face and stood up with #87 painted in blue and green on my left cheek. The kicker is the obnoxious pink heart surrounding it. I'd say at least I don't have Olaf on my face, but Carter seems incredibly proud of the cartoon snowman that covers his cheek.

He gestures to a stone retaining wall. "Wanna sit and have our cheesecake?"

"You've had two cinnamon buns and a corn dog. How are you still hungry?"

He pats his belly. "I'm a big boy."

He certainly is, and the corn dog is the only thing I've eaten since breakfast, so I let him pull me down beside him, and we enjoy our dessert in silence.

"Do you need a ride home later?" he asks after a minute. "I can take you."

My belly does this odd flip, and I can't pinpoint the exact reason. It could be because the thought of being alone in a car with Carter later tonight makes me both anxious and excited, or it could be because I'd rather he didn't see where I live, the shoebox-sized house that fits me perfectly.

"No, thank you. I should get going after this."

"What? Already? No, you can't." He gestures at the towering pine tree currently being wrapped in lights. "You have to stay for the tree lighting. We could do something else after this too. Go somewhere, maybe."

"It's getting late."

"But you don't have to work tomorrow," he argues, or whines. Little bit of a pout too. "You're on vacation."

"I don't know . . ." I've already stayed longer than I planned to.

I've seen Carter get behind a microphone and make the crowd laugh. I've seen him engage with every child who's tugged on his hand, whether for photos or signatures or a simple chat. I've seen him be a friend, a leader, a community partner, and through it all, he's worn the most genuine smile. If I'm being honest, I'm not sure it's a side to him I was ready to see, even though Cara insisted it existed somewhere behind the egotistical playboy attitude.

And I guess that's the thing: just because he's got this sweet, goofy side doesn't mean the playboy side doesn't exist. You can be both, and you can have both. But if I'm going to have him, I don't want both. The longer I stay, the more I see, the easier it becomes for me to fall.

And I refuse to fall when nobody's going to be waiting at the bottom to catch me.

"I don't think it's a good idea," I finally murmur.

Disappointment flashes in his eyes. "Why are you so opposed to hanging out with me?"

"It's not that. It's . . ." My bottom lip slides between my teeth as I stare at my feet. "I'm not interested in a one-night stand. I've told you that."

"So you wanna go on a date?"

Well, now I can't *not* look at him. "You don't date, Carter."

"Right. Not typically. But that's not what I asked, Olivia."

I can't focus. Everything feels hazy, like a thick fog I can't see through to the other side. Because that's what this is. I hear his words, but I don't know what lies on the other side of the actions. It's like choosing to jump when you can't see the ground.

"Liv?" Carter squeezes my fingers. "Do you wanna go on a . . . date?" He tacks on a barely audible *fuck*, peering up at the sky as he tips his head side to side, the bones in his neck cracking, as if simply saying the four-letter word is painful enough.

Which only serves as a reminder that a date would be a waste of time, both his and mine.

"I have no desire to go on a date with you just to let you fuck me at the end of the night and then promptly watch you publicly parade around town with a different girl glued to your hip every other day of the week, leaving me feeling used and tossed aside."

A simple *no* would have sufficed, which is what I'd meant to say when I opened my mouth. Instead, I word-vomited all over him and embarrassed myself by revealing how easy it would be for him to hurt me.

Ultimately though, it is what it is. I don't know how him well enough to make another choice. Carter's not been secretive about his intent. Besides being forthcoming with wanting to get me in bed, the guy also proudly splashes his personal life all over the papers. What am I supposed to think when he controls his own narrative and that narrative screams *fuckboy*?

"I'm sorry. I didn't mean to be insensitive. It's just—"

"It's all I've given you. You don't have to apologize." Carter's thumb sweeps over my knuckles, and I watch as he traces the shape of each finger. "So you don't want to hook up, but you don't want to date either? I guess I'm a little confused."

"That's fine," I insist, maybe a little stubbornly. "I'm the only person who needs to understand my decisions. You can have anybody you want, Carter."

His laugh is hollow, long fingers skimming the sharp angle of his jaw. "I can't, clearly. Because what I want is you."

"You only think you want me because I said no, and you're not used to it. It's the thrill of the chase."

He gnaws on his lip. "That's what I thought at first too. But now I'm not so sure. Who knows; maybe I'd be good for you."

I hear the words, and I'm trying so hard to focus on them, but it's impossible to hold back my snicker any longer. "I'm sorry.

I know this is a serious conversation, but you've got that damn snowman on your face."

Carter dips his head, covering his smile with the hand he runs over his mouth. "Will you please just stay for the tree lighting? We're having fun. There's no sense in ending it now. I'll order you an Uber to take you home so you don't have to worry about what might happen if we're alone together in a dark car later."

"I'm not worried—"

"You are. You're fucking transparent, Ollie. 'Cause I'd probably try to kiss you, and you'd probably let me." He leans back, blowing out a deep breath. "And who the fuck knows what happens after that." A soft, easy smile. "So stay, please. No funny business, I promise."

I'm quickly learning that the only thing I'm good at saying no to is his request to get me naked and in his bed. He's incredibly persuasive, especially when he pulls those dimples in, or when he gives me those puppy dog eyes.

That's how I wind up standing next to him nearly two hours later—well after Adam's smooshed not one, not two, but *three* pies into his face—as the sun finishes dipping into the horizon while we stare up at the massive tree, waiting.

My frosty breath puffs out in front of me, and my teeth clatter as a shiver rolls through my body. With the sun gone, the winter air feels unbearably frigid.

Carter shifts from beside me, disappearing from view. A moment later his arms come around me, pulling me back against his chest, encasing me in his warmth. My body stills at the contact, but inside, every nerve ending fizzes.

My arms lift, floppy-eared puppy mitten–sheathed hands gripping his forearms where they wrap around me, and I sink into the moment, letting myself forget about the expectations, the fears, the lines.

Carter chuckles, his chin resting on top of my head. "Cutest fucking mittens I've ever seen."

The tree comes to life, multicolored lights twinkling, making this December night glow as the crowd around us *ooh*s and *aah*s.

"It's beautiful," I whisper.

Carter's arms tighten around me. "Yeah. Sure is."

With the tree lit and the park emptying, Carter walks me to the car idling by the curb.

I look at the fancy, all-black SUV. "I know you ordered the luxury option."

"Prove it, pip-squeak."

I giggle. "Thanks for today, Carter. It was fun."

He nods, rubbing the back of his neck. "What, uh . . . what are you doing on New Year's Eve? There's a team party. Cara and Emmett will be there. Maybe you could come."

"Oh, I don't—"

"Do you already have plans?"

"Well, no, but—"

"Then you'll come." He folds his hands together beneath his chin. "Please, Ollie. It'll be fun." He blocks the car door. "I won't let you leave until you say yes."

I roll my eyes. "Okay, fine. I'll be there."

He punches a fist through the air. "*A-ha!*"

"It's not a date," I remind him quickly, poking his shoulder.

He shakes his head, hands up. "Not a date." He opens the door and gestures for me to climb in, and then proceeds to reach over and buckle me in. He tucks my box of cinnamon buns on my lap and pulls back, scratching the back of his head. "Um, Ollie?"

"Yeah?"

"I'm sorry for upsetting you Friday night and making you feel like I bailed on you."

"I'm sorry I actually *did* bail on you."

"I'm not sorry you were jealous."

"I wasn't jealous."

Carter grins. "Green looks so good on you."

"Shut up." I smile up at him. "I'll see you on New Year's Eve."

He nods. "Not a date."

"Not a date," I repeat.

Then he shuts the door, hits me with two finger guns, and yells, "It's a date!"

9

DOGS > GIRLFRIENDS AT CHRISTMAS

Carter

I HAVE A LOVE/HATE RELATIONSHIP with Christmas.

Growing up, it was my favorite season. Yeah, it wasn't just a holiday; it was a whole damn season.

It started in November when the Vancouver air would chill enough for my dad to kick on the furnace. Christmas music started playing through the house as soon as Remembrance Day passed. We'd barely have our Halloween decorations down, and Mom would pull out all the Christmas bins from the attic.

She'd kick her holiday baking off with chocolate peanut butter balls, even though the Christmas before she swore she'd wait until later. The earlier she baked, the more we ate, and two weeks before Christmas, she'd be a mess in the kitchen, freaking out over having nothing left.

But my favorite was the first Sunday in December. We were a busy family, always on the go between my sister and I, both of us competitive athletes, even as kids. But on that first Sunday, we cleared our schedule every year. We'd start off at our favorite diner for breakfast, and I always got the Oreo pancakes. Then we'd head to Merry Tree Farms, where we'd trudge through fields in search of the perfect Christmas tree.

Dad had a thing for Christmas trees. No less than nine feet tall, and wide enough that we could all fit around it. It had to fill the front window in our living room *just right.* He'd spend minutes examining a tree only to suddenly say *nope* and head off to find another. My sister and I were always competing to find the perfect tree, the one that would impress our dad. One year, he bought two because he said we both picked perfect ones.

When I was ten, he showed me how to use the saw, and we cut the tree down together. I helped him carry it back to the truck, and together we loaded it into the bed of the F-150.

When we got home, Mom would crank the Christmas tunes, make a platter of sandwiches, and the four of us would decorate the tree together. Then we'd all pile onto the couch with mugs of hot chocolate and a tray of Christmas goodies and watch *The Santa Clause.* When I was younger, I always wished my dad would take Santa's place like Tim Allen did in the movie. He promised to take me to the North Pole with him if it ever happened.

I loved everything about Christmas.

But we lost my dad seven years ago and Christmas has never been the same.

Cutting the engine in the driveway of my childhood home, I stare up at the lackluster house. There's not a single light or decoration to indicate what time of year it is. Every year I offer to put them up for my mom, beg her even, but she just gets this sad smile and says, "Maybe next year."

Still, she tries to give us pieces of the Christmas she thinks we want, even if the effort leaves her covering up the ache in her chest, pretending like every Christmas without my dad by her side doesn't kill her. I hate watching her like this, seeing her so broken when she deserves so much love.

"What are you looking at?"

The quiet voice to my right makes me jump, like I somehow forgot he was here. I smile at my friend, his weary blue eyes moving slowly like he's trying to see what I'm seeing, even though he can't.

"How do you know I'm looking at anything, old man?"

Hank is eighty-three years young and began losing his vision at fifteen due to Leber hereditary optic neuropathy. It affected his left eye first, and a few months later his right. Though he can perceive shadows, he's been legally blind since before his sixteenth birthday.

Hank taps the spot between his eyes with two fingers. "Third eye. Some people call it mother's intuition."

"You're not a mother," I remind him, in case he's forgotten.

His deep laugh lines transform his weathered face with his hearty chuckle. "Your mother let you put up lights this year?"

"Nope." I sigh, stepping out of the car and into the falling snow. I let Dublin, Hank's guide dog, out of the backseat before helping Hank.

"It's hard, you know," he starts softly, slipping his hand into mine while I guide him to Dublin's lead. "Living without your soul mate. Holidays without them. New years and birthdays. Heck, listenin' to the evening news without them is hard. It's all hard, Carter."

I know that, of course. I've watched my mom struggle year after year. And Hank knows because he lost his high school sweetheart to cancer fourteen years ago, seven years to the day I lost my dad. It's how Hank and I met, on the worst day of my life.

I shake the snow from my toque before stepping inside and kicking my boots off. Dublin waits patiently by Hank's side as I help him with his coat, and I smile at the way he shifts on his paws, ready for permission to bolt into the kitchen. He's the sweetest golden retriever in the world, but probably the worst trained guide dog.

Well, maybe it's not the training that's so bad, but how lax Hank is with him. Dublin's always on when he needs him, but Hank doesn't like keeping him in working mode too long. He says dogs should be allowed to be dogs. Hank's fairly independent, and I think more than anything he got Dublin for the companionship, the emotional support.

Hank sniffs the air. "If you think you're gettin' some of that turkey before me, Dubs, you're mistaken, big fella." Once he's got his cane out, he gives his dog a pat. "Go ahead."

Dublin skitters across the old hardwood floors, sliding past the opening for the kitchen before he reverses and disappears inside. Laughter erupts from the room, my mom and sister gushing over their favorite dog.

A moment later my mom emerges, sliding into the living room, face more lit up than the half-assed Christmas tree in the corner of the living room. Her gaze sweeps over me and Hank as she smooths her hair, and she leans to the side, peering around us.

"Oh." She frowns. "Only you two?"

"Only us two? Were you expecting someone else?" I tug her into me, enveloping her in a hug. She smells like cinnamon and syrup, bacon and turkey, the same as every year, which is how I know my Christmas morning is off to a good start, even though she sighs at my question.

"No, nobody else." She presses up on her toes, kissing my cheek. "Merry Christmas, sweetheart." She embraces Hank. "Merry Christmas, Hank. I'm so glad you could make it."

"Where would Dublin and I be if we weren't spending Christmas with the two most beautiful women in Vancouver? Thank you for having me, Holly."

My younger sister saunters into the living room, leaning against the kitchen door frame, wearing that signature Beckett smirk my dad gave us. "Mom was hoping you were going to surprise us by bringing your girlfriend." Jennie pops a chocolate peanut butter ball into her mouth. "Her exact words were, 'wouldn't that be the best Christmas present ever?'"

I cock my head at my mom, raising my brows. She's wearing this grin, half sheepish, half guilty, a sprinkle hopeful, but she still swats my shoulder.

"Oh, don't give me that look, Carter. I *know* that look. I *invented* that look! You're hiding something."

"I'm not hiding anything." I move by her, wrapping Jennie's entire face in some sort of headlock, which she promptly tries—and fails—to wriggle free of. "I don't have a girlfriend."

Jennie lands a punch to my gut, then flips her braid over her shoulder. "That's what I said. Nobody would ever want to date you."

"*Please*. I'm a hot commodity. Everyone wants a piece of me."

She rolls her eyes as she greets Hank with a hug. "Yeah, it's called alimony." She barks a loud laugh in my face and then squeals when I lunge for her, dropping to the floor to use Dublin as a shield.

"Well, since your sister brought it up . . ." Mom shifts her tortoiseshell glasses up her nose, that hopeful expression never waning as she rocks back and forth on her toes. "Who's the girl you've been pictured with?"

"What girl?" Heading into the kitchen, I find the widespread platter of Christmas goodies. I drop a chocolate peanut butter ball in my mouth and quickly follow it up with a snowman sugar cookie. "Dere are wots of girls," I mumble around my bite, then swallow. "You know how I feel about variety."

"Carter, for heaven's sake. Swallow before you speak, and you know damn well which girl I'm talking about."

I shrug, and she plants her hands on her hips, lips pursing.

"Don't feed me that bullshit. It's been two weeks of pictures of you two. Slow dancing at the bar last weekend, at your fundraiser two days ago." She arches a brow. "How like you to wait until your sister and I leave to bust out your date, by the way."

Well, that's not what happened. I saw Olivia *after* they left.

She gestures at me with the sweep of both hands. "*And* you dedicated your goal to her!"

"Oooh, *her*."

"Yes, *her.* And then in your postgame interview, you said, 'That's Olivia.'"

"Right." I tap her nose. "That's Olivia."

Something dangerous and scary flits across her gaze before she flicks me right between the eyes.

"Ow! What was that for?"

"I *know* that was Olivia, because that's what you said in your interview, smart-ass! I want to know *who* Olivia is. You've never done that before, dedicate a goal to a girl."

"Untrue." I point at the only ladies in my life, even if I'm considering adding another one to the mix. Why? They're fucking complicated; these two right here prove exactly that. "I've dedicated plenty of goals to you two."

Mom snaps a tea towel at me when I reach for another cookie. "You're really getting on my nerves lately, Carter Beckett."

"I've always been there, Mom."

I study her closely for a moment, noting the way so much of her excitement has drained. There's a disappointment that lingers, pulling down the corners of her mouth, dulling the spark in her eyes. I don't like that I've somehow crushed what little bit of happiness she managed to find today.

I nudge her shoulder. "You didn't really think I was going to show up here with a girlfriend, did you?"

Her cheeks flush and she waves me off. "Of course not." Her gaze shifts to the table in the dining room, then back to me. I follow it, finding the fifth place setting when there should only be four.

"Aw, Mom, c'mon."

She rushes into the dining room and quickly picks up the dishes. "It's nothing. I don't know what I was thinking. I thought maybe . . ." Another wave of dismissal. "Nothing. The fifth place setting was for the dog, actually."

Jennie comes up behind me and tugs my ear. "Would you get a girlfriend already? Quit breaking Mom's heart. I'm sure there's someone out there that will look past all your humongous fuckboy-sized faults."

"Oh, Jennie." Mom presses a hand to her forehead. "Would you quit calling your brother a fuckboy?"

"He prefers ladies' man," Hank supplies.

"*Yeah, I do*," I whoop. "That's my guy!"

"And ladies' man is just a nicer name for fuckboy."

Jennie snickers and leads Hank out of the kitchen, leaving me and my mom alone.

"You know, Carter, I've never said anything about your choice to . . . to . . ." She's got this flail-y hand thing going on, flapping around her face like she's trying to figure out a nice way to say her son sleeps around. "To do whatever it is you're doing with so many different women," she finally settles on. "But I hate to think you're missing out on something incredible, something special." She lifts one shoulder, wearing a smile that manages to be sheepish, sad, and nostalgic all at once. "Something like me and your dad had."

I pull her into me, winding my arms around her and holding her tight. "How are you doing today, Mom?"

"I'm okay." A staggered inhale followed by a raspy exhale that hints at the lie. "I miss your dad, Carter. I miss him so much."

My eyelids fall shut as if that'll stop the pain. It won't. My mom's pain is my own.

"I know, Mom. I miss him too." I press my lips to her hair and squeeze her a little bit tighter, smiling faintly at the big, blue totes sitting by the stairs, *Christmas* scrawled on them. "The bins made it out this year."

"I couldn't open them," she admits. "Just sat there and stared at them. But . . . it's a step, right? Even if it's a small one?"

"It's a step, Mom."

As we stand there in the silence of the kitchen, holding on to each other while the Christmas music drifts all around us, I make her the only promise I know how to make.

"If I find something like you and Dad had, the last thing I'll do is let it get away from me."

10

CARTER'S PALACE OF LOVE

Olivia

THIS IS THE KIND OF house you see in magazines, the kind you spend your life dreaming of. Where the idea that something like this could one day be yours isn't so far-fetched.

Nestled back in a gated community in North Vancouver, with a driveway I swear spans the length of my high school, the sprawling two-story house sits at the base of Mount Fromme. Large gray stone, slate-blue siding, and wooden pillars work together to make this home the masterpiece it is, and the backdrop behind it—the sea of dark green forest capped with snow, the peaks of the mountaintop, the trillions of stars you can't see anywhere else—makes it utterly breathtaking.

"You gonna stand out here all night or come in?"

I drag my gaze off the backdrop and try to ignore the butterflies that erupt in my belly when I find Carter on the front porch, leaning against a pillar, hands tucked in his pockets, an easy smile on his face.

I've never been so attracted to him as I am in this moment. Dark, fitted denim, a deep green and blue plaid button-up, untucked and with the sleeves rolled. Chestnut waves lay in a tousled mess atop his head, and he's so effortlessly handsome it nearly hurts.

"Cara and Em left you out here to fend for yourself," he says.

"So you thought you'd save me?"

His grin grows as I step toward him. "Nah. I'm the one you need saving from."

"Ah, right. Big, bad Carter."

He flexes his bicep, kisses it, and pumps his brows. "I am big."

I climb the two steps to the porch and enjoy the way his eyes gleam when I step into him. "But you're not all that bad, are you?"

"So bad," he murmurs.

"Really?" I run the tip of my finger along the collar of his shirt. "Because there's a picture of you with Olaf painted on your cheek that says differently."

His gaze darkens. "Don't remind me you had my number painted on you last week."

My fingers curl around his shirt, bringing him closer as I whisper, "The first thing I did when I got home was scrub that bad boy right off."

A feral sound rumbles in his throat as his eyes narrow, and with a snicker, I back away, peering around the covered porch.

"This house is incredible."

"I know." He zeroes in on my dress beneath my open coat. "So is that dress." He holds his sleeve up to my stomach. "We match."

"Looks like we do." I won't tell him I slipped on this dress tonight because the color reminded me of his eyes.

"Come on." He slings an arm around my shoulder and leads me toward the door. "Before you freeze and we have to strip down and rely on body heat and cuddling to warm you back up."

"Carter Beckett doesn't cuddle," I reply, looking with wonder around the expansive front foyer. It's as grand inside as it is outside, and everything feels . . . right. Homey and warm, like the only place you'd be content to be during a snowstorm, snuggled up on the couch in your pj's with your hot chocolate, a classic Disney movie, and the people who matter most.

"I'd cuddle with you."

"You're pulling out all the stops, aren't you?"

Instead of responding, he starts peeling my coat off, and I shift the container in my left hand to my right when he requires that arm.

"What's this?" he asks, taking it from me once he hangs my coat.

"It's nothing special. They're bacon-wrapped water chestnuts with a sweet and spicy glaze. They're—" I stop midsentence, watching as he tosses one in his mouth, humming.

"So good," he mumbles, tongue running along his lower lip to catch the lingering sauce.

"You are a never-ending pit, aren't you?"

The lopsided smile he gives me brews a fire in my belly, and his next words stoke it. "I can go all night, baby."

I clear my throat. "They're for the host. Cara said all the food's been catered in, but I thought I'd bring something anyway as a thank-you for having me."

"Oh. Well, thank you. And you're welcome." He takes my hand and makes to drag me down the hallway.

"What?" My eyes move around the foyer once more, this time focusing on the faces in the photos. Though he's many years younger in most, I'd recognize that face anywhere. "This is your house?"

"Uh-huh. As dazzling as I am, don't ya think?"

"It's . . . it's beautiful. Why didn't you tell me it was your house when you invited me?"

"Didn't I?" He shrugs and takes my hand again, tugging. "Oh well. Let's—"

"Wait a second."

Carter's body stills and he looks at the ground. The expression he wears is cautious and nervous as he slowly swivels my way, like he knows exactly where this is going.

"I thought you had a condo downtown. You said you could carry me there on your back in eight minutes."

"Right. I did, uh, say that."

"Or am I mistaken?"

"No, you're not, uh . . ." He scrubs the back of his neck. "I do have a condo downtown. I just don't live there. I live here."

My nose scrunches. "Then why would you have a condo?"

I can tell he doesn't want to answer. Or maybe he just doesn't know what to say. The man looks like a deer caught in headlights.

I lift my brows, waiting, barely noticing Garrett as he comes trotting down the staircase. "Carter? Why do you have a condo if you don't live there?"

"Condo?" Garrett repeats, wrapping me in a hug as he moves by us. "You mean Carter's Palace of—" He slams his jaw shut, eyes wide as his gaze ricochets between us.

"Carter's Palace of what?" I urge.

"Don't," Carter warns him lowly. "Don't you dare."

A beat of silence stretches between us, the tension palpable.

"Love," Garrett whispers. "Carter's Palace of Love." He cowers from Carter's menacing stare before dashing down the hallway, calling his apology over his shoulder. "I'm sorry, okay? I don't lie well under pressure! *Don't hurt me!*"

With my arms pinned across my chest, I hold Carter's stare. His is a mixture of afraid and amused. He shouldn't be amused. He should be 100 percent terrified, because right now I'm thinking of kicking his ass.

"Out of curiosity, what line were you going to feed me if Garrett hadn't accidentally outed you for having a Palace of Love, where you take all your special friends?"

"They're not my special friends. They're not even my friends. *You're* my friend. And you're special."

Oh for the love of— "Carter."

He cringes. "Maybe I would've told you I sold it?"

"Oh, so you would've lied?"

"What? Ugh." He sighs, slumping. "No, I wouldn't have lied."

"So you'd have told me the truth, that you have a condo down-town for easy access to fuck after your games?"

"No, I—ahhh." He claps both hands to his face, dragging them down in slow motion. "This feels like a trap. You wouldn't have liked either of those answers." He lets out a deep breath with a low *whoosh*. "I would've told you that you're the first woman I've ever had to my house who hasn't been a family member or a friend's girlfriend. That I'm happy to have you here, not there, and to spend some time getting to know you better tonight."

I know what he's doing. He's trying to deflect from the negative, to turn his fuckpad into a positive because I'm the special one who's made it here instead. He seems good at that, seeing the positives, even if right now it's to talk himself out of a corner. But the truth is I've never been very good at being an optimist. I'm not a pessimist, either, or at least I don't think so. I'm just a realist.

He tucks my container under his arm and takes my hands in his. "Can you forget about all the preconceived bullshit for tonight? One night, Ollie. I know I've got a reputation, and I know I'm not an angel. Let's pretend none of that exists and enjoy our date."

"It's not a date."

"And we'll pretend you're not jealous."

Sigh. And he was doing so well.

I flick his collarbone before strutting by him. "Get over yourself, Beckett."

His hearty chuckle trails behind me, and of the sentence he mutters to himself, I only catch the words *ass* and *dress*.

I swivel on my heels. "What did you say?"

The grin he flashes has me believing he's the devil in chiseled marble. There's not an innocent bone in that muscled body of his.

"I said you look stunning tonight in that dress." That's not remotely close to what he said.

Long fingers lacing through mine, he tugs me along behind him.

"C'mon, pip-squeak. Let's go have a drink."

I can't think of a more awful, reckless, deliriously alluring idea.

So naturally, I follow him.

I COULD DIE A HAPPY woman in this kitchen.

I don't know if it's the sprawling midnight blue cabinets, the brick backsplash, the double-wall oven, the shiny marble countertops, or the stone fireplace in the living room that's visible from here. All I know is if I took my last breath standing right here, that would be okay.

"You look like you're in heaven."

A fizzy red drink appears in front of me, cranberries and limes bobbing around, and I waste no time bringing the glass to my lips as Carter drops his elbows onto the island.

"I'm pretty sure I have this kitchen saved on my dream home Pinterest board."

"What's a Pinterest?"

"What's a—" Sighing, I shake my head. "Never mind."

Carter's grin goes from self-assured to a little wobbly as he pulls open a drawer. His hand swallows a small brown package, and he clears his throat. "Hey, um, this is maybe kinda weird, but I got you som—"

"*Olivia!*"

Carter slams the drawer closed, his cheeks flaming as Adam yanks me into his side. I keep my eyes on Carter, dying to know what's he's hiding in there.

"Carter said you were coming, but none of us believed it."

Garrett raises his hand. "I said you'd be here. Bet everyone a hundred bucks." He pulls a wad of hundreds out of his jeans, fanning them at his face. "Thanks for showing up."

Emmett pulls one bill free and stuffs it in my hand. "Ollie gets one of these since she made it happen."

Cara steals a bill. "And I get one because I brought her." She pats Adam's shoulder. "Did you know you're Liv's favorite Viper?"

His face lights, and he runs a palm down his proud chest. "Really? Me?"

"Yep." I ignore the look of betrayal on Carter's face. "You're like a brick wall out there." He's also incredibly endearing. Every time he's complimented in a postgame interview, he gets all shy and looks away from the camera.

"Ollie played hockey for fifteen years," Carter tells him.

"Really? I want you to tell me you were a goalie, but you're fucking tiny." Adam folds his lips into his mouth. "I'm sorry. Tiny's not a bad thing, it's just—"

"Not good for a goalie, I get it. I tried for a year when I was eight." My nose wrinkles. "It was the worst. I'm not built for the guilt that comes with losing. I'm too sensitive and couldn't separate myself from the loss. I'd cry the entire car ride home because I'd blame myself."

"I get it. Some losses are harder than others but it's always a bit easier when I've got these guys to lift me up after."

"Is your girlfriend here? I haven't met her."

"Oh, uh . . ." Adam palms his nape. "No, she wasn't feeling up to it tonight. Maybe next time. She'd love you."

You'll hate her, Cara mouths over his shoulder, and the look everyone else wears, including Carter, tells me the same.

"I'll look forward to meeting her." I nudge Garrett. "What about you? Anyone special?"

"Nuh-uh." He gives me a lazy grin and a wink. "Why, you lookin' for a midnight kiss?"

Carter scoffs. "You can't kiss my date at midnight!"

"For God's sake, Carter, this isn't a date."

"You can't kiss my not-a-real-date-but-actually-is-a-real-date at midnight!"

Garrett leans into me, mouth at my ear. "Full disclosure, I've got five hundred bucks riding on you kissing him at midnight."

Before I can respond, an eruption of cheer comes from the dining room, and Garrett claps his hands together.

"C'mon, Liv. Let's play beer pong." He tows me toward the crowded room where a gorgeous spalted maple table is covered in red cups and ping-pong balls. "You can be my partner. We'll make Carter and Adam *weep*."

Carter trails in behind us, hands tucked in his pockets, and I follow his glower to Garrett's hand on my hip.

Oh my. Mr. Beckett is jealous.

His gaze meets mine, and he saunters over with a fierce look of determination while Garrett and Adam fill six cups each with beer, arranging them in the shape of a triangle on opposite ends of the table.

His fiery stare burns every place on my body it touches. "Care to make this interesting?"

My fingers run up the line of his buttons. "What did you have in mind?"

His gaze bounces to my mouth. "I win, and I get your midnight kiss."

Behind me, Cara snickers. It's been a few years, mind you, but in university, Cara and I were the queens of the beer pong table. We went entirely undefeated our sophomore and junior year.

"And if I win?"

"You won't. My motivation is too high."

I admire his tenacity; I'll give him that much. Trailing my finger down his torso, I stop just above the waistband of his jeans.

My single drink has gone straight to my head, because I'm seriously considering the possibility of me sticking my hand down there later. "Humor me."

"What would you like?"

I'd love a foot rub and to be politely railed into the new year if I'm being honest, but the request that comes out of my mouth is so much tamer. "You have to take me to see *Frozen II*." I'm dying to see it and I figure he'd rather be caught dead than at a public movie theater with a girl, watching a Disney princess movie.

The group around us groans, as if they know something I don't.

Carter just grins, pulling those dimples right in. "Deal." He brushes my curls off my face, tucking them behind my ear and gripping my neck. "Joke's on you, Ol." He touches a tender kiss to my jaw, making me tremble. "I love Disney movies and I get to take you on a date. Now I win, regardless of the outcome."

Carter is good, as expected. So are Adam and Garrett.

But I'm better.

When Garrett and I win the first game, Carter quickly declares it's a best-of-three scenario. And when we win the second game, too, it's suddenly the best three out of five.

When I sink the first ball during the third round, Garrett lifts me into the air while the crowd hollers.

"I've never seen Carter lose at anything so many times in a row before," Garrett whispers, his hand on my back.

Across the table, Carter watches us, jaw tight, eyes dark. I can't tell if it's losing that's brought on this response, or the way Garrett's been so blatantly flirting with me the entire time.

Ping-pong balls soar through the air as we trade points back and forth, until there are only two cups left on each side. With tensions high and Carter up next, Emmett calls out to me.

"Eh, Ollie, hold up! You dropped something!" His brows quirk, and I follow his pointing finger to a load of nothing before he hits me with a sneaky wink.

Message received.

Look, I'm a woman. I may be small, but what I lack in height I make up for in hips and curves. I've also been told I have a killer ass, something Cara likes to remind me of with a gentle *pat-pat* whenever she strolls by me.

I tend to be a little self-conscious about the softness of my edges, the roundness of my ass, all things that have come via a healthy obsession with spending endless hours scrolling through desserts on Pinterest, or watching inspirational baking videos on Instagram, and then trying to recreate them. But the truth is most men find all those dips and curves irresistible.

And Carter Beckett? He's definitely most men.

Right now, he's poised over the table, gaze flitting between the cup he's aiming at and me. When I smile, he smiles back, soft and sweet. I almost feel bad for what I'm about to do.

Almost.

"Oops." Turning my back on him, I bend over, right down to the ground, lingering there for a moment, just long enough to hear what I want to hear.

Ping . . . ping . . . ping.

"*Fuck!*"

Adam chucks a ping-pong ball off the table. "Are you fucking kidding me, Beckett? You got distracted by an *ass!*"

He drags both hands down his face before gesturing at me. "It's one bangin' ass!"

Carter's wayward ball rolls to my feet and I shoot up, holding it above my head. "Got it!"

Adam gently bangs his forehead off the wall, groaning, and

Carter's wearing the sexiest scowl I've ever seen. The alcohol in me dares me to kiss it right off.

Emmett claps my hand, howling with laughter, and Garrett grabs my face, kissing my forehead with a loud smack. He sinks his own shot with ease, then rubs my shoulders while he talks strategy in my ear.

"Just take it slow. Take a deep breath. Don't rush your shot. We've got it in the bag. Any cup, Liv, any cup."

Cara claps a hand to my ass. "Let's go, baby!"

I set my eyes on the cup I want and get into position. I'm confident, and it's warranted.

"Oh, Carter? I went a hundred and eight games undefeated in university." Eyes locked on his, I send the ball soaring, grinning when I hear that plop as it sinks into his drink, the crowd around us exploding with cheers.

Adam sinks to the floor, Carter grips the edge of the table, dropping his head, and Garrett spins me in his arms.

Drunk me realizes whatever I'm feeling for Carter is much more than an attraction to all his sexy bits, and I don't really know what to do with that. Logic tells me to run, to shut it down before it becomes more, because this man will break me. *Il*logic says, *Eh, fuck it, let's give it a shot*.

I'm not sure which one will win, but the bold part of me swings two arms around his neck and says, "How does it feel to lose, big boy?"

Something daunting and feral flashes in his eyes, and when his fingers wrap tenderly around the base of my throat, pulling me closer, I know his next words are true.

"Trust me. The last thing I've done is lost."

11

THE FINAL COUNTDOWN

Carter

"You got your ass handed to you."

"Three times in a row."

"How does that feel, Carter?"

I shove my hand in a face. I'm not sure whose, because every single one of my friends' faces has been in mine in the last thirty seconds, after I watched Olivia's ass disappear behind the bathroom door. "Shut up. No, I didn't. I feel fine. I didn't—she didn't—fuck." I hold my palms up, half shrug, half surrender. "Okay, but is it technically losing if—"

"*Yes.*"

"Okay, well, you didn't all have to say it at once." I look at Cara. She's checking out her pointed red fingernails. "You knew."

"Knew what, fuckboy?"

"That she was gonna win."

"Yeah, I knew. Of course I knew. She was my beer pong partner for four years. Girl can do a mean keg stand too." She pats my chest. "No kiss for you."

"I'm gonna kiss the fuck outta her in the back row at the movies."

"Ha! You think I trust you to be alone with my bestie in the dark? Em and I are coming with you." She gestures at Adam and Garrett. "You boys wanna come too?"

Garrett groans. "I had to take my sisters to see it over Christmas."

"Perfect, so you're in. And—"

"Nobody's coming," I growl. "You trust me."

Cara laughs. One of those dramatic ones, where she slaps at her thigh and wipes beneath her eyes. "Carter, I love you, but the last thing I do is trust you with my best friend."

I sweep my arms out. "Well, what the fuck? Why not?" I wouldn't trust me, either, if I'm being honest. It's not that I have bad intentions, it's just that I kinda . . . don't know what they are, at least not past spending time with her.

"I don't want to say something mean."

"Just say it, Care. I'm a big boy."

She heaves a sigh. "If *manwhore* were a word in the dictionary, you'd proudly pose for the photo. If Olivia goes out with you, kisses you, etcetera, it's because she has feelings for you and wants to explore them. You do all those things for fun with people who mean nothing to you. And that's fine; if that's what you want to do, you go ahead. I'm just saying that as long as you're on two totally different pages, if you plan on doing the same thing you've been doing all this time, chances are she's going to end up getting hurt."

"And if I'm not? If I'm not planning on . . . on . . ." Christ, I can't even finish the sentence. The thought alone of anything more than a casual fuck makes my skin crawl.

What if I fuck it up? What if I'm terrible at it? What if I hurt her?

"Why does he look like that?"

"He looks like a sad, lost puppy."

"Looks more like constipation to me."

Adam slings an arm over my shoulders. "Leave my guy alone. He's got a crush, that's all."

A crush? My throat squeezes. "Psssh. No I don't." *Do I?*

"You do, Carter. That's why you haven't left the bar with a single woman lately."

"Maybe I needed a break. I've been tired."

"That's why you bought Olivia cinnamon buns and cheesecake and talked her into getting her face painted with you last week. That's why you stood there with your arms around her during the tree lighting, just because she shivered, and that's why you invited her to a party at your house, even though you never have mean-ingless hookups here. Because Olivia means something to you, and you, my friend, have a crush."

Well, *shit*. He might be right.

What the hell do you do with a crush?

YOU FOLLOW HER INTO THE bathroom, that's what you do with a crush.

Well, I didn't follow her *in*. She's already inside, and I'm waiting out here to surprise her.

The door opens and Olivia slips out, head down.

"He's just a man," she mumbles to herself. "An incredibly beau-tiful and irritating man."

Oh, I like where this is going. My hands wrap around her waist—just one, actually; the other claps over her mouth to stifle her scream—and I walk her back into the bathroom, locking us in.

"*Carter.*" She swats my shoulder. "Why are you always sneaking up on me?"

"Let's skip that and circle back to what you were saying about an incredibly *beautiful* man."

I should start keeping track of how often she rolls her eyes or plants her fists on her curvy hips. They draw attention to all the right areas but all the very wrong ideas.

Her eyes are the warmest shade of brown with tiny flecks of gold, like smooth, melted chocolate, and when she peers up at me from beneath those thick, dark lashes, all I can picture is the way she'd look below me, our eyes locked while I bring her right to the edge before inevitably throwing us both over.

And those hips—*fuck me, those hips*. Wide and full, leading up to a teensy waist and down to a stellar, round ass. All I want to do is grab hold of those hips, burn my fingerprints right into them as I pin her to the mattress and drive inside of her, watching her fight to breathe as my name leaves her lips.

"I also said irritating. Or did your selective hearing kick in? And hey." She claps in my face then gestures at her own. "I'm up here, Beckett."

"Just admiring your dress." I've done it at least a hundred times tonight. It's a deep, forest green that clings to every dip, leaving little to the imagination, except whether she blushes all over. I hope one day I get to find out.

"Is that why you trapped me in the bathroom?"

"Nah, I trapped you because there's no way you would've willingly let me come in here with you if I'd asked." Leaning back against the sink, I incline my head toward the edge of the bathtub. "Now sit your ass down so we can talk."

She sits, but she sure as hell drags her ass about it, and I smile at her bare feet, her sparkly gold toenails. She ditched her heels about three seconds into the first round of beer pong and I have a feeling they won't be making it back on.

"Don't like being too high off the ground, huh?"

Her nose scrunches in the most adorable way when she giggles. "I hate heels, period. I've spent most of my Christmas break in sweats, and I kinda wish I'd worn them tonight."

"I have some sweats if you want to change. I can take you upstairs and show you where they are."

"How kind of you. And I assume they're in your bedroom?"

"Yep. They'd be big on you, so I'd need to help you dress to make sure we cinch them just right, obviously."

"*Obviously.*"

"We wouldn't want them to accidentally fall off."

"Oh God no. That would be a disaster. I'd just be standing there in my panties."

I run a hand across my jaw, shrugging. "And then I'd need to wrap you in my body, carry you right back up to my bedroom so nobody could see you. Honestly, it's giving me the heebie-jeebies just thinking about it. We should probably stay in the bedroom where we're safe." I stand, offering her my hand and heaving a drawn-out sigh. "C'mon, Ol. Let's go."

A wide grin blooms, brightening every bit of her face, and when she smacks my hand away, I chuckle and sink down beside her.

Olivia watches the way I spread my hand out right next to hers, and when my pinky slides against hers, she doesn't move away. Instead, she licks her lips. "Garrett bet on us kissing."

"Yeah, I know. I didn't take the bet."

"You, Mr. Confident, didn't bet on yourself getting a midnight kiss? Why not?"

"Because I don't bet against myself, but I don't like to lose either. I can't get a good read on you. At first, you did the opposite of everything I expected you to do. You turned me down, told me to go fuck myself, slammed the door in my face, and the last thing you wanted to do was spend any time with me at all. But now I'm getting better at figuring you out, like some of the stuff I think you're feeling, and you smile at me more and laugh a lot, but that means I see your confusion as well as you do. You don't know what you're going to do until you do it, so I have no fucking clue anymore."

"And what am I confused about?"

I shrug. "Me. Maybe you're wondering which version of me is the real one, and whether it's okay to like that version."

Olivia stares at her toes, worrying her bottom lip. "Hmm."

I nudge her shoulder with mine. "Did I hit the nail on the head or am I way off about what's going on here between us?"

Wide eyes move between mine, searching. "You don't like me, Carter."

"I think I do, yeah."

She laughs, an exhausted, frustrated sound. "You can't even say the words."

I swallow the tightness in my throat that feels a little bit like fear and try again. "I like you, Olivia."

Something in her expression jars me. It's tender but guarded, lost but begging to be found. She wants answers, but she's not sure she'll buy them. "How do you know you like me?"

"Besides the fact that my chest got tight whenever Garrett was touching you?"

"You were jealous?"

"I've never really been jealous before so I can't say for sure, but I briefly thought about decapitating my right-winger, so, yeah, I think I was."

Her gaze warms, softening. "I'm sorry. I would never knowingly put you in that position. You must realize the irony of the situation though, no? You saw another man with his hands on me once. Twice we've been at a bar together where you've expressed interest, and twice you've ended up with another woman's hands on you." She holds up a hand, stopping me before I can argue. "It just happens, I know. But it happens because that's the narrative you've created for yourself, Carter. I mean, how many women have you slept with since we met?"

"None," I answer truthfully and without hesitation.

A snort of disbelief. "Bullshit."

"What reason would I have to lie?"

"To get me into bed." The *duh* hangs heavy in the air between us.

"I've never needed to lie to get a woman into bed before." As soon as the words leave my mouth, I realize how it sounds. Olivia is already halfway to the door before I catch her wrist. "Stop. Stay, please." I run an aggravated hand through my hair. "Look, I don't know how to talk about this kind of stuff, which is hard for me, because I don't filter my words before they leave my mouth, but if you give me a minute, I'll get there."

I wait for her to sit back down, and then try again.

"What I mean is I've never needed to lie about how many women I've been with. It's never been a secret because of the way I've lived my life. Women know what to expect with me. And you know, clearly, because that's the reason you've been dead set on avoiding me like the plague. Why would I lie now? It won't get me anywhere. You'll just add *liar* to the list of cons under my name."

She nibbles her lip. "I don't . . . I'm not keeping score or anything."

"That's bullshit and you know it. The odds were stacked against me the moment I approached you."

"Well, to be fair—"

"Yes, I asked you to go back to my condo and fuck, I know. Not a great first impression. If I could take it back, I would."

"Why?"

"Because then maybe you could get past all the other shit and we could move forward."

She honestly could not look more confused. She's also seriously lacking her sassy comebacks. Part of me worries I've broken her. "What in the world are you talking about?"

I gesture between us. "This. Me and you." I drive a hand through the air like an arrow. "Forward."

"Is there a me and you, Carter? A forward?"

"I . . . I think so."

"You think so," Olivia repeats slowly. "I don't have time for *I think so*'s. Nor the energy to wait around while you figure out what you want from me, especially when the chances are pretty damn high that you figure out a couple weeks down the road, once I'm already in well over my head, that what you want is not a relationship."

My expression must hold all the disappointment I feel, because her warm hand cups my cheek, guiding my gaze back to hers.

"I'm sorry. I didn't mean to sound rude. I'm just not sure you understand, Carter. We're worlds apart."

My gaze floats down her face, over her high cheekbones, the dainty freckles that paint her nose. She's so beautiful, sometimes I think it hurts. "Are we?" I finally ask.

"*Aren't we?* We want different things."

"What if we don't?"

"Can you tell me honestly that what you want is a serious, committed relationship? Because I don't do casual, Carter. I'm not built for it, and I have no desire to waste my time on something that doesn't have the potential to move forward."

"I don't know," I admit. "All I know is being with you here feels nice, and it felt nice last week too. Don't you feel it too?"

A beat of silence lingers between us, and my pulse thuds in my ears while I wait for her to answer, to tell me I'm not alone in this.

She brushes a stray wave from my forehead and smiles. "I do. But as it stands, Carter, I think that's all we're on the same page with. Does that make sense?"

I nod slowly, wetting my lips. "Does that mean if I wanted to try to be in a relationship, you'd let me try it with you?"

She chuckles, a bit anxious, a bit exasperated. "You realize you're making it sound like tryouts, you know? A relationship is something two people try together, yes, but I'm not a test run to see if being in a relationship is something you actually desire. You need to decide what you want first before you go after the girl."

"What if the only thing I'm sure about wanting is you?"

She sweeps her thumb over the indent in my chin. "Sometimes wanting something isn't enough."

I SPEND THE NEXT TWO hours trying to pretend like my gaze isn't exactly where it is: glued to Olivia.

I watch the effortless way she connects with my friends. I watch her put her heels back on just to ditch them all over again two minutes later in my kitchen. I watch her dance and drink and play games, and I watch her fucking *laugh*. Fuck, is she ever spectacular when she laughs, head thrown back, eyes squeezed shut, her milky skin stained pink as her curls cascade down her back.

I rub at my chest, trying to soothe the tightness that stretches across it when one of my teammates touches her lower back, bending to whisper in her ear. All this jealousy I'm feeling tonight is throwing me off-kilter; I don't know how to handle it.

But Olivia catches my eye, the corner of her mouth lifting as she sidesteps away from him, and for some reason, that's it. For some reason, I know: no isn't an option when she's involved.

Because I can do better, *be better*, and I can do it for Olivia. I *want* to do it for Olivia.

Maybe that's why I get a wild idea when Ryan Seacrest tells us there's only two minutes to midnight, even though I lost our bet.

Maybe that's why I straighten off my spot on the wall, catching Olivia's wild, anxious gaze. I see the apprehension, the way she spins, hands in the air like she has no idea what to do. She starts slipping off toward the hallway, but Cara grips her arm, yanking her back.

Olivia's gazes crashes into mine.

And suddenly there's only thirty seconds to midnight.

And I start moving.

And she's still freaking the fuck out, feet cemented in place, eyes gigantic saucers that only grow rounder with each stride I take, eating the distance between us.

Fifteen seconds.

"Carter," Olivia whispers, gripping my wrists when I take her face in my hands. "What are you . . . what are you doing?" Her eyes bounce between mine, full ruby lips parting to let her tongue peek out, swiping across, getting ready, because she knows *exactly* what I'm about to do.

Ten.

"I—I . . . Carter, I—"

"Relax, Ollie." I rake my fingers through her soft curls, and when I bracket her jaw in my hand, I swear I hear her heart thumping.

Five.

My thumb skims her lower lip. Her eyes flicker. "Can I?"

Four.

Three.

Two.

One.

"Yes."

12

"PAY UP." —GARRETT

Carter

THERE'S A PART OF ME that would like to say nothing happens when our lips finally meet for the first time. That it's the same as it always is: no sparks, no flames. That there's a sinking feeling in my stomach, an anchor that drops to the very bottom as fast as it can when I realize this is nothing new, that I'm right back to feeling like the type of love my parents shared doesn't exist for me, that I'll never find it. That I'm okay with that, the way I have been all these years.

A part of me would like to say that's what happens.

But I can't.

Because when I haul Olivia into me, when her hands slip up my arms, over my shoulders, fingers plunging into my hair, when our lips touch—*fucking finally*—my entire body comes alive. My world explodes with color, my hands on her face trembling with desire and need, with shock. I want more. *Need* more. I don't see how I'll ever get enough of this, of her, of us. She's a drug, and I'm addicted off my very first hit.

Her lips part on a sigh, vanilla and brown sugar begging my tongue to reach out and take a taste. We meet with a hot, wet sweep that makes me groan, and I sink into the feel of her, until there's nowhere left to go.

Everything around us dies down to a gentle simmer, the frantic drum of my heart drowning everything else out. Nothing matters except this woman in my arms, the way her mouth moves fluidly with mine as I swallow every one of her whimpers.

Olivia pushes forward, forcing me backward until my calves hit a chair. When I fall onto it, she falls with me, climbing into my lap and plowing her fingers through my hair, as if she has no intention of letting go.

My hands glide down her back, gripping her waist, and when her hungry mouth moves over mine, I suddenly become aware that the room is silent. I crack one lid, spying Cara's astonished, slightly irritated face. Emmett's nervous gaze bounces between his girlfriend and me. Adam hits me with two thumbs up and a grin, and Garrett starts trying to collect his winnings.

Locating Olivia's fingers in my hair, I twine them through mine and pull our hands to my chest, pressing one more kiss to her lips.

And one last one.

Okay, *one* more. Just for good measure, because fuck me, she tastes like the best kind of sin.

"Ollie," I whisper when she goes in for more. "Ollie, we have an—"

"*Fuck yeah*," Garrett whoops out. "I'm five hundred bucks richer!"

Olivia's eyes flip open, wide and horrified. "Oh." She touches trembling fingers to her lips, cheeks igniting. "Oh my God."

"Hey." I run my palm down her back. "It's okay. Just a kiss. Not a big deal."

"I'm sorry," she whispers. Before I can ask what for, she slips off my lap and disappears with Cara.

"Mind your business," I toss out without any heat at everyone else as I cross the room, Emmett hot on my heels.

"*You fucking kissed her*," he hisses.

"*She said I could*," I hiss back.

He shoves my shoulder. "Do you like her?"

I jam my elbow into his ribs. "Yes, I fucking like her."

"*Shhh!*" Clapping a hand across my mouth, Emmett pushes me against the wall. With a finger on his lips, he gestures down the hall, where Cara's voice filters from.

"You like him." It's more accusation than anything.

"Of course I like him, Cara. He's charming and funny and makes me smile in this irritating sort of way and I'm losing my damn mind because I'm totally falling for Carter Beckett."

Hell yeah she is. Charming? *Check.* Funny? *As fuck.* Make her smile? *Straight from my bucket list.* Emmett rolls his eyes as I jerk a fist into my side in celebration.

I peek around the corner, frowning when Cara leads Olivia and all her compliments away. When she returns five minutes later, it's without my favorite brunette.

"Did she leave?" Shit. I fucked this up somehow, didn't I?

Cara crosses her arms, tapping her fingers. "What's your endgame here, Carter?"

"Endgame?" What the hell does that mean? I wanted to kiss her, so I did. I like her and she likes me. Why is everyone making such a big deal about this?

I mean, sure, kind of a silly question, all things considered. I'm not what you'd call boyfriend material.

But maybe . . . maybe I could be, for her.

"Yes, Carter, endgame. What's your plan?"

"I want to . . ." I scratch my head. I want to see her again. I want to take her to that Disney movie. I want to kiss her some more, maybe snuggle on my couch while we watch TV in front of the fireplace and I play with her hair, 'cause it's soft and it smells nice. "I want Olivia." *Plain and simple.*

"You want *every* girl."

"It's not the same, Cara. Not with her."

It's never really been about wanting so much as it's been about satisfying an urge, slapping a temporary bandage over a void.

Because the truth is, though I promised my mom I wouldn't let a love like my parents' get away, there's a big part of me that not only expected to never find it, but didn't want to either. When you love someone so wholly, it makes you weak. You risk pieces of yourself that you can't afford to lose.

With Olivia, the ache doesn't feel so startlingly empty. I don't know why, and the thought alone scares the shit out of me.

I'm not sure what Cara sees in me, but her expression softens. She sighs, squeezing my arm. "Ollie went upstairs to take a breath. Give her a couple of minutes, 'kay?"

I do. I give her five minutes, then ten. The longer I pretend to be interested in any conversation, the antsier I grow. By the fifth time I've opened the fridge for no reason, Adam sighs.

"Just go get her, man."

"*Fuck yeah.*" A six-pack of beer in hand, I take the stairs two at a time and rush into every spare room, frowning when I come up empty.

A sliver of golden light pours out through the cracked door at the end of the hall, along with the faint smell of burning cherry-wood. Slowly, I step into my bedroom.

Olivia's not here, but a frigid gust of wind blows through the glass doors leading out to my balcony, sheer curtains ruffling with the breeze, and I follow the smell of fire outside.

There, on the outdoor lounger set opposite the built-in stone fireplace, curled up beneath a blanket, is just the person I'm looking for.

Orange flames dance, illuminating the soft lines of her face, the gentle heave of her chest, the swell of her ruby lips. With her hands curled under her chin, Olivia sleeps soundly, the sweet sight crushing like a weight on my chest.

I've never had a woman here who I wanted something from. Never allowed a woman to be vulnerable enough in my space to fall asleep. Never had to work so hard to push down the longing that makes me itch to climb in behind her, pull her into my chest, and just fucking . . . *be*.

Until Olivia.

As I sink down to the cushion beside her, I find myself wondering if everything is always going to be *until Olivia*, if this is that point in my life where everything changes. The thought is as thrilling as it is confusing and frightening.

Olivia's toes press against my thigh, and I feel the sharp bite of her freezing skin through my jeans. Covering her feet with the fuzzy blanket, I squeeze, trying to warm them before this west coast winter can inflict permanent damage on the cutest toes I've ever seen.

Her feet flex in my grasp, arms stretching over her head like a sleepy kitten. Dark lashes flutter, giving way to bleary eyes. When the confusion fades, she drops her head back onto the cushion with a groan.

"Please tell me you didn't catch me sleeping on the balcony off your bedroom."

"I didn't catch you sleeping on the balcony off my bedroom."

She huffs a laugh and sits up. "I wasn't snooping or anything."

"So how did you end up in my bedroom, and then on my balcony, and curled up beneath my blanket, which was on my bed, by the way?"

"I . . . I . . ." Her cheeks flush as she takes a breath, then just goes for it. "I was overwhelmed and I couldn't think straight, so I came up here for some quiet and I got curious and the lights were on and your bedroom wasn't what I was expecting and then I found this and the coals were still hot and this fucking view, Carter, it's absolutely incredible and I was just staring at it and I hope you're not upset with me for invading your privacy and falling asleep."

Upset with her? I'm not upset with her. I'm just fucking *staring* at her, this breathtaking masterpiece, so wildly contradicting with the way she spits fire and sarcasm while simultaneously caring too much about what people think.

And honestly? I fucking adore her.

I take her hands in mine, squeezing them gently. "Hey, pip-squeak. Take a breath. Don't be sorry." I gesture to the crackling flames, the sea of stars swimming in the night sky, the endless trail of pines leading up to the peaks of the mountains. This view right here is why I bought this plot of land four years ago. "I get it. It's impossible not to get a little lost when you're looking out at all this. Kind of realize how small and insignificant our problems are. It's my favorite place to be when I need peace." When I need to forget who the world thinks Carter Beckett is and remember who I actually am, or who I want to be, maybe.

Olivia watches me carefully, and I wonder what she sees. Is she able to see past the image I've carelessly created for myself? I think she is. I'm less sure that her decisions aren't fueled by that image, though.

She gestures at the beer, a silent question, and I nod, watching as she twists the cap off two, one for each of us. She sips quietly for a minute before asking, "Why did you come after me?"

"Because I haven't been able to get you off my mind all night. If I'm being honest, I haven't stopped thinking about you since you walked out on me at the bar."

She nibbles her lip. "Do you know what scares me about you, Carter?"

Everything, probably, but hopefully something I can fix. "What?"

"That I honestly don't know whether you're being genuine or if you're just trying exceptionally hard to get into my pants."

"It's a dress," I tease, tugging on the sleeve wrapped around her delicate wrist. Her unimpressed face tells me it's not the time for jokes.

The short and truthful answer to her worry is both. I genuinely care about her and want to spend time with her, but I would also throw myself at her feet if it meant she'd let me destroy her body, because I want to absolutely wreck her.

I mean that in the most respectful way possible, of course.

"You make me think," I admit.

She does a half eyeroll. "Because you aren't used to having to work for it?"

Christ. Like, I fucking get it. Nobody trusts me with Olivia, her included, because I fuck around a lot. Nobody thinks I have it in me to change, to want more, to treat a girl right.

Draining my beer and ditching it on the table, I scrub my face. I don't know what to do and it's unnerving. I never have to second-guess myself on the ice. I've worked damn hard to earn the respect of my teammates, their confidence in me as their captain. I do my best not to let them down, but right now, I feel like I'm letting myself down. I don't know what my next move should be. How the hell do I get her to trust me enough to give me a shot here at something, *anything*?

Olivia touches my knee. "I'm sorry, Carter. My sauciness is my best defense mechanism."

"I see that." And I get it.

"I meant what I said earlier. I do like you. I just . . ."

"Don't trust me. And why would you? Why would anyone?"

Olivia's eyes flicker and drop. Tentatively, she wraps her fingers around mine. "I'm really sorry, Carter."

She doesn't have anything to apologize for. It's my own fault. Emmett always told me my fucking around would come back to bite me in the ass. I always figured he meant an accidental pregnancy with a puck bunny, though I'm careful as hell. Birth control and a condom or I'm not going in. I didn't think in a million years he meant that the only woman I've ever wanted would ultimately not go for me because of my past.

But here she is, having already admitted her feelings for me, the only thing standing in our way being my less-than-stellar history with relationships, or rather, lack thereof.

So, I guess I need to work on changing her mind, give her a reason to trust me, even if it's slow and takes me all damn year. I'll be her friend first, and I'll be good.

For Olivia.

13

OPRAH & OOPSIES

Carter

"So I guess that means no making out in the back row at the movies, huh?"

She giggles. "We don't really have to go."

"What? No, fuck that. *Frozen II*, right? We're going." I find my phone and flip through to the cinema app. "Let's pick a date right now. I'll grab tickets."

"But—"

"Listen. Are you telling me never, Ollie, or are you open to the possibility of a future if I prove you can trust me?"

"Hmm . . . I guess I did beat you three games in a row . . ."

"I let you win," I lie, then clap my palm over her mouth when she opens it to argue. "Okay, I leave for a series in two days, so we can go when I get back."

She rips my hand away, bringing our joined hands to her lap, and scooches closer, hanging over my phone. She taps on a date. "That Friday could work if you guys are off."

"We are." It's our bye week, actually, which is our mandated five-day break. It's going to be a busy weekend for reasons neither Cara nor Olivia knows about yet, but will by tomorrow.

"But it's a Friday night, so if you're, um . . . busy, then I totally—" Her mouth shuts when I hit the purchase button.

I tap her nose. "It's a date, pip-squeak. Now drink another beer and tell me where in Ontario you grew up."

Olivia sinks against me with a wistful sigh. "I'm from Muskoka."

"Ah, cottage country. No wonder you fell asleep out here."

"We don't have mountains, but this is . . . *wow*. It's the only time I've seen as many stars as I used to every night at home."

"How'd you wind up all the way out here?"

She sets her beer down, bouncing side to side, and her face lights like she's gearing up to tell me her favorite story.

"Okay, so, my brother—he's four years older than me,"—she touches my hand—"came out here for school and decided he never wanted to come home again. When I graduated from high school, I came to spend the summer with him and his girlfriend—she was pregnant, one-night stand, but now they're married." She waves a hand around. "You know, true love, fairy-tale bullshit. But anyway, not the point."

I could listen to her tell stories all day.

"So I came out here, and honestly, I fell in love. I spent two months hiking and exploring, and I didn't want to leave. I was all set to go to Toronto in September, but Kristin—my sister-in-law, she's fantastic—was working at the university, pulled some strings and got me a meeting with admissions. It was sheer luck they'd had someone pull back their acceptance the day before, and I got in. Flew home the next day, packed up my whole life, and drove out here three days later with my dad. I got assigned Cara as a roommate and that was the end of that. There was no turning back. She'd never let me leave now."

"I imagine Cara would be on the next plane out, ready to chase you down and drag you back here by your hair if you tried to leave her."

"My mom's tried a couple times. She still pretends she's mad at me for leaving. I was seventeen and such a quiet kid, a real homebody.

The thought of moving to Toronto for school and being away from my parents terrified me, and suddenly I was moving across the country on a whim."

She leans forward, gripping my hand. I don't know why she gets so animated when she's telling a story, but I love it. It also feels like she's dropping her walls, which I can definitely get behind.

"Mom refused to say good-bye when we left, wouldn't look at me, hug me, nothing. But then she chased the car down the street, screaming at my dad to stop. She sobbed in my arms for twenty-seven minutes before she let me go. My dad timed it."

I make a face, one that makes her giggle some more. "Sounds like something my mom would do." I sigh. "No one will ever love you the way an overbearing mom does." Or a supportive dad. You know, the I'm-your-biggest-fan kind. I had one of those, and I miss him.

An hour and a half later, the beers are gone, and Olivia's buzzing happily beside me, a permanent lazy grin etched on her face.

"Think my party's over," I murmur after several minutes of slamming car doors, hollering friends before they climb into cabs.

Olivia sighs, laying her head in my lap. I don't hesitate to bury my fingers in her hair, twirling the tip of one curl around my finger while trying not to think about how it might feel to wrap all of it around my fist and bury another body part inside of her.

I *try* not to think about it, but I'm a man, and she's one hell of a woman.

"I didn't mean to hog you up here," she tells me.

I smile down at her. "Wouldn't spend my new year any other way."

"I'm not ready to leave," she admits softly.

Fan-fucking-tastic, because I'm not ready to watch her go.

"Then don't. Sleep over."

She throws an arm up, pinching the first bit of my body she can get her grubby little fingers on. It happens to be my nipple.

"Ow, you little shit." I smack a protective palm over my injured nipple. Olivia doesn't look the least bit apologetic, so I curl overtop of her, tickling her ribs while she squeals with laughter until she's a wheezing mess, writhing around on my lap, tears threatening to spill down her cheeks. Holding her wrists over her head, I drop my face until the tips of our noses touch.

"No pinching," I whisper.

I want to do it, but it's her that tips her chin, brushing her lips across mine. Just barely. Just enough to remind me how much I like kissing her. How this is unlike anything I've ever felt before.

Taking her hand, I lead her into my bedroom.

"Think of it more like a slumber party. We could watch a movie, and you can sleep in my bed. I'll take a spare."

I pull her toward the four-poster bed, enjoying the way she shuffles along behind me as if trying to disguise her eagerness.

"Come on, Ollie." I pat the mattress. "Have a feel."

Her wide eyes bounce between me and the bed. Moving behind her, I press her palms to the mattress, covering her hands with mine.

My lips touch her ear. "It's a Hypnos. Oprah sleeps on one."

She makes a sound deep in her throat, one I someday hope to hear while we're rolling around together, naked, preferably in this very bed. She peers at me over her shoulder, licking her lips before taking the bottom one between her teeth.

"But . . . I don't . . . have any pajamas . . . Or a toothbrush."

"I'll get you both."

Her fingers dust across the soft bedding, her chest sinking lower to the mattress with the gentle guide of my hand on her lower back.

"I'll make you breakfast in the morning and maybe we could . . . talk . . . more."

She presses up on her toes and rests a knee on the mattress. "What will you make me?"

"Waffles. French toast. Bacon. Eggs. I'll make you a fucking turkey dinner if you want, just get in the damn bed."

Olivia snickers, fisting the covers. I grab her hips, tossing her onto the bed. She rolls onto her back, starfishing in the middle of the bed.

"Oh *fuck*," she moans, sweeping her arms out. *Ah, shit.* My poor dick, jumping around behind my zipper. "This is amaaaziiing."

I know that, of course. Cost me fifteen grand, taxes in. Worth every penny.

Hands in my pocket, I watch her with a smile as she rolls around, testing it out. She's not bothered when the door handle jiggles, or when Cara calls out to her.

"Livvie? You in there, babe?"

"Uh-huh."

"Uh-huh? Well, get out here. We're going home."

Olivia sits up, looking to the door, then me, like she doesn't know what to do. If it was my choice, I'd keep her here until she had to go back to work. We'd also be naked the entire time, trying out a few choice gymnastic moves.

"If you don't want to stay, it's okay," I tell her quietly.

She cocks her head, studying me. "Um, I'm going to . . ." The corner of her mouth lifts. "Stay."

I clap my hands together and scream out a silent *yes!* before divebombing the bed, wrapping my arms around her, rolling her around in some sort of weird hug while she squeals with laughter. I jog across the room to my dresser, pulling out a T-shirt and a pair of sweatpants. I hold the pants up in question; they're going to swallow her whole. She makes a face and shakes her head.

"What the fuck? Carter Beckett, are you in there?" Cara shakes the handle. "Carter, open this fucking door right now! Em, kick it down! Keep your dick out of my best friend's palace!"

Throwing my shirt to Olivia, I hit the lock and whip the door open, gesturing at my body with the sweep of my arm. "I'm fully dressed, and my dick is in my pants, right where it belongs, thank you very much."

Cara appears both unimpressed and shocked. Emmett, on the other hand, grins from ear to ear as he pokes his head in. He doubles over with laughter, clearly wasted, when he spies Olivia on the bed.

"Oh my God," Olivia croons, on her knees in the center of my bed, holding my shirt to her body. "Care, look! He gave me his shirt to sleep in. It's gonna be a dress on me!"

Cara holds her hands up. "What in the fuck is going on here?"

"I'm just gonna sleep." Olivia ditches the shirt and lifts the blankets, sliding beneath them. Her head disappears between the pillows until all I can see are her arms, which she holds high in the air. "I kicked Carter Beckett out of his own bed. Somebody take a picture! I don't think this has ever happened before!"

It hasn't. I do a lot of shit with Olivia I've never had a desire to do with anyone else.

Emmett dives for the mattress, snuggling up to Olivia as he holds his phone above their heads, snapping a picture while they snicker. I kinda wanna crawl in there.

Scratch that. I *really* wanna crawl in there. And kick my best bud the hell out.

Cara points a terrifying finger in my face. "I'm too drunk to yell at you. If you hurt her, be prepared to eat your own dick. I've heard it's huge, so it's a good thing you have a big appetite." Scary eyes move between mine. "Got it, Beckett?"

Holding up two fingers, I pledge, "I solemnly swear I will not hurt Olivia Parker."

She pats my chest and turns back to the bed where her best friend and boyfriend are still bouncing around. "It's like I have kids sometimes." She stalks over, dragging Emmett off the bed and kissing Olivia's cheek. "Have fun, be safe, and don't make any ill-advised decisions."

Olivia salutes her. "Yes, Mom."

Cara rolls her eyes but laughs, and Emmett shuts the door with the pump of his brows. A minute later, the front door opens and closes, leaving the house eerily quiet.

I never thought I'd be here tonight, alone with Olivia, especially not in my bed.

Her curls are a wild mess, blankets pooled around her waist. She's like the antichrist, sitting there in bed, everything about her dark—hair, gaze, dress—a stark contrast to the fluffy white bedding. Nothing but filthy, downright naughty thoughts run through my mind. *Antichrist.*

I clear my throat. "You just gonna sleep in your dress?"

Her grin is slow, all devil, as she slips out of the bed. "I was waiting for Cara to leave so I could peel it off."

I swallow my tongue, watching her stroll toward me with all the confidence in the world. And I get the hell out of the way.

"'Kay. I'll, uh . . ." I thumb toward the door. "Give you some privacy."

I reach for the handle, and Olivia's hand comes down hard on the wood, slamming it shut the moment it opens. She turns the lock, and suddenly the energy in the room is about as electrically charged as the nine inches of titanium straining behind my zipper right now.

I puff out a heavy exhale, sagging at the click of the bathroom door behind me. Sinking to the edge of the bed, I stare up at the ceiling, praying for some much-needed self-restraint.

"Uh, hey, Ollie," I call out weakly. Shaking my head, I drag my hands down my face. "I think we should talk about, um . . ." *Fuck, this is painful.*

"I like you," I blurt for at least the second time. I'm talking to a door. "I was thinking . . . maybe we could . . . I could maybe . . . maybe you can learn to trust me, you know, give me a chance, if I show you . . . you can trust me . . ." It's barely a whisper by the time I reach the end because I have no idea what the fuck I'm doing.

Silence.

And then: "Tomorrow."

I leap to my feet. "What?"

"We can talk tomorrow. After you make me a turkey dinner for breakfast."

Fucking *yes.* I look down at my main man. He's not deflating any time soon. He's about as excited as I am. "Hear that, big buddy?" I whisper eagerly to him. "We're fucking gettin' somewhere!"

"Carter?" Olivia calls. "Can you help me?"

Dashing across the room, I pause at the bathroom door. Before I can ask if she's decent, she opens the door, yanks me inside, and tries to kill me.

"I need you to unzip me."

Fuck. *Fuck, fuck, fuck, fuuuck.*

"Carter." Olivia's fingers twine with mine. "I need you to look at me if you're going to help me."

Oh. Right. I'm looking at my feet. I chuckle. It comes out a fuckload anxious and high-pitched. I run my hand down my chest before twirling a finger in the air. "Turn around, gorgeous."

Our eyes meet in the mirror, and she smiles. It's cute and a little loopy, and when her teeth sink into her lower lip, I grin. She's the cutest, and I wanna keep her.

I sweep her curls over her shoulder, trailing a finger down her neck to her dress, right where her—

"Uh, Ol. There's . . . there's no zipper back here. Your dress is . . ." I pull on the soft fabric, watching it stretch from her back with ease, giving me a glimpse of the flawless skin below. "Stretchy."

"Oh, right." Her ruby red lips part with a beam, goofy and beautiful. "Oops."

Oops?

This is also the moment I catch sight of the satin blush bra on the corner of my bathroom countertop.

Oh, fuck. Oops is fucking right.

I'm about to make a big fucking *oops.*

14

DOOMSDAY

Olivia

I'M NOT ENTIRELY IN MY right mind.

It's part alcohol, but mostly delirious, undeniable attraction to the man currently standing behind me, slack-jawed at the sight before him.

The sight is me, braless, asking him to take my dress off.

And in case he's not certain of what I'm asking, I guide his hands to my hips, up to the dip of my waist. "Guess you can just slip it off then."

Who am I? I don't know. A girl who's going to take life by the balls, I guess. Or rather, Carter Beckett. I'm going to take Carter Beckett by the balls.

This feels like one of those ill-advised decisions Cara warned me about before walking out of here.

But the thing is . . . I want him. I like him, despite everything.

I guess I've decided the fallout is something I'm willing to deal with, because here I am in Carter's bathroom, asking him to undress me.

Maybe it was his defeated expression when he talked about the lack of trust everyone has in him. Maybe it was him asking me to stay, promising me movies and breakfast. Maybe it was him sitting there next to me, absolutely riveted while I rambled on. He wasn't

Carter Beckett, egotistical hockey phenomenon and ladies' man. He was just . . . Carter.

And I like him that way, when all the walls fall away. Maybe that made me feel special. Maybe it put some stock in his words. Maybe . . . maybe I trust him a little more than I did when I walked through the front door several hours ago.

I don't know. The only thing I do know is I can't fight this anymore. I'm tired.

He looms over me, fingertips digging into my waist like he's finally holding something he's always wanted. It's a sight I want to remember, the way he can't take his eyes off our reflection; the way he breathes so deeply, like he can barely contain himself.

Beyond that, there's an apprehension, a hesitation to take this step. So I tip my head back, fingers dancing up his neck, and he dips his face, smiling.

"Can I kiss you?" he whispers.

I nod, and his mouth descends. It's tender and soft, teasing and tasting, lingering, and I want more. More of this, more of him. I sink my fingers into his waves, tugging him closer, and when his tongue laps at mine, he steals the whimper right from my throat.

His hand coasts up, over my breasts, wrapping gently around my throat to hold me there, my mouth his to explore.

He breaks away, drawing my gaze to his. It's dark and heady, like I'm the only thing he's capable of seeing, lulling me into a fake sense of security. I want him to have my body, and I want to pretend he knows how to keep all of it safe.

"Look at you." He strokes my lower lip. "You're so fucking small and delicate, I'm afraid I might break you."

"I'm not made of glass, Carter. You don't have to be gentle with me. In fact, I'd prefer if you weren't."

My ass is on the counter a second later, legs wrapped around his waist, my curls wrapped around his fist as he pulls my head taut.

His mouth hovers so close to mine that I can't tell who each erratic breath belongs to as we breathe each other in.

Rough fingers scrape up my thigh, slipping below the hem of my dress, pushing it up until it pools around my hips. He wraps a hand around my bare waist, and my entire body trembles.

Carter's heated gaze dips to the space between us, the damp spot in the center of my panties, and his throat bobs. He watches me closely, brushing his thumb over my clit as it cramps with need.

"Carter," I whimper, and his mouth collides with mine.

He shifts against me, a slow grind that makes my head fall. His mouth slides up my throat, hot, wet kisses that have my hips lifting, desperate for friction. He gives it to me, hands sliding beneath me, kneading my ass, pulling me closer.

Gentle nips trail my jaw until his lips find my ear. "If we do this, Olivia, there's no going back."

No going back from what? If we do this, it's the beginning of something. Something intimate and feral, and maybe something more, but more than likely, the beginning of the end.

A murmur of grief echoes in my chest, reminding me that this isn't me, that I want so much more than fleeting nights and good-byes. The steady, quick thud of my heart tells me to give up the fight just for tonight, to embrace it for what it is: one night of guaranteed passion with the man I can't stop thinking about.

Tucked deep below all that is the part of me with very real fears and insecurities, the part that's been comparing myself to the women wrapped around his arm in every picture.

But the chemistry between us buzzes like a live wire, making it impossible for me to think clearly right now. I know what I want, and what I want is this man—inside of me, all over me, taking, possessing, over and over.

So I tell him, "If you want me, you can have me."

With one fell swoop, I'm on my feet, back pressed to his chest, my dress in the clawfoot tub in the corner, next to the immaculate glass shower. Rough hands grip my hips, his gaze raking over me like hot coals. Soft lips press tender kisses across my shoulder, down the slope of my spine as Carter hooks his thumbs into my panties and slowly lowers himself to his knees, taking the lace with him as he goes.

His warm mouth slides up the back of my thigh, and when one hand slips between my legs where my heartbeat has found itself, I squeeze my eyes shut and hold on to the edge of the counter for dear life.

"You're nervous," Carter murmurs.

Nervous, drunk on raw desire, terrified of the generous helping of honest to goodness feelings that scare the shit out of me . . . All of it swirls inside me, grabbing hold of my heart, clenching it like a fist.

"Fucking stunning." The words are a wonderous whisper as his fingers glide through the wetness spread between my thighs from behind. He stands, kisses my neck, and holds my gaze. "Flawless." He palms one breast, rolling my taut nipple. His teeth scrape my ear. "How wet are you?"

"Oh God." The answer is *drenched*, and he knows it. "Touch me," I beg. "Please, Carter."

"Look at me." When I do, he drags his fingers through my slick slit before sinking one inside. "Fuck." His mouth opens on my shoulder as I cry out his name. "Such a wet fucking pussy."

His fingers wrap around my throat as he thrusts inside of me, an achingly slow plunge that has me pleading for more. Flames spark in my stomach, like I'm teetering on the edge of a volcanic eruption.

He adds another finger, filling me wonderfully, a steady drive that picks up speed, ferocity, until the heel of his palm slaps against my ass with each thrust.

His chest rumbles with approval as I take everything he gives me, including the words he forces down my throat when his mouth takes mine. "Good girl."

Everything inside me comes to a rolling boil, spilling over as he releases my neck to work the tight bundle of nerves at the cleft of my thighs, smiling against my skin when his name explodes off my lips.

Without hesitation, he flings me over his shoulder, hand on my ass as he marches into the bedroom and tosses me onto the bed. He smiles when I giggle, arms sweeping over the bedding as I bury my head in the fluffy pillows.

"I never want to leave this bed."

He tears his shirt overhead, steps out of his jeans, and crawls over me, kissing the corner of my mouth before I have time to admire how beautiful his body is. "So don't. Think I could keep you forever."

I bury the feeling that fuels in my chest and burns in my belly way down deep inside me, because that's a dangerous thing to think he might mean. I may be slightly intoxicated, but I'm 100 percent positive Carter Beckett is a man I could fall in love with.

I'm not a one-night stand girl; I've already said that. For me, sex comes after feelings. I might have failed to mention that I rarely catch feelings. It's a blessing or a curse; I haven't decided yet. I look for a real connection and those are hard to come by. It also means that in my twenty-five years I've only had sex with two men, quite the contrast from Carter's list.

"Hey." He guides my gaze to his. "Where'd you go? Kinda disappeared on me there." Soft lips trace my jaw until he buries his face in my hair. "And why the fuck do you always smell so good? Like banana bread, freshly baked. I wanna devour you."

Desire takes flight like butterflies in my stomach, a heavy ache between my thighs.

"The only problem is I don't know where to start. I wanna be everywhere, all at once. Like . . ." His fingertips dance over my breast, and he drags his thumb over my nipple. "Here."

He dips his head, circling my nipple with his tongue, and if I wasn't already dead, I am now.

"But I also wanna be . . ." His mouth coasts a slow, torturous path down my stomach, every bit of me shaking with anticipation. "Here."

His mouth continues its leisurely path, sucking on my hip bone, staining my skin. He settles his face between my legs, alternating the wet slide of his tongue and the press of his lips as he glides up my thighs.

"And here," he whispers, finishing at the juncture of my thighs.

"Fuck." His breath crackles like the fire outside, and I can't breathe. "Here, Olivia? Here's where I wanna be most."

With one languid stroke, he licks me from bottom to top, and *fuck fuck fuck*, when he sucks my clit into his mouth, I can't. I plow my fingers through his hair as he tosses my legs over his shoulders, buries his face between my legs, and does what he promised: fucking devours me.

The way he eats me is nothing short of ferocious, a meal when he hasn't eaten in days, hot lashes of his tongue paired with searing kisses as I cling to him, grinding against his perfect face.

"Fuck," I moan, back arching as he thrusts two fingers inside me. "Carter, I—I . . . I can't."

"You can."

He's relentless, a savage intent on showing no mercy as he watches me climb higher, and when he throws me over the edge, I clap a hand across my mouth to stifle my cry.

Carter tears my hand away, pinning my wrists above my head as he looms over me. "Slap that hand back there again and I'll tie both of them to the bedpost. I wanna hear you scream my name when you come with me inside you. Got it?"

Oh shit. Yes. I nod, five hundred times, and he grins.

"No sassy comebacks, Ol? Did I break you?"

I press my lips to his, whispering against them. "You haven't broken me yet, but I'm hoping if I'm a good girl, you will soon."

"Fuck." He brackets my jaw, dark eyes fixed on mine. "I wanna give you whatever you want."

"Wreck me, Carter."

Our mouths collide in a frenzy, scraping teeth, sliding tongues, bruising touches. I shove him down to the mattress and straddle his hips, because I need a minute to properly admire the masterpiece that's Carter Beckett. He's broad and firm, solid, corded muscles moving lithely beneath golden skin. I trail the tip of my finger down the etched path in his torso, then further, through soft curls that disappear below the waistband of his boxer briefs.

"You're so beautiful," I murmur.

"Me?" There's something in his gaze, something obscure and yet so vulnerable, like he wants me to see it but doesn't know how to show me. "You're fucking immaculate, Ollie."

My heart races, nerves squeezing my throat. If it weren't for sheer desire to let go and feel the weight of his need for me, mixed with the drinks we've consumed that's lowered both our inhibitions, I might hit pause. We need to talk, but when all I can see is his body below mine and that heady look in his eyes, I don't remember how to communicate.

"Hey," he whispers. "What's wrong? You wanna stop, we'll stop. I'll snuggle the shit outta you and we can watch a movie. I'm cool with that."

"I've only had sex with two people," I blurt out. "I only sleep with people I care about."

If he's surprised, he doesn't show it. Instead, he cups my cheek, kisses me softly, and says, "I'm sorry I can't say the same. But I can tell you honestly if I only had sex with people I cared about, I'd be losing my virginity tonight at the age of twenty-seven."

Surely that can't be right. There's no way I'm the only person he's ever—

"I've never felt this way about anyone before. Never, Ollie. I just want you to consider . . . consider giving me a shot. Consider me. That's all I want, Ol. A chance with you." A gentle kiss sweeps across my knuckles. "We can talk more about it in the morning." He lifts me off him, pulling me against his chest as he settles us beneath the blankets, stuffing his face in the crook of my neck as he murmurs, "Banana bread."

"Carter." I'm so lost, which is not at all what I want to be when I'm this turned on. "What are you doing?"

"Snuggling you." Clearly, and he's doing it well. I'm surprised; pretty sure it's his first time. "I've never been a snuggler before." *There we go.* "I think I'm fucking fantastic at it." *And hello, arrogance.*

"You're doing impressively well. But what are you *doing*?"

" . . . Stopping? Isn't that . . . isn't that what you want?"

"When did I ever ask you to stop?"

"You said . . . I . . . well, I guess you . . . didn't."

"You're right. I didn't." I push him down and straddle his lap, rolling my hips over the cock that's fighting so damn hard for freedom.

Carter's mouth falls open, hands balling into fists at his sides before he grabs hold of my hips, stopping me. He shifts me, just enough to reveal that I've drenched his boxers. Dipping my hand between my thighs, I run two fingers through my pussy. They come away soaked, and when I slip them between my lips, it's not me who moans, but Carter.

"You said you wanted to hear me scream your name when I come. Are you going to make me or not? If you're not up for the challenge, I can take care of myself."

Without warning, he flips me to my back, pinning me below his weight. His teeth graze my throat, up to my ear. "Mouthy girl. You wanna be wrecked, do you? I can make sure you don't walk out of here if that's what you really want."

"Prove it."

I'm on my hands and knees before I can comprehend how I got there, and Carter's palm lands swiftly against my ass, a burst of pain and pleasure rushing through me, pooling between my legs.

"*Fuck*, this pussy." He climbs off the bed and pulls me to the edge. I hear his underwear hit the ground, but all I feel is the plunge of his fingers as I gasp, clawing at the sheets. He pulls out, leaving a trail of wetness along my hip when he flips me to my back. All coherent thoughts promptly exit my brain at the sight of him standing there completely naked, fisting his cock in his hand.

"Holy shit." I'm not sure *wrecked* is the right word for what Carter's going to do to me. Totally destroy, yes. Obliterate, I think so. He's so smug, that self-assured grin growing as my eyes widen when he starts stalking toward me, thick, muscular thighs flexing with each step.

I crawl backward when his knees hit the mattress, that *thing* dangling between his legs, dragging across the bedding. Aside from the wild beat of my heart, the only other thing I can hear is the slowness with which it slithers across the bed, alerting me to my impending doom.

"I—I . . ." For the love of God, what the hell am I trying to say? I give up on words, instead spreading my arms out, palms facing each other, before I make a tiny *O* with my pointer finger and thumb. I shake my head and shrug. "It's not gonna fit."

Carter's chuckle is way too ominous for my liking, and I'm still doing the crab walk. My hand slips and I start tumbling over the edge of the bed, legs in the air. He catches me before I can do any damage that might potentially and prematurely end this trip to heaven/hell that I'm so looking forward to, even though Carter's packing a goddamn missile that's going to blow my vagina to smithereens.

Taking hold of my ankles, he drags me beneath him, his cock brushing against my swollen clit. He drops his hips, a slow grind that steals the air from my lungs. With a fistful of my hair, he brings my mouth to his, the hot lash of his tongue doing nothing to ease the apprehension his next promise brings.

"We're gonna make it fit."

Pushing my legs wider, he runs his fingers up my soaked pussy, then coats his cock with my wetness. The sight is so filthy, so beautiful, I nearly miss his wicked grin when he asks, "Any last words?"

I shake my head.

"Good. Hold on."

His smile slips, a lust so dark, so feral clouding his eyes. When he slams inside me with a single punishing thrust, my entire world fades to black. My mouth opens and he swallows my scream before it can escape.

"Oh my God," I cry, tearing into his shoulders, clinging to him as he fills me. "Wait, Carter, please."

His body stills, trembling, and he grips my throat like he's afraid if he doesn't hang on to something he won't be able to control himself.

But he's so big, so thick, so heavy, and every inch of me feels so tight, stretched beyond belief.

He drops his forehead to mine, chest heaving. "I'm sorry, Ollie."

The pain wanes, a delirious fullness that spreads like flames, heat licking at my skin. I snag my lip between my teeth, moaning as I arch off the bed, taking him a little bit farther as I adjust to his size. My nails rake down his arms, eyes rolling to heaven, as his hips start rolling, a slow grind that coaxes every knot inside me loose, until everything starts unfurling.

His anxious gaze bounces between mine, seeking instruction, permission, *control*. Control I'm willing to give.

"Fuck me, Carter. Please."

A snarl rumbles deep in his chest as he drops me to the mattress and does exactly what I asked: *fucks me*.

His skin slaps against mine as he pistons inside me, so deep I swear I can feel him in my belly. His touch is rough, fire that singes everywhere it touches, branding me as his. Each roll of his pelvis sends sparks through my clit, each plunge of his cock deeper and harder than the last, until I feel weightless. I'm nothing but bones and sheer pleasure burning through me from head to toe, lighting me aflame from the inside out.

Carter's fingers tangle in my curls, dig into my hip, keeping me in place as his body dominates mine.

"Fuck," he growls against my neck. "Fucking love fucking you." He slides a wet kiss across my mouth. "I want more, Ollie. I'm gonna take it."

I don't know what more I can give, but then he lifts my leg and throws it over his shoulder, grabs onto the headboard, and pummels into me with everything he has.

"Pill," he grunts out. "Are you on—"

"*Yes*."

"Can I—"

"God, *yes*."

A throaty, pleased hum rumbles as he drives faster, and I cry out his name, palms sliding over the knotted muscles on his back. There's nowhere else to go, but when my hands find his ass, I squeeze him closer anyway, begging for *harder*.

"Harder? Haven't we covered this? I want to keep you, not break you."

I shove him to the mattress and sink down his length before he can protest. My head falls backward with a cry of unbridled pleasure, and Carter hisses, lifting me up and slamming me back down on his cock, over and over.

Leaning upwards, he takes my nipple into his mouth as I ride him, sucking, nipping, and I nearly yank his hair right out of his head. The look he gives me when he shifts back, brushing my clit, sends me straight off the deep end, and I come all over his cock.

"One more," he growls, pulling me off him. He flips me onto my belly, pulls my head taut, and jerks my ass into the air before he thrusts back inside me. "You're gonna give me one more."

One more? I can't. I fall to the mattress, boneless and limp, but Carter hauls me back up, his whisper pressed to my ear.

"We're done when I say we're done."

"Carter," I whimper.

"Fucking love when you say my name." His wet mouth glides up my neck, teeth grazing the shell of my ear. "Now scream it."

He drives himself forward, once, twice, three more times, and when he hits that spot I can never seem to find, every nerve ending sizzles and pops. I rip the sheet right off the bed and do what he asked: scream his name.

Carter explodes inside of me, and I swear I've never seen a sight more beautiful than this man coming, burying his cry against my slick neck.

He pulls out, tugging me into his side as he collapses to the mattress, and the empty feeling is so profound, I wonder if I'll ever be that full again.

I place my palm over his chest, feeling the steady thrum of the heart below. Carter covers my hand, and a startling warmth crawls up my chest to that vital organ I'm meant to keep safe.

"Can I keep you?" he asks.

"Yes." My heart skitters to a stop at the simple answer spoken without thought, and only when Carter tilts my chin and captures my mouth a kiss does it restart.

It's in this moment that I realize how earth-shatteringly fucked I am.

15

IS THIS KARMA? I DON'T LIKE HER

Carter

"Oh shit. Fuck. Shit, shit, shit."

Cracking one lid, I try to pin Olivia's panicked voice. I was having the very best dream. Olivia under me, over me, her lips, her hands, her perfect tits. The sooner I find her, the sooner I get to live out the dream in real life.

Rolling onto my back, I sweep an arm over the empty spot beside me. It's still warm and I can smell her all over my sheets, like a fresh batch of cookies. I wanna eat her right up.

"Come back to bed, Ollie." I scrub my eyes, riding out a never-ending yawn, finally sitting up when I hear a loud crash followed by a string of curses.

Olivia's stark naked, lying in a crumpled heap on the floor.

I lean over the bed, smiling. "What you doin' down there, baby?"

Her lips part with what looks like—but cannot possibly be—horror, and she moves her hands over her stellar tits. I didn't expect the shyness this morning, sans alcohol, but I guess it makes sense.

Hanging halfway off the bed, I rest a palm on the hardwood and reach out to her. I need to get her back up here so I can fuck her back to sleep.

I swear I had a goddamn epiphany last night while my sword of thunder was buried nine inches deep inside the most insanely stunning woman I've ever sparred with. I never wanted to leave, and this morning, I still don't. I hope she's okay with that, because I'm pretty sure she just got herself a shadow.

The shadow is me. I'm gonna be glued to her leg like a horny, unneutered dog for a long-ass time. Maybe forever. I don't fuckin' know. I only know I'm not letting go.

But she scoots backward, snapping her jaw shut. "I'm *not* your baby."

Okay, so Olivia's not a morning person.

"Do you need coffee?"

Whoops. Wrong question.

I resist the urge to hide under the covers, instead offering her a gritty version of my delightfully charming smile that I think she loves/hates. It doesn't seem to be having the desired effect.

She jumps to her feet, snatching the blanket off my body and wrapping it around herself.

She makes a throaty sound, wide gaze glued to . . .

My dick. He's happy to see her this morning, giving her the ol' one-eyed salute as he bobs around.

"Good morning," I say with a chuckle, swiveling my hips, making him dance. "All of me is happy to see all of you."

Christ, she's hard to crack this morning. Not even a smile, just a hand slapped across her eyes.

I cock a brow. "You know he got well acquainted with your palace last night, right?"

Olivia sure is making a lot of sounds today. This one is all whimper-moan, right before she makes a mad dash for the bathroom, slamming the door behind her.

But I'm not shy, so I slip out of bed and stroll right through that door.

I run a hand down my torso, giving it a little scratch before I fist the base of my cock, looking at the beautiful girl wrapped in a sheet, her dress in one hand, phone in the other, enormous brown eyes set on me.

"What the fuck are you doing? We should be in bed, cuddling." *Or fucking.* "And this . . ." I trail a finger along her collarbone until I reach her fist where she's clutching the sheet tight to her body. "I don't care where this goes, as long as it fucking *goes.*"

I tear the sheet away, letting it pool at our feet. With two handfuls of her ass, I hoist her up to me, wrapping her legs around my hips before I press her against the glass shower. I bite back a groan at the feel of her hot, soaked pussy pressed against me.

"You're gonna need to cancel any plans you have." I drag slow, wet kisses up her neck, then nip at her chin. She's got the tiniest dimple there, right in the center, and I love it. "I'm keeping you all damn day."

Olivia's mouth opens like she's going to say something, maybe argue with me the way she likes to. Instead, our mouths collide. She clings to me, fingers plowing through my hair, back arching, hips rolling.

"Perfect," I grumble against her lips. "Christ, Ollie, you're fucking perfect."

Her breath snags, and she shoves against my chest, pushing me away.

I'm confused, but I almost always am when it comes to her, because I can't read her mind.

But wait. Maybe we're just— "Are we roughin' it up?" I ask with a smirk, prowling toward her. I'm into it. I'm into everything as long as she's part of it. If she wants to push me around, I'll push her right back.

Like, nicely. But not too nice.

"What?" She shakes her head, hands out between us. "No, Carter. Stop. Please."

Stop? What? No. I don't want to. But I do, of course.

"Are you okay?" I look her over with a slow sweep. It gets heated on the way down and I wind up making three passes. "Did I hurt you last night?"

I reach for her right hip, brushing the four round bruises that match my fingertips. Twisting her, I find my thumbprint on her backside. She's covered in a fuckton of tiny purple hickeys, too, drawing a possessive growl from my chest.

Mine, my brain shouts out, and my cock twitches in agreement.

"No, you didn't—" She stops, covering her face before pushing by me, pulling her dress over her head. "I have to go."

She forgoes the bra, choosing instead to hook it onto her wrist before searching the floor, looking for the thong I peeled off her last night, I assume. I neglect to tell her that it's in the pocket of my jeans, half buried under the bed.

I scratch my head. "Go where? Do you have plans? I thought you were gonna stay for breakfast."

Olivia ignores me, giving up on the hunt for her undies. She heads for the door, yanking it open and barreling down the hall, and I'm so fucking lost.

I throw on a pair of sweats and fly down the stairs behind her, spinning her back to me. "Are you gonna say anything?" Her eyes are trained on my torso. "Or look at me?" I blow out a frustrated breath and plow my fingers through my hair. "Fuck, Ollie, I'm so confused right now."

"I have to go," she whispers.

"Go fucking where?" It comes out louder than I intend, and Olivia flinches. I take a deep breath, and taking her hands in mine, try again. "I'm sorry. I'm just a little lost. You said we were gonna talk about us, and—"

"*You* said that, not me."

I blink down at her. She's still not looking at me.

"You-you-you—" Christ, is this really happening right now? Am I stammering? "You agreed! You said we'd talk after breakfast!"

"We both had too much to drink." Her excuse is weak and she knows it. "I don't think we knew what we were doing."

Bullshit. "Fucking look at me if you're gonna lie to me, Olivia."

Her eyes snap to mine, and I don't like what I see. They're red rimmed, her bottom lip wobbly. What the hell is going on? This is so damn simple. There's no reason to cry, because I'm right fucking here, wanting her, like I have from the moment I saw her. I may not have any experience with relationships, but I know well enough that this shit I'm feeling isn't one sided. This situation she's putting us in right now? Neither of us wants to be here. And yet, she's doing it anyway.

"So that's that? Just another one-night stand? Thanks for the sex, see you never?"

"It's what you want," she tries to tell me, clutching her phone to her chest.

"You don't know the first thing about what I want. If you did, you wouldn't be turning your back on me and walking out of here right now, claiming this was just sex that means fuck all to me, or to you. That's bullshit. You know it and I know it." I'm not afraid to argue with her. I'll do it all damn day if I think she's wrong, and right now, she is.

She ducks around me, heading for the kitchen, stepping into the heels she left there. "I have to go, Carter."

"No, you don't. You're refusing to communicate. Here I am wanting to talk about what the hell is going on between us, and there you are, trying to run away."

"There's nothing—"

"Don't you fucking say there's nothing going on between us!" I'm shouting again and I hate it. I get worked up easily and I'm really on edge right now. I thrive on control, and right now, all

I'm doing is losing all semblance of it. This girl owns me—*for some fucking reason*—and I refuse to let her make the wrong decision for both of us.

So I stalk toward her, backing her against the wall. Shattered brown eyes meet mine, and I push her hair off her face.

"Stop it. Stop pretending like you aren't scared out of your mind right now, like that hasn't been the only thing holding you back this entire time. I can see what's right in front of me, and that's you, beautiful, sarcastic, smart, strong, sensitive, and fucking *scared* of the way you feel for someone you never wanted to have feelings for."

Her phone slips from her shaking hands, and I catch it before it can hit the ground. My face fills the screen, except it's not only mine. Over and over, picture after picture of me with my arm wrapped around a different woman, heading into my condo, into hotels.

The worst part, by far, is the headline, the one with today's date beneath it.

"New Year, Same Carter: Carter Beckett's Twelve Hottest Conquests and What We Can Expect of Him This Year"

I look to Olivia. The weight of the turmoil she wears, the sympathy, the fear, all of it is heavy, turning down the edges of her mouth, guiding her gaze down.

"This isn't me." I tip her chin up, stealing her gaze. "This doesn't have to be me."

"How can you promise that?" she whispers, her voice cracking. "We barely know each other. You admitted last night that you didn't know if a relationship was what you wanted." She shakes her head, gesturing at her phone in my hand. "I can't compete with that, not even in my own head, which is where it's most impor-tant. You may think I'm strong but I have no qualms admitting I'm way too insecure to pretend how many gorgeous women you've been with doesn't fucking terrify me, that I wouldn't be constantly waiting for you to get bored of me." She presses her fingertips to her forehead like she's got a headache. "You have a condo for sex."

That's not actually why I have it, but I'm not wasting time on that distinction right now.

"None of those women mean anything to me, Olivia."

"I got so wrapped up in you last night, lost so much control, that we didn't think to wear a condom. That's so reckless."

I rub at my neck. "I don't have girls here, Olivia. Ever. I wasn't lying." Maybe it's a piss-poor excuse, but I don't have a single condom in the house. I do keep one in my wallet, but that was stored down here in the entryway table, and in the heat of the moment . . . "Are you not on the pill?" Fuck. Didn't I ask her this?

"I'm on the pill, but . . ." She trails off, glancing at my crotch.

"I'm clean," I mutter. If I sound defeated, it's because I fucking am. She's never going to get over my past. "That's the first time I . . ." First time I went in bare, but I don't finish that thought out loud. "I get tested." My throat is tight and dry. "I don't want you to go. I like you, and you said you like me too."

"I *do* like you. I like what you've shown me, but there are other things . . ." She squeezes her eyes shut and shakes her head. "I wish I could overlook everything else and jump right in. But I don't know how, Carter, because when I look down, there's not a single part of me that can see the ground. I don't want messy and scary. I want steady and sure."

Steady and sure, got it. I can be steady and sure. I can figure it out.

"Listen, I know I'm not boyfriend material, but I can try. Really, I can. I'll be good. I'll-I'll—"

She places her hand on my chest, stopping me. "I don't want you to change for me, Carter. This, us . . . It was a mistake."

Ouch. I step back, rubbing my palm over my chest, trying to soothe the sudden, sharp pain.

Olivia's gaze softens. "I'm not trying to hurt you."

"It sure as hell doesn't feel that way," I bite back, because everything fucking hurts.

"I'm sorry. I really am."

"You don't have to be sorry. You just have to trust me."

Her shoulders slump. "I wish I could, but I don't know how to." She takes my hand in hers, clutching it to her chest. "We're not right for each other."

"How do you know that? Everything has felt right since I met you. It hasn't been easy, but it's felt right."

It would have been naïve for me to think it would be easy, that we'd be able to fall into some sort of . . . relationship. But after last night, I thought she'd at least consider it. Consider me. I'm fucking trying here. I've decided what I want. Isn't it supposed to be easy from here on out?

I understand the hesitation, the fear. How can I not? The media isn't blowing smoke; my reputation is exactly the way it's been painted. She's allowed to be terrified. *I'm* terrified. I'm in unchartered waters here. I'm scared I'll hurt her. I'm scared I don't know how to be a partner. I'm scared that this could . . . work. I'm scared that she could be my forever. Christ, that's petrifying.

But right now, I'm most terrified that she's going to walk out that door and never come back.

"I don't know," she admits. "I don't know anything except that I'm too afraid of walking into something that feels like a heartbreak waiting to happen. It's like running into a burning building, Carter. We're too different, and the only way this can end is up in flames."

"Sometimes different is good," I argue quietly. "I like different."

The corner of her mouth lifts with a sad smile, and I know. She's leaving, even if there's a part of her that begs her to stay. Even if all of me begs too.

"We shouldn't have had sex," I whisper. She told me last night that she couldn't trust me enough to move forward, and yet when everything fell away for a few hours, all the insecurities, the apprehension, the hopeful part of my brain thought those things might be gone forever.

But fears don't disappear overnight. Even I know that.

"No," she agrees, squeezing my hand. "We shouldn't have. And I'm sorry, because I'm the one who initiated it. I took something I wanted but told myself I couldn't have. You would have never pushed me into it."

And then we wouldn't be here, with her walking out on me like she has every intention of putting too much space between us, distance I don't want at all. If I give her space, will she come back?

"Is it forever?" I ask as she slips her arms into her coat. "Good-bye?"

Her watery eyes meet mine, searching as silence hangs heavy in the space between us. All I can hear is the rapid *thump thump* of my angry, bruised heart. She doesn't want it to be forever, but I can tell by the look in her eyes that it's the way she thinks it needs to be, so before she can answer, I beat her to it.

"You leaving right now doesn't change how I feel about you, and it won't change your feelings for me either. I know you're hoping they'll disappear so you don't have to deal with the way I've been living my life, but they won't. Running from things you're afraid of won't get you very far."

I head back to the kitchen, pulling open the drawer I slammed shut in a hurry when Adam swept Olivia into his arms last night. I take out the small package wrapped in brown paper with little white stars, the burlap bow tied around it with a tiny jingle bell. I tried wrapping it myself five times over before I finally enlisted my sister's help.

I meet Olivia at the door, and a lump forms in the back of my throat as I take her in one last time. Even when she's leaving me, she's still beautiful.

"Do you need a ride?" I ask.

"Thank you, but I ordered an Uber."

I nod as she steps onto the porch.

"Ollie?"

The quiver in her hands tells me it's taking everything in her not to fall apart right now.

"Just so we're clear, you're the one who's walking away right now. This isn't what I want."

I tuck the small gift into her hands, watching her forehead crinkle in surprise. "Merry Christmas."

16

FEEDING MY FEARS

Olivia

MY LIFE FEELS LIKE IT's hanging on a delicate balance, swaying back and forth with my own indecision, my desires tipping the scale on one side, and my fears on the other. Both are heavy, and I can't get a handle on either. Instead, everything feels ready to teeter and crash before inevitably going up in flames.

Except things might have already gone up in flames.

I can continue to blame alcohol for decisions made, but the truth is simple: I felt weak. I explored a man I've been slowly getting to know, and I consciously gave in. To the magnetic pull, the raw desire, the genuine connection. I let my body and my heart lead.

The truth is, I'd closed my eyes and jumped. As I fell asleep with his body locked around mine, keeping me warm, I told myself to breathe, that we'd figure it out together in the morning.

And yet when the warm sun touched my skin and woke me, my heart hammered with apprehension at the hand splayed over my belly, the face stuffed in my neck. My hands shook, but I closed my eyes and willed the fear away.

I'd wriggled out of his arms and played on my phone while I waited for him to wake, and the first thing that looked up at me when I opened Instagram was his smiling face as he ushered a leggy brunette through the doors of a high rise, his hand on her ass.

I'd made the mistake of finding the article, where they'd lined up Carter's top twelve fucks of the year, rating them based on things as trivial as facial attributes, physique, fashion, and jobs.

Fear whispered that I'd never be able to stack up.

Fear reminded me he had a separate home to bring his one-night stands.

Fear screamed in my face that I wouldn't be enough to keep a man like Carter interested.

Fear told me to run, to leave before he could hurt me.

Fear is a funny, fickle thing. It's there to protect you, to keep you from getting hurt, tells you to back up before it's too late. But it weighs you down, keeping you from moving forward, like feet stuck in mud. And more often than not? You get hurt anyway. Sometimes, like today, you hurt the person you care about in the process too.

The thing is, I'm allowed to be scared. But Carter stood there, begging me to stay, to communicate, to give him a damn chance. And instead of sitting with my fear, talking through it, I gave it wings, tied myself to it, and watched it take flight with me attached. I let it control me, and I hate that.

Truth is, I don't know how not to. I don't know how to put my heart on the line for a man who's never been interested in a relationship. I don't know how to open myself so wholly to someone who may not, in the end, be able to reciprocate, to keep my heart safe.

I just . . . don't know. That's the reality of life sometimes.

I swipe a tear from my cheek as soon as it falls, because through all the indecision, they still feel unwarranted. But every time I read the note in my hands, my eyes prickle all over again. I've yet to put the small piece of cardstock down, the smell of cedarwood and citrus clinging to it, a scent I'm not ready to lose.

So I read the note for the seventh time.

Olivia,

Merry Christmas and Happy New Year.

I know this year will be the best one yet, because I met you.

Carter

The kicker? The tiny heart scribbled next to his name.

The lump in my throat dips to my chest, making everything tight. I place my palm over the ache, willing it to go away, but it doesn't.

Giving up, I admire the rose gold chain in my hand. It's not a necklace, but a lanyard for my school ID badge. The delicate chain breaks every few inches with small diamond-encrusted hoops, a matching rose gold whistle hanging off a clip.

My thumb rubs methodically over the words etched into the pendant connecting the chain to the clip. *Miss Parker* it says on one side. Turning it over, I smile through my quickly blurring vision at the words on the back: *World's hottest teacher.*

But my favorite part? The tiny hockey skate charm that dangles next to the whistle. This gift is thoughtful and practical, beautiful, and I walked away, leaving him to start a brand-new year by himself, when all he asked me to do was stay, to trust him.

It's not a question of trusting his intentions. I know him well enough to understand that he doesn't lie. If he did, he'd probably be better at talking to women, or more specifically, me. In fact, if he lied, I might've found myself in his bed that first night we met.

When he tells me he'll try, I believe him. It's that I don't know if I can trust that he's really thought this out, that something has absolutely changed for him in the last twelve hours that's made him suddenly ready for a relationship.

I don't want to be a girl whose face gets splashed on the tabloids, sprinkled all over social media, labeled and judged when he might change his mind. Heartache is hard enough to deal with privately; I have no desire to be forced to do it so publicly.

My phone lights up on my bed, and I swallow hard when Cara's face pops up. She'll want details, ones I'm not ready to share. That means admitting how deep I've already fallen, how I acted out of fear, and that I'm not sure I can make it right because I'm not sure I'm brave enough to try this.

Cara's never scared of anything. She knows what she wants and goes after it without a second thought. I wish I were that sure of myself.

I clear my throat and lift my phone to my ear. "Hey, you."

"Hey, babe! You still at Carter's? We're coming to see you two. Put some clothes on. And don't try to tell me you didn't get down and dirty with him. Your bad intentions were written all over your face while you were bouncing around in his bed."

The laugh I force is cringeworthy. Despite my dad's insistence that I'm highly dramatic and would make a good actress, I'd make a shit one. I have big feelings, which makes them difficult to swallow down.

"I'm at home, Care."

The line goes silent for so long, I check my screen to make sure the call is still connected. It is. The muffled sound of her directing Emmett to my house instead of Carter's comes before her vicious words.

"What did he do? His ass is fucking grass, Liv, I will kill him. I swear, I'll do it. I'll go to jail for you."

Her fierce, protective nature is what makes her such a good friend and person to have in your corner. I'm just not sure she should be in mine right now. She'd never leave, because she's always been my shoulder and me hers, but she won't humor me and tell me I was right if she thinks I was wrong either.

"I appreciate your ferocity, but Carter did nothing wrong."

"Then why are you sad?" The words are quiet and tender, a stark contrast from just a moment ago. "I'm pretty sure Carter had plans to keep you all day. Em and I heard something about a turkey dinner."

A genuine laugh bubbles in my throat. I wipe a tear away. "He promised turkey. And movies and snuggles and talking."

"But you're not with him."

"No."

"It's okay to be scared, Ollie," she assures me softly, reading me the way she always does. "We all feel that way sometimes. We're gonna get through it, okay? Whatever that looks like."

My heart swells, grateful for the love I have. "Thanks, Care." I clear my throat and wave a dismissive hand around. "Anyway. Enough about me and my self-inflicted problems. What's up? Why are you coming over?"

The instantaneous way she perks up is obvious, a palpable energy that leaks through the phone. "I guess you'll have to open your front door and find out."

The line dies at the same time knocks sound on my door.

Okay, it's not knocking. I'm pretty sure there's an entire body being slammed into the door.

I scoot out of bed and head down the hall. The moment I open the door, a body collides with mine. Long limbs wrap around me, taking me to the ground, and I nearly drown in Cara's blonde locks.

She pulls back, blue eyes alive with excitement as shoves her hand in my face, an obnoxiously huge and utterly stunning diamond pressed against the tip of my nose.

"*Hi, maid of honor!*"

17

OREOS, SOUL MATES, AND FUCKUPS

Carter

I'M A SHIT ACTOR. THESE past few days have done nothing but prove that. I don't know how to shake what I'm feeling—the confusion, the fucking anguish. I feel like a lost puppy, and I know I look like one too.

Mostly because Garrett keeps poking my cheek and saying so every time he catches me frowning. Admittedly, it's often these days. I don't know how to talk to my friends about the way I'm feeling. I think they all expected me to simply move on. To be honest, I kinda hoped I'd move on too.

I don't have to be an expert to know that relationships are hard. All I have to do is look around this bar at my teammates. Guys that aren't ready to settle and give up their freedom. Ones that can't find a partner who's in it for them and not their money. Of the few that are married or in serious relationships, only a couple are faithful. Sometimes it feels like there are more shit examples than there are good.

A seed of envy roots in my stomach as I watch Emmett grin down at his phone. Sometimes I think I might want what he has, for my whole life off the ice to be wrapped up in a girl who makes me happy, someone I can be myself with.

But then I catch sight of Adam as he checks his phone for the umpteenth time tonight, frowning at the lack of messages from his girlfriend. The same girlfriend who hasn't been to a single home game in over a month, who rang in the new year alone because she didn't feel like coming. Adam had what Emmett has, and now it feels like he just . . . doesn't.

I nudge him with my elbow when he tucks his phone away. "Everything okay with you and Court?"

He sighs, running a hand through his hair. "Honestly, I have no clue. She's so distant. Never wants to do anything and hardly answers my messages when I'm away. You know how she said she wasn't in the mood for your party? When I got home, she was wasted, getting undressed from wherever the fuck she'd been."

Fuck. "Did you talk to her about it?"

"Tried. She said I was making a big deal out of nothing and slept in the spare room. The next morning, she refused to talk about it."

I don't know what to say. I have, like, zero experience with adult relationships, that much is clear by now. I've basically been fucking my way through my twenties without a care in the world, other than ensuring I have a rubber secured to my dick before I stick it somewhere hot and wet. I have nothing of value to add to this conversation. It's probably best I keep my mouth shut because if I say anything, it'll probably be *dump her*.

So instead, I tell him I'm sorry.

This is why I don't do relationships. They're complicated and messy and it seems like people spend 99 percent of the time being miserable, jealous, angry, or worried.

There's a reason the only thing I'll settle for is something like my parents had.

Because it was pure. It wasn't ugly, bogged down by never-ending resentment or toxicity. Mom used to tell us those smooth bits came with time, that nothing is ever perfect in the beginning, and even when they seem perfect later on, they're not. But to me, to any outsider looking in? It sure as hell looked perfect.

I watched my dad spin my mom around the kitchen every day of my life until I moved out. I listened to their stories, their laughter. They loved hard, and it was palpable. I could always feel it as much as I could see it.

But my mom's been living with a broken heart for the last seven years, only I don't think *living* is the right word. She's been surviving, and barely.

And that's terrifying. I can't imagine loving someone that much, losing your other half and not knowing how to go on. I'm not interested in feeling that level of hurt. I can barely handle keeping my mom afloat some days.

Now here's Adam, the kindest guy I know, with the biggest heart, and he looks like he's already going through it, even though he's still with his girlfriend.

So maybe Olivia walking out on me was for the best. The last thing I need to do is go and fall in love or whatever the hell you do in relationships, only to inevitably wind up like Adam, or worse, like my mom.

I don't want to be fractured; I want to be whole. And maybe being whole by yourself is better.

The thought settles uncomfortably in my stomach, like my body's fighting it, telling me to hang on, but my brain doesn't know that we can. By the time the guys and I make it back to the hotel for the night, I don't know whether I'm closer to being over Olivia, or have somehow managed to fall harder for a woman I haven't seen or talked to in days.

"You're extra into those Oreos lately, eh, buddy?" Adam's eyes shine as he watches me tear open a package and stuff two in my mouth while simultaneously pulling on sweatpants.

We kicked ass in Calgary earlier tonight, no thanks to me. I racked up six penalty minutes, got an earful from my coach for being a shitty leader, and now that I've had a beer and a platter of nachos to myself, I fully plan on stuffing my face with sugar and collapsing on the couch.

"Can't stop, won't stop," I mumble around my cookies. Fudge dipped today. I like to switch it up, and all flavors are good. Except carrot cake. I love carrot cake, but in my cookie? No fucking thanks.

"He's eating his feelings." Garrett pats my belly. "Aren't ya, big fella?"

I hit him with a judo chop when he reaches into my package. "Get the fuck outta here." I kick my leg out, hitting his stomach, keeping him at bay.

"Share," he whines, making grabby hands at my cookies. "I want some."

Rolling my eyes, I toss a cookie in the air, watching as Garrett eagerly catches it in his mouth. Emmett chuckles, flopping down on the couch and pulling out his phone.

Things have been a little weird with him. He said Olivia and I shouldn't have had sex, and I know that, but sometimes hindsight is twenty-twenty. Other than that, he's been more on the reserved side. This is the guy that went streaking with me through downtown Vancouver after our NHL debut and a shit ton of booze. He's not reserved.

"Emmy!" Cara's voice drifts from Emmett's phone, where he's got her on a FaceTime call. "I miss you. Show me your di—"

"I'm with the guys," Emmett cuts her off quickly. "Please don't finish that sentence."

Cara pouts and then quickly lights when she spies me over his shoulder. "You sucked tonight, bud. Stay out of the penalty box."

I flip her the bird and twist another Oreo apart.

"What are you doin', babe?" Emmett slips a hand up his shirt, rubbing his torso. It's a strategic move, I think, because he grins at Cara and wags his brows.

She traces the shape of her lips with her finger before snapping out of it, shaking her head. "Livvie and I are having a sleepover and getting wine drunk."

My heart stops at her name, and so does my hand, on my way to my mouth, waiting, drooling, ready for that icing, and hopefully a shot of Olivia. Instead, I get a shot of the coffee table, littered with wine bottles, empty take-out containers, and junk food.

A sly smile crawls up Cara's face before she turns the phone. "Say hi, Ol!"

Olivia's got her hair piled on top of her head in a bun messier than the one my sister always wears, the one I tell her looks like a bird made a nest on her head. She's wearing the rattiest hoodie I've ever seen, covered in paint splotches and holes, and she's so fucking beautiful it *hurts*.

Her wide eyes lock on mine, cheeks blazing, hand hanging there in midair, holding on to a . . .

A goddamn Oreo.

Woman's my fucking soul mate.

The silence is ear-splitting, everyone watching to see how this plays out. Garrett rips open a bag of Doritos in slow motion, gaze ricocheting between me and Olivia as he brings a chip to his mouth at the literal pace of a snail. The drawn-out crunches have me considering all sorts of violence, and Adam's body vibrates as he tries to hold back his laughter. Emmett makes this cough-snort sound, body shaking until he finally can't hold it in anymore.

Emmett and Adam fold over with laughter, and Olivia tugs the collar of her hoodie up to her nose, dropping her gaze and her cookie. My heart sinks with every inch she moves farther away from me, though she's not really here anyway.

"I have to go to the bathroom," she says quietly, slinking away, leaving me wondering when I'll see her next.

The camera toggles back to Cara. "Man, she is gonna kill me for that later."

Garrett shoves a handful of chips in his mouth and shrugs. "Well, you did say you wanted to see her."

See her? She can't even fucking look at me. This is nothing like the reunion I had in mind.

Everything about this fucking sucks.

I'M STOMPING OFF THE ICE before the buzzer finishes ringing, throwing my gloves off the second I shove my way into the change room.

"*Fuck!*" Tearing my helmet off, I make my way to the sink, where I let the water run past the point of frigid before splashing it over my sweaty face. My skin feels like it's sizzling, and every bit of tension I'm carrying knots in my back, my chest.

"*Beckett!*"

My head drops at my name, my grip on the sink tightening until my knuckles turn white.

"Over here. Now!"

I follow my coach through the change room, past the apprehensive stares of my teammates, until we round the corner, giving us a fake sense of seclusion. They may not be able to see us, but I know from experience they'll be able to hear every single word of this verbal beatdown.

"What the hell has gotten into you?" Coach's eyes blaze, face red and twisted. "We're only twenty minutes down and you've spent five of those minutes in the goddamn penalty box again!"

"It won't happen again, sir."

"Tell that to your fucking team. You're their leader and you're letting them down. We're down a goal because of the shit you pulled out there!"

His anger is justified. My head's up my ass tonight. I'm distracted, even more so than I've been this last week. Seeing Olivia on the video call two nights ago, how she couldn't get away from me faster, it fucked me up more than I care to admit.

I've been turning away every woman postgame at the bars. I've been trying so hard, been so good, in hopes that she's watching, that she'll see me changing and her fear will disappear. It's not working, and that she's becoming such a distraction despite the distance makes my head such a cloudy, jumbled mess of a place to be.

One night. *One damn night* with this girl and I'm fucking wrecked. Why the hell can't I shake this?

I don't know what Coach sees on my face, but there must be something there—defeat, probably—because his gaze softens.

"Look, Carter, I can tell something's going on with you. This isn't you. You're more levelheaded than this on the ice. You never fail to lead, but lately your head isn't there. You gotta shake this."

I'm fucking trying.

"I don't know if you've switched up your routine or something, but whatever it is, go back to what you were doing before. That was working for you. Find the Carter Beckett we all know and love."

But what if I don't love that version of me? What if I don't want to be that Carter Beckett anymore?

That's what everyone wants though, so that's what I give them.

I head back to the ice for the second and third periods, and I whip my ass into gear. I manage to stay out of the penalty box, score a goal, and get an assist, leading our team to another victory. Coach is happy after the game, even if I'm not.

"Carter! Can we grab you for an interview?"

I'm hell-bent on ignoring the reporters waiting in the hallway as we make our way back to the change room after the game, but Coach wraps his hand around my padded elbow, stopping me.

"He'd love to chat."

Burying my groan becomes near impossible as recorders and cameras are shoved in my face, denying me privacy.

"You struggled there that first period, Carter," one reporter says. "Seems like you've been struggling a lot."

Dragging a hand through my sweat-soaked hair, I sigh. "Uh, yeah, I've, uh, been feeling a bit off lately. Getting over a bit of a bug. Trying to get my butt in gear though," I add with a forced grin.

"You turned it around in the second and third. What changed?"

"Um, I—"

"Is it Olivia?"

My hand stops its skim of my jawline at the mention of her name. "Pardon?"

"Olivia. The girl from a few weeks ago. You dedicated your goal to her and were seen dancing together the same night. It looks like she was the same girl you had with you at the fundraiser for The Family Project, but she hasn't been seen since."

My jaw tightens. "What's your question?"

"Did you two break up? Were you dating? Or was she just another flavor of—"

"I'm not talking about Olivia."

"Can you tell us her last name? Who is she to you? What does she do?"

"Un-fucking-believable." I squeeze my eyes, a dark chuckle rumbling beneath my breath. With a step forward, I tower over the reporter who has the nerve to keep pushing. I don't like being pushed, and the way he stumbles backward a half step tells me he finally sees that. "Olivia's personal life is none of your damn business. Drop her name, because I can guarantee you my bite is as vicious as my bark." The crowd clears as I push through to the change room. "Interview's over."

My warpath doesn't end there. In fact, my frustration amplifies, my anger, my fucking confusion. I hate this, and I don't know how to change it.

This isn't me; Coach is right. I need to do something to fix this, and I need to do it quick. That's why I make a beeline for Cara as soon as I step inside the bar after the game.

But Emmett beats me to her, spinning her around as she takes his face in her hands and kisses him. Just over a year together and they haven't lost that spark yet. I think they're one of those lucky couples who never will, the easy kind where everything falls into place right from the get-go.

Cara sets her phone down before the two of them head off to the bar, and I slide into her spot. I'm not entirely proud of myself as I scoop her phone up, ready to pluck Olivia's number from it. Maybe luck is finally on my side, because the screen is already opened to their message thread.

Cara: Ur date rope you into breakfast
tomorrow or what?

Olivia: Duh. Is it even a real date if it doesn't
end with breakfast?

Blood drums in my ears, the words in front of me sending a raw ache through my chest as awareness settles over me. She's moved on, on from whatever the hell this was, or whatever it wasn't. Because it wasn't ever anything, was it? Nothing more than undeniable chemistry and physical attraction, paired with some foolish notion that a relationship might be something I wanted, that Olivia and I might be good together.

Why the hell did I ever think this was a good idea?

Coach was right. This new me isn't working. The old Carter Beckett wouldn't give two shits about this. He'd bury his feelings in something hot and wet.

And that's exactly what I'm going to do.

My gaze sweeps the bar, bouncing around all the hopeful stares until I find what I'm looking for.

Tall. Platinum blonde. Winking and wiggling her fingers at me. The exact opposite of Olivia.

"Mr. Beckett." She trails a glossy black nail down my tie before slinging her arms over my shoulders. "Don't you look handsome."

My eyes close at what I'm about to do, like they don't want to see this train wreck of a decision go down. "Wanna get outta here?"

She wraps my tie around her fist and hauls me closer. The perfume she's wearing is suffocating. "I got a new tattoo," she whispers.

"Cool." I swallow the tightness in my throat. "Can't wait to see it."

Another repeat offender. Brandy or Mandy or fucking Candy. I don't know or particularly care. All I know is I've fucked her before and it was decent enough. Hopefully decent enough to knock me off whatever this hellhole of a rollercoaster I'm stuck on is, because I don't wanna ride this fucking ride a second longer.

"Let's go." I hate myself the second I clap my hand over her ass, and even more when I slip my hand into hers and tug her out the door.

This winter is kicking my ass. Mountains of snow and frigid air that slaps at your cheeks, neither of which are typical of a west coast winter. Part of me keeps equating the way I'm feeling to those winter blues people talk about, but as I stalk down the sidewalk with Candy Brandy's hand in mine, I know it's because this hand doesn't feel right.

None of it feels right.

I don't have a single clue what I'm doing right now, why I thought this might be the right way to deal with the way I'm feeling. No fucking shit Olivia didn't trust me to change. This right here proves I'm the same guy fucking his problems away. The feeling that my dad would be so utterly disappointed in me hits me like a truck.

My condo comes into view up the road, and panic races up my spine at the sight of cameras waiting to see who I'm bringing home tonight. I'm so tired of having my picture splashed everywhere, my private life on dispay. I don't want to be this person anymore, so careless. I want to be the steady person someone can count on. I want to be the person *I* can count on.

I shove my fingers through my hair, tugging at the ends as I come to a stop. "What the hell am I doing?"

Brandy—*Mandy?*—slides her palm beneath the collar of my coat. "Me, in about two minutes."

I shake my head, tension coiling in my shoulders. Pressing my palms into the cold brick of the storefront we're stopped in front of, I heave one deep breath after the other. Gently, I bang my forehead against the wall. Maybe it'll knock some sense into me.

"I'm sorry. I can't do this."

"What? You're the one who—"

"This was a mistake." I take her hand in mine, leading her back toward the bar. "C'mon. I'll take you back."

Her hurried steps match mine, and when she peers at me out of the corner of her eye, I remember why I liked her enough to go back for seconds. Because although she barely knows me, she sees me as a human being, not only a meal ticket. "You okay?"

"I'm . . . I . . . I don't know. I fucked up."

"Can you fix it?"

"I don't know how to fix my past."

She smiles. "Playboy ways coming back to bite you in the ass?"

"Yup." I groan, closing my eyes as my name is shouted from behind us, and I hear the rustle of people jogging to catch up to us, see the flash of cameras as they catch my back. "Fucking ruthless," I mutter.

"*Carter! Over here!*"

Just as we reach the bar, my vision goes stark white, blinded by flashing cameras.

"The first girl you've been seen with this year! No more Olivia?"

"Who's the beautiful girl?"

Shielding my eyes from the bright lights, I reach for the door.

Except Mandy wants to talk.

"Sandy," she tells them with a bright smile, waving at the camera. *Huh. I was close.* "With an i-e. Sandie with an i-e." *For fuck's sake.*

I tug on her hand. "Let's go." I need to go home and screw my head on straight before it explodes.

"So the rumors weren't true?" a reporter calls. "About you and Olivia? She was nothing more than another—"

"*Enough!*" I roar, twisting back to the cameras. My chest heaves with a fury so deep, one I don't know how to handle. It shakes my whole body, begging for release, and it's about to get it if they say her name one more time. "Enough about Olivia! Leave her name out of your damn mouth!"

Sandie shoves me through the doorway. "And for the record," she shouts, "there's nothing going on here. He was being a gentleman and walking me back to the bar. Get a real job."

"Uh . . ." I blink down at her. "Thanks."

"No problem. Now if you'll excuse me, there's a martini calling my name." She struts away, pausing to glance over her shoulder. "Oh, and Carter? You can't fix your past, but if you want a different future, all you have to do is choose it."

From across the bar, I feel the weight of everyone's gaze on me. I don't meet them; I can't handle the disappointment, not when I'm already bogged down with my own self-loathing. I head straight for the back exit, the cold air a welcome reprieve this time as I lean against the wall and just fucking *breathe.*

I hear the click of the door, and without opening my eyes, know who it is. They let me stand here with my thoughts for a moment before speaking.

When I finally open my eyes, the sympathy reflected in their stares throws me for a loop.

"She's on a date." The words are more shattered than feels reasonable.

Cara frowns. "Liv?"

I nod. "I saw your phone," I admit, cringing as her sympathy shifts to annoyance. "She said she was gonna have breakfast with him too."

"Oh, you fucking . . ." She groans, fishing her phone from her purse. "Carter, I swear to God." She flashes me her screen, a photo of Olivia and a small girl who looks remarkably like her smiling at the camera. "That's her date. Her seven-year-old niece. They're having breakfast because she's got her for the weekend."

A wave of relief rushes through me. "She's not seeing someone?"

"No, you dork. She's hung up on you and trying to work through her self-doubt and insecurities with the public life you've been leading."

I hang my head. "She's going to hate me now."

"Why?" Garrett's brows tug together. "You didn't do anything with that girl. We all heard her yell it. Should you have left with her? No, probably not, because you know as well as we do that it's not what you really wanted."

Adam lifts a shoulder. "The important part is that you stopped yourself before doing something you'd regret."

"She'll never trust me now. Nobody thinks I'm good enough for her."

Emmett holds a hand up, shaking his head. "That's not at all true. Were some of us hesitant to let you get close to her? Absolutely, I can admit that. Because this right here is out of character for you, at least when it comes to women. You've been my best bud for nearly ten years, and not once have you pursued anything serious."

I rub the back of my neck. "You've barely talked to me lately. Kinda thought you were mad at me."

"I'm not mad at you, dude, and there's not a single part of me that thinks you're not good enough for Olivia. Far from it. I just feel stuck in the middle a little. It sucks, because I love you two and you're both hurting. I understand why she's afraid, and at the same time I can see how much you like her. I want you guys to be happy, and I think it would be cool if you were happy together, but I don't think pushing Olivia to be ready is the right thing to do either." His shoulders pop up and down. "It sucks all around."

"Then help me," I beg. "I'm trying here. I hate feeling like this. I've decided what I want. Isn't it supposed to be easy from here on out?"

Cara's head rolls over her shoulders with an exasperated laugh. "I love the fuck out of you, Carter, but are you really that daft when it comes to relationships? Things don't suddenly fall into place because you've decided you want her."

"But that's how it worked for you guys."

"No offense, but if Em had half the reputation you did, I probably would've made him work a little harder. But just because we fell in love right from the beginning doesn't mean it hasn't been hard. We've had to choose each other every single day, put aside our differences and work together to compromise, to build a life together. Maybe it looks like everything simply fell into place for us, but we've worked hard at this, and with any good relationship, you will. You're taking two lives and merging them. That requires a lot of work and a strong commitment. Is that what you want?"

"Yes." It's strange what a simple three-letter word can do, one spoken with so much certainty, the weight that lifts with the epiphany that comes with it. Yes, I want to choose Olivia, over and over again. I want to work for it, for us. I want to be better, not only for her, but for myself too.

Cara loops an arm through mine. "Then let's get you your girl back, Mr. Beckett."

18

DON'T GO BACON MY HEART

Olivia

You probably think there's no reason one would *need* to kiss their partner during a twelfth grade gym class, but you'd be wrong.

Just shy of eighteen years old and they've got a better love life than me.

"Aw, *c'mon*." I hike a brow as the kissing turns into an aggressive game of tonsil hockey. "Okay, ladies, that's enough."

I prop my fists on my hips as Lucy and Jean ignore me. It's my own fault; I'm way too friendly and lenient with my students, and it sometimes backfires. I've lost count of how many times I've broken apart public displays of affection.

"Nope. Nope, nope, nope, nope." I clap my hands five hundred times until they stop. "Here's an idea: wait until class ends."

They break away with a laugh, and Lucy tosses her arm around my shoulders. "Sorry, Miss Parker. You're the only cool teacher at this school."

"Don't try to butter me up with that cool teacher bullshit." I shove a set of pylons into her hands. "Set these up along the red line, please."

"Aw, man." Jean groans. "Not shuttle sprints."

"Yes, shuttle sprints. This is a fitness class, Miss Ross. You joined it of your own volition."

She crosses her arms and frowns, scuffing at the floor. "Lucy made me."

"Oh, the things we do for love."

Lucy jogs back over after setting out the pylons. "You okay, Miss Parker? You seem a little, I dunno . . ." She waves a hand around my face. "Sad, lately."

"Me? Sad? No, I'm totally fine. Super-duper fine." *Super-duper fine, ladies and gentlemen.*

Paul swaggers over, dropping his elbow to Lucy's shoulder. "Yeah, what gives? You've barely laughed at any of my jokes."

"Maybe you need to work on your material."

"Please. I'm funny as fu—" He pauses at my arched brow. "Frick. Funny as frick."

"Right, well—" The gym doors burst open, and I clap a hand over my eyes and sigh as a gorgeous, leggy blonde sweeps into the space, all eyes on her as she tears off her oversized sunglasses. "For shit's sake. *Cara!* You can't just barge in here! I'm in the middle of a class!"

She flicks her wrist. "Class dismissed."

"What? No! No, class isn't dismissed." I point at my students, all twenty-one sets of eyes bouncing between me and Cara. "Stay!"

Cara slumps theatrically. "C'mon, Miss Parker. It's the last class of the day. Let these kids have some fun. Be cool."

"I'm cool! I'm fun! We have lots of fun here!" I look around for validation, pinning my arms across my chest when I don't get it. "Fine. Go. But anyone who's late tomorrow is doing burpees."

Tapping my foot, I watch as my students high-five my best friend. This isn't the first time this has happened, and it won't be the last. Cara works on nobody's schedule but her own, and my principal has a crush on her, so she strolls through those gym doors way too often.

Cara flashes me what I'm sure she thinks is a charming grin before gesturing to my office. "Step into my office, Miss Parker."

"It's *my* office," I huff, then dash forward in an unsuccessful attempt to beat her there.

She sinks to my chair, twisting back and forth, fingers steepled at her chin. "To what do I owe the pleasure?"

"You are so incredibly irritating, you know that?"

She grins. "I really do, but I figured we were overdue for a work visit. Plus, those kids love me."

"Because they get a free period every time you show up."

"I'd make a great teacher." Her eyes sparkle, and the way they linger on me unnerves me. Cara's always had a way of seeing right through me. "What's your plan for this weekend? You can't avoid him, you know. He's going to be there."

I flop down to the chair across from my desk, legs over the armrest. "Who the hell manages to throw together such an extravagant engagement party only two weeks after the engagement?" I don't touch on the fact that tomorrow night was supposed to be mine and Carter's movie date.

"I have my connections."

Her connections are that she owns her own event planning business, is absolutely unstoppable in party-planning mode, and when she needs something she doesn't have—like, say, a venue on such short notice—she knows how to be persuasive. And I don't mean flirty; I mean utterly terrifying.

"In fact, he's the best man, so you're gonna be walking down the aisle together at the wedding."

The noises I make are not a coherent response. They're mostly a string of grumbled curse words that make Cara grin.

"C'mon. What's going through your mind? You're keeping so much bottled up. I need you to talk to me."

I tug on the sleeves of my sweater. "I know he didn't do anything with that Sandie girl, and he's allowed to be with whoever he wants; I'm the one that walked away. But it's still scary, you know? He meant to hook up with her. It was his first knee-jerk reaction." I look away. "I can't help but wonder if he'll always try to hurt me when he's angry with me, but at the same time, I know I hurt him first."

"Sounds like you've both made some decisions recently based out of fear."

"It feels like this vicious circle. Like a carousel that won't stop. I want to climb off, but I don't know how to get it to slow down."

"Yes, you do. You need to decide to leave it all where it is or move forward." She walks to the whiteboard that hangs on the wall, picking up a marker. "So here's what we're gonna do." She scrawls *Carter Beckett* across the top of the board, underlines it three times, then draws a stick figure with a giant penis. I'm going to need to erase this immediately. She finishes with a heart on the left and a frowny face on the right.

"We are *not* making a pros and cons list."

"Think of it as a list of likes and dislikes." She taps the frowny face. "Now, things you don't—"

"He's a playboy."

"Previous . . . fear . . . of . . . commitment," she scribes, which is not at all what I said.

"He's arrogant, cocky, and flashy." Except the second the marker touches the board, I stop her. "Wait. I think I kinda like that. He's . . . proud. Charismatic. Confident. I think they're good qualities. I wish I was as sure of myself as he is." Then we likely wouldn't be in this mess.

"Hm. Interesting." She adds them below the heart. "You're obviously very physically attracted to him."

"Duh. I wanna tap that man like a maple tree."

"And he's funny."

I nod, running the tip of my fingernail across my lower lip. "He makes me laugh a lot, and he's kind of a big goofball. He makes me feel good about myself. He's painfully honest, and I like the way he smells and the way he plays with my hair. And when he looks at me . . . when he looks at me, it's like it's only me and him. I like the way he looks at me. I like that his house is his escape, that he likes to stare at the stars and the mountains and forget the noise. He has the prettiest smile and the best dimples, and he was so sweet with the kids at the fundraiser and such a good sport at taking pies to the face, and he's a good friend, and—" My heart patters so fast, I stop, laying my hand over it. Through it all, Cara watches me with a soft smile.

"Bet he's a good snuggler."

Warmth spreads from my belly and up into my chest as memories play over in my head. The way Carter hauled me against him after each round, his face in the crook of my neck as his lips painted my skin, his hand on my throat as he kept me right where he wanted me, one arm wrapped around me so tight, like he was afraid I might slip away.

Cara touches the hockey skate charm hanging from my lanyard, smiling before gesturing at the board. It's full below the heart, a stark contrast to the frowny face. "Looks like you have your answer."

I wring my hands, my throat tight. "I know I do. But that doesn't make it less scary. His past was his present only a month ago. My fears are logical and warranted, aren't they?"

"I understand, Liv. It's impossible to ignore the caution signs, especially when they're constantly being thrust in your face everywhere you turn. Carter's never shied away from his decisions, or from them being splashed about so publicly. It's unnerving, and of course it's going to make you question his intentions. At the end of the day, though, you're letting fear of the unknown dictate your life." She reaches forward, giving my ponytail a little tug. "So are your fears warranted? Absolutely. But it's up to you to rise above them, to step outside your comfort zone and put yourself out there, if you want to explore this thing with Carter. What do you think?"

I sink down to the chair, my cheek propped on my fist. "I can't stop thinking about him. Everything feels natural with him, and he pushes me to open up. For someone so assertive, he's always been incredibly patient with me. I think . . . I think I'd really like for both of us to give this a chance, if he still wants that."

Cara snorts and pulls out her phone, showing me a text thread with a contact labeled *World's Most Annoying Man*.

is ollie ok? i don't want her 2 be upset about that girl.

does she hate me?

do u think she wants to talk maybe 1 day soon?

maybe i could send her flowers???? roses? sunflowers? seems like a bright flower kinda girl.

i think i miss her, care. this sucks.

"Safe to say he still wants to give it a shot, Liv." She leans against my desk, nudging the toe of my shoe with hers. "I'm proud of you. Going after what you want sounds easy, but sometimes it's just fucking scary. I think leaving when you did gave you the chance to step back and gain some clarity on the intensity of your feelings and what you wanted."

The school bell rings, and Cara slings her purse over her shoulder and tosses my things at me.

"Did you get your dress sorted for Saturday?"

I groan as we slip out the gym doors. "I've been to the mall twice this week and I can't find anything."

"All right, off to the mall we go. You need my expertise."

"I don't have time for a Cara-sized trip to the mall. I've gotta be home by five. Jeremy's dropping Alannah off."

"Oh, sweet Livvie. We'll be in and out in a half hour. I promise you."

We're in and out in seventeen minutes.

Cara towed me into a store, waltzed up to a rack, picked a dress in nine seconds, shoved me into the change room, and then made every single employee come look at how "fucktacular" I looked. Truthfully, I couldn't disagree, hence the seventeen-minute trip.

Now she's invited herself over for dinner, hell-bent on getting my niece riled up before bed. Alannah's sleeping over because tomorrow is Take Your Kid to Work Day, and she begged me to come to school with me so she could boss around the big kids.

"I'll be quick," Cara promises as she pulls into her driveway. "Just need to grab something. Why don't you come in and say hi to Em?"

"If you're going to be qu—"

She slams the door, gesturing through the windshield for me to follow her, and with a sigh, I follow my bossy best friend.

I should've known it was a trap.

Because when she shoves me toward the kitchen, instead of only Emmett, I get the impossibly large frame of Mr. Beckett, frozen while he stares at me from halfway inside the opened fridge, jaw dangling.

"Hey! Hi! Olivia!" He's yelling; I don't know if he realizes. "G-good," he sputters. "You look good!" Still yelling. He slams the fridge door and drops his elbow to the countertop, nearly missing his chin when he tries to prop it up in his palm.

I look down at my outfit. I'm in my running shoes, a pair of leggings, and a hoodie with my niece's hockey team's logo on it. My hair's in a messy, low ponytail, tucked beneath a toque, and I look like I spent the day teaching fitness, which is exactly what I did. Carter looks like he spent the day lounging on the couch and still belongs on the cover of *GQ*. His charcoal sweatpants hang low on his hips, highlighting what I know to be an entirely too-impressive package, and his Vipers shirt clings to his flawlessly sculpted torso.

"Oops!" Cara sashays into the room. "Carter! Totally forgot you were here!"

"Uh-huh," Emmett muses. "Forgot." His air quotes are perfectly placed. "We're gonna order pizza. You ladies staying?"

"Can't," Cara tells him, which is good, because I certainly can't speak. "Send some to Liv's. We're eating there."

Carter and I are having an epic stare down. I can't look away, nor do I really want to.

Until Cara takes my hand, dragging me toward the door.

My mouth quirks, and I give Carter a tiny wave. "Bye," I whisper.

His entire face shatters with a cheek-splitting grin.

"*Wait!*" Both hands come up as his body does this weird rock-swivel thing, like he has no idea what he's looking for. Then he launches into the living room and returns a moment later, sliding across the floor in his socks, two cookies in his hand. With a shaky grip, he holds them up to me. "Oreos."

My God, he's freaking adorable.

It's impossible to ignore the zing that passes from his fingers to mine when we touch. This man is a live wire and my entire body sizzles when he's around.

He dashes ahead in his socks, now sure to be soaked from the snow, and pries open the passenger door for me. As we back out of the driveway, he watches us from the front porch, that ridiculous, over-the-top grin never waning.

"Man's in love," Cara mutters, and the whole way home I can't help wondering if that might be our future someday.

We're not in my house for two minutes when the front door swings open, a gangly brunette flinging her sleepover bag into the wall when she sweeps her arms out with an extravagant flourish.

"I'm here, baby!" Alannah twirls, stopping with wiggling fingers in the air.

"Jazz hands? Really?"

Her giggle fills my small house, and she bounds over to me, leaping into my arms and tackling me into the wall. It's short-lived, thank God, because when she spots Cara, it's game over.

My brother finally makes it through the door, looking from them to me. "Alannah *and* Cara? Good fucking luck to you." He sighs as his daughter sticks her hand in his face, because she's his human swear jar.

Alannah tucks her money away. "Mummy and Daddy said they're gonna take a nap tonight after Jemmy goes to bed since I'm not gonna be home, since, ya know, I stay up *way* later than him." Jemmy is her little brother Jeremy. Yes, my brother named his son after himself. I call my nephew Jem, and most of the time, my brother Asshole.

Cara lifts her brow. "A nap, Jer? You sure you're not trying to make a third?"

"Fuck no." Another sigh, another dollar for his daughter. "I forgot how hard babies were. I'm done."

"You should get snipped."

He claps a hand over his crotch. "Don't threaten my boys."

A teenager appears at my door, two pizza boxes in his arms. "Uh, Cara . . ." He clears his throat when Cara appears behind me. "There's a message here . . . it says he, uh . . . can't wait to destroy your kitty when you get home."

Cara smiles, taking the pizzas. "Romance is alive and well," she boasts happily, disappearing into the kitchen with Alannah.

Jeremy takes another step inside, frowning when his shoulders shake. "It's freezing in here, Ol. Furnace broken again?"

"Guess so," I murmur, moving to the thermostat. Fifty-five. I press at the buttons, waiting for that sound that lets me know the furnace is whirring to life, but it never comes, so I smash on them some more, giving my brother an awkward grin when nothing happens. This thing is broken 80 percent of the time, he's fixed it for me at least three times, and I've had it professionally fixed four times. My cheeks burn. "I'm sorry."

"Why are you apologizing?"

I rub my arm and look down at my feet. "Because it's freezing in here and Alannah's staying over. It was working when I left for work this morning, I promise."

Jeremy rolls his eyes and tugs on my hoodie. "Load her up in your ratty sweats before you go to bed. She won't break."

"I'm tough as nails, Auntie Ollie." Alannah peeks out from the kitchen, flexing her biceps and growling like a bear, a slice of pizza between her teeth.

I follow Jeremy down to the basement, nibbling my thumbnail as he plays around with the furnace. When he sighs, I know the verdict isn't good.

"Hate to tell you this, Ol, but this thing is toast. You need to replace it."

Fantastic. Obviously a furnace is on the list of things I can afford right now.

"Kris and I can help you out."

I shake my head. He's bailed me out before; a new furnace is where I draw the line. "I have some emergency money saved up," I lie.

His brows quirk, and I think he believes me. Then he pulls me in for a hug on his way out the door, and whispers, "You're a terrible fucking liar."

I find Cara and Alannah spread out on the living room floor, pizza covering the coffee table as they flip through Netflix.

"There's a special pizza for you," Cara tells me.

I pad into the kitchen and lift the lid on the box, huffing a laugh at the single topping. Bacon. *Real* bacon. An unholy amount; curly, crispy edges, tiny bubbles of grease, and a smoky aroma that overloads my senses in the best way.

My phone vibrates in the pocket of my hoodie, and I press play on the video from Emmett.

It's of Carter, loading up a plate with pizza while he sings.

"Don't go bacon my heart! Mmm, mmm! I won't go bacon your heart! So, *oooh*, *oooh*! Don't go bacon my heart!" He flops onto the couch with a sigh. "You think Ollie likes the extra-extra bacon pizza I ordered her? I bet she found the most bacon-y slice." He chuckles, dropping half a slice of pizza into his mouth. "I can't wait to see her at the party Saturday. Maybe I'll line my pockets with bacon."

The video goes black at the same moment realization hits, and my heart races at the knowledge that I'm already well in over my head.

"You look scared again."

I glance over my shoulder and see Cara leaning against the door frame. "I'm terrified," I whisper.

"What scares you the most?"

"That I'm going to fall in love with him."

Cara laughs, one of those irritating, mocking laughs. "Oh, Ollie." She strolls over, stealing a slice of my extra-extra bacon pizza, taking a bite. "I hate to tell you this, but if you're scared of falling in love with him . . . you're already halfway there."

Her words take root in my head, and I keep turning them over late into the night. When Alannah and I are on the way out the door the next morning, I haven't stopped thinking of them, or of Carter.

My phone buzzes, and I tap on Emmett's text as I head down the steps.

> **Emmett:** Theater 4, row L, seats 10 & 11.
> Tonight at 7:30.

> **Emmett:** He's still going.

The frigid January air warms as I reread the details, the seats Carter meticulously picked for our movie date while we curled up by the fire on his balcony—last row, dead center.

He's still going.

A strange but welcome calm unfurls in my belly, climbing into my chest, allowing my shoulders to unstack. I feel lighter somehow, like a weight has been lifted. The weight of my fear, maybe, or my indecisiveness. Both of those things have the power to drag you down like anchors, and I'd been letting them pull me under since the first time that man gave me butterflies.

Alannah tugs on my hand. "Why are you smiling so big, Auntie Ollie?"

I fix the Vipers toque on my niece's head, covering her ears. "I'm just happy, honey."

She grins up at me. "Happy looks good on you."

Feels damn good too.

19

GOOD SURPRISES

Carter

Hope is one of those funny things, kind of like time.

Time either races or drags; there's no in between. When things aren't going your way, time stands still. You feel stuck, rooted in place, and your feet won't move in the direction you want to go. These past twelve days, I've wanted one of two things: to either get the girl or get over the girl. The former was preferable, but with each day that dragged on, I would've taken either just to get rid of the heavy cloud hanging over my head.

And then she fucking smiled at me, and it's like somebody hit the button on a stopwatch and time restarted, flew forward. Now I'm racing into the weekend, eager to see her.

Hope works the same way. Everything feels slow and dark without it, like a night spent waiting for the sun to rise.

And then suddenly you see her, the brilliant bloom of her smile, the way her eyes come alive as they collide with yours from across the room, and everything changes. The door swings open, showing you the sunshine outside, the hope, and you step right into it, feeling the warmth kissing your skin like the heat of her stare.

I'm still not a superfan of this brutal, biting cold, though.

"Why couldn't we stay in your apartment?" I whine to Hank as we amble down the street. "It's too cold to be outside."

"Dublin needs exercise. And you, quite frankly, need to quit all this bitchin' you've been doing. This is why I always say that Jennie is the superior Beckett sibling."

"Superior Beckett sibling, my ass," I mutter, guiding Hank down to a bench in Stanley Park.

I've known Hank for over seven years now. We came across each other purely by chance, or so it seemed, at a time when I needed him most. He stopped me from making a mistake that could've fucked my life beyond repair and ended my career before it had really gotten started, and he's been a constant ever since, one of my best friends despite the nearly sixty-year age gap. He's my family, and there's never been a part of me that hasn't appreciated how lucky I am to have him.

Hank sips his coffee. "You haven't been yourself lately."

I stare out at the English Bay. The bitter winter we've been graced with has turned the water into sleek blue ice, and under the bright sun, it glitters. "Not really."

"Got that girl on your brain. The pretty brunette."

I glance at him, a smile on my lips. There's no point in asking him how he found out about Olivia; he keeps more tabs on me than the paparazzi. "I do."

"You sleep with her?"

I huff a chuckle. "How the hell do you know that?"

"You're a manwhore, Mr. Beckett. You sleep with everyone."

"Hey." I nudge his shoulder with mine. "Play nice, old man."

Hank chuckles. "I can tell you like her."

"I do." Too much, probably. Too soon. I don't know. Is this how this goes?

He gives Dublin's ears a ruffle. "So, what's the problem?"

"The problem is I'm a manwhore who sleeps with everyone."

Hank's silence gives way to a too-broad grin. "Sure it's not your ugly mug?"

"I'm nice to look at and you know it."

The week after we met, Hank asked if he could touch my face. He said it was something he liked to do to put a face to the voice. He also said he wanted to see what all the fuss was about. I still remember the impressed sound he made before he told me my features were perfectly symmetrical. When I laughed, his fingers slid across my dimples and he said, *Ah. Dimples. That's why you're so popular with the ladies*. But the best part? When he was done, he told me the face-touching bit was a bunch of bullshit Hollywood threw into movies to romanticize visual impairments, and I'd fallen for it without a second thought. Not only was I pretty but gullible too.

"The lady on the sports channel says you're the hottest thing since sliced bread. I think she must be blinder than I am."

I bark a laugh and follow it with a sigh. "Do you think her leaving was a sign that I'm better off alone?" The words taste foreign and sour, though up until a month ago I had no intention of ever wanting more.

Hank snorts. "I don't believe you're actually such a cynic when it comes to love. You've got a big heart. You don't really want to be alone the rest of your life, do you?"

"For a while there, I kinda thought I did."

"That's no way to live your life. You have a lot to offer someone, Carter, and while it's important to be able to be happy on your own, having another person to amplify that happiness, to share it with along with all the other special moments, that's what life's all about. That's where it really starts to get fun."

"I might hurt her." As angry and confused as I've been, I understand too. I've taken whatever bits of Olivia she was willing to give up, and when I decided I wanted her for more than one night, I expected her to take me at face value. I never gave her the certainty she wanted, the security she needed. I just asked her to close her eyes and jump.

"Hurting someone and getting hurt are risks you take in love."

My head flops back with a groan. "Stop saying that word."

"I love saying *love*. It's my favorite word." He claps my knee. "So tell me why today is different."

"Different? What do you mean?"

"Well, we covered why you haven't been yourself lately, but today? Today you're a little bit more yourself."

I think about yesterday, how I couldn't take my eyes off her, the confirmation that my feelings were very real stacked behind the way my entire body buzzed at her proximity, the way I longed to just fucking . . . *touch her*.

"I saw her last night. Only for two minutes, but she smiled at me. Three times she smiled at me. And she let me open the car door for her, and she waved good-bye, and . . . I think that's good, right? I think it means she might give me a chance. Do you think she's gonna give me a chance?"

Hank chuckles softly. "You don't give yourself enough credit. It's not only the girl that needs to give you a chance; it's yourself. So, tell me . . . you gonna win her back?"

I grin at him, squeezing his hand. "Do I ever lose?"

"Not typically, no, as much as I hate to admit it. I've never met a more pompous man."

"You love me." I'm still grinning like a jackass and I know he can hear it.

Hank sighs. "I do. And I'll love you more if you add another beautiful lady to my life."

"I'm trying. I promise."

"Well, try harder. The Carter Beckett I know fights for what he wants and doesn't take no for an answer." He twists my way, those hazy blues drifting over me. "Unless you've gone soft. Have you gone soft, Carter?"

"Hell no."

"Then get your ass in gear and get your woman."

"Aye-aye, captain."

"I'm blind in both eyes. I don't wear a patch."

"What? I wasn't—forget it. You're unreal."

"You love me," he parrots back.

"I do."

"Then you'll get me Thai food for dinner and make that girl your woman."

I salute Dublin, who cocks his adorable golden head at me. "Thai food and a saucy, mistrusting woman, coming right up."

IT'S NEARLY SEVEN AS I stand out in the cold, looking up at the theater. It's a Friday night, the place is packed, and I'm kicking myself for being here. Going to the movies in public seemed worth it when Olivia was going to be sitting beside me, but now I'm alone, and it hits me for the first time that alone isn't at all what I want to be.

And yet here I am anyway, and I don't know why. Maybe I was holding on to hope that things would get sorted in time for our first date. That I would get to sit next to her and whisper irritating things in her ear and make her laugh, and when it was good and dark, I'd slip my hand around hers, lace our fingers together, and feel the world right itself.

Instead, I pull my toque over my head and walk inside, hoping nobody notices me.

"Just the one?" the kid behind the counter asks as he scans the ticket on my phone. "You've got two tickets there."

I clear my throat. "Yeah, um—"

"Two, please and thank you."

I twirl at the soft voice, and my heart tries to escape out of my throat when I spot the brunette who's been occupying every bit of space in my head.

She licks her lips and takes a tentative step forward, hands wringing at her stomach, and when she opens her mouth to say something, I beat her to it.

"You came."

A beam like sunshine explodes across Olivia's face, and I swear she's radiating from the inside out.

"Hi, Carter."

20

FORWARD

Carter

CAN I TOUCH HER? I don't know if I can touch her.

I keep reaching for her hand, then letting mine hang there in midair before pulling it back, dragging it over my thigh. It's all clammy, so she probably doesn't even want to hold my hand anyway. But I want to hold hers.

Olivia's being a good sport, pretending not to notice how anxious I am. She keeps her eyes trained on the movie trailers in front of us, but every time I look at her, the corner of her mouth quirks as she tries not to laugh.

"I'm so hot," I blurt, tugging at the neck of my hoodie. I fan at my face. "Are you hot?"

Amusement dances in her eyes. "No."

"Oh. Just me then." Leaning forward, I tug my hoodie over my head, and Olivia grunts as my elbow connects with some part of her body. "Oh fuck." I shove my hoodie in her lap and stick my face in hers, running my hands over her arms, lifting them, searching for . . . bruises? I don't fucking know. Christ, I'm a fucking mess. "Did I get you? Are you hurt? Are you okay? Sorry my hands are so sweaty." I twirl one in the air, then point to the ceiling. "It's the heat. I think they've got it cranked all the way up. Want me to ask them to turn it down?" I push on the armrests, climb to my feet, and thumb down the row. "I'll ask them to turn it down."

Olivia grabs a fistful of my shirt and tugs me back down to my seat. "The temperature is fine, Carter. I know you're nervous, but—"

"Nervous? Me? Psssh." I wave a flappy hand through the air. "*Please*. They call me Mr. Confident."

She doesn't even bother to fight her smile. "Uh-huh."

I sink back in my seat, knee bouncing as I stare at the screen. This particular theater is relatively quiet considering how busy the place is. Perks of seeing a kid's movie after they've all gone to bed, I guess. Anyway, I kinda wish it was busy. Maybe I'd have something else to focus on other than how fucking nervous I feel.

She's here. She came, all on her own. What does that mean? Is this a date? Does she want to, like . . . move forward? With me? I won't fuck it up. I'm gonna be so fucking good, and I'm gonna show her how much she can trust me.

"Carter, I—"

"I'm gonna go get snacks," I half yell, leaping to my feet before promptly tripping over them, catching myself against the row in front of us.

"Are you o—"

"I'm fine," I call, scurrying down the row. "Snacks. Snacks, snacks, snacks." I bury my face in my hands the second I burst into the hallway, leaning back against the wall. What in the fuck is wrong with me? She's, like, half my size. Why am I scared of her suddenly?

I pick the longest line at the concession stand, relishing in the time alone to screw my head on straight, but by the time I get to the counter I accidentally order so much food, they have to put my candy and chocolate in a popcorn bag so I can carry it all.

"Thanks." I wrap one arm around the XL popcorn, the other around the bag of treats, and carefully pick up a drink in each hand. "And by the way, it's hot as balls in theater four. You should maybe think about turning the heat down."

The kid behind the counter blinks slowly. "We keep all our theaters set at sixty-five degrees."

My brows rise as I give him a pointed look. "Yeah. Fucking scorching."

My heart climbs into my throat as I climb the stairs to Olivia in the back row. Her eyes shine with laughter as she unfolds my seat for me so I can sit down with my hands full. I place the bag of candy in her lap and she snickers as she peeks inside it.

"This is a lot of food."

"Yeah, I eat when I'm nervous. And all the time, really. And I remember the day after we met you said you like sweet over salty, so I got chocolate and candy, but we're at the movies, so we need popcorn too. Do you like popcorn? I didn't know what you wanted for a drink, so I got a root beer and an iced tea, and you can have whichever you want, or we can split them both if you want some of each and don't mind sharing germs or whatever, but if you don't want my germs, then that's cool, and we can—"

"Carter." Olivia lays her hand on my arm. It's soft and warm and all I can hear is my heart. "Take a breath. I love chocolate, candy, and popcorn. I like both root beer and iced tea, so I'm okay with either, but we can share if you'd like, because I don't mind your germs. Okay?"

"Okay."

"Thank you for this. And thank you for the extra-extra bacon pizza last night."

"Did you find the most bacon-y slice?"

She smiles, and I think my heart stops. "I did, but it was hard, because there was so much bacon. My dream come true."

"I asked them to use the real stuff, not the crappy crumble."

"It was incredible."

"Okay." I nod. "Yeah. Good."

The lights dim, a quiet hum fading to silence that makes my skin crawl as I'm forced to go back to pretending like I don't want to take Olivia's face in my hands and kiss her.

I'm someone who gets completely enraptured in Disney movies. My sister and I spent entire weekends laying on makeshift pillow beds on the living room floor, watching every Disney movie in our extensive collection. At nighttime, my parents would cuddle up on the couch behind us, and if we begged enough, they'd agree to let us sleep out there, stay up and watch the movies. I can count the times we made it to midnight on one hand, and more often than not, we woke up in our own beds.

And yet right now I can't focus on a single thing happening between Anna, Elsa, Kristoff, Sven, or Olaf.

By the time we're a half hour into the movie, Olivia sets the treats down, and I follow her lead, placing the popcorn down too.

I can't get my knee to stop bouncing, and I'm itching to do something with my hands, namely hold one of hers. Instead, I yank my toque off and plow my fingers through my hair, tugging on the strands.

Olivia reaches out, gently pulling my hair free, bringing my hand down to my lap, where she slowly twines her fingers with mine.

"Okay?" she asks on a whisper.

I stare down at her hand in mine, so tiny, so soft, *so fucking warm*. Then she gives me a tender smile, and just like that, the frantic race of my heart slows to a steady gallop, the tension in my shoulders dissolving.

"Okay."

"YOU REALLY THOUGHT OLAF WAS going to die there, huh?"

"He *did* die, Ollie. Elsa brought him back to life, thank fuck. I would've rioted." I nearly cut off the circulation to her hand by gripping it so tight while I waited, hoping the funny snowman would reappear.

"Can you imagine if Disney movies were as cutthroat now as they were when we were growing up?"

I shudder, squeezing her hand as we step outside. "There was so much trauma back then."

"But it shaped us. I wouldn't be who I was if Scar didn't toss Mufasa off that cliff, you know?" She releases my hand, stuffing her toque over her curls and pulling her floppy-eared puppy mitts from her coat pocket. "Thank you, Carter. I had a lot of fun."

"Me too. I'm glad you came." I rock back on my heels, smiling down at her as she smiles up at me. I don't want to say good-bye.

She tilts her head down the street. "Um, I'm gonna go grab a tea at the coffee shop down the road."

"Oh. What a coincidence. I was also about to go there and get a tea. Guess we can walk together. Maybe grab a seat at the same table."

"You drink tea?"

"Never."

Olivia laughs, and my memory really didn't do it justice. I wrap my gloved hand around hers as we head down the street, snow-flakes falling from the sky, clinging to her lashes, the tips of her hair. My own snow angel.

"I guess you're used to this kinda winter, huh?"

"We got our asses kicked every winter in Muskoka, but they were the most gorgeous winters. Towering, snow-covered pines, and frozen lakes that looked like glass. My brother and I would walk to Willow Beach and play hockey where the lake was frozen solid." Her nose wrinkles. "But I think I've grown too accustomed to these west coast winters, because whatever's going on lately with this weather is really doing me in. I'm this close to taking Cara up on her offer to finish the season in Cabo."

"Nah, you don't wanna do that. You'd have to listen to her and Em have phone sex every night. Trust me, it's not something you wanna hear. I've been subjected to it for way too long on our road trips." I nudge her shoulder with mine. "Plus, that sounds like a lot of days without me, which would ultimately suck for you. Imagine how dull life would be without my antics."

Olivia laughs, a soft sound as I open the door to the coffee shop. It's quiet in here, a few people sprinkled throughout, chatting lowly and sipping on hot drinks.

"What do you want?" Olivia asks, pulling out her wallet.

"You're not paying."

"I'm paying."

"*I'm* paying."

"You paid for the movies and the snacks."

"Yeah, 'cause you kicked my ass in beer pong and I owed you a night at the movies. It's the same night, so it counts."

"Carter—"

I level her with a look, and it must be charming as hell, because she sighs, tucks her wallet away, and tells me she wants a London Fog Tea Latte.

"Good girl." I press my lips to her blushing cheek. "Go sit down. I'll bring the drinks over."

I bring cookies and muffins, too, and Olivia looks at me like I have five heads when I set everything down on the table.

"What? If you don't finish it you can take it home with you. Or I'll eat it. I'm always hungry."

"Are you still nervous?"

I shake my head, breaking a ginger molasses cookie in half, sliding the other half over to Olivia. "I don't think so. Not anymore." I study her, the slight curl of her shoulders as she plays with her cookie. "But now *you're* nervous."

"A little bit," she admits. "We need to talk, and normally I'm good at talking but . . . sometimes I feel kind of foggy around you."

"Is that because you're confused?"

"Yes." She shakes her head quickly when my face falls, touching her fingers to the back of my hand. "Not about the way I feel about you. I just think . . . I think my mind is always going in two different places, thinking about everything that could go wrong, but everything that could go right too. It's hard to focus, and I get lost in this space in between, where I'm just . . . scared and confused."

"I get that."

"You do?"

I nod. "I think I was thinking the same thing, but maybe in different ways. I didn't know how to step forward, because I'd never gone that way before. And then when I wanted to, you wanted to leave, and it was confusing." I look down at my hot chocolate, and when I meet Olivia's gaze again, so much vulnerability shines in her eyes. "I might have been confused about why we were on different pages, but I understand your fears. I just wish you would've stayed and talked. We could have tried to figure it out together."

"We could have," she says. "But I honestly don't think it would've been effective. I couldn't wrap my head around what was happening. I think I needed to step away to evaluate my feelings, how fast and strong they came on, and my priorities, though I wish I hadn't hurt you in the process." The tip of her forest green nail taps on her mug. "Could we try to figure it out now? Or is it too late?"

"It's never too late, Ollie. But maybe . . . maybe we should take it slow. Or try to, at least. You know, proper dates and stuff, where you can learn to trust me."

"I would like that, Carter."

"Kissing doesn't qualify as slow, though, in case you were wondering."

"Oh really? Are we talking innocent pecks or—"

"Tonsil hockey."

Olivia snorts a laugh, my favorite kind. "That feels fast to me."

"Well, you have little legs. It makes sense that you think everything I do is fast. Something for you to work on, I guess."

Brown eyes roll as she shifts back, slinging one leg over the other and tossing her curls over her shoulder. "And you can work on earning your tongue in my mouth."

My eyes hood. "A challenge? I love a challenge."

She hides her smile behind her mug. "And I love watching you lose."

"Oh, I never lose, Ol."

"Right. Just at beer pong."

A growl rumbles low in my chest, and when Olivia snickers into her tea, I smile.

"I really like you, Ollie."

Tenderness swims in her eyes as her shoulders drop. "I really like you, too, Carter. Thank you for being patient with me and giving me some time."

The truth is, I think I'd give her anything she ever needed; all she'd have to do is ask.

And when we finally amble out of the coffee shop at midnight, strolling hand in hand down the street, I wonder if *she's* what I've been needing all this time. It feels that way.

"Save me a dance tomorrow?"

"You can have as many dances as you like."

I tug her toque down a little lower, covering her ears. "What if I want them all? I've never been good at sharing." I brush her hair over her shoulder, knuckles skimming her cheek. "You're not gonna let me kiss you right now, are you?"

"No, I'm not." She tugs on my coat, guiding my face to hers so she can press a kiss to one of my dimples. "You need to work on your self-control if we're going to do this slow, Mr. Beckett."

"Fine, but I've never been good with self-control." I watch as she climbs into her car. "That rule was more of a guideline anyway. And you wanna kiss me too!"

"Of course I do." She winks. "But I want to watch you lose more."

21

HOLY FUCKBALLS

Carter

I SEE HER THE SECOND she walks through the door.

You can't miss her. Gorgeous little thing that stills in the doorway, my heart stops beating at the sight of her.

I watch Emmett wrap her in his arms before he starts sliding her coat off, revealing the dress that took Olivia three trips to the mall to find. Don't ask me how I know that.

She's stunning, but she always has been. She could be wearing my hockey bag zipped up to her neck with armhole cutouts and she'd still be the most beautiful woman I've ever laid my eyes on.

Actually, that doesn't sound half bad. I make a mental note to ask her to pose naked with my hockey equipment in the near future. I'm gonna take a fuckload of pictures of that woman. My phone's gonna be full of Olivia.

But she's not wearing a hockey bag. Fuck. No. This dress. Sweet, holy fuckballs, *this dress*.

"Shit." I don't know if it's Garrett or Adam who breathes the only word I can think of. They're both staring, brows slowly climbing their foreheads as they follow the line of her petite body down, down, down, and then back up, gazes lingering on her plunging neckline the same way mine does.

I gulp. "Yeah."

Draped in crimson lace, Olivia looks as tempting and mouth-watering as a candy apple. She's forbidden fruit, and I want to devour her.

I fight a groan as my eyes bounce around her perfectly hugged curves, the way the lace clings to her waist, slips down her luscious thighs, before flowing out around her knees. She's three inches higher in those sparkly gold heels that match the barrette in her hair, styled in thick waves.

There's an air of confidence about her tonight. Maybe it's because that dress makes her feel as stunning as she is all that time, or maybe because we fixed things last night. Maybe because she's hell-bent on making me lose control, ready to watch with a smile. But if I had to guess by the simple rise and fall of her chest, I'd say she's a little nervous underneath it all.

Me? I'm totally in control. I've got this.

I'm not goofy Carter tonight. I'm wearing an impenetrable mask she won't be able to . . . penetrate? Fuck. I dunno. Now all I'm thinking about is penetration.

Totally in control.

Except—*fuck me*—when she spins and flashes me the red ribbon that threads over the smooth, milky skin on her back, I die a little on the inside.

"I'm deceased," I mutter, adjusting the quickly swelling lump between my legs. *Not now, sword of thunder*, I mentally tell my dick. *Stand down, big buddy.*

"She's dressed to kill." Adam's gaze slides my way. "You should probably take that as a sign. She's in control." He sighs. "Girls are always in control."

"*I'm* in control," I growl lowly.

Because here's the thing about me: I'm persistent. Fierce. Voracious and so boldly confident. When I set my sights on something I want, I don't rest until I've got it. Olivia Parker is no different.

I may have had her once, but once will never be enough, not with her. I want her over and over. I want to fucking own her, make her mine, every damn inch of her, for nobody but me.

I'm aware that's a little caveman of me.

But here's the other thing: I don't fucking care.

Except then Olivia peeks at me from over her shoulder, dark lashes fluttering, and she slowly—*so damn slowly*—skims her fingers over the curve of her hips, the swell of her round ass, the dip of her teensy waist, all while her lower lip slides between her teeth.

Fuck. I'm not in control. I'm not in control at fucking all.

Olivia

Oooh, holy fuckballs. *Don't look, don't look, don't look.*

He's in a suit. A full suit. Three-piece, midnight blue. My God, it could not fit him any more perfectly. Hugging his broad shoulders, tapered around his sharp, lean waist. Holy crap, those thick, muscular thighs. I remember those bad boys pinning me to the mattress as he—

I fan at my face with two flappy hands.

I need to stop. I need to not. I need to . . . Crap, I don't know. I think I need to mount that man in a bathroom.

"Hot?" Cara asks, whispering in my ear. She's ethereal tonight in her skin-tight white lace, blonde hair falling in thick waves down her back, hips for days and an ass that matches. Like always, my best friend looks perfect.

"Yep. Super hot in here. Is the furnace on? You should ask them to turn it down. Air-conditioning, maybe. Hot."

"We're in the middle of a deep freeze that Vancouver hasn't seen in years, you have no heat at home, and you want them to turn on the air-conditioning?" She follows my darting eyes and smirks at my still-flapping hands. "Maybe you need someone to put out your fire."

"Huh?" My eyes snap to her, then back at Carter, and nearly roll out of their sockets when he catches me staring, and unfortunately flapping. "Help me," I beg Cara. "I'm supposed to be in control. *He's* the one that's supposed to give in."

"I'll tell you what I *can* do." She stops a waiter with a tray of champagne, pours one glass into another, then repeats. She swipes both full-to-the-brim glasses off the tray and hands one to me. "I can get you drunk."

We clink our glasses, and as that first sip of bubbly slides down my throat, I let out a deep breath. By the time I'm finished with my second glass, Cara disappears to mingle. I should slow down, but then Garrett ambles over with a frosty beer in each hand, and who would I be to turn that down?

He wraps me in a hug, one hand on my lower back when he releases me, and I swear his gaze lights with fear when it darts over my shoulder, right before he yanks his touch back.

"You hockey men sure clean up nice, don't you?" I fix the knot of his tie, hanging low and too far to the right. "It's nice to see you."

He's got such a great grin, so happy and carefree, kinda like a cute dog. "Yeah, we've missed seeing you around. Some slightly more than others." His mouth dips to my ear. "Hey, wanna spike Carter's blood pressure?"

"What did you have in mind?"

He sets our beers down and holds out one hand, a sneaky smile spreading. "Dance with me."

With a giggle, I slip my hand into his and follow him to the dance floor. His palm rests gently on my lower back as he twirls us across the space, the heat of Carter's gaze touching my spine everywhere it goes.

"Can't take his eyes off you," Garrett whispers. "Looks like he's contemplating which of my body parts he should remove first."

When I laugh, he grins, spinning me out, pulling me back in. "You been keeping up with the team?"

"Of course. Your goal against Vegas on Tuesday? Chef's kiss."

His face lights, chest swelling with pride. "Yeah? Right through the five-hole. What about you? Carter told me you coach the girls' volleyball team at your school."

"He talks about me?"

"When he's not being a mopey ballsack? Yeah, he talks about you all the time."

I can't imagine a mopey version of Carter. He's so upbeat all the time, charismatic and boisterous. A sudden wave of guilt rushes over me.

"Yeah." Garrett taps the corner of my frown. "That's exactly how he looked. You two are made for each other."

"I—I don't—are you—my volleyball team lost in the semifinals, and do you think we're really made for each other? He's Carter Beckett and I'm Olivia Parker and I'm so short and he's so tall so are we even all that compatible, body parts that don't line up and stuff like that?"

I take back what I said about his cute puppy grin. This one is *all* jackass. "That was the most impressive round of word vomit I've ever heard. But I'm gonna need you to get your head in the game. I've got money riding on Carter being the first to crack, not you."

"I'm scared you made the wrong bet."

"I believe in you, Ollie."

That's great, but as the song ends and he leaves me, it's becoming more and more clear *I* don't believe in myself. I'm unraveling, and I haven't even spoken to the man responsible for my demise.

I sigh, scooping my beer off the bar, intent on finding a corner to hide in so I can end this night without any more self-inflicted damage.

Of course, I bounce off something hard on my way, my drink splattering over the edge of my glass.

"Shit, I'm so sorry. I'm a mess tonight. I wasn't watching where I was going. Did I get you . . . wet . . . *Oh-God-shit.*" Those last three words come rushing out in one puff of air.

"Oh God shit," Carter hums, one hand in his pocket, the other wrapped around a crystal glass. "That's a new one."

My legs are shaking. I'm not joking. And when Carter brushes his fingers over my collarbone, sweeping a curl off my shoulder and letting it slip through his fingers, I squeeze my eyes shut.

What the fuck is happening? I was perfectly fine last night, and so utterly in control when I walked through this door earlier. Is it the alcohol? It's the alcohol. Carter's definitely not making me weak. He's not . . . *winning.*

"You got your hair cut."

I smack my glass against my head, which I grab with both hands, as if to ask, *this hair*? "Today."

"Today?"

"Yeah, I got it done today." I only realize I'm borderline yelling, the way he did the other night, when his brows quirk. I swallow and try again, this time in a whisper. "I got it cut this morning." I make scissors with my right hand and snap them twice. "Snip-snip."

Oh God. Carter might be winning.

"Hm." He tucks my hair behind my ear, the tip of his finger skimming my sparkly gold barrette. His eyes don't leave mine as he swirls the liquid in his glass and tosses it back. He sets the empty glass on the bar before taking my half-full beer and ditching that too.

And he walks forward.

Not walks. *He prowls.* He prowls forward, and I slink backward until I've slinked all I can slink.

His fingers ghost over the dip of my waist as he dips his face to mine, and my heart slams against my sternum like it hopes he might kiss me. Instead, his lips pause at my ear.

"Excuse me, Miss Parker." His breath is warm and spicy with sweet notes of vanilla and caramel as it rolls down my neck, and his gaze falls to my lips as they part on a shuddering inhale.

The wall behind me suddenly opens, and I stumble into complete darkness.

Carter flips the light switch, illuminating the extravagant bathroom we've entered.

And then he hits the lock.

My heart sputters like Red Rhonda, my slowly dying car.

Broad hands seize my hips as he spins me toward the vanity, slapping my palms down on the counter. My exposed skin singes at the feel of him, the heavy weight that presses into my lower back. The tips of his fingers dance up my forearms, circling my biceps when he grips me. His nose brushes up my neck, settling at the shell of my ear.

"You started off so good," he murmurs. "So strong. You walked in here like a woman with all the confidence in the world, batting these lashes, running your hands over these fucking curves, and I thought for sure I was done. All my self-control flew out the window."

He drags his mouth down my neck, one hand splayed over my belly, the other gliding down the outside of my thigh until he fists the hem of my dress. The lace scrapes softly against my skin as he pulls it up, and I arch away from his body, pushing myself toward his hand.

Fuck control and fuck slow. I just want him to fuck *me*.

Dark eyes crash into mine through the mirror, and when he smiles against my shoulder, I know he's got me. He knows too.

"But then you gave yourself away. You're adorable when you're a mess, you know that?"

The pad of his thumb traces the edge of my silk panties, and a trembling breath escapes my lips, sparks fluttering throughout me.

"Do you want me to touch you?"

"Yes," I gasp. "Please."

A satisfied hum crawls up his throat, and his mouth opens on my neck. I sink into him, fingers finding his perfectly styled waves.

Then he pulls back, taking his scorching touch with him, leaving me gaping in the mirror.

I twist, watching in horror as he adjusts the lump in his pants, straightens his tie, and fixes his hair. "What are you doing?"

"Heading back out there."

"But you . . . you said . . . I said . . ."

"You said you wanted me to touch you. And maybe I will. Tomorrow."

"Tomorrow?"

"After we go for lunch."

"L-lunch?"

He nods, tucking his phone in my hands. "Address, please. So I can pick you up tomorrow for our date."

"I—"

"Now, Olivia."

Oh look. The feminism has left my body.

I scramble to enter my address under the weight of his stare, and when I'm done, he sweeps me into the noisy hallway.

Tipping my chin, he presses a tender kiss to the corner of my mouth. "You're fucking stunning, Miss Parker."

Cara launches herself through a horde of people as I watch Carter disappear. She grips my shoulders and shakes, making my head bobble. "What happened? You guys were in there for, like, ten minutes." Her gaze travels down, noting my flushed cheeks, my rumpled dress. "Oh my God. You had sex in the fucking bathroom!

I knew it! *Garrett!*" she screams into the crowd. "You owe me, Em, and Adam a hundred bucks each!"

"Fuck that!" he screams back from the abyss. "There's no way she gave it up that quickly!"

IT'S BEEN THREE HOURS AND I'm wondering when Carter's going to cash in on the dance he made me promise him last night. There's no shortage of hockey players who want to dance tonight, that's for sure. I've been spinning around the dance floor all night, but the man I really want to dance with seems perfectly content to watch me from afar.

I'm exhausted, a little dizzy, and tipsy enough that I can't stop giggling. If he doesn't ask me to dance soon, I'm going to be asleep in the coat closet.

All he's given me is lingering stares, smiles hidden behind the rim of his glass, grazing touches over the small of my back as he leans around me at the bar to order a new drink. I'm on edge, which is exactly where he wants me.

"Your feet must be killing you by now," Adam says as we sway back and forth, my hand in his. "Have you taken a break?"

"You guys don't seem to have that word in your vocabulary."

He laughs. "Fair enough."

"I can't wait to get home and climb into a bubble bath."

"With a good book and a glass of wine?"

"Maybe sans wine." I'm sure my flushed cheeks say it all. "I've had my fair share tonight."

Adam twirls me out and pulls me back in, laughter shining in his eyes as they flick over my shoulder. "I love making that man jealous."

He moves us in a slow circle so that I can see Carter, perched against a wall with a handful of his teammates. His eyes bounce around me and Adam, the positioning of our hands—which is pretty damn innocent; the man has a girlfriend, though she's not here—before coasting back to me.

A crooked grin blooms on his face, pulling in his deep dimples, and he sets his glass down, straightening off the wall.

Adam chuckles. "About damn time. He's been trying to convince us all night he's in control." His blue gaze dips to mine, his smile so full of kindness. "I'm really happy you two are giving this a go. He's been hung up on you since day one, singing nonstop. He's so damn excited to spend time with you tomorrow. The rest of us are excited for him to stop whining."

"Don't listen to Adam," Carter's low voice rumbles behind me. "He doesn't know what he's talking about."

"He blew up our group chat the second you drove away last night, Ollie; trust me."

"All right." Carter steps between us. "Enough of that. My turn."

"I was beginning to think you weren't going to cash in on your dance," I say as he hauls me against his chest, one hand on my back, the other holding mine.

"I wanted to be your last."

"Mmm. Your friends are tattling on you."

"Maybe they're full of shit."

"Maybe." I twine my fingers in the waves at the nape of his neck. "But I don't think they are. I think you missed me, and I think you bragged about last night to your friends."

Forest green eyes gleam. "Some of my arrogance is rubbing off on you."

"I bet you'd like to rub something else off on me."

Carter guffaws, and it feels like my single greatest accomplishment ever. "So naughty, Miss Parker. It must be the heels. The added height gives you added confidence." His mouth dips to my ear. "But you know what happens when you've been naughty, don't you? You get punished."

"Mmm. By who? You?"

"Only me. Do you want to be on your knees when you get punished, or over my lap?"

My heartbeat thrums, settling between my legs, and butterflies erupt in my stomach, swirling so violently I feel dizzy. I need to go home before I accidentally beg this man to fuck me on the bathroom sink. I have higher standards than that.

Or do I? No, I don't think I do.

"What's the matter, Olivia? You seem like you're wavering."

I press my lips together. "Nope." *Yes.* "I'm just . . . tired. Super tired. Time to go home."

Before I can change my mind, I kiss his stunned cheek and jet toward the coat closet. Once I've said my good-byes to the future bride and groom, I brave the cold. There's a fresh dusting of snow covering the sidewalks, kissing my toes, and my teeth clatter as I pull up the Uber app on my phone.

A lavish limo stops out front, and when the driver opens the back door and gestures inside, my brows jump. I point at myself, and he smiles, nodding.

"Oh, no. You must have me confused with someone else. I'm—"

"Get in." Carter tugs my phone from my hand, sweeping me toward the limo with his hand on my back.

"But I—"

"Get in the car, Olivia." His leather-gloved thumb brushes my trembling lower lip. "Your toes are going to fall off, and I want to make sure you get home safe."

"Yeah. Okay." My head's bobbing but my feet aren't moving, so the man grips my waist, lifts me off the ground, and places me on the backseat. He slides in next to me, spreading his legs, and when he recites my address into a speaker, I snort. "Are you checking to make sure I didn't give you a fake address?"

"You wouldn't do that. You like me too much."

Rolling my eyes and crossing my arms, I stare straight ahead at the divider that hides us from the driver, ignoring Carter as he pull his gloves off, lays them over his lap, and fucks around on his phone. But ten minutes in, he hasn't paid me a damn bit of attention, and if I don't get to be in control, neither does he.

"Are you seriously checking the sports updates right now?"

A sneaky smile tugs at his lips. "No."

"You're being an ass."

"You don't mean that."

I sling one leg over the other. "You're right. You don't know how to look at me without losing control. I get it. This is easier for you."

There it is.

He tucks his phone away, electric green eyes dropping to my lips as he moves toward me, lithe and deadly. "You saying I don't know how to play the game, Parker?"

"Apparently not this one, Beckett."

"Think you can play better than me?"

I check my nails. "Isn't that what I've been doing?"

His hand wraps around my throat, shoving me down to my back as he hovers above me. His hips drop to mine, the tips of his fingers searing my skin like an open flame as they drag up my thigh, slipping beneath my dress.

His mouth paints the column of my throat with wet kisses, nipping the edge of my jaw, lingering at my ear. "Prove it."

A raw ache unfurls between my legs as he pulls away, grazing my clit through my panties when he shifts my dress back into place.

He spreads back out in his seat, looking way too damn pleased with himself, smiling down at the motherfucking sports updates again.

The car rolls to a stop seconds later, and I jump out, slamming the door behind me.

"Ollie," he calls, chasing after me. I hate that it comes out a chuckle, and I hate even more when I slip on a patch of ice on my porch steps, sending me flying backward, right into his stupid, hard chest. He sets me down at my door, and I've never wanted to wipe a grin off someone's face more than I do right now. "Did I win?"

"No," I grumble, kicking off my heels. "I haven't kissed you."

Still grinning, still way too smug. "We're supposed to be taking this slow."

"I know."

"So no kissing."

"Right."

"Would it make you feel better if you won?"

"I don't—"

Carter swallows my words with his mouth, his fingers plunging through my hair as my back hits the closet in the front hall. His hand slides up my leg, beneath my dress, wrapping around my bare hip as I grind myself into him.

"Fuck slow," he growls. "I can't do slow. Not with you."

God, I don't want slow. I want to crack this whole thing wide open, the chemistry, the passion, the fire. I want to give him all of me and take all of him.

Carter pulls away, fighting to breathe as his gaze rakes over me. Something blooms there, something vulnerable and cautious. "I . . . I missed you while you were gone."

With my hand on his cheek, I promise, "I missed you while I was gone too."

There's that megawatt grin, perfect teeth, and deep dimples, and before he leaves, he dashes back down to the limo, jumps over the icy step, and returns a moment later with a small blue box that he presses into my hand.

He places a lingering kiss on my lips. "Sleep tight, Ollie girl."

I stand over the kitchen counter after he leaves, lifting the lid on the blue box. Inside is a cupcake, and the tiny flag that sticks out of the frosting tells me it's maple pecan, topped with maple buttercream frosting and bacon crumble.

The note scrawled under the lid sends my heart into overdrive.

I got you the most bacon-y one.
xo Carter

22

I'M NOT ANXIOUS; I'M IN CONTROL

Carter

"Stop smiling like a jackass."

"You can't prove shit, old man."

Hank finds my face, shoving it away. "I know you like the back of my hand, Carter."

Chuckling, I finish rearranging the food on his plate before sliding it over to him. "Steak is at twelve o'clock, scrambled eggs at three, hash browns at six, toast with jam at nine."

"Why don't you go ahead and tell me why you're smiling." He gestures at me with his fork. "Does it have anything to do with why you showed up three hours early today and we're having breakfast instead of lunch?"

Dublin's head whips back and forth between me and Hank, watching every disappearing bite. Poor guy's got a puddle of drool so big gathering at his feet that I'm beginning to worry might be a slipping hazard, so I let him eat a breakfast sausage from my hand.

"You feeding my damn dog again? You spoil him." Hank grabs a piece of steak, smiling when Dublin devours it.

"I have a date today."

Hank's fork pauses in midair, his mouth hanging open. He doesn't have to look so shocked. I'm date-worthy. I can date. It's not a big deal.

"Olivia?" he finally whispers. "You got the girl back?"

"Obviously."

He claps his hands together before reaching out to grasp mine. His smile is so broad, so genuine, that mine grows too. "I knew you would, Carter. Didn't I tell ya, Dubs? I told you Carter would win her back. You said he was clueless, but I knew better." He pats Dublin's head. "You shouldn't talk like that about him when he's not around, buddy. He's an okay guy."

I narrow my eyes, shoving bacon into my mouth.

"Did you kiss her?"

"Mhmm. Didn't mean to, though." A perfect example of how in control I am, which is to say not the fuck at all. Frankly, it's a miracle I didn't fuck her in the bathroom at the party.

"What the hell do you mean you didn't mean to? Who doesn't mean to kiss a beautiful lady they're trying to win over?"

"I'm trying to take control."

Hank snickers into his napkin. It spirals quickly, until he's keeled over the table and everyone is looking to see what's so funny.

"Control? You? A man?" He slaps a palm down on the table. "Carter, let me tell ya something, son. In a relationship, the only person ever in control is the woman. She always—always, always, *always*—has the power. She owns you and those dangly things between your legs." He cups both hands side by side, around imaginary balls, I presume. "The sooner you realize that the better."

"I don't think so. I did a pretty good—"

"No, you didn't. You kissed her even though you didn't mean to. Why? Because she has the power. Because you took one look at that pretty face and you crumbled to the floor at her feet. And you always will, because you'll put her before anyone and everything else."

Well, that's kinda scary. Hockey's always been my priority. Olivia couldn't possibly overtake it.

. . . Could she?

"When do I get to meet the special lady?"

"If I want to keep her around?" I sip my milkshake. "Never."

He chuckles, tossing a balled-up napkin at me. "Son of a bitch."

Hank and I head out for a walk before I take him home, helping him settle in his La-Z-Boy. Dublin tucks himself into his side while I get Hank set up with his audiobooks. He loves listening to smutty romances. He says it's the only action he gets anymore.

"Have fun on your date, Carter. Don't do anything I wouldn't do."

I look down at the cover of the book that's displayed on the tablet I got him two years ago for his birthday. *Fifty Shades Darker*. "I don't think we need to worry about that."

His hand searches for mine, and when I take it, he squeezes. "Love you."

"Love you, too, you dirty old man."

I'M NOT ANXIOUS; I'M IN control. There's a difference.

If I were anxious, would I have gotten here twenty minutes early and stayed in the car?

Maybe.

If I were anxious, would I just be staring up at Olivia's house?

. . . Also maybe.

It's not as if I don't know *how* to go on a date. It's not like I have very real feelings for her that scare the living shit out of me. If I were anxious, would I—okay, I'm fucking anxious. But it's not a big deal. Everyone feels this way before their first date, right? Whether they're sixteen or about to be twenty-eight.

Right? Right.

Plus, the startled half scream I hear when I finally ring the doorbell says Olivia's just as anxious.

"Shit. He's early. I'm not ready."

I glance at my watch. I'm one minute and thirty-two seconds early. And as I mentioned, I've been here for twenty minutes, sitting in my car. I got out three times, made it up the front steps, then hightailed it back to the car.

But it wasn't because I was anxious.

Olivia still hasn't answered, so I ring the bell again, three times in quick succession, grinning at the curses flying from her mouth as her footsteps stomp closer.

The door swings open, revealing Olivia in all her glory.

In her pajamas.

She's wearing an oversized University of BC tee with a hole on the side of her waist, and a pair of striped long johns that are so long they completely cover her feet, except for her pink toes. I did tell her to dress casually when I called this morning.

"This is slightly more casual than I was going for, but we can make it work." I shake the snow off my toque and step inside. "You're rocking the whole I-woke-up-like-this vibe." I wink. "Kinda makes me wanna take you back to bed."

One of the things I like about Olivia is I never know what I'm going to get. Sometimes she's quick with the sassy comebacks, and sometimes, like right now, she just stares up at me while her face floods with heat.

I thought I was nervous? Psssh.

"Oh my God," she whispers. "I haven't said a word yet, have I?"

"You're just kind of staring at me," I confirm.

She buries her face in her hands. "I'm a fucking mess this morning."

"That's okay. It makes me feel better about it taking me four tries to actually knock on your door."

"I thought you were in control."

"Can I tell you the truth?" Hooking a finger beneath her chin, I tilt her face up. "I've never felt so fucking powerless. That's why I'm gonna kiss you now instead of waiting until the end of our date like I promised myself I would, okay?"

She smiles, and I press my lips to hers, desperate to taste it. It's tentative at first, a slow exploration, testing the boundaries. But then her lips part on a sigh, letting me sweep in, and she fists my coat when her knees buckle.

"Ol," I whisper against her lips.

"Mmm."

"Go get dressed."

Her grunt is as unimpressed as her glare, and I watch her ass bounce in those thin pants as she struts down the hall and disappears.

I take in the small entryway, smiling at the lanyard I gave her for Christmas that's hanging beside her coat, two keys and an ID badge attached.

I'm kinda nosy, so it only takes me a minute to find her skates. My thumb glides over the blade, pleased to find them sharp, and I slip out the door and tuck them in my trunk before she notices I'm gone.

I peel my coat off, trying to ignore the biting chill in the air as I wander into the living room. There's a stack of romance novels on the coffee table that would likely pique Hank's interest, next to a stack of graded tests on the female reproductive system, and the pen that rests on top has perfect teeth marks engraved in it.

There are a cluster of picture frames on her TV stand, and I find my favorite one immediately. Olivia is sitting in front of a Christmas tree, a smiling baby in her arms—*terrifying*—and that small brown-haired girl from Cara's picture glued to her side. Her smile is the biggest I've ever seen it, shining all the way up in her eyes, and I want to make her that happy.

"That's my niece and my nephew," Olivia tells me from the doorway. "Alannah and Jem."

This woman before me is so effortlessly gorgeous I don't know what to do with myself, and when she fiddles with her hands, blushing, I just want to scoop her up and take her home.

"I'm sorry it's so messy in here."

Her timid whisper is weighed down with vulnerability, like she's ready to start letting me in. What doesn't sit right with me is that she seems worried that I might not like all of her once I know her.

I take a seat on the couch, patting the cushion beside me. "Come here."

She nods, but remains rooted in place.

"One foot in front of the other," I tease.

A goofy grin lights her face, and she claps a hand to her forehead. As soon as she's within reach, I pull her down to me.

"I know we talked on Friday night, but I think we should air everything out so we can start fresh and keep on with those explosive kisses, yeah?" I give her hand a squeeze when she doesn't answer. "Ollie?"

"Oh! Oh my God! I answered in my head. Yes, I wanna kiss you. Oh crap." Her eyes widen and she jerks her hands back. "I mean, I want you to kiss me. No!" She grips her own face. "Talk! I want to talk! Oh fuck. This is awful."

"You're fucking adorable when you're nervous." I twirl a curl around my finger. "I just need to know how you're feeling."

"I'm scared," she admits. "Scared that your feelings are temporary."

"I spent nearly two weeks trying to convince myself they were temporary, to let go of them and let go of you after you walked out. It didn't work. They got stronger somehow, and that was really confusing, especially when I thought you were on a date. I didn't know why it was so easy for you to move on, but impossible for me."

"It was just Alannah," she assures me. "She spends the weekend here sometimes and we go on all these dates, like out for lunch and to the movies."

"Cara told me. If I'd just asked . . ." I scratch the back of my head, heat rushing to my ears. "Are you mad at me for what I did?"

Olivia covers my hand with hers. "No, Carter. I know you were hurting and you were trying to fix it."

"I was so disappointed in myself. Just for considering it for even a minute. I didn't know how to handle what I was feeling."

"Sounds like we both need to be a little more patient with ourselves."

I watch our fingers tangle, admiring the perfect way they seem to fit together. Then I swallow and go for it.

"I want to date you, Ollie. I want to take you for dinner and go see Disney movies and dedicate my goals to you without feeling bad about it. I want us to give this a real shot."

"That's a big change for you."

"One I'm ready to make if it's me and you."

Her cheeks flush, teeth skimming her bottom lip. "I'm kind of an all-in type of person, Carter. I have to be able to envision a future with someone before I decide to take the next step. It's why a genuine connection is so important to me, and I feel like I have that with you. So if that scares you . . . I just want you to know."

I think about the lanyard I picked up on Christmas Eve, the day after the fundraiser, because I knew I wanted to get her something. But it was the words I wrote that meant the most to me. I was looking forward to the new year, because I was looking forward to a year with her in my life.

"I'm all in, as long as it's you I'm all in with." My lips meet hers with a gentle, sweeping kiss, brushing her hair behind her ear when we part. "Are you still scared?"

"Yes."

"What are you most afraid of?"

"Falling," she answers quietly and without hesitation.

"I'll catch you."

"Promise?"

Bringing her to me, I sear her with a kiss that feels every bit like a future I never knew I wanted.

"Promise."

23

I'VE BEEN COCKBLOCKED

Olivia

IS GETTING WINE DRUNK AT lunchtime frowned upon? Because it would make being on the other end of Carter Beckett's undivided attention a hundred times less intimidating.

Honestly, I don't know if he's watching every bite of food I put in my mouth because he's waiting for me to let him finish it, or because he genuinely can't take his eyes off me. If I had to guess, I'd say it's a mix of both.

"Uh, excuse me."

Carter's eyes flick up at the interruption, a group of college boys hovering by our little corner booth.

"Can we get a picture?"

This is the fourth group to ask. Carter's response has been the same every time.

"I'm having lunch with my girl right now, so I'll catch you on the way out."

The *my girl* comment does the same thing it's done every other time: kisses my cheeks, wraps around my neck, and tumbles down my spine, settling like a heavy weight at the cleft of my thighs.

And Carter does what he's done every other time: watches me with the proudest grin, making me squirm, and murmurs, "Huh. Wonder what that blush is for."

This time, when I roll my eyes, he chuckles and aims his brows at my plate. "You gonna finish that?"

"And here I thought you were watching me eat because you couldn't get enough of me." I sigh, pushing my plate across the table.

"Oh, that's absolutely why. You're the first thing I've been hyperfixated on since I discovered hockey." His hand slips below the table, fingertips dancing up my thigh. I'm riveted, focused on the movement while he carries on talking like he isn't lighting my nerve endings on fire with a simple touch. "Been fixated on the way these thighs fell open for me, eager to let me taste you. On the way they shook when you came all over my face."

My heartbeat races as his fingers drift higher, and when he glides them over the seam of my leggings, right over my clit, I ball my napkin in my fist.

"Fixated on the way this pretty pussy squeezed my cock so good, like it never wanted to let go. Fixated on the way your mouth opened when you came, the way you cried out for God." He strokes me firmly, until my belly clenches and my thoughts vanish. And then he pulls his hand back, diving into my food, leaving me wanting and furious. "Thanks for sharing, Ollie."

I somehow manage to give him the cold shoulder for the rest of our meal, incredibly proud of myself when we step outside, even if I am going to have to resort to my battery-powered boyfriend when I get home.

Carter catches my hand, spins me into him, and dips me. "I'm sorry I teased you, Ollie girl. Please forgive me." His words dissolve on my tongue like sugar, and I hang on to him for dear life, because if he's been fixated on me, I've been fixated on him too.

"*Olivia!*"

My eyes flip open as Carter hoists me back up, sweeping me behind his back as several cameras invade our space.

"Carter! Is Olivia your girlfriend?"

"Are you officially off the market, Mr. Beckett?"

"What's your last name, sweetheart?"

"Fuck off," Carter growls. "You don't get her last name. You don't get shit." His fingers lace harshly through mine as he tugs me into his side and down the street, my face aimed at the ground.

I trip over the curb when I scramble toward his car, and he catches me before I can face-plant on the asphalt. My feet don't touch the ground as he hauls me toward the passenger side, stuffing me inside.

Carter is in the front seat and has us around the corner before I can count to five. He pulls over down the street, pulling my mitts off my hands and bringing my knuckles to his lips.

"I'm so sorry. Somebody must've posted a picture at the restaurant." He takes my face between his hands, looking me over as if I might be injured. "Are you okay?"

I nod. "I don't . . ." I don't know how to say it without hurting his feelings.

"You don't want to be a girl in pictures with Carter Beckett."

"I'm sorry."

"Don't be sorry, Ollie. But it will happen, as long as we're together. There's a bright side to it all, though. Now there's photographic evidence that I'm dating the world's hottest teacher."

I snort a laugh, only because he seems so sincere.

"It'll get old quick, I promise. I can see it now." He swipes a hand through the air in an arc. "'Carter Beckett, seen for the tenth night in a row with hot-as-hell high school teacher.'" He squeezes my hands. "Trust me, princess, it'll get boring fast."

My nose scrunches. "I'm not a princess."

He pulls into traffic, winking at me. "You're my princess."

I roll my eyes to distract from the fact that I might like the ridiculous nickname. "What are you doing for the rest of the day?"

It's my not-so-subtle way of asking if our date is over, but before he can answer, the car speaker rings, *Hank calling* lighting up the dashboard.

Carter's brow furrows before he accepts. "Hank? What's up, buddy? Miss me already?"

"Carter." Poor Hank sounds distressed. "You still on your date?"

"Just heading to our second destination." Carter flashes me a devilish smile and winks again. "What's going on? You okay?"

Hank sighs. "I'm sorry to interrupt. Hi, Olivia."

"Hi, Hank," I push out after a moment of stunned silence. *He knows my name.*

"Carter, I took a little tumble getting out of the shower."

"Shit." Carter looks over his shoulder, hits his blinker, and turns left from the right-hand lane. "Are you hurt?"

"It's nothing serious but I'm having some trouble getting up on my own. Could you maybe—"

"We'll be there in ten."

We get there in seven because Carter drives a shit ton on the erratic side. He enters the five-story apartment building with a key, and once we ride the elevator up to the top floor, he uses another key to enter the suite.

"Hank?" Carter storms through the small apartment. I follow him, crashing into his back when he comes to a sudden stop. "Are you fucking kidding me, old man?"

A man—Hank, I presume—with a full head of fluffy white hair and weathered blue eyes grins up at us from where he appears to be entirely too relaxed, a whole lot amused, and awfully proud in his easy chair, the cutest dog I've ever seen curled up at his side.

"Tricked ya. You're too damn gullible." Hank carefully climbs to his feet, his golden retriever following. He grasps a long stick in one hand, holding the other out toward Carter, who takes it in his own, but not before giving him a playful punch to the shoulder. It's at this moment I realize Hank has a visual impairment.

"Wanted to meet the beautiful Miss Olivia before you have a chance to mess it all up and scare her away."

"Your confidence in me is inspiring." Carter rolls his eyes, leading Hank over to me. "I hoped to hold off on introducing you to him, Ollie, Hank likes to do whatever the hell he wants."

I arch a brow. "Like someone else I know."

"Ha! I like her already!" Hank elbows Carter's hands away and reaches forward. I slip my hands into his and he squeezes. "I had to meet the girl who's made my friend here a miserable dud for a few weeks while she kept him on his toes, made him work for it."

"I'm happy to meet you, Hank. This has turned into the best date I've ever had." The dog at his feet whines, begging me for attention. "May I pet your dog, or is he working?"

Hank waves me off. "Dublin's never really working. Laziest guide dog you've ever met. Go ahead, Dubs. Get your kisses."

Dublin drops to my feet, rolling around, and I sink to my butt so I can give him all the loving.

"Dublin? Like Ireland?"

"Yeah," Hank says with a wistful smile. "Reminds me of my sweetheart."

Carter hands me a frame with a black-and-white wedding picture. The bride and groom couldn't be more in love, that much is obvious by the way they're laughing. He plops another photo in my lap, this one colored. I recognize Hank's face, his fluffy hair, though it was light brown back then.

Carter taps on the beautiful redhead tucked into Hank's side in the photograph. "This is Hank's high school sweetheart."

"Ireland?"

Hank nods proudly, eyes misty. "Beautiful, ain't she? She saved my life."

"And mine." Carter's hands are in his pocket as he toes at the floor with his shoe. He gives me a sheepish smile, one I'm not used to seeing, and I hope one day he'll feel safe enough to share his story with me.

I trail a fingertip down Ireland's long, ginger waves. "She's got the most gorgeous smile."

"I remember the exact shape of her lips, and the tiny dimple she had just off to the right of her mouth." He touches the spot on his own face, then claps his hands. "Can I feel your face, Olivia?"

"No, no, no." Carter shakes his head. "Don't fall for it, Ollie. I did, and when he was done, he told me it was all bullshit. Just wanted to see how gullible I was, which, as it turns out, is very."

"You're no fun," Hank grumbles as Carter helps me off the ground, and then directs Hank down beside me on the couch. "I already know you're five foot one, have tiny freckles on your nose, eyes the color of chocolate, and hands that fit perfectly in Carter's, always warm."

Carter's cheeks burn bright. He's so cute it hurts.

Hank's fingers find my braid, twirling the end of it. He twists to Carter. "What color? Describe it to me."

Carter's green eyes glitter as he drinks me in. "Dark brown, like rich, smooth coffee. The kind that wakes you the hell up, that you crave in the morning and all day long." His gaze drifts to a curl that brushes my cheek, before lingering on my lips. "With a little bit of caramel drizzle that leaves you licking your lips, begging for another taste."

Oh crap. I'm horny. My lady bits are buzzing.

Hank lays my braid back over my shoulder. "Smells like banana bread."

"*Right?*" Carter throws his arms out. "Thank you!"

"Well, can you squeeze some time with this old man into your date? I made snacks." He gestures to the coffee table where a bowl of Doritos and a platter of Oreos sit. I like Hank.

Carter checks his watch. "Well, we're already too late to make the movie."

"Movie? We watched it on Friday."

The grin he wears has my heat crawling up my neck. "Trust me, gorgeous; we weren't gonna watch it this time."

"A-ha!" Hank claps a hand to Carter's knee. "That's my boy!" He throws his arms around our shoulders. "Guess you're stuck with me this afternoon. I've never been a cockblock until now."

"Don't get used to it," Carter mumbles, but—

"Hang on." I lift the tablet off the coffee table, and as I flip through the books in Hank's audio library, I wonder if I've just found my new best friend.

"Hank," I murmur, turning to him.

"Oh no," Carter whispers, eyes flicking to the tablet.

"What is it?" Hank asks, head moving between us.

Carter swallows. "Olivia just found your smut collection."

24

MY PANTS HAVE LEFT THE BUILDING

Carter

BY THE TIME WE LEAVE Hank's, the sun is already dipping into the horizon. I'm typically someone who loves winter—present year excluded; this shit is too cold for me—because hockey has always been my life, but I hate the shorter days, the fleeting hours of sunlight. I always feel like I'm rushing to get things done before the sun sets, like right now.

We've got one more stop on our date that depends on daylight before we head back to my house for dinner and cuddles. Potentially naked cuddles. I haven't decided yet. I've realized slow isn't a word in our vocabulary, but sex is something I can hold off until we're both ready to take that step.

"When's the last time you skated?"

"Yesterday," Olivia answers distractedly.

We're not far from my place, and she's got her face nearly pressed against the window as she stares out at Capilano Lake. It's always breathtaking, but especially now, faded rays of sunshine glittering off the ice.

Olivia manages to pull her gaze away. "I coach Alannah's hockey team."

"You—" I accidentally slam on the brakes, bracketing my arm across Olivia's chest to catch her. "Sorry, sorry. I just—you just—I think I might love you," I joke, except I'm possibly, *maybe*, halfway serious. "That's amazing. Can I come see a game?"

"Absolutely not."

"Why the hell not?"

"Because all you'll do is distract the girls and the moms."

"Hmm. I see your point. This face is highly distracting. Don't get me started on this body."

God, I love when she rolls her eyes. So tiny and ferocious. "You're so ridiculously full of yourself it's ridiculous, Beckett."

The tip of my finger dances up her thigh. "You can be full of me too if you play your cards right."

She laughs and shoves my hand off her thigh, only to twine her fingers with mine and set them back in her lap. "Who the hell raised you?"

"Mama Beckett would take offense to that, Olivia." *She'd apologize profusely and tell me to keep my filthy mouth shut.*

Which reminds me, Mom's gonna have a field day when those pictures of Olivia and me hit the news. I make a mental note to pretend like I have no idea what she's talking about when she inevitably calls me about it, just to grind her gears.

Once the car is parked, I tug Olivia over to a bench overlooking the lake. It's covered in a thick layer of glass-like ice, the slowly sinking sun making it dazzle like crystal. The snow-dusted pines shine in the sleek reflection, and everything is white, powder blue, and deep forest green.

Olivia's so enthralled she doesn't notice her skates in my hands until I kneel at her feet. When she smiles, it's the most beautiful sight I've ever seen. "We're going skating? Here?"

"You got it, princess. You said you grew up doing this back home. Figured this might be a nice way to bring a bit of home to you."

Her eyes shine with gratitude. "Thank you, Carter. This is, hands down, the best date ever."

My chest puffs with pride. "Knew I'd kill my first date."

With our skates on, I help Olivia down to the ice and watch as she takes it all in, speechless.

Most areas of Vancouver don't typically get cold enough to freeze over so completely, but this winter is an exception. Right now, as Olivia twirls slowly, gazing with wonder out at all this little slice of heaven has to offer, I couldn't be more grateful for the cold.

"I've never seen something so beautiful." Her smile is so dazzling, it hits me right in the stomach like a sucker punch.

"Yeah. Me neither."

Her lashes flutter as she takes her bottom lip between her teeth. "Who do you think is a better skater, me or you?"

I scoff. "Please. I'm way faster."

"I said better, not faster." She skates away from me, leaning forward on one foot before she jumps into the air, spins, and lands on her feet. She sends up a spray of snow when she stops in front of me. "Hockey on the weekends and figure skating during the week until I was ten."

"I'll take your ass to the ground, Parker."

There's a happy thump in my chest when Olivia throws her arms around my neck. She's finally given up that shyness from earlier today. I love seeing her like this, her walls coming down, her simply . . . being herself, with me. Me, being myself with her. It's easy.

I rub the tip of my nose against hers. "Wanna race?"

"No way. Your legs are, like, three times the length of mine." She spins away from me. "Unfair advantage."

I skate toward her, loving the way her hips swing with every backward stride. "Afraid I'll win?"

"I could skate circles around you, Mr. Beckett."

I incline my head toward the small green boathouse that sits in the middle of the lake, connected from one shore to the next by a narrow wooden dock. "First one there and back."

Her fingers crawl up my chest. "When I win, will you rub my feet? They're gonna be sore from kicking your ass."

I capture her mouth with mine. "So arrogant."

"Guess you're rubbing off on me."

"Oh, I'll fucking rub off on you." I catch Olivia's waist as she tries to spin away from me, hauling her right back. "We gonna do this or what, pip-squeak?"

"Definitely." She touches her lips to the corner of my mouth. "But there's something I want to do before I humiliate you."

I don't have time to ask what that is before her mouth opens on mine. Hot, wet tongue lashes, nipping teeth and bruising grips, this kiss is nothing but starved. I'm about to toss my ridiculous idea of anything *other* than naked cuddles out the window when she starts tugging on my zipper.

"What do you think you're doing, Miss Parker?" I barely manage the words, because she slips her hand down my pants and wraps her fist around my cock, which is now hard as fuck. "Fuck."

"Can't a girl put her hands on her man?"

"Yup. Yeah. That's . . . *fuck*. Hands." My head whips between the trees and my car. Do I wanna push her up against a tree and fuck her, or watch her slip around on the leather seats in the back of the Benz? Tree is more accessible. Do we need to take our skates off? No, I think I can make it work. I've got thighs of steel.

"Carter?"

"Yeah, baby?"

"You're gonna lose."

"What?" I nearly cry when her hand disappears. "What are you—*Olivia*!"

Her piercing cackle echoes across the lake as she takes off like lightning. I'm too stunned to care when my jeans start slipping over my ass, and I'm proud to say that by the time Olivia reaches the boathouse and starts flying back toward me, my pants are around my ankles.

Because that girl can fucking *skate*.

She's still laughing like a hyena when she jumps into my arms and crashes her lips against mine. "Ready to rub my feet?"

I'm ready to rub something, that's for fucking sure.

I DON'T THINK I'VE EVER realized the power a single person could have on someone. Because here on my balcony, with Olivia's warm body tucked into mine, her cheek pressed to my racing heart, I've never been happier. There's no part of me that wants to climb on a plane in the morning and leave for three days, and the realization is staggering.

The flawless beauty sprawled out in my lap is decked out in my clothes, head to toe. My Vipers hoodie, a pair of sweats that swallow her legs, my thickest socks covering her feet as we curl up next to the roaring fire, Olivia with a cup of the tea I ran out to buy this morning so she can have it whenever she's here.

Every minute of this day has been perfect, from Olivia's hand in mine as we skated across the lake, to the way she stood by my side at the stove, watching me cook dinner, right down to the way she tightly wrapped her arms around me when I showed her the stash of tea I'd run out to buy just for her.

I pull the elastic from her braid and run my fingers through her curls. "Hank didn't scare you off today, did he?"

"Are you kidding? That guy really amps up your cool factor. His smut collection is the most impressive thing I've ever seen."

Right. My eighty-three-year-old best friend and my ... *Olivia* ... might have started an impromptu book club today. They're starting with some book called *Follow Me Darkly* or something. I have no desire to get tangled up in that, except apparently blindfolds are involved, so, like, maybe.

But still: "My sword of thunder is the most impressive thing you've ever seen."

She tips her head back, wide gaze locking on mine as silence hangs between us. Then she laughs in my face. "You do not call your dick your sword of thunder."

"I absolutely call my dick my sword of thunder. You know why, Ollie? 'Cause he brings the thunder." I take her chin in my hand. "I don't appreciate your laughter right now."

Folding her lips into her mouth, she pretends to lock them and throw away the key. "You and Hank seem really close. Have you known him your whole life?"

"A little over seven years," I murmur, wrapping my arms around her, gazing out at the mountains, the stars that paint the sky. "He saved my life."

"You said that earlier, that his wife did."

Because she did. I may have never met Ireland, but she saved my life the day Hank found me, and I'll never think otherwise. But the only people who know how Hank came to be in my life are my family and my very best friends, so maybe that's why I pause.

"You don't have to tell me, Carter. You're allowed to have boundaries, and it's okay if this is one of them."

But what if I don't want to have any boundaries? What if I want to show her all of me?

"The day I met Hank, my dad was in a car accident. It was barely five in the morning, and the driver was still drunk from the night before." Grief settles like a heavy weight on my chest, and for a moment, it's hard to breathe. "He died on impact."

It's the smallest, simplest thing, but when one of her hands tangles with mine, and the other moves to lay over my heart, any apprehension I feel melts away. If I want her to know me, well, this is maybe the most important piece of my puzzle.

"I was supposed to play in Calgary the following night. My dad was driving down to watch because it was my first game as an assistant captain. I offered to fly him out but he said he wanted to take the scenic route. I should've . . . I should've made him."

Olivia presses a kiss to my palm. "It's not your fault, Carter."

"It's hard not to think that way sometimes, though. Especially that day." The only person to ever blame me for my dad's death is me. It's a heavy weight to carry, even though I'm not the one who chose to get behind the wheel after drinking all night long. Hell, I've seen the struggle in my own sister's eyes, wondering if our dad would still be here, if he'd one day be able to walk her down the aisle if it weren't for me playing hockey.

"It was after eleven when my mom's body finally gave up the fight. I carried her to bed and sat with my sister as she cried herself to sleep. And then I . . . I went out. By myself. I didn't want the responsibility of taking care of them when I didn't know how I'd even be able to take care of myself. Hank was there. Kept cracking fucking blind jokes. I tried to ignore him but he kept throwing peanut shells at me every time I started to doze off." I run an agitated hand through my hair. "I was just fucking . . ."

"Heartbroken," Olivia whispers.

"Yeah." My voice cracks as I hug her tighter. "Just a heartbroken mess. I didn't think he had any clue who I was. He couldn't see, after all. And then I made the stupidest decision I've ever made. I stood up and grabbed my car keys."

Olivia sucks in a jagged inhale, swiping away a tear that runs down her cheek.

"Hank slapped his cane against my knee so fast before he stabbed the end of it into my stomach. I remember exactly what he said to me next."

I think back to that moment, the one that saved my life, and maybe so many more. I remember those light blue eyes moving over me, the fury that I've only seen Hank wear that one time as he slipped off his stool, his hands moving over my chest until he found the neck of my shirt and gripped it.

"'I know you're not about to drive, Mr. Beckett,' he said. 'You've had way too much to drink and have too much to lose. There are people here who depend on you. Don't make a stupid decision that you'll regret the rest of your life, if you even live to see it, just because you're hurting right now.'"

Silent tears stream down Olivia's face as she turns, fingers pressing into my jaw as she presses the softest kiss to my lips.

"That day was the seventh anniversary of Ireland's death. Hank was sitting there at midnight drinking a glass of chocolate milk because he'd had a dream during his afternoon nap and claimed that his dead wife said somebody might need his help. He'd been sitting there since six in the evening, waiting. Said he knew it was me he was waiting for the second I sank down on the bar stool next to him."

Olivia sniffles, hiccupping against my chest. I pull her face up to mine and smile at the way she tries to slap her tears away.

"I'm sorry for crying," she cries, wrapping her arms around me and burying her face in my neck while I smooth my palm down her hair. "I'm so thankful for Hank and Ireland and you."

"Me?"

She nods. "For letting me see the real Carter Beckett. For being the type of man who carries his mom to bed. For having a man in his eighties who loves dirty books as one of your best friends. I'm grateful to be here with you."

I'm a little lost for words, so I capture her mouth with a kiss. If I attempt to talk, there's a good chance that a lot of words I'm not ready to say about how I feel for her are going tumble out, which is ridiculous. Disregarding all the weeks that came before, it's been one day.

There's no denying that whatever we've got between us feels right. I hope she feels it, too, because in this moment I'm acutely aware that these feelings are going nowhere fast.

For the next hour, we stay by the fire, trading stories, laughing quietly while she stretches out opposite me, enjoying the foot rub I'm giving her through my socks. She keeps jerking her foot away and giggling every time I hit a certain spot in her arch, so I peel the thick socks off and throw them over my shoulder, revealing her pink toes.

"Do you have a foot fetish I'm not aware of?" Olivia asks when I press my lips to her arch.

"No. I have a *you* fetish. And I'm dying to see if your feet are . . ." I nip her arch. "Ticklish."

Olivia flies off the back of the couch and nearly hammers me in the face with her foot when my teeth nibble on her sensitive skin. "Stop it! *Carter!*"

But do I stop? No, of course not. I find all her ticklish spots, until I'm satisfied that her laughter is forever ingrained in my brain, and also that she could kick my ass if she really wanted to. *Though she be but pint-sized, she is fierce*, or whatever the saying is.

"You're such an ass," she mutters as she snuggles into my chest.

"Yeah, but I'm *your* ass." A rustle draws my attention down below, and I drop my voice, nudging her cheek. I point out at the clearing where a fawn is emerging, each step slow and cautious as it looks around. "Look."

Olivia gasps, scrambling over my lap to get a better look, gripping the railing. "Oh my gosh. It's just a baby."

A shadow moves behind it, and a much larger deer emerges from the trees, rooting around in the snow. "And there's Mama."

"So incredible," Olivia murmurs wondrously.

"Like you."

She turns her smile on me. "Are you trying to charm me, Mr. Beckett?"

"I've been trying since I met you."

She slings her arms around my neck, straddling my hips. "You're getting pretty good at it, as much as it pains me to say. Much better than 'I wanna put you in the penalty box.'"

"Still can't believe that didn't work. But I think if I'd had five more minutes—"

"I would've rearranged your face. Yes, you're absolutely right."

"Feisty girl." I slip my hands beneath the hoodie she wears, palms sliding up her back, and the chill makes her shiver. "You like putting up a fight, and I like it too." I flick my tongue over the spot below her ear. "Makes me wanna slap your ass and fuck you until you scream.

I think my favorite sound is Olivia's whimper. I enjoy the way her skin warms with the sound, her body buzzing as my lips move against her neck. I rip the collar of my sweater to the side, exposing her shoulder to the cold air, and cover it with my hot tongue.

"*Carter.*" There's that whimper again. Goddamn, I love it.

I pull the hoodie over her head, exposing her soft curves, the gem in her belly when her shirt underneath rides up. It's getting late and I have a flight in the morning. I know I need to take her home so she can get some sleep before work, but I won't see her for a few days and I'll be damned if I'm going to leave this city without a little taste.

So I kiss her stomach, peel those sweatpants off her legs, wrap her around my body, and cart her to the bed, sinking to my knees in front of her.

She threads her fingers through my hair, fisting it when her head falls back with a moan as my mouth coasts up the inside of her thigh. There's a little wet spot in the center of her pale purple panties that makes me want to rip them right off.

So I do. I destroy that scrap of satin and bury my face between her legs like she's the first meal I've had in days. Olivia collapses on the bed, legs winding around my neck as she pushes me deeper into her, hips arching, crying out for more as I fuck her with my tongue.

She's coming apart at the seams, melting into my mouth with every flick and slide of my tongue, the way my teeth graze her clit. My fingers crawl beneath her shirt, finding her taut nipples, and when I give one a pinch, she gasps, arching off the bed. Her legs quiver as she yanks on my hair, and I know she's close.

Climbing to my feet, I flip her over, pulling her to her hands and knees, dragging her shirt up her back and my finger down her spine, watching her shiver. My palm curves over the swell of her full ass, and I dip two fingers inside her, dragging her wetness through her slit until I find her clit, swollen and begging for attention.

"You're so wet, Ollie. Do you like when I touch you?"

"Please, Carter."

"Please what?"

She buries her face in the mattress, hiding the sound she makes. I plow my fingers through her hair, fisting it, and I pull her back up.

"Tell me you want me to fuck your pussy with my fingers."

"Carter," she whimpers.

"*Say it.*"

The hushed demand has her gripping the sheets, and when I tease her clit, she sobs, "Fuck my pussy with your fingers, *please.*"

I sink two fingers inside of her without hesitation, holding her down while I pump in and out. Her ass juts backward, slapping against the heel of my palm as she begs for more, for harder, faster.

"That's my girl."

Fuck, she's a sight to be seen, ass in the air as she writhes and moans, fisting the sheets so hard she starts dragging them right off the mattress. She feels like velvet, plush and soft, so fucking warm, and when those walls tighten around me, I slow my roll, plunging at a deliberately leisurely pace, one that takes all of three seconds to drive her wild.

"Please, Carter," she cries. "I wanna come."

"Is that right, gorgeous?"

"Ye-e-esss." The word is a garbled mess as she shudders, body quaking.

"You wanna come," I whisper against her ear. "And I want you to earn it." I release her hair and pull my fingers from her sopping heat.

"*What?*" *Uh-oh.* My beautiful girl isn't happy with me, even less so when I lick her arousal off my fingers.

"Get some pants on. I'll take you home."

She slips off the bed and falls to her ass. I barely manage to bite back my snicker, but she looks like she's ten seconds away from murdering me, and the world needs more Carter Beckett.

I'm waiting by the door when she comes storming down the stairs in my sweatpants and hoodie five minutes later.

She shoves a finger in my face. "Wipe that arrogant smirk off your face before I wipe it off for you."

I follow her to the kitchen, watching her gather her things and shove them into her purse. "You're still mad, huh? But you can't be. I'm going away for three days. You're gonna miss me."

She pins me with a patronizing smile. "And that's the only reason you're still breathing right now."

I tear her coat from her grip the second she pulls it out of the closet, throwing it over my shoulder. Angry Olivia is my favorite Olivia.

I circle her wrists, pinning them to the wall on either side of her head as I work my mouth up her throat. "You want me to fuck you?"

"Screw you," she tosses out without any real heat. All that heat is stacked in her dark gaze.

"I'd love to. All you have to do is promise me you'll still be mine in the morning." Releasing her wrist, I push down her pants and dip my hand between her thighs. "Better yet, tell me who owns this pussy."

"I'm not going anywhere, Carter." She pulls my face from her neck, her eyes gleaming. "And I own this pussy."

"The fuck you do." I unzip my pants and pull out my hard cock, pressing it against the most addicting pussy in the world as I hoist her up to me. "Try again, princess."

Her hips arch off the wall, grinding against me. "Right now? You do."

"That's fucking right." I look between us, the way we're so nearly connected, my throat suddenly thick, chest tight. "I haven't been with anyone but you, Ollie. It's just you for me. Nobody else."

Her hand settles on my cheek. "There's nobody but you, Carter."

With a wicked grin, I slap her hands above her head and pin her to the wall with my hips. "I'm about to unleash two weeks of pent-up sexual frustration on you." I press my mouth below her ear. "You're gonna have my cum dripping down your legs for the next twelve hours, at least, and that'll be the only thing that gets me through this trip without you."

Olivia cries out with unrestrained pleasure when I drive inside her, tears my shoulders apart with her nails as she unravels, and I accidentally put a fist through the drywall when I violently come inside of her.

Oops.

25

AM I WALKING FUNNY?

Olivia

DO YOU EVER HAVE THE feeling everybody is talking about you?

All morning, I've been telling myself that I'm just being paranoid, but the hushed whispers, the stares that follow me through the hall seem pretty telling.

That or Carter really *is* rubbing off on me, and I just assume everyone is obsessed with me.

I make a pit stop in the bathroom on the way back from my break to check my outfit for the third time this morning in case there's a hole or a giant stain. Honestly, I wouldn't be surprised if I were wearing a sign on my back that said, "I fucked Carter Beckett and I liked it," especially when I exit the bathroom and see the football coach do a double-take.

"Miss Parker."

"Hey, Mr. Bailey." I swat his hand away when he ruffles my hair. He thinks it's hilarious that I'm five foot one and teach high school fitness to a bunch of boys that tower over me. I think it's hilarious that he's balding at twenty-eight.

"How was your weekend?"

"Great. Fantastic. Awesome." I could probably stop but my mouth keeps running. "It was super fun." *I got nailed so hard I felt it in my soul.* "How was yours?"

His smirk is more irritating than Carter's, only because it's lacking the sexy. "I bet it was. Have a good day, Miss Parker." He winks before heading upstairs, leaving me wondering about that comment as I push through the gym doors.

I'm moving a little slow today because, as I've said, I got fucked straight into the ground last night. And the kitchen counter. The couch. Against the front door. And, uh, on Carter's lap in his car.

So, anyway, my legs are jelly, which means my senior boys are dressed and waiting for me when I stroll in five minutes late.

"Miss Parkerrr, you're late."

"Are you limping? What kind of freaky shit did you get up to this weekend?"

I shove my finger in his face. "Watch it." Sinking down to the bleachers, I kick my heels off and swap them for my runners. Wincing at the pain that runs up my right hamstring, I curl over my knees and grip my calves.

"Feeling sore, eh?" Brad grins down at me. "Musta been a killer weekend."

"Mind your business," I hiss, but take his hand when he offers it to me, pulling me off the bleachers. "Okay, let's get—" I plant my fists on my hips, glaring at my boys, snickering behind their hands. "Are you seriously whispering about me while I'm standing right here?"

Travis Duke steps forward, phone out. "Miss Parker, is this you?"

"Is what me?" My own phone starts vibrating in my back pocket, and I ignore it, leaning into Travis, so I can get a look at—

"*Holy-fuck-shit.* Oh my God." The words leave my mouth before I can stop them, and my hands fly to my lips. I don't know if it's to keep more words from spilling out or because I might vomit.

I rip Travis's phone out of his hands.

"They're great pictures. You look hot."

"No wonder your legs hurt today. That guy's fucking massive."

"And you're so tiny. Probably wrecked your—"

I slap a palm across the mouth that's still talking, because please don't finish the sentence. My phone won't stop buzzing, my heart is thundering, and I can't formulate a single thought other than *oh fuck*.

I yank out my phone, ready to hoof it across the gym, but instead I swipe across the screen and accept the call just to get it to stop fucking vibrating.

"I didn't take you for a puck bun—"

"Don't you *dare*," I growl, reeling on Brad. He backs himself up against the wall, hands in the air as I step into him. "Finish that sentence and see what happens, Brad, I *dare* you. I may be small, but I will put you in the ground and bury you six feet deep. Nobody will find you, Brad. *Nobody*."

A husky yet anxious chuckle is the only sound echoing off the empty gym walls right now, and it's coming from my phone, which has somehow found its way on speaker. "Uh, Ollie?"

I turn off the speaker and slap my phone to my ear. "Carter?" Spinning away from the boys, I throw my magical finger up over my shoulder, because I sure as shit don't miss the whispered words, *Miss Parker, Carter Beckett,* and *fucking* the favored ones.

"Hey. Hi. It's, uh . . . yeah, it's me. Carter . . . Beckett." He breathes out a quiet *fuck me* that somehow manages to tip the corner of my mouth despite this entirely fucked-up situation, because he's so adorable when he's nervous. "Are you okay? I'm guessing . . . I mean, did you see the, um . . . pictures?"

Did I see the pictures?

"There's an article too." I scan Travis's phone screen, rendered speechless by the sight before me. Me and Carter from every angle, knee-deep in a rigorous game of tonsil hockey on the sidewalk yesterday.

Carter sighs. "Yeah. The article. But . . . it's . . . you look beautiful," he tries. Another sigh. "Are you . . . are you okay?"

I'm too busy reading this ridiculous gossip article to answer him.

Olivia? Is That You?

Remember back in December when Carter Beckett, captain of the Vancouver Vipers, dedicated a goal to the mysterious brunette and couldn't keep his eyes off her the entire game? (Yes, Mr. Beckett, we all noticed!) They were seen later that night dancing the night away—a new recreational activity for Beckett—before she disappeared off our radar for several weeks. Well, she's back, and we sure missed her.

Beckett, seen here with Olivia, last name unknown, stopping for some ultrasteamy PDA—in broad daylight, folks!—after wrapping up with an intimate lunch at West Oak on Sunday. I guess they missed the memo that Sunday is the Lord's day.

Is Beckett finally ready to change his ways, or will old habits die hard? Only time will tell if little Miss Olivia is enough to keep the man who can't be tamed interested.

Stay tuned!

"*Ohmyshitfuck.*" I shove Travis's phone against his chest, bringing my shaky fingers to my mouth. *Is Olivia enough?* What the fuck? Stupid tears sting my stupid eyeballs, my heart rattling in my chest.

"Olivia?" Carter murmurs. "I'm sorry I'm not there with you for this. But it's . . . it's different, right? Even the article said so."

The article said I might not be enough, that's what it said.

"Hey," he whispers. "Talk to me."

I force myself to breathe. "I have a class right now, Carter. I'll call you later, okay?" I end the call as soon as he gives me the okay, then turn back to my boys. "Uh . . . do a . . . sit. Just sit. Five minutes. I need five minutes." I need more than five minutes to get a handle on myself, but it's a start.

Shutting myself in my office, I pace back and forth. I've got over twenty text messages and half of them are from Cara. The latest one is a picture of me and Carter, except Cara's drawn a heart around us and written *hubba hubba* across the top. I wish I could find the humor in this situation, but right now I'm struggling. It's ridiculous, I know. I was there yesterday; I knew pictures were taken.

Four texts from Carter come in rapid succession, and not even the ridiculous name he gave himself in my phone last night does much to ease the anxiety unfurling inside me.

World's Sexiest Man: r u ok ollie???

World's Sexiest Man: i'm sorry. i wish i could be with u right now.

World's Sexiest Man: call me later??

World's Sexiest Man: plz don't be upset. now everyone knows. it'll be ok. i'll make it up 2 u. promise. *tongue emoji* *eggplant emoji* *peach emoji*

As if he won't settle until he makes me smile, he sends one more.

World's Sexiest Man: ur still my princess, even if ur mad at me 4 showing u off *kiss emoji* *heart emoji*

And then another message pops up.

Jeremy: Ur coming over for dinner tonight. Apparently we have some catching up to do.

*

THE TENSION AT THIS DINNER table is more palpable than the steak I'm currently hacking apart.

I glance up to find my brother's glare locked on me. I scowl right back and keep on sawing, maybe a little more aggressively than necessary, because I want him to think he did a shitty job cooking these bad boys up. He didn't. My steak is perfect.

"Overdone," I murmur, just to piss him off.

"Like hell," he scoffs.

"So," my sister-in-law, Kristin, starts, eager to ease the hostility.

"Daddy's mad at you, Auntie Ollie," Alannah says matter-of-factly. "I dunno what for. Carter Beckett is *everything*." She sets her fork down and starts ticking his excellent qualities off on her fingers. "He's rich, he's the best skater, he scores, like, a thousand goals, *and* he's, like, the cutest boy in the whole world."

I point my knife at her. "He's funny, too, and his favorite cookies are Oreos."

Alannah gasps. "Those are *my* favorite cookies!" Folding her hands together in prayer at her chin, she pouts. "Will you please tell your boyfriend that we have the same favorite cookies?"

He's not my boyfriend, but I nod anyway. "Of course."

"Does he like to dunk 'em in milk like me? Does he eat them whole? Or does he twist 'em apart and lick the icing off?" She twirls her ponytail around her finger, staring dreamily into space, eyes twinkling. "I wonder . . ."

"Well, you'll never find out, because you'll never meet him." Jeremy pushes back from the table, picking up his plate and mine, even though I'm not finished yet. I lunge for it, but he spins away. "Auntie Ollie is breaking up with him."

A loud, disbelieving, that's-fucking-hilarious laugh escapes me. "Absolutely not." First of all, tell that to Carter. Secondly, no. No freaking way. I like him, I have him, I want to keep him.

I should probably tell him that. Carter, not Jeremy. Because I was kind of stuck in freak-out mode all afternoon, had to have Cara talk me off a cliff about pictures and meaningless articles, and then came right here. We haven't had a chance to talk, and I know he's worried about me.

Jeremy loads the dishwasher and slams it shut. It bounces back open and I snicker. The glare he shoots me is a nine out of ten on the menacing scale. I'd have done better.

Kristin touches my hand. "Don't worry. I won't let him hurt you." Her voice drops. "And Carter Beckett is *so* sexy. I need all the gory details." She pokes the inside of her cheek with her tongue. "*All* of them."

"*Kris!*" Jeremy's booming voice has us jumping. "Come on! No! You're supposed to be on my side!" His arms are all flail-y. He looks desperate. I bite my lip to keep from laughing.

"I'm always on your side, honey."

"Thank y—"

"But there are no sides here. Olivia's an adult. She can date whomever she likes."

"Are you fuck"—his eyes slide to his daughter, her wide gaze bouncing between the three of us—"*freak*ing kidding me? She's gonna get hurt." He waves a hand over me. "I mean, literally, your, uh . . . *thingie* is gonna be hurting. He probably gave you gonorrhea or something."

My ears blaze as I look away. I'm about to tell him Carter's clean, but then I realize I don't need to justify anything to anyone.

"I'm not going to stop seeing him because you disapprove, Jeremy."

Standing, I pull my nephew out of the contraption he's bouncing around in and hug him close. Based on the fist he's trying to stuff into his mouth, he's teething something fierce.

"Want me to feed him?" I ask Kristin. Pulling Jem's shirt up, I tickle his belly before giving him a big, wet raspberry. He giggles like crazy, spit bubbling from his mouth.

"That'd be great, Liv, thanks. His bottle is in the fridge if you wanna—"

"No." Jeremy rips Jem from my grasp and deposits him into Kristin's lap. She couldn't look more irritated, and when he turns away from her, she slices her finger across her neck while glaring at the back of his head. "You're not using my son to distract from the fact that you're dating the world's biggest manwhore."

Alannah's nose scrunches. "What's a manwhore, Daddy?"

"That's what Auntie Ollie's boyfriend is, sweetheart." He pats Alannah's head, patronizing smile directed at me.

"He is not." I throw my arms across my chest. "Not anymore."

Jeremy laughs, a tired sound, as he drags both hands down his face. "You can't honestly believe you're the girl Carter Beckett is going to change for."

The snide remark wraps around my heart, squeezing like a vise. Because to me, that sounds a whole lot like *you're not enough.*

I clear my throat and reach for Alannah, kissing her hair before moving toward Jem and Kristin. "As fun as it is to listen to how my own brother thinks I can't possibly be good enough for a man like Carter Beckett, I'm gonna get going."

"Aw, Liv, come on. I didn't mean it like that."

"You meant it exactly like that," I say quietly, trying to mask the hurt.

Kristin glares at him. "You're being an ass. Apologize to your sister or find somewhere else to sleep tonight."

"You can sleep with me, Daddy!" Alannah shouts excitedly, then frowns and plants two fists on her hips. "But only after you say sorry for hurting Auntie Ollie's feelings."

Jeremy follows me to the door, his big, stupid feet clomping behind me. "Ollie, come on. I didn't mean that you're not good enough."

"That's what you said. And that's what the article said too." My bottom lip quivers without my permission. Jeremy's never been good with tears. That's why his arms go up, all frantic, desperate to stop them before they start.

"No, no, no, no! Olivia, *no*. You're enough! You're too much! Too good!" He throws his head back and groans at my watery eyes. I won't lie, I have the power to stop them now that he's crumbling, but I let them come, just to get some slack. "*Ollie*. Fuck."

His arms come around me, rocking us side to side. I hide my victorious grin in his chest.

"He makes me happy, Jer." Pulling back, I wipe the theatrics from my eyes.

"I want you to be happy. I do, Ollie. But I don't want you to get hurt."

"I'm a big girl. I can handle it." I 100 percent can*not* handle it. But I'm learning to trust him.

"Are you sure you like him? Like, if there's even a shred of doubt—"

"I like him. A lot. No shreds. Not even one."

His gaze sweeps my face before he nods. "Yeah, okay. Fine. I'll give him a shot." He takes my hand, tugging. "Now quit this I'm-leaving bullshit. Your nephew needs to be fed."

Giggling, I skip back through the living room, scooping Jem out of Kristin's arms and kissing his cute little nose.

Alannah throws her arms around my waist. "I can't believe my aunt is Carter Beckett's *girlfriend*. All the girls on the team are gonna be *so* jealous."

She stays up way later than a seven-year-old should to watch the game, and when Jeremy walks me to the door later he hands me his Vipers jersey, the one with Carter's last name on it.

"What the hell do you want me to do with this?"

He grumbles at the ground, rubbing the back of his neck.

"Pardon?"

Jeremy throws his hands in the air. "I said can you get your stupid boyfriend to sign my stupid jersey!"

There's no hiding my smirk at this turn of events, and the last thing I see before my brother slams the door in my face is the mega roll of his eyes.

26

DID I DO IT RIGHT?

Carter

I DON'T WANNA BRAG, BUT I'm playing phenomenally.

Mending things with Olivia lit a fire under my ass, and the puck I just buried in the net for the second time tonight is proof.

Emmett jumps at me with a chest bump that smashes me into the boards, and when I fall to the ice, the rest of my team piles on top of me.

It may have been the game-winning goal. In overtime.

Did I say I didn't want to brag? Oh. Well, I lied.

"Outstanding playing from you tonight, Carter," praises one of the reporters crowding me outside the change room when I make it back there.

"It's a team effort, like always." I snag Adam's jersey and tug him over. "*This guy*. Where the hell would we be if it wasn't for him?" I shake his cage before he starts pulling his helmet off. "Best goalie in the league."

"Adam, you got that last assist tonight. How's that feel?"

"Always nice to help lead my team to a win." He smiles, running his hand over his puffed chest. "Carter's always ready for a pass up the boards, waiting to take off."

Take off. Ha. Reminds me of what I did to Olivia's clothes last night. I wonder what she's doing right now . . .

Adam nudges me in the side, sending a pointed glance toward the reporters. *Oops.*

"Sorry, can you repeat your question?"

"I asked if the girl you were seen out with yesterday has anything to do with your stellar performance today?" The reporter gestures with his hand like he's trying to remember her name. I doubt he's forgotten; it's splashed all over the sports world today, along with her breathtaking smile. "Olivia, I think her name was."

I smile, straightening off my stick as I clap Adam on the back. Olivia doesn't want the world to know her, but I want everyone to know she's mine. "Have a good night, everyone." I wink at the camera. "Hi, Ollie."

My mood sours when I pull out my phone in the change room and find there's still no word from her.

Soured isn't the right word. I'm anxious, I think. Should she be messaging me more? Did I message her too much today? Am I being overbearing? Is this how this goes?

I glance at Adam. He's wearing the same expression as he stares down at his phone: disappointment. He sighs and stuffs his phone away; there's no word from Courtney again.

But that's different, isn't it?

Or is it?

Emmett strolls out of the shower with a towel wrapped around his hips, eyeing me. "Everything okay?"

"I don't know. I think maybe Olivia might be mad at me?" I shrug. "I don't know." I already said that. "I haven't heard from her very much." If I was in town, I'd simply show up at her house. But I'm, like, seventy-two hours away from seeing her, which I hate.

I get a face full of Emmett's dick when he drops the towel, reaching for his boxers.

"Fuck's sake." I shield my eyes with my hand. "Tuck that thing away."

He chuckles, giving his hips a little roll. "Cara said Liv was upset because the article said she wasn't enough to keep you interested."

Olivia? Not enough? Well, that's fucking ridiculous. "But she—"

"I know, but she's a girl." He taps his temple. "This shit gets inside their brains and lays eggs. Anyway, Care said her brother wasn't happy and was making her go over. Probably why you haven't heard from her more."

"Not happy about what?"

Emmett levels me with a look but it's Garrett who snorts and answers. "Somebody would have to restrain me if you tried to get with one of my sisters."

That's unnecessary. His sisters are way too young for me. Also, they're basically Garrett in female form. "I don't see the issue."

"Put it this way. If you had a daughter, would you want her to—"

"Nope. No way in hell. Got it." No need to finish that sentence. I would chop the dick off any man with a history like mine who tried to get near my daughter, and then I'd lock her up until she was thirty. Maybe even thirty-five. All-girl school would probably be a good option. Unless she likes girls. Fuck. Nowhere is safe.

Okay, so maybe I get what her brother's deal is. But I'm not gonna be like that anymore. Olivia's the only girl I wanna get down and freaky with. I won't hurt her; I know it.

But I'm distracted the entire ride back to the hotel, staring down at my phone, composing and deleting a message to Olivia three times before I finally tuck my phone away.

"Do me a favor," Emmett says as we head into the bar in the lobby. It's rammed and rowdy and I kinda don't want to be here. "Remember how it looks to be surrounded by girls who throw themselves at you. Doing nothing isn't enough. You have to actively do anything *but* nothing."

"What the hell does that mean?"

"It means it's easy for someone to snap a picture of you standing next to a girl who's touching your arm and headline it 'Carter Beckett: Cheating Already.' Be aware, that's all. You have someone else to think about now. A picture like that would embarrass Olivia."

"Right." I honestly couldn't feel more dense right now. How is it that I need to have this explained to me at twenty-seven? Either way, I'm thankful for his warning, because the second we sit, a girl throws herself in my lap.

I'm not sure my reaction is the best. I throw my hands in the air and scream, accidentally shoving her off my lap and to the ground when I rocket to my feet and yell out, "*I have a girlfriend!*"

After a few deep breaths and a chance to assess the situation with my friends laughing around me, I help the stunned girl to her feet. "I'm so sorry. I didn't mean to push you."

"It's okay." She giggles, right before she attaches herself to my torso.

Uh . . .

Gripping her biceps, I lift her gently off her feet, sidestep a shitload to the left, drop her back down, repeat, "I have a girlfriend," and head back to my table.

"Girlfriend, eh?" Adam pumps his brows. He's already got deep-fried pickles; how the hell did that happen? "Goin' straight for the big guns?"

I swipe a pickle off his plate and smother it in ranch sauce. "What do you mean?"

He shrugs. "I thought you were just dating."

"Isn't that the same thing?"

Garrett and Emmett snicker, and Adam hums around his food, shaking his head. "You have so much to learn about women, young grasshopper."

"I'm three years older than you."

"And yet I'm years ahead of you mentally."

"Fuck you." I steal another pickle to distract from the fact that he's right.

"Until you've had this particular conversation, Olivia's not your girlfriend. She's a girl you're dating, which means you're getting to know each other, seeing if you're compatible, if the feelings are real enough to turn this into an actual relationship."

What the fuck? I already know we're compatible. She's not afraid to call me out on my shit and I'm not afraid to put her in her place. Which, last night, was on the ground while I fucked her senseless. Also, she laughs at all my jokes. And her smile makes my own grow. And her hand feels really nice tucked into mine. Like, *perfect*. Plus, I can swallow her entire body up in my arms when I hug her.

And feelings? I know mine are real enough. It's the only explanation as to why I couldn't get over her after she walked away. Are hers . . . not?

"It also means she's free to date other people at the same time," Garrett adds. "You're not exclusive without that label, and you don't get that label without a conversation."

"What? No. Other people? No." She's not allowed. I forbid it. I fire off a text to her before I can make my fingers stop.

> **Me:** R u seeing other ppl???

My phone vibrates as soon as I hit send, and I hit accept without checking the name first.

"Ollie?" The level of frantic in my voice right now needs to go. I clear my throat and try again with a little more gravel and indifference. "Olivia? Hey."

"Did you seriously only pick up because you thought I was your girlfriend? You've been ignoring me all damn day, Carter Beckett!"

My chest deflates. "Hi, Mom." I didn't purposely ignore her. Her texts started rolling in while I was on the phone with Olivia earlier today, trying to tame this whole article debacle before shit could hit the fan, which it did anyway. And then I got on a plane. "How's the most beautiful girl in the world?" *Over fifty,* I add in my head.

"Don't you try to butter me up, Carter, I swear." *Oops, she's mad.* "You're mad."

"You're damn right I'm mad, honey!"

"You sound less mad when you call me honey." *Don't poke the bear,* my dad would say. But I like to poke. "Is it that time of the month already? I'm sure I have another week before you and Jennie and your synced-up cycles start attacking." *Poke, poke.*

"Oh, you little—" The words dissolve into a groan, and I can practically see her shifting her glasses up so she can rub her eyes. "Somebody needs to straighten you out, and it might be me."

"But I love you, Mummy," I mumble distractedly around a pickle, reeling her back in. "You're my favorite."

"Nobody gets on my nerves quite like you do." She sighs. "Do you really have a girlfriend?"

"Yes. Maybe. I don't know." *I'm confused.* "Apparently I need to have that conversation with her and not just assume so."

She snickers. "You've always been relentless. I'm sure you'll convince her."

"Damn right." *I'll fuck the answer out of her if I need to.*

"Are you happy, honey?"

Heat creeps up my neck. "I'm out, Mom."

"Answer the question, Carter."

"Yes."

"Yes what?"

I drum my fingers on the table. I'd like to say nobody's paying me any attention, but there are three sets of eyes glued on me.

Four, if you count the girl on Garrett's lap. And that's *not* counting the people around us who can't believe they're in the same bar as the Vancouver Vipers.

So I hold my phone closer to my mouth and grumble out what she wants to hear.

"Pardon me? I didn't hear you."

"Yes, I'm happy!"

"Oh, sweetheart. I hope I didn't embarrass you in front of your friends."

I LAST A WHOPPING THIRTY-TWO minutes after I hang up with my mom. Long enough to drain a beer, devour a plate of nachos, and watch Garrett make out with a random fan.

I've got a mouthful of toothpaste when my phone rings on the bedside table. I dash out of the bathroom and dive across the bed, knocking my phone to the floor when I see Olivia's name on the screen.

"Shit." I roll off the bed and hit accept on the FaceTime call five thousand times. "Hey. Hi. You. Olivia." It comes out super gurgly because of the toothpaste. I hold up a finger. "Hafta spit."

I take her with me into the bathroom to rinse my mouth out, before flopping onto the bed, throwing a hand behind my head, and flashing her a grin. "Hey."

"You're already in bed? I thought you'd be at the bar."

I lift a shoulder like I wasn't pining over her down there. "I was for a bit, but I'm tired."

"Oh. Do you want me to call you tomorrow instead?"

"No! I mean . . ." I clear my throat. "No, that's okay. I want to talk to you now."

"I want to talk to you now too." She's in bed, too, tired but so damn beautiful as she fiddles with the strings of the hoodie she's wearing.

"Are you wearing my hoodie?"

She tugs on the neck, her mouth and nose disappearing into it. "I like it. It smells like you."

"How do I smell?"

She grins. "So good, like I wanna bury my face in your chest and soak up your hugs, every single second of them."

Sweet Christ. "You know, you're kind of a softie. Quite the contrast from the sassy brunette who's told me to go fuck myself who knows how many times."

Her cheeks tint. "Shut up."

"Like a kitten. An attitude bigger than you, but underneath it all, you're just a big, soft ball of cuddly fluff."

She rolls her eyes, but she's not trying hard enough to hide that smile. I see it. Her lower lip slides between her teeth as she fiddles with the messy topknot on her head. "Hey, I'm sorry I kinda disappeared today. I know it's silly, because I knew they took pictures. But I forgot, I guess, after everything else yesterday. And . . . I didn't like the way the article made me feel."

Her honesty is refreshing, and I appreciate it. I'm tired of misunderstandings and miscommunications. I need to know how she feels so I can help her through this shit. Being in the spotlight is new for her, so I need to be patient while we navigate this part of our relationship.

Relationship. Oooh, that word tastes funny. Kinda like it.

"I should have prepared you better."

Olivia shakes her head. "No, Carter, you didn't do anything wrong. I kinda lost my head there for a bit, but I didn't mean to make you question whether or not I was seeing other people."

I wave her off. "Pfft. You didn't." But also: "Are you?"

Her face ignites with laughter, and my insides do a little dance. Adam was wrong. This girl's my girlfriend; I know it.

"I only have room for one goofy, demanding, arrogant man in my life."

I run a palm down my proud chest. "And it's me?"

"It's you, Mr. Beckett."

I whoop my fist through the air. "Undefeated, baby!"

Oooh-ho-ho, no one's as good at making Olivia laugh as I am, I swear.

"I miss you," I tell her quietly. "Is that weird? Should I be telling you that? Or keeping it to myself? You don't have to say it back. Don't be pressured or anything. I just—"

"Carter."

"Yeah?"

Olivia lays her cheek on her pillow, her smile sleepy and sweet. "I miss you too."

"You do?"

She rubs her eyes. "Yeah. It's rather irritating. I wish you were here with me, but instead I'm alone. Cold." The last word is a lazy mumble that tumbles off the tip of her tongue as her eyes flutter closed.

"I'd keep you warm, baby."

"Mmm, I know. Bear."

"Bear?"

"Mhmm." She stifles a yawn. The whites of her eyes are red, hiding behind her hooded lids, her smile dazed. "You're like a grizzly bear. Warm and snuggly. Cute."

"I think you mean huge and powerful." I flex a bicep and growl.

Her tired giggle is a slow song I want to dance to forever, restarting my heart.

"You're gonna fall asleep on me, sleepy girl." I turn off the light as Olivia's eyes fall closed for the last time, her chest rising and falling steadily, face lit by the gentle glow of a lamp somewhere over there, right where I wanna be.

I can't take my eyes off her.

"Carter?" she calls suddenly, the words thick with sleep. Her eyes are still closed, and I think she might be dreaming.

"Yeah, princess?"

"What if I fall in love with you?"

"Then I'll fall with you, too, Ollie girl."

27

BEDTIME BURRITO & A SURPRISE GUEST

Olivia

I HAD A DREAM ON Monday that I told Carter I was falling in love with him.

Only it might not have been a dream.

Because when I woke up Tuesday morning, it was to a bleary-eyed Carter smiling up at me from my phone, where he'd apparently been all night. I fell asleep on him and he didn't want to hang up on me, he told me. The call lasted until my seven a.m. alarm woke us both up. I'm so fucking impressed with my iPhone battery.

The words I might have muttered in my sleep came rushing back to me, and I fumbled over an apology for any sleep-induced ramblings he might've heard without coming right out and asking if I dreamed it.

Two days later, on Wednesday morning, I'm still nervous when his name lights up my screen. Like right now.

"I need a picture of you," he says in way of greeting, shaking out his bedhead waves.

"Good morning to you too."

He grins. "Morning, princess. I can't wait to wake up next to you all weekend."

Yeah, apparently that's happening. He flies out next Monday and won't be home until Saturday, so I'm pretty giddy about spending the whole weekend together. Also, my house is frigid.

Not having to sleep in several layers of clothing will be a refreshing change of pace.

I cover my yawn and try to shake away the sleep. I'm tired because Carter and I were on the phone until after midnight.

His eyes hood. "Yawn that big in my bed and I'll put something rock hard and throbbing between those pretty pink lips."

"Your mouth and mind are equally filthy, Mr. Beckett." I'm trying to get used to it, and it certainly doesn't help he spends all his free time dirty texting me while I'm at work.

"That brings me back to the picture. I need one, Ollie. I had to jerk it to those paparazzi pictures last night after you went to bed. My sword of thunder and I would forever be in your debt, princess."

I refuse to wrap my head around that name. Sword of thunder, that is, not princess. I'm mostly managing to ignore all the princesses, and what does it say about me if I admit that I actually *like* them?

"You must be the only man on this earth who has named his penis."

"That's not true. Garrett calls his Lieutenant J—"

"*Shut up, you fucker!*" The pillow Garrett chucks at Carter's head is the cherry on top.

"Poor Garrett."

Carter guffaws. "Poor Garrett? He could've taken an eye out!"

"You're indestructible, Carter. Quit whining."

There's that smirk. He flexes a veiny bicep. "Yeah, I am pretty indestructible. You know what's not indestructible though? Your p—*hey!*" Another pillow to the face, this one knocking him sideways.

"Thanks, Garrett," I call.

"Welcome!"

Carter rubs the side of his head. "I'll be home late tonight so I won't get to see you."

"Oh. That's okay." It'd be more convincing if I weren't frowning.

"And I'm watching Jennie dance tomorrow night, so I won't see you until Friday at the game."

"Who's Jennie?" I quell the urge to ask him why he's watching her dance; this jealous streak that's lit a fire in me is driving me wild.

"Jennie's my sister. She's a competitive dancer at SFU and she's got a show tomorrow night. Also, I enjoy this little green-eyed monster that's been hiding inside of you."

"I wasn't jealous," I lie, then return my attention to his sister before he can call me out on it. "That's impressive."

"Yeah, she got a full ride out of high school. Been dancing her whole life." He chuckles, scrubbing at his jaw. "My parents had no life outside of taking us to dance and hockey. We spent more time in the car traveling to practice, games, and recitals than we spent in our actual house. My dad always said—" His cheeks flush, and he waves me off. "Ah, forget it."

"What did he say?"

Carter drops his gaze to his lap before lifting it back to me. "He said we'd understand why they were willing to give up everything for us when we had our own kids someday."

I wish I could've met Carter's dad. In the little bit he's told me, it's clear he was a wonderful husband, a supportive father, and that he shared Carter's sense of humor. Apparently those two were quite the irritating pair around his mom and sister. I can't even begin to comprehend what Carter's gone through over the years, but the heartbreak still lingers thick in the air when he talks about his dad.

I can't help but wonder how Carter would be different if his dad were still here. I like him the way he is, but would he have gone through years of casual, meaningless sex if his dad hadn't passed?

Except if he hadn't, there's no way we'd be where we are right now, the two of us. Aside from his undeniably good looks, Carter is goofy and hilarious, charismatic, kind, and passionate enough to make you feel like he's lit you on fire. There's no way he'd be single. Hate it all I want, but that past of his is the only reason we're able to give this a real shot right now.

"Do you want kids?" Carter asks me suddenly. "Or no kids? Do you hate kids? You probably hate them, working with them all day and whatnot. No, that's silly. You love them; you coach your niece's hockey team on your own time."

Nothing is more adorable than Carter when he's anxious and rambling. Regardless of being a natural at this dating stuff despite never having done it before, it's clear he's so out of his element, second-guessing everything he says or does.

"I'd like to have kids one day," I tell him.

His throat bobs as he nods. "Cool. Yeah, cool. Me too. One day."

"Carter?"

His face lights. "Yeah?"

"I have to get dressed for work."

"Oh. Okay. Yeah. I can't wait to see you Friday, Ollie. I'm gonna score you a goal and blow you a kiss on national television."

"I could definitely do without the national television bit."

He flashes me that devilish grin, hitting me with a wink before we hang up, which is not the reassurance I was looking for. Then my phone buzzes, and I sigh at the text.

World's Sexiest Man: on a scale of 1-10,
how mad will u be if i call u princess on
national TV?

IT'S AFTER ELEVEN WHEN I finally crawl into bed, feeling particularly mopey and a little frustrated with myself for being that way.

I survived fine on my own before Carter yet now I can't go more than a few hours without talking to him.

The team boarded in San Jose at five, and though I know it's too late to see him, I guess I was hoping Carter would call when he got home. But one last look at my phone shows me what I already know: he hasn't called or messaged since my workday ended.

I scoop his hoodie up, breathing in his scent as the thick cotton wraps around me. Even though I'm wearing thermal long johns and tucked under three blankets, my body still shakes with a shiver, so I grip the blankets to my chest and roll across my mattress, wrapping myself up like a bedtime burrito.

I'm right on the cusp of unconsciousness when the pounding starts, jolting me awake with a yelp. It stops for only a moment before starting again, quicker, harder, and I jump out of bed.

Except—blanket cocoon. I can't move my legs, nor pull my arms free fast enough to save myself from face-planting.

"*Ow*," I moan, rolling onto my back and ripping my arms free so they can clatter to the cold hardwood where I lie, lifeless and bruised. "Fuck me."

And there's that damn knocking again. I swear I hear a faint *Liv, Liv, Liv, Liv*, so I roll to my stomach and army crawl across my bedroom floor. Using the door frame to pull myself up, I shake the blankets off my hips and head down the hall.

If I were more awake it would probably occur to me to not answer the door at nearly midnight. Instead, I scrub the sleep from my eyes, slide a hand under my sweater to scratch my belly as I yawn, and throw the door open.

"Oh. I *am* dreaming." I touch my face; it really does hurt from the dream face-plant. "That's good. This won't bruise." I swing the door shut and turn to head back to bed.

Except it doesn't close, and the man at my door sweeps inside, catching my elbow.

"I can see why you'd think having someone as handsome as me show up unexpectedly at your door in the middle of the night would make you think that, but no, you're not dreaming." Carter's grip tightens as he hauls me into him. "And you just tried to slam the door on me when I've been missing you for three days, so I'm gonna need you to open up that pretty mouth of yours and lemme taste you, gorgeous girl."

28

WHO TURNED THE HEAT UP?

Olivia

THERE'S A HOCKEY BAG ON my front porch.

A pair of sticks, too, and when a brown leather weekender bag falls to my floor, the soft thud kickstarts my heart.

But the six-foot-four hulk of a man in front of me still doesn't seem real.

"Carter?" Popping the buttons of his wool coat, I slide my hands inside, pressing my palms to his chest. He's solid, so damn warm, and when I press my nose to his chest and inhale, he smells good too. My gaze rises, finding his, amused and curiously soft, and I launch myself into his arms, wrapping my legs around his waist as I crush myself to his body. "You're here."

"I'm here. Flight got delayed and I thought it was too late to call but then I was miserable and I . . . I wound up here." He smooths my hair from my face, hesitant eyes moving between mine. "Is that okay?"

I drag his mouth down to mine, answering him with a kiss. "I missed you."

"Fuck, that sounds so good." His hands glide down my back, cupping my ass. "Why do you have a blanket wrapped around your ankle?"

"What?" I untangle my limbs from his body, and sure enough, when he sets me on my feet, the corner of my blanket is wrapped around my ankle. "I got tangled in my blankets," I murmur as he hauls his equipment off my porch, throws it into my living room, and kicks his boots off. He slips his tie over his head, grinning when he slips it over mine, winding it around his fist and dragging me into him for a scorching kiss.

"I'm starving," he whispers against my mouth, pressing me against the wall. "For you." His tongue glides against mine, slow and hungry, and my knees wobble. Then he claps a hand to my ass and pulls me to my kitchen. "And for food. You got any?"

I'm fixated, watching as he tugs his shirt from his pants and rubs his hand over his rippled torso, checking out the contents of my fridge. He glances over his shoulder, hitting me with a dazzling smile as his gaze coasts my body.

What is he doing? Did he just come for a midnight snack? Is he . . . staying?

"Would you get rid of that damn blanket before you hurt yourself? If I have to take you to the hospital tonight, it'll be because I impaled you too hard with my cock and fucked you into a coma, not because you tripped on that fucking blanket and broke your ankle."

Well then. That's one way to turn up the heat in here.

And I'm taking too long, apparently, because Carter bends and unwraps my ankle.

"There. You're safe." He pulls my leftovers from the fridge, inhales, and moans. "Fuck, this smells so good. Can I?"

The second I find a fork, he yanks it from my hand and digs in. I genuinely don't think he's even breathing, just shoveling my Cajun chicken pasta into his mouth.

I shake myself out of whatever trance I'm in, smiling at the way Carter licks the fork after he's finished. "Guess I'm eating cafeteria food tomorrow."

He freezes. "This is your lunch? Aw, Liv. Why didn't you tell me?" He sets me on the counter and pulls my legs around him, stuffing his face in my neck. "I ate your lunch. I'm so sorry. I'm a big boy, though, and I was practically wasting away."

I snort a laugh, but it quickly dies a whimper when his mouth opens on my throat.

"As much as I love you in my clothes . . ." His fingers dip beneath the hem of his hoodie that I've been living in, brushing against my skin. "This hoodie needs to fucking go."

It's on the floor a second later, and everywhere his gaze touches singes my exposed flesh.

"This tank top," he growls, brushing his thumbs over my nipples, taut against the thin material. His fingers dance down my belly, finding a hole by my waist. "I fucking love this tank top. But I'm gonna ruin it."

The quiet night fills with the sound of my top shredding. The cool air dances over my flesh, and I shiver when my body erupts with goose bumps. Carter frowns, examining my fingernails, an interesting shade of blue, though they have no nail polish.

His own shoulders shake, and he rubs his hands up and down my arms. "It's freezing in here, Ol. Can I turn up the heat?"

He's on the move before I can tell him not to bother, and I follow him to thermostat in the front hall, picking his sweater up and covering myself back up.

"Forty-nine? Ollie, it's only forty-fucking-nine degrees in here!"

Humiliation burns my cheeks as he tries the buttons.

"Why does it say heat mode off? And why won't it let me turn it on?"

My gaze falls. I grip one arm with the other. "My furnace is broken."

"Shit." His hand runs along the edge of his jaw. "For how long?"

"Um . . ." I scratch my temple. "A week or so?"

"A week? Olivia! You can't—that's not—" He cups my face. "Fuck. That's too cold for you, Ollie."

"Hence the outfit." I gesture at my bundled body. "And the blanket wrapped around my ankle."

"Where's your furnace?" He points to my basement door. "Want me to take a look?"

I grab his hand, stopping him, because Carter doesn't wait for anyone, which means that as soon as the question left his mouth he was already halfway to the door. "You can't fix it. My brother already looked at it. It's been in and out since last winter. I need a new one."

"Oh. Are you . . . are you gonna do that? Replace it?"

My ears burn. I can't look at him. I shift on my feet, fiddling with the bun on top of my head. "I'm saving."

"You're saving?"

Tears of embarrassment prickle my eyes, and I look away before he can see. "I can't afford it right now. Please drop it."

"I—"

"If you're cold, Carter, you've got five fireplaces at home to warm you up."

The corner of his mouth quirks. "Seven."

"What?"

"I have seven fireplaces."

Heat pools in my cheeks, enough to keep my warm tonight. "I'm sorry I don't have any," I whisper as I move by him.

"Hey." His palm wraps around the nape of my neck, gently guiding me back to him. His eyes hold nothing but sincerity. "I'm gonna need you to tell me why you got so upset back there."

"Because you said—"

"I know what I said. I asked you if you were going to replace your furnace." He watches me take my lower lip between my teeth. "Are you embarrassed that you can't afford it?"

I focus on his chest, the flawless skin peeking out from his opened buttons. Even in the middle of winter, he's such a perfect shade of sunset gold.

"Look at me, Ollie." He pulls the tip of my thumbnail from my mouth, where I hadn't noticed it migrated, and brackets my chin between his fingers, forcing my gaze to his. "You never need to be embarrassed about that. You work hard, and you're doing the best you can. I'm proud of you, and I hope you are too."

My heart thuds quietly, my chest tightening at the sweet words, the compassion he holds in his steady gaze.

"It's hard not to compare myself to someone like you," I admit. "I know we're on different playing fields, but everything you have is so beautiful, so incredible, and—"

"Including you, Ollie. You're so beautiful, so incredible, all of you. Don't you get that everything else doesn't compare? I'd trade it all in for you."

Butterflies take flight in my stomach, and when I lay my cheek on his chest, I can breathe again. "I like your fireplaces. All seven of them."

Carter chuckles, twisting us back and forth. "I'm gonna snuggle the shit outta you tonight and I run hot, so you won't need all these clothes anyway."

"You're staying over?"

His expression says *duh* but his mouth says, "All I wanna do is fuck you into tomorrow and fall asleep with my girlfriend in my arms."

Oh look, there's my heart, beating in his hands.

Judging by the pink tint painting his cheekbones and the way he's pulled his lower lip into his mouth to gnaw on it, I'd say this exceptionally large and confident man standing before me is currently feeling shy.

"Girlfriend?"

He nods, scratching at his head. "Is that okay? I know I want to be with you. I know we're compatible. I don't need time to see if this will work, if I'm serious about you. I already know all that.

I want you to be mine and I don't want to share you with anyone else. So be mine. Please."

My hand slides along the stubble lining his jaw. "How are you single?"

"Because you've been playing hard to get for the last seven weeks, give or take. Because you're keeping me standing here, waiting around for an answer to my question when the answer seems pretty obvious to me."

"Pretty obvious, huh? And what's the obvious answer?"

"The obvious answer is yes, because you're obsessed with me. You can't stop thinking about me and my pretty eyes. And my dimples." Hot breath rolls down my neck. "You *love* my dimples."

"Your arrogance never fails to amaze me."

"What you mean is confidence, and you love that about me too."

I wind my arms around his neck, fingers curling into his hair as he hoists me to him and heads for my bedroom. "Is that so?"

"Uh-huh. I know you like the back of my hand." He lays me on the bed and steps back, working the buttons of his shirt before he slips it off, revealing his impeccably chiseled torso, that deep *V* that runs like a trail of raw desire right down to where it disappears in his pants.

"What am I thinking right now?"

"That you want to come," he replies simply, ditching his pants on the floor. His boxer briefs follow quickly, and a heady need unfurls in my belly as his knees hit the mattress. "Around my fingers, on my tongue. All over my cock."

My heartbeat settles between my thighs, and something raw and feral squeezes in my throat as he prowls toward me. He hooks his fingers in the waistband of my pants and drags them down my legs. His rough palm scrapes over my torso, squeezing my breast. A moment later, the sweater I'm wearing is on the ground, leaving me naked and exposed.

There's something about the heat stacked behind his gaze, so dark, so starved, that makes it hard to breathe when he looks at me.

I reach for him, but his palm lands on my collarbone, forcing me backward.

"Ah-ah, pretty girl." Tender lips find the delicate skin of my inner thigh, tasting. "You haven't answered my question yet."

Fuck. What was the question again?

He trails the tip of his finger up my slit, and my head falls back with a moan when he grazes my clit.

"God, *yes*."

"Yes? Is that your answer or are you simply letting me know you enjoy the way I touch you?" His half-lidded gaze holds mine as his tongue traces around my aching center, making it cramp with need. "Be more specific, Ollie. Are you mine?"

He sinks one finger inside me, achingly slow, and all thoughts leave my brain.

"Yes," I cry. "Yes, I'm yours."

"Ding, ding, ding," he whispers. "Right answer."

My back arches, my hands in his hair and his name on my lips when he buries his face between my legs. His mouth is a wet dream, his tongue a lethal weapon, and I'm ready to let this man destroy me.

And *oh God*, does he ever do it well. Thrusting fingers, grazing teeth, and a wicked tongue that never quits, I come undone with an explosive orgasm that leaves my legs quaking.

Not until Carter crawls up my body do I realize his hands are trembling.

Catching my breath, I stroke his cheek. "What's wrong?"

"I like you so much," he blurts. "I like everything about you. Is that right? Is it okay to tell you how much I like you or am I supposed to keep it to myself? Tell you once and never talk about it again? Tell you every single day? I don't know, Ollie; I'm new at this. All I know is I really wanted to tell you, and also, I'm super fucking terrified." He rests his forehead against mine and breathes. When his eyes open, the fear in them tells me I'm not alone. "I don't wanna mess this up."

I turn my head, kissing the inside of the palm that rests against my cheek. "I like you so much, too, Carter. And I don't think you'll mess it up. You're already so great at it."

"Yeah? I mean, I'm great at most things, so—*hey*!" When I deliver the first whack to his shoulder, he captures my hand and pins it above my head. "Don't make me tie these hands behind your back," he whispers against my lips. "I have no idea what I'm doing, Ollie."

I don't either. I've been in two serious relationships, yet I've never felt what I feel for Carter. This intensity that vibrates between us, the magnetism that draws us closer and closer, it's as confusing as it is addicting. I can't find a pause button, and it's daunting.

You're not supposed to fall this quickly.

Carter settles onto his side, pulling me back against him. "Slow and steady tonight, 'kay? I just wanna feel you." He lifts my leg, guiding his cock between my thighs. I grip the sheets as he pushes in, and his fingers lace through mine. His mouth sweeps down my neck, across my shoulder, teeth pressing into my skin as he rocks his hips against mine. "Every inch of you. It's all my favorite. You're my favorite. My princess."

A shudder leaves my lips. "That nickname is ridiculous, but I think I love it."

He releases my hand, running his fingers up my arm, then down my side. Fingertips dig into my hip as his pace quickens, each thrust deeper, more powerful than the last. He strokes the tight bundle of nerves at the cleft of my thighs, and I forget my name.

"You want another one? What about pumpkin? How 'bout it, Liv? You wanna be my pumpkin pie?"

"You're too much." I barely manage an eye roll, and Carter swallows my breathy laugh with his mouth.

"I think you wanna be my pumpkin."

"I wanna be your anything."

His hand glides up my belly and closes over my throat, angling my face toward his, his movements never slowing. "How about my everything?"

My heart stops beating at those simple words. Carter doesn't dare tear his gaze off mine as he keeps moving, driving forward, panting. His forehead creases, eyes closing for only the briefest moment before his mouth devours mine in a kiss so fierce, so hungry, I feel it right down to the tips of my toes. I cry out his name, and he buries mine in my neck when the world shatters around us.

Carter crushes me to him, folding me in his arms. Beyond the soul-crushing orgasm that makes it hard to catch my breath, the feelings I have for him are suffocating me right now. I bury them in my throat, and my face in his heaving chest.

Then his stomach grumbles, and he rolls on top of me. "I hate to ruin this moment but I'm hungry again."

"You are a bottomless pit. I made blueberry muffins. They're in the—"

He leaps off the bed with a squeal—yes, a squeal—and I watch his bare ass disappear into the hallway faster than I've ever seen this man move when he's not on skates. He returns thirty seconds later with his cheeks and hands full. "Found 'em."

"—pantry. Wow. Three muffins, huh?"

"Four," he mumbles, pointing at his chipmunk cheeks. He swallows, offering one to me. "One's for you." He pulls it back into his chest. "Unless you don't want it. Then I'll eat it."

"Carter—"

"Yeah." His head bobs as he kneels on the bed, tearing one muffin apart. "You're right. Sharing is caring." He stuffs a piece between my lips and flops onto his back, legs hanging over the edge. "Your bed is too small for me."

"It fits me just right."

"That's because you're pint-sized."

"And you're monster-sized."

He looks down at his crotch, swiveling his hips, making my favorite of his muscles dance. "Hear that, big guy? We're monster-sized."

I shake my head. "What in the hell have I gotten myself into?"

He chuckles. "Did your kids give you any more trouble after Monday?"

Pouting, I snuggle into this side. "One of my boys called me a puck bunny."

"He sure did, and you lit him the hell up for it. I knew you could back all that sass up." His fingers trail a slow path up and down my spine. "Everything else go okay? Em said your brother was upset."

I gnaw my lip, but when he tilts my head, bringing our gazes together, I sigh. "He wasn't happy at first. He wanted me to stop seeing you."

"Oh." His gaze falls, but I touch his cheek, bringing him back to me.

"Then I told him how happy you make me, and that was all that mattered."

Green eyes move eagerly between mine. "Yeah? I really make you happy?"

I grin, so wide my cheeks hurt. "What do you think?"

His own grin is detonating as he brings my lips to his. "I think I love your smile more than anything in this world."

When he turns out the light and holds me tight against him, I realize he was right earlier when he said I wouldn't need all those layers to keep me warm. All I need is him and the fire that fuels in my belly when he's with me.

His lips dot my shoulder with kisses as he sings softly, those same words he sang to me back in December while he held me in his arms and spun me around a crowded dance floor.

"I'm so lucky to be the man who gets to keep you by his side, Ollie." Burying his face in my neck, Carter makes a soft, happy noise. "Goodnight, pumpkin. Like you."

"Like you, too, Carter."

It's only seven in the morning and my Thursday is already shaping up to be as fantastic as my Wednesday night, because Carter's body is still wound around mine.

"No," he growls, thick and husky as I try to slip free when my alarm goes off. His hand closes over my throat, hauling me back to him, and he throws a leg over me, a quiet hum of satisfaction rumbling from his chest. "You stay with me."

"I have to go to work, Carter."

Long fingers skim down my belly, pushing their way between my thighs. "You feel hot. Sick day."

I turn in his arms and kiss his sleepy face, his dark lashes resting against his cheekbones. "You keep sleeping. I'll leave my spare key in the kitchen."

"Can I eat more muffins?"

"Are you gonna eat them all?"

He sighs. It's a resigned sigh, but pleased, like he's happy I know him well enough to ask the question. "Yeah. Yeah, I am."

I think he's asleep when I'm ready to leave a half hour later, so I don't bother saying good-bye. That's a mistake; he screams my name from bed when I open the front door.

I lean against the bedroom door. "You rang, sir?"

He reaches up, curling his fingers into his palms. "Need a hug and a kiss."

Oh my God, *he's adorable.*

I sink into the crushing hug, that full feeling that comes with it, and when he releases me, he gives me a pat on the butt.

"Have a good day, pumpkin." He rolls himself into a perfect burrito, muttering to himself about the size of my bed and the ungodly temperature in my house.

My day only gets better when my lunch is hand-delivered by someone who looks suspiciously like the limo driver who gave me a ride home last weekend, and even better when I pull out the bacon carbonara and slice of chocolate cheesecake topped with an Oreo.

When I get home from work, it smells different. Cozy, somehow, or maybe it's just knowing Carter was here. Either way, I smile to myself as I take off my coat and head to the kitchen.

The bright display on my counter has my stomach somer-saulting. Pink, orange, and yellow tulips fill a glass vase, but it's the note that makes me happiest.

> *Pretty and bright, just like you.*
> *Can't wait to wake up with you this weekend.*
> *Like you lots,*
> *Carter*

I fan at my face, trying to disperse the heat rushing to it right now. When that doesn't work—*I'm freaking sweating right now*—I yank off my sweater. But I'm still hot, so I start pulling my leggings over my hips and—

Why am I hot?

My eyes flick to the thermostat. Hesitantly, I take one step toward it, then another. Another, and my heart nearly pounds out of my chest when I finally look at it.

Seventy-two. It's seventy-fucking-two degrees in here. Quite the stark contrast from the frigid air that's been circulating for the past several days.

I get halfway down the basement stairs before I turn and run up them again. Two more tries before I finally make it down. My jaw dangles, my hand shaking on the railing as I gawk.

At the shiny, brand-new furnace that absolutely, 110 percent, was not here this morning.

29

DON'T POKE THE CRAZY LADY

Carter

THIRTY-SEVEN MINUTES.

Huh. Not the longest I've sat here and waited by any means, but definitely not the shortest. I'm not surprised. This is the norm in this household. Has been my entire life.

Still, I groan, running two aggravated hands through my hair before dragging them down my face in slow motion. "Mommm, come onnn," I beg, slumping against the couch. "Let's gooo."

"I'm not done putting my face on, Carter!" she shouts back.

"You don't need a face. Your face is perfect." I'd tell her she was prettier than Beyoncé if it'd get her ass out here. Except I've tried; it doesn't work.

Flopping down, I sprawl over the couch. "I don't understand why you can't be ready when you tell me you'll be ready."

Mom is famously late for everything. Jennie's bad, too, but Mom is unmatched. Dad used to throw her over his shoulder and cart her out of the house, which is precisely why I told her Jennie's recital starts at five, not 5:30 like it actually does. A little white lie goes a long way in ensuring we're on time for absolutely anything that requires leaving the house.

"And I don't understand why you still expect me to be ready when I tell you I'm going to be! You should know me better by now."

She sticks her head into the living room. She's got mascara on her left eye only, making it look ten times bigger than the right. I make a face and cower away. She rolls her eyes and flips me the bird but drops her mascara wand in the process.

"Karma," I murmur, earning myself a flick to the forehead. I swat my hand around, but she runs down the hall, cackling.

"*One more minute*," she sings.

I sigh, pull out my phone, and do what I've been doing for the last hour: check to see if Olivia's messaged me.

She hasn't, not since she finished her lunch and sent a picture of her licking an Oreo, which, obviously, is now her contact picture.

I lay my phone on my chest and fold my arms behind my head, crossing my ankles. If I have to spend my days waiting on women, might as well get comfy.

My eyes pop open when my phone starts vibrating on my chest. The picture of Olivia licking her cookie shines on my screen and I scramble up to sitting.

"Hi, Ollie girl." My ten-outta-ten grin melts into a frown at her sad expression. "What's wrong? Kids got you down?"

There's a crash somewhere behind me, and three seconds later my mom comes skidding into the living room, breathless, both eyes finally done. She points at my phone and mouths *Olivia? It's Olivia?* Then she jumps up and down, covering her mouth with both hands.

She's fifty-two, in case anyone's wondering whether my mom is, in fact, an adult.

I smoosh my phone into my chest. "Really? *That's* what gets your ass out the door?"

She grins, settling on the floor, legs crossed as she stares up at me with wide, innocent eyes.

"No," Olivia says into my chest. I pull my phone back to find her rubbing at one eye. "Well, not really. Your typical short jokes and all that." She pulls her bottom lip between her teeth, looking at her lap. "Carter. We have to talk."

"Uh-oh," I muse with a chuckle. "Someone's in trouble." I balk at the unimpressed look on her face. "That was stupid. I don't know why I said that. It's me. I'm in trouble."

I'm lucky Olivia finds my goofiness endearing, because at least I get the twitch of her mouth when she tries not to smile. I count it a win, like I do every time she fails at being mad at me. But I want to see that full beam, feel the way it lights me up like sunshine. So I pull my dimples in and try again.

"You look gorgeous. So gorgeous. Flawless, really, but you always are." I gesture at my hair before popping my chin on my knuckles. "Did you do something new to your hair? Suits you. You're the best girlfriend out of all the girlfriends I've ever had. My favorite."

Those mocha eyes narrow dangerously before Olivia erupts with laughter. My mom's bouncing around on her ass, hands clasped beneath her chin. I hold my foot out, trying to shove her away. It doesn't work; she's too persistent.

"I'm the *only* girlfriend you've ever had."

"Right." *Charming grin? Check.* "'Cause you're my favorite."

Her eye roll is one of my favorite things about her, because I love her sass, her feistiness. Olivia works so damn hard to keep that oversensitive side tucked inside, but I see it.

"Why is my house so warm?" she finally asks, playing with that plump lower lip.

I run a palm over my proud, puffed-up chest. "I'm sure I'd have no idea about that."

"Carter . . . you bought me a furnace."

My mom becomes a cat, clawing at my legs, nails digging in hard enough to warrant a silent scream from me as I hide my phone and keel over, pushing her off me.

"Furnace?" Mom whisper-yells. "You bought her a furnace?" She claps her hands ten thousand times. "I knew you'd be a giant suck!"

"Shut up," I hiss, tossing a pillow at her face. She dodges it, picking it up and clutching it to her chest while she grins like a fool. She's way too invested in my love life.

I turn back to Olivia. It's a mistake. Or maybe the furnace was a mistake.

"Oh shit." Those brown eyes turn the most interesting shade of hazel, shining with hints of gold and mossy sage as they widen and fill with tears. "Baby, no. Please don't cry. Why are you crying?" *How do you help someone who's stuck in your phone?* "I don't know what to do. Are you okay? Do you need me to come over? Help me," I beg my beautiful, sensitive girl.

"I can't afford to pay you back right now," Olivia cries, swatting at her cheeks. She buries her face behind a couch cushion when her tears don't slow. "I'll set up a payment plan," I think she mumbles. Hard to tell when she's smothering her face like that.

My mom's rocking back and forth on the ground, clapping at my knees. *I love her*, she mouths. I push her away with my hand on her face.

"It's a gift, Ollie. And take that pillow off your face."

She rips it away. "A gift for what? It's not Christmas! And you got me a Christmas gift and I got you nothing! I ran out on you!"

"Birthday?" Fuck, should've tried Valentine's Day. I distinctly remember Olivia telling me she turned twenty-five in October.

"My birthday's in October!"

"I wanted to do something nice for you and give you something you weren't able to give yourself right now."

She wipes the back of her hand across her eyes, hiccupping.

"If your cute little toes froze off, I don't know what I'd do with myself."

"I don't want you to think I'm using you for your money."

"I don't know how I could possibly think that. It's a gift."

"Nobody's ever done anything like this for me before."

She should probably get used to it; I'm gonna spoil the shit out of her.

"I didn't want you to be so cold, pumpkin."

She melts at the nickname, finally granting me that smile I've been dying for. "Thank you so much, Carter. I . . . you're . . . I really want to hug you right now," she finally settles on.

"Oh my *God*!" Mom shouts out, collapsing dramatically onto her back before pouncing on me. "I can't help it! She's adorable!"

"*Mom!*"

A power struggle promptly ensues as she tries to steal my phone. An elbow soars through the air, hammering me in the nose as she throws herself over my lap and grabs for my phone.

"I just . . . wanna . . . say . . . *hi*! Gimme the phone, Carter!"

"Get your grabby hands outta here!"

I manage to catch one flail-y arm and pin it behind her back. She huffs, blowing her bangs off her forehead with her famous mom-scowl. The anxious giggle coming from my phone has both of our heads turning to find Olivia watching us with curious amusement.

"Oh God, this is my worst nightmare," I accidentally mutter out loud, wincing when my mom flicks me in the temple. "You already met Hank; it's only a matter of time before someone scares you away."

Mom gasps. "You introduced her to Hank before me?" She jerks my phone out of my hand and smiles softly. "Hi, Olivia. It's so wonderful to meet you."

"Hi, Mrs. Beckett," Olivia says with a bashful, wobbly smile. "I'm sorry. What a terrible first impression. I'm not usually this emotional."

My accidental snort earns me another glare, this one from my girlfriend.

"Don't worry, honey." Mom thumbs at me. "This one cried at every single Disney movie. He's always been a big softie."

"Anyone who didn't cry when that old lady drove Tod out to the forest and left him there is a monster," I argue.

I don't know how it happens, but a minute later my mom's already asked Olivia what her plans are for Easter and if she'll be joining us on our family trip to Greece this summer.

"Okay, Mom, say byyye." I grab my phone back and lock myself in the bathroom. Sinking down to the edge of the tub, I run a hand along my jaw. "So, that just happened."

Olivia snickers. "If your family had a TV show, I'd watch it."

"We'd be the next Kardashians, and I'd be Kim, obviously." I smile at the way her eyes crinkle with her laugh. "Are you upset with me? About the furnace? Maybe I didn't think it through."

When I woke up alone earlier this morning, my nipples were sharp enough to cut ice, my balls trying their damnedest to crawl up inside me. I had a heating company on the phone six minutes later and paid an obscene amount of money to get them out there today. I couldn't help myself. I want to take care of Olivia however I can and I'm lucky enough to be in a situation that allows me to do that.

"I'm not upset with you. I'm just shocked. It's such a big gift. Are you sure you don't want me to pay you back? I can put aside a little from each paycheck and—"

"No way. From me to you. That's what a gift is."

She sniffles and I'm worried she's going to cry again. I'm not good with tears. They make me feel helpless and overwhelmed.

"Thank you so much, Carter. I'm sorry I wrote you off when we first met."

"Don't be." I'd be lying if I said I wish she hadn't. We could've been screwing like rabbits and loving on each other all this time.

"Things happen the way they do for a reason. If you hadn't shot me down, this here might not have been. I already can't imagine my life without you in it."

Her bottom lip does an almost imperceptible tremble. "Stop it."

"Stop what?"

"Being so . . . perfect.."

Oh, *hello*. My chest puffs with pride. "That's why they call me Mr. Perfect."

"You're lucky your cuteness overrides your smugness."

"You make me feel smug." My phone buzzes, warning me that I need to get my mom's ass in gear. "I'm sorry, Ollie. I gotta get going. Call you tonight?"

She nods. "I'm gonna go through my closet and throw out all my holey sweats and long johns now that I'm not living in the tundra."

I head to the front door where my mom's putting her shoes on, thank *fuck*. "That's cool. You're not gonna need them anymore anyway. We're gonna sleep naked so I can touch you all night long."

"Oh, Carter, for heaven's sakes." Mom frowns, hands on her hips. "Can't you keep it sweet for more than two minutes?"

"You said that in front of your mom? *Carter!*"

I wink. "Bye, pumpkin pie. Like you lots."

Her blush amps all the way up to ten before she mumbles out her response, and when I shove my phone in my pocket, my mom's giving me the heart eyes.

I slip my feet into my boots. "Can I help you?"

"Pumpkin pie?"

"Yeah, whatever."

"You have nicknames for your girlfriend."

I grunt in response.

Mom pokes my chest. "Don't grunt at me."

I grunt again, just to piss her off, except it has the opposite effect and now she's got this little smirk glued to her face.

"Carter loves his girlfriend, Carter loves his girlfriend," she sings.

"All right. That's enough with you. I'm pulling a Dad."

"Carter, don't you d—*ah!*" Her shriek turns into a fit of giggles when I haul her off her feet and toss her over my shoulder like she's a sack of potatoes, the way my dad always did, her laugh the same.

"I love you, honey."

"I love you, too, Mom."

"I CAN'T STAND HIM."

"Carter," my mom warns. "Watch it."

I gesture aggressively at the way that douchebag is handling my little sister. "I hate the way he touches her. Like he fucking owns her or something."

I plaster on a fake smile as Jennie and her dance partner move through the crowd toward us. As soon as she's close enough, I yank her out of his grasp, enveloping her in my arms.

"You were awesome, Jennie."

Mom rocks her back and forth in a suffocating hold, and the second she releases her, Jennie's partner swoops back in, wrapping his stupid arm around her waist. Jennie watches the way my gaze zeroes in on his hand, covering her snicker with a cough and stepping away from Mr. Twinkle Toes.

"Wasn't she beautiful out there tonight, Carter?" Twat-waffle Simon says.

"She always is." Stepping between them, I angle her away from him. "You should go solo."

"I had a solo performance in the first half." Jennie squeezes my hand in warning. "Remember?"

"Yeah, but permanently. You should ditch pairs." I lean into her, whispering, "Jerkwad's bringing you down."

She pretends to hug me. "You just hate him."

Fucking *obviously*.

"Who you hooking up with tonight, Steve?" Believe it or not, I'm kind of a dick sometimes. If I don't like you. And I don't like Simon, which is why I sometimes, *occasionally*, call him by the wrong name. He fucks every girl he dances with and he's had his sights set on my sister for four years.

"I could ask you the same thing," he replies with a smile so self-assured I want to punch it off his face.

"I have a girlfriend."

"Right. So I've heard." He checks his fingernails. "Can't be all that serious, knowing your history."

My jaw ticks. "It's serious."

"Okay." Jennie claps her hands. "I'm starving. Dinner?" She loops her arm through mine before anyone can respond, waving at Simon over her shoulder before leaning into me. "As much as I love this macho, overprotective brother bullshit, I'd prefer you *didn't* kill my dance partner before I graduate."

"Is he fair game after graduation?"

"I couldn't care less what you do to Simon Syphilis once I've got my degree in my hand."

"Oh, for the love of—" Mom shakes her head. "You two are ridiculous."

I know I definitely am, because when I drop them off two hours later and am alone in my car, I'm in the same position I was in last night after I got off the plane. Drumming my fingers on the heated steering wheel, I hesitate for only a moment before I throw the car in gear and head in the opposite direction of where I'm supposed to be going.

Ten minutes later, I'm standing in front of Olivia's dark, quiet house. I should probably call her, but instead I stick the key she left me this morning in the lock. The door creaks as I step inside, quickly shutting out the cold. A dim light flicks on from her bedroom down the short hallway.

"Hello?" Olivia calls, followed by a scuffle, a bang, and then a quiet *fuck me*. Five seconds later, she pokes her head out of the doorway from her spot on the floor. The brightest beam blooms when she spots me. "Carter."

"What are you doing on the floor, pretty girl?" I help her to her feet, smiling at the blanket that's tangled between her legs. I don't know what in the hell she's doing to keep getting wrapped in this thing that it refuses to let go.

She flings her arms around me and smashes her face into my chest. "I didn't know you were coming over again."

"Neither did I." I drop my lips to her nose when she rests her chin on my chest. "Kinda just happened. Again."

"Are you sure you're not here to return my key?"

"Nope." I swing her up into my arms. "Thought I'd check on your new bedtime outfit." Dropping her to the bed, I trail one finger down her thigh, stopping at her ankle. She's in only a pair of purple boy short panties and a loose T-shirt that shows off one creamy shoulder. "I'm a big fan."

I tug my clothes off and climb into bed behind her. Slipping a hand beneath her shirt, I cover her warm stomach and inhale her smell. She's my favorite scent, like the Sunday mornings my mom used to spend baking muffins for our school lunches. She smells like the most intoxicating version of home, and I'm addicted to the feeling that comes with it.

"You must know you're never getting that key back. It's mine now. Already on my ring."

"You can have it," she whispers as I pull her shirt over her head.

"Good, 'cause I wasn't asking."

My fingers dip into her panties, making her moan, and her hair tickles my skin.

"You never ask for anything," she rasps, bucking against my hand as I push two fingers inside her.

"Nah, only for you to be mine."

Her hand curves over my nape as she angles her face toward mine, begging for a kiss. I give it to her, because I always will. "I'm yours."

My mouth tilts as I look down at my stunning girl. Her eyes squeeze shut with a moan as I sink inside her. Taking her chin between my fingers, I silently beg her to look at me again. The feeling that floods my chest and overwhelms my entire body when she does is dizzying.

Olivia's soft lips coast my jaw until she finds my mouth. "My heart's never felt as happy as it does right now."

Her words tumble tenderly off her tongue, and I empty everything I have into this woman my heart beats for.

30

AND DON'T POKE THE FUCKING BEAR EITHER

Carter

WHAT KIND OF CELEBRATION DO we think Olivia will enjoy best when I score for her tonight? The obvious answer is a sneaky wink, but she chose me, so she has to know she chose flash. I do everything with flare, not in the shadows.

Except Olivia, for obvious reasons. I do her in the shadows. Though I like to think I do her with flare, as well . . .

Nabbing a loose puck, I fire it off the boards as I scan the seats behind our bench, searching for Olivia. Her coat is draped over her seat, next to Cara's, so I know they're already here.

"Word on the street is you bought your girl a furnace." Emmett hip checks me into the boards and steals the puck, twisting and hammering it off toward an unsuspecting Adam, whose blocker goes up just in time to deflect it.

Garrett chokes on air. "Pardon? A furnace?"

"Her house was fucking freezing." I pull a puck from between his legs, flip it onto the tip of my stick, and Emmett whacks it off before I can show off.

"A brand-new furnace," Garrett muses. "Huh. We sure she's not using you for your money?" Emmett and I sandwich him between the two of us and the boards. "Okay, okay! I was joking!"

"Eh! Boys! Save it for the other team!"

My head lifts at Cara's voice, and I grin like a total loser when I meet Olivia's entertained gaze. I shove Emmett out of the way, hop over the boards and up on the bench, and slap my gloves against the plexiglass as Olivia makes her way down the aisle. She's wearing the Vipers tee I had waiting for her in the limo I sent to pick her up, and it wraps around her waist like a sin, the little gem in her belly button peeking out when she moves to sit down.

"Ah-ah-ah," I tsk. "Gimme a spin, gorgeous."

Her cheeks turn an adorable shade of rosy pink. "Carter."

I smile, twirling my finger in the air. Olivia rolls her eyes and holds her hands above her head—bag of popcorn in one, beer in the other—showing off the most spectacular backside. I resist the urge to bite my knuckles, only because my gloves stink, but goddamn, that *87* and *Beckett* decorating her back are really doing something for me.

I press my visor against the glass. "I'm so hard right now."

"Beckett!" Coach shakes my helmet. "Stop flirting with your girlfriend and get your ass back on the ice for warm-up!"

"Just telling her about the goal I'm gonna score her."

All I want to do is show off for my girl. I know she loves it, even if she's rolling her eyes at most of my ridiculous antics.

Three minutes into the second period, Garrett jumps on the ice a moment before me, grabbing the puck as it slices across the red line. He calls my name as I leap over the boards, and I tap my stick on the ice three times to let him know I'm here. The puck hits the curved blade of my stick without any effort from Garrett, his eyes bouncing between the net and the defenseman who's about to get in his face.

"On your heels, Beckett!" Emmett hollers from my left, alerting me to the forward who's hot on my ass.

I slam on the brakes and watch as the left-winger goes flying by me before he realizes I'm not with him anymore. In the second it takes him to twist back around, I spin by him, looking for my guys.

"All you!" Garrett shouts from the side of the net, ready for a rebound. "Stuff it in, baby!"

My left leg slides back as I wind up, and my stick hits the puck with a crack like lightning. The fans hold their breath as I let that bad boy soar, and when it smacks off the crossbar with a ding so loud it echoes before falling down into the net, the entire arena explodes.

"Bar down, baby!" I shriek, throwing my arms up.

"Fucking snipe show, bud!" Emmett roars, tackling me into the boards, where Garrett and our defensemen pile on top of us.

Olivia's on her feet by the time I climb back to mine, clapping and hollering with Cara. I skate by the bench, bumping gloves with my teammates, and she flashes me a beam brighter than the red light that's still flashing on top of the goalie net.

I stop in front of her, and her eyes widen, smile evaporating, replaced by a look of pure horror as my sticks rise in slow motion.

Don't you dare, Olivia mouths.

But Cara's jumping up and down, shaking Olivia's shoulders, just *daring* me to.

So I do. I point my stick at her, bring my glove to my lips, and blow Olivia the biggest, loudest smooch I can muster, sending it out into the arena as the crowd goes wild. Her cherry red face lights up the jumbotron for the second time in her life, and because I'll never learn my lesson, I scream, "*That's my fucking princess!*"

They replay my goal on the big screen three times as I lean on the boards and rehydrate, chatting with the guys. When I line up at the red line for the face-off, I sneak another peek at Olivia. She's got her feet up on the glass, sunken halfway back in her seat, one hand covering too much of her outstandingly gorgeous face. She narrows her eyes. They get extra squinty at the grin I flash her.

"*Fuck me*." Lucas Daley, centerman and assistant captain for Seattle, whistles as he glides in a small circle, stick across his hips. "Can I have her?"

"What the fuck did you say?"

"When you're done with her." He glances in Olivia's direction. "Can I have her?"

My teeth clack when I slam them together. "I don't plan on being done with her."

His disbelieving snort has my neck cracking, straining left to right. He's trying to get me riled up and I can't let that happen, especially with Olivia here.

"You've fucked her, now I'm waiting for you to do what you do best and chuck her."

"Fuck off, Daley," Emmett flicks out with disinterest.

"Or what? Your buddy here gonna knock me out?"

"If you don't stop running your mouth?" I skate forward until my chest touches his. "Yeah, that's exactly what I'm gonna do."

The ref pushes an arm between us. "All right, gentlemen. Enough of that. Let's get this shit on the road."

I take my place on the ice, shaking off the anger that's tumbling off my shoulders in waves as I get ready for the face-off with Daley. The ref bends, the puck in his hand hovering over the blue dot.

"Jesus, fucking look at her, would you?"

With a sigh, the ref straightens, scrubbing a palm down his face. I barely register it, too focused on Daley, his gaze glued to my girlfriend, who happens to be watching us while she pulls on her bottom lip.

"She's a tiny, slutty little puck bunny, isn't she? I'm gonna rip her in two."

Before I know what's happening, my gloves and stick are on the ice, fists balled around the neck of Daley's jersey, my face in his as I haul him close.

"Say one more fucking word about her and you're gonna be spitting chiclets." My pulse hammers in my ears, chest swelling with rage. I'm a volcano, teetering on the edge of eruption. Nobody will be able to stop me once I start.

A smug grin spreads across Daley's face as he drops his stick and tosses his gloves.

"Keep it clean and quick," the ref tells us, clearing the space around us.

The atmosphere in the arena is wild. These fans live for fights, love watching Carter Beckett lose his shit on occasion, which is exactly what's about to happen.

Dropping my grip on Daley's jersey, I keep my fists up as we start spinning in a slow circle.

"Are you clean?" His gaze flicks to Olivia. "Don't like to wrap it when I fuck a girl who looks like that. Wanna feel every inch of—"

My fist connects with his mouth, his head snapping backward, shutting him the hell up. He sputters, wiping the blood from his cracked lip before he chuckles.

"She looks terrified. Think she's worried I'm gonna knock you on your ass, Beckett?"

His fist swings, connecting with my shoulder when I dodge the punch. I lunge for him, grabbing hold of his jersey and dragging him toward me.

"You're still talking, but I'm not the one bleeding."

Daley twists when I swing at his face again, and I tug his jersey over his head, knocking his helmet off in the process. I let my fist fly once more, cracking him in the nose, blood splattering my knuckles. He dives for me, grabbing my jersey as we go tumbling to the ice. His fist flails, crashing against the corner of my mouth as my helmet pops off and I roll on top of him. My hair slaps against my forehead as I send my fist flying forward, once, twice, three times.

"*Beckett!* Enough!" The ref skates toward us, the linesmen flanking him. "Up! Both of you! It's over!"

Gripping Daley's jersey, I yank his face to mine, chest heaving. "You won't fucking touch her."

I glance up at the woman in question as my punishment is handed to me over the speakers: five minutes each. Olivia's anxious gaze is set on me, knees bouncing, the tip of her thumb in her mouth like she's gnawing on her nail.

Cara shovels popcorn into her mouth and hits me with two thumbs up and a holler. "Fucking right, Beckett! Knock 'em dead, baby!"

Sighing, I sink to the bench in the penalty box, running my fingers through my drenched hair, our trainer joining me to clean my lip.

Chris dabs at the corner of my mouth. "Never thought I'd see the day where Carter Beckett fought over a girl. Was it worth it?"

"She'll always be worth it."

"Whatever it takes to keep your girl safe?"

"Whatever it takes." A promise I intend to keep.

"You sure she's staying the whole weekend?" Garrett picks up the backpack in the back of the limo. "Doesn't seem like she brought much."

Olivia's a minimalist, I think, so that's probably why. But instead I say, "Because she's not gonna need any clothes while we're at home."

Adam huffs a laugh, stretching his legs out. "I miss those good old days."

Emmett arches a brow. "If the days aren't good, Woody, then you gotta do something about it. That's not right, bud."

"I don't know what else to do. I feel like I've tried everything. I managed to convince her to meet us at the bar, at least."

First time in, like, four months, I say in my head. I don't know what the hell is going on with Adam and Courtney, but something sure as hell isn't right.

I spot my gorgeous brunette the second we step through the door. She's leaning over the bar, chin propped on her fist, eyes on the TV above as it plays a highlight of my goal. I ditch my coat in the booth Cara's set up at, drop a kiss to her cheek, and make a beeline for Olivia.

"Your ass is out of this fucking world," I murmur, dropping my chin to her shoulder as my arms come around her.

"Mmm." She reaches back, threading her fingers through my hair as she tips her head to the side, letting my lips meet the soft, warm skin on her neck. "You're so romantic."

"I'll show you romantic." I slip a hand under the front of her shirt, covering her belly, and dip the tips of my free fingers beneath the waistband of her jeans. "I'm gonna shred these jeans when we get home. Burn 'em in the fire."

"What will I wear?"

"My naked body, draped over yours, while I fuck your brains out."

My favorite ass rubs against me. "All weekend?"

"All. Damn. Weekend." I nip the edge of her jaw. "You're gonna beg me to stop."

"Why would I do that?"

I hum a laugh, turning her toward me. "If you wanna get a head start, we can sneak off right now to the bathroom."

"You'd never fit in the stalls."

"I love when you talk about how massive I am. It only pumps my ego."

"You know damn well I'm not talking about your dick."

"You love my monster dick," I tease, squeezing her ass as my tongue sweeps her mouth.

"I do." Her thumb brushes against the cut on the corner of my mouth. "But you know what I don't love?"

I drop my head backward with a deep belly groan, eyes squeezing shut. "You tricked me. I thought I was gonna get away with it."

Olivia lifts one perfect brow, pinning her arms across her chest. "You're in trouble, Carter Beckett."

My gaze hoods. "I love it when you talk teacher to me, baby."

"Don't sweet-talk me. It won't work."

"It won't?" Tugging her back onto me, I kiss her neck, wet slides and nipping teeth until I find her ear. "What about kisses? Will those work?"

"No." It's more gasp than word so I'm calling bullshit. "Carter." A whimper, probably due to the way my tongue flicks out, tasting the skin below her ear. Her fingers dig in, squeezing my biceps as she leans into me like she needs my body to keep her upright. It's cool; I'll always support her.

Olivia groans, melting into me.

"Impossible not to give in to me, right?"

"I hate you," she mutters without any heat.

"Nah. You love me." I feel the heat of my accusation creeping up her neck, and I hide my smile in her hair when I crush her to me for a hug. Lacing my fingers through hers, I scoop her beer up and tug on her hand. "Come on, pumpkin. I want everyone to see me with the gorgeous girl from the jumbotron tonight."

"And that's another thing!" She throws her free hand in the air. I love her little temper tantrums. "You embarrassed me *again* tonight."

I shove her into the booth and slide in next to her. "You call it embarrassing you; I call it showing you off. How else would the world know you're mine?"

Cara cocks her head, watching us. "You're still mad at him?

Even knowing now why he fought? I'd be on my knees for Emmett in a heartbeat."

I clear my throat and tap Cara's shin with my foot before slicing my hand across my neck twice. *Ix-fucking-nay*, I mentally scream at her.

"Oh. You didn't tell her."

"Tell me what?" Olivia looks between us. "What didn't you tell me?"

"Uh . . ." I scratch my head, searching for something, anything other than what she's asking. "That you're . . . my . . . I . . . looove you?"

Huh. Kinda feels like I just satisfied an urge to say words that are 1,000 percent too early to actually say. Weird.

Her frown says she doesn't find it particularly funny. "Carter."

"Ollie girl." I take a sip of her beer, holding her gaze.

"He fought for you," Cara blurts, then slaps both hands over her mouth like the urge was uncontrollable. "Sorry. So sorry."

Sighing, I sink back in the booth, gaze narrowing on Emmett, actively looking anywhere but at me.

"Carter?" Olivia touches my arm. "What does she mean you fought for me?"

I lift a shoulder and let it fall. "It's nothing, really. Daley just said some shit I didn't like."

"Said he wanted to split you in half with his dick," Cara blurts again.

"*Care!*" Emmett holds his hands up in a *what the fuck* kinda way, eyes wide, while Garrett and Adam choke on their drinks. "Babe, come on."

"I'm sorry! I can't help it! Isn't it hot, though? He defended your honor! There was blood everywhere! It was a war, and you were the prize."

"She was never up for grabs." I squeeze Olivia's knee beneath the table. She's exceptionally quiet, staring up at me. "You okay?"

"I'm bored, Adam," a familiar voice cuts in. A redhead appears at Adam's side. "Let's go."

"Already? It's only—we just—I mean, we only just got here." He frowns, reaching for his girlfriend's hand. She pulls it away before he can take it. "You haven't met Carter's girlfriend yet. Olivia." He gestures at Olivia, who glues on a bright beam. "This is Courtney."

"Hi," she tosses out, rude as fuck as she ignores Olivia's outstretched hand. She smirks at me. "Girlfriend, huh?" Adam's eyes widen, and Courtney rolls hers before taking Olivia's hand, giving it a quick, flimsy shake. "I'm gonna go get another drink with my friends then."

"Sorry, Ollie," Adam whispers, ears beet red, eyes downcast. "She's not usually so . . . she's . . . I'm sorry."

Olivia gives his hand a squeeze. "Don't worry, Adam."

The night's kinda fucked from there. Adam's in a sour mood and everyone's quiet and tired. Olivia's tucked into my side, her hand on my thigh when her head hits my shoulder only forty-five minutes later.

I press a kiss to the crown of her head. "Wanna go home so I can worship your body?"

"That sounds nice," she says with a soft, happy sigh.

She takes off to the bathroom after we say good-bye, and I gather our coats and follow to wait for her. I learned my lesson after the last time she went to the bathroom in this bar.

The skin on the back of my neck pebbles, and a moment later Satan saunters into the dark hall.

"Carter," Courtney drawls, sidling up next to me. "How long's this girlfriend thing gonna last?"

I shift on my feet, ignoring the booze oozing off her. She hasn't set foot back in our booth since she disappeared after her stellar performance earlier tonight. "As long as she keeps me."

"Come on. You and I both know that's not you." She drags the tip of her finger up my neck, and I swivel, crowding her space.

"What the fuck are you doing? You're dating one of my best friends. I have a girlfriend. Get your hands off me."

Her eyes gleam as she winds my tie around her fist. "Poor Carter. No fun for you anymore now that you've got your balls in a vise. Is your girlfriend not up for sharing? What a drag."

I lower my face until the tips of our noses nearly touch. "Walk. The fuck. Away."

With a wink, she strides off, a little too much swing in her step, and I run an agitated palm down my chest.

I don't know what the fuck has gotten into her in the last six months. I've never had an issue with her until a pool party at their place last summer when she followed me inside the house and slipped her hand up my shirt. When I asked her what she was doing, she said she saw the way I looked at her. I still don't have a clue what she was talking about, but I turned around and left without the beer I'd gone in for.

The longer I stand here, the more restless I become. My shoulders feel tight and rigid, and I've got a headache brewing behind my eyes. I don't know if I need sleep, caffeine, or simply Olivia, but I decide a quick glass of ice water will do while I wait, so I guzzle one down at the bar before heading back toward the bathrooms.

A leggy brunette straightens from her spot on the wall when she sees me. She's mildly familiar, but I can't place her.

"There you are."

I swallow my sigh. "Do I know you?"

"You showed me the view from your penthouse while I was pressed up against your bedroom window." Slinging her arms around my neck, she murmurs, "I hear you're ready for seconds."

31

WHEN PUSH COMES TO SHOVE

Olivia

"So you're the girlfriend, huh?"

Courtney's blue eyes watch me in the mirror. This is only the second thing she's said to me ever, but I don't think I like her very much.

I turn my eyes back to the sink. "I'm the girlfriend."

"It's so nice to meet you, Ophelia."

My reflection smiles at hers as I scrub my hands. "You too, Chloe."

Her eyes narrow. "Courtney."

"Pardon?"

"My name is Courtney."

"Oh my gosh. I'm so sorry." Pulling a paper towel from the dispenser, I dry my hands. "I must have forgotten. It's been such a long, busy week at work. What is it that you do?"

Her gaze coasts down my body, then back up. Leaning over the counter, she reapplies her crimson lipstick. "My boyfriend's rich. I don't need a job."

Don't think it, don't think it, don't think it.

. . .

Poor Adam. Damn it. I thought it.

"I wouldn't quit your job just yet," Courtney gives me her unsolicited advice. "You wouldn't want to make any rash decisions that you might regret later."

"I don't plan on quitting my job."

She blows out a theatrical sigh of relief. "Oh thank God. It's for the best, really, knowing Carter and all." She squeezes my shoulder in a patronizing sort of way. "You know, because you're not his usual type."

My jaw flexes, and she calls out to me one last time, right before I can escape.

"So convenient how close his condo is to the arena and bar, right? Great way to get all those girls he fucks back there quickly."

Something angry and uncomfortable claws at my chest, and I work to keep my voice steady. "I've never been there, so I wouldn't know. We spend our time together at his house."

Courtney turns back to the mirror as if she hasn't heard me. "Bye, Olive."

"What a bitch," I mutter, pausing outside the bathroom to take a deep breath and shake away the fear she's trying to feed me, the insecurities she's trying to plant back in my head where I don't want them. She wants me to think I'm nothing special to Carter, that I'm the same as everyone who's come before me. She wants me to be as miserable as she clearly is, and I don't know why. I can't imagine a life with someone as kind as Adam Lockwood being anything less than perfect, and life with Carter is shaping up to feel the same.

Though I'd prefer if I didn't find him at the end of the hallway with a tall brunette, her hands on him.

I take a cautious step toward them, catching the tail end of their conversation, which happens to be something about being fucked up against a window.

My gaze moves between them as I quietly call his name. "Carter?"

A wave of relief runs through Carter as he exhales, and he reaches out to pull me into him, clutching me tightly. "Hi, baby," he whispers, pressing his lips to my cheek.

"What's going on?" It's not me who asks; it's the willowy brunette. "I thought we were going back to your place?" She looks me over. "Is she coming?"

"What? No?" Carter's head wags rapidly. "Ollie, I didn't say that, I swear. I went to get a drink of water and when I came back she was here and—" His brows pull together as he turns to look at her. "Who told you I was ready for seconds?"

Ready for seconds? A deep pit of jealousy opens in my stomach, the ache so raw, so ugly, I lay my hand over my belly, right where it hurts. He's been with her before, this stunning woman with legs that go straight to heaven.

I hate this feeling. The envy is bitter, and I close my eyes as I try to wipe away the image of them together, the comparisons I'm already cataloging in my head as I study her. I tell myself not to do this, not to deep dive into this hole. I can't live in a place where I'm constantly wondering if somebody else was better, if he kissed their lips while he brought them to the brink.

"She did," the woman murmurs, forehead creased as Courtney emerges from the bathroom with nothing but a glance in our direction before she strides away. The brunette presses her fingers to her forehead. "Oh my God. I'm so dense. Courtney told me you were asking about me but couldn't remember my name. She said you were back here and I . . ." She closes her eyes and shakes her head. "I'm so sorry," she whispers before she moves by us.

"Ollie." Carter guides my gaze to his. "I promise I didn't do anything. Courtney came back here and she was touching me and—"

"She was touching you? Without your permission?"

He nods. "I told her to leave me alone."

"I'm sorry, Carter. That's not okay." I squeeze his hands. "Are you all right?"

"I'm fine. It's you I'm worried about."

"I just want to go home."

"Then let's go home."

Carter helps me into my coat and takes my hand, towing me through the bar. It takes me all of two seconds to spot the rude redhead that seems to be finding humor in our tired expressions.

"Leaving already?" Courtney purrs. "Shame."

Carter tenses, his mouth opening, presumably to tell her to go fuck herself. That's what I want to say, at least.

So I put my hand on his chest and beat him to it.

"You're a bitch," I tell Courtney, though I suspect she knows as much. "You're rude and miserable and I don't know what right you think you have to pull the shit you did."

Her jaw clenches, eyes searching for Adam across the crowded bar.

"Adam deserves so much better than you; I hope one day he realizes that. Touch my boyfriend without his consent again, and it'll be an entirely different conversation."

I'm not entirely sure what I mean by that, but the threat lingers in the air regardless. I'm not normally a physical person. I've only gotten into one fight in my life and it was on the ice. I was fifteen years old and the victim of a plain old mean girl. After two and a half periods of dealing with her physical and verbal aggression, I finally let my temper get the best of me.

My point is this: girls can be mean, and if push comes to shove, I can be mean right back. I grew up with an older brother who never went easy on me. I was in a headlock 90 percent of my childhood.

We don't stop to say our good-byes, and when we step outside I expect Carter to call for our ride. Instead he starts pulling me down the street, through the falling snow and the howling wind as it slaps at our cheeks. I'm struggling to keep up, my sneakers slipping on the icy sidewalks, and Carter finally slows, tucking me into his side.

"Sorry," he murmurs, pausing to press his lips to my cold nose.

He's anxious and worked up; it's not hard to tell. The problem is that I am, too, and I'm afraid we're about to feed off each other's energy. I'm angry. Angry for him, for having to put up with unwanted advances, unconsented touches. Angry at Courtney for not appreciating what she has, for inserting herself where she doesn't belong. Angry at myself, because I can't stop thinking about Carter's upcoming road trip. I can't go to the bathroom without women throwing themselves at him. It's not a stretch to assume I'm going to be lying awake, wondering how many girls are propositioning him each night, putting their hands on him.

Carter swipes a key card through a slot on a sky-high building, and I take in the elegant lobby as he tows me across it.

"Is this your condo?"

"Mhmm." He sweeps me into an empty elevator and punches in a five-digit code before it springs to life.

The heat stacked in his gaze when he turns on me is new, and when he presses me against the wall and opens his mouth on mine, my heart races in a way I don't like.

His touch is rough as he works my coat off, his kisses hungry and needy, and when the elevator opens, he walks me backward until we're stumbling into an apartment.

I don't have a chance to look around, because he kneels before me and tugs my shoes off, hoists me up to him, and carries me down the hall. He sets me down on a cold bed in a dark room, the clink of his belt buckle, the soft thud of his pants hitting the floor, the heavy, jagged rise of my chest with each staggered inhale, all of it too loud in the silent room.

Fragments of silver moonlight slip through the window, casting shadows that only aid my unease. I make out the shape of a lamp on the bedside table, yanking the cord to bathe the room in a dim glow.

My heart races as I take in the room. Perfect, but empty. No pictures, no personal touches. Not lived-in and homey like his bedroom in his house. It's sterile and white, pristinely kept, and I hate every cold inch of it.

There's a starved look in Carter's eyes as he grips my ankles and drags me toward him, like he can't wait another second, like he's been deprived for weeks on end.

Has he?

I close my eyes and shake my head as if I can shake the notion right from it.

Carter rips my shirt overhead and jerks my jeans down my legs before wrapping them around his waist. Pressing himself against me, he groans. "Fuck, baby, I want you. So badly."

"Stop!" The demand comes without warning. There's a wild drum in my ears, and a pulsing in my temple that won't ease. "I—I—I can't. I can't, Carter." I scoot out of his hold, jump off the bed, and back myself against the wall, my hand at my throat.

"Hey," he whispers, brows pulled down. "What's wrong, princess?"

"Don't. Don't call me that."

He approaches me like I'm a feral animal, caged and terrified. "Talk to me, Ollie, please. What's wrong?"

"I—I—I can't, Carter. I can't be with you." My trembling gaze lands on the bed. "Not there. Not where you've . . ." Not where he's been, night after night, with girl after girl.

His gaze flickers, softening. A moment later, I'm wrapped up in him, my face buried in his chest as I beg with my brain to hold on to my tears. I don't want him to see them, to see this part of me, weak, scared, and so fucking vulnerable.

His palm runs slowly over my back, tender and reassuring. "I'm sorry, Ollie. I'm so sorry. I wasn't thinking." With my face in his hands, his patient gaze searches mine. He presses a lingering kiss to my forehead before fixing my shirt back over my head. "I'll get the car, okay? We'll go home."

I don't know what makes me do it, why I want to torture myself, but while Carter calls his driver, I open the drawer of the bedside table. Mass amounts of condoms spill out, phone numbers scrawled on paper, punctuated with lipstick kisses.

I bring my trembling hand to my mouth, creeping to the living room. It's as stark as the bedroom, and when I open the side table drawer, I'm graced with more condoms.

"He'll be here in ten minutes." Carter steps into the room, fully dressed, eyes on his phone. He comes to a full stop when he looks up, eyes moving between my face and the drawer of condoms I'm staring at. "Olivia . . . I haven't been up here since—"

"Why did you bring me here?"

"I . . ." His gaze holds mine as he searches for a reasonable excuse. "I didn't think. I just wanted to be alone with you. I didn't want to wait."

"Do you miss the life you had before you met me?" The words are out of my mouth before I can swallow them down, but God, the weight of them is so heavy, and I'm tired of carrying the worry in the back of my mind. I think I've been trying to convince myself that my fears are no longer warranted, that Carter's been great for a whole week and I have nothing to be insecure about.

But that's just it, isn't it? It's been a week. I walked away from him for very real reasons, very valid fears, and just because I want them to leave doesn't mean they simply get up and walk away.

And God, do I wish they would, because I can't stand the way his face crumples at my words, but it's always been simpler to disguise my pain and worries than to admit them.

Still, I always assumed that the right relationship would be all smooth sailing, a puzzle that falls together painlessly.

But Carter's been the exception to every rule, every familiarity. He's the axis that spins my entire world, and it's dizzying and unnerving for one man to hold so much power over me.

I tell myself not to do this, not to spiral through this endless loop of doubt. I can't live in a place where I'm constantly wondering where the media will rank me on his list of conquests.

And yet the article from only days ago plays over in my head, the speculations, the inclination that I can't possibly give him what he really needs or wants. Pair that with the fleeting time we've managed to spend together over this past week, and this position where I stand right now in the very place I never wanted to be, like all the women before me, all of it only heightens my insecurities, my fears. I've always been confident in who I am as a person, what I have to offer someone. Except now half of North America is watching, placing bets on how long it will last.

And so, for the thousandth time, I realize, in all honesty, I don't know if I am enough.

I don't want to find out the hard way.

I need him to help me through this, but I don't know how to ask.

"Do you want your freedom back? Is that what you bringing me here was about?"

Carter's eyes cloud over, a stormy night that steals the brilliant green in his forest. "Don't. Don't do that. Drop the act for, like, five minutes, okay? I know you're trying damn hard to pretend like you're some tough chick whose feelings aren't hurt by seeing me with someone else, by that fucking article from Monday, by seeing all this"—he gestures around the condo, at the condoms—"but I fucking see you. I know you, Olivia, so be real with me. If you're scared, tell me you're scared, but don't spew your accusations like they're the truth just because you're too afraid to come right out and admit it."

He twists away, scrubbing his hands over his face before running them through his hair, a sound of exasperation coming from his throat. Anger, sorrow, defeat . . . it's all there when he turns back to me.

"You said you were all in. You said that, Ollie, but I gotta be honest, this thing you're doing feels a whole lot like you've already got one foot out the door, ready to bail as soon as things go sideways. And I can't . . . I can't do this."

I clutch at my chest, right where it feels like it's cracking wide open. Then the tears come. They fill my eyes, pooling until I can't see. I refuse to blink, because if this is it, if it's over already, I don't want to let him see them come tumbling down my cheeks. I don't want to show him how hard I've fallen so quickly.

His hand closes over mine, leading me to the door. He slips my coat over my shoulders and helps me back into my shoes. When he walks me out into the hallway, the tears spill down my face, betraying me.

I won't look at him. I can't. Not in the elevator while he tenderly holds my hand. Not when he leads me through the lobby or out into the cold night, murmuring a quiet warning for me to keep my head down as I barely register the flash of camera lights. Not when he helps me into the limo and slides in next to me, all without a word. I stare out the window at the passing landscapes as I cry silently for the relationship that's over so soon, the only man I've ever felt so deeply for, my insecurities that led me down a deep, dark hole I can't climb out of. Not now that it's over, that I've repeated too many mistakes because trust didn't come easily enough, fast enough.

My eyes widen when we drive past the street that will take me home, and I finally turn to Carter. "You-you . . . he missed the—"

He doesn't look at me. "You're coming home with me."

"But we—"

"We fought." His eyes collide with mine. Something tender flickers in them, something unsteady, like maybe . . . maybe he's scared too. "That doesn't change anything."

I stay quiet, staring down at my lap, at the agitated finger he taps on his knee.

Until he twists back to me.

"You know what would happen if I took you home right now?"

My lips part to give him an answer, though I don't really have one. He cuts me off anyway.

"First of all, it would be the last thing I'd want to do and the last thing you'd want too; let's be honest. I'd leave beyond angry with myself and you'd pretend you were done with me, that it was for the best. Then you'd get inside, put on your pajamas, have five minutes to cool down, and realize you're angry with yourself too. You'd cry over our fight, like you're doing now, because you'd feel bad that you hurt me with your words. And me?" He gestures at himself as he looks me over, watching my tears continue to fall. "I'd get home, be pissed at myself for letting you walk away, leaving you when you're upset and vulnerable, that you're once again dealing with the consequences of my reckless past choices. And I'd get in my car and drive all the way back to you."

He captures my chin, dipping his face to mine.

"I'd throw you over my shoulder if I had to, but I wouldn't need to, because the second you saw me, you'd fling your arms around me and cry. And you know what I'd do, Olivia?" His nose touches mine, trailing the length of it. "I'd hold you. I'd kiss you. I'd tell you it was okay, that I forgive you for the words you said when you were hurting and scared. Then I'd ask you to forgive me for acting without thinking, for bringing you back here and contributing to a narrative that only feeds your fears."

With a low sigh, Carter sinks back against the seat, letting his head fall backward. "You wanna fight, get your self-doubt out, that's fine. But you're gonna do it with me, at my house, together."

His searing stare swings my way. "I refuse to let you push me away again."

32

HALF OF HER HEART

Carter

HOW CAN SHE THINK I'D give up so easily?

She's letting her insecurities take hold, root in her brain and force her words. Those intrusive thoughts dare her to try, to see if I care enough to fight for this. They tell her I don't, that I'd rather walk away, but they're wrong. *She's* wrong.

The sword she wields is double-edged, and she hurts herself whenever she hurts me.

Truthfully, I think part of what scares her is that I'm *not* going anywhere. Alone, she's free to hide within herself. If I'm by her side, she's forced to step outside of herself, to face the insecurities that want her to self-destruct.

As afraid as she is that this might go south, she's just as scared that it won't, that it'll work. So am I. Forever or never—both of those thoughts are terrifying.

I drop my watch to my dresser and tug my tie loose. I don't know why the fuck I put this thing back on when we left the condo, and right now it feels suffocating.

Olivia hovers by the bed, watching me. Her eyes grow bigger with each step I take in her direction, and she stumbles backward when I stop in front of her. I catch her around the waist, her hands trembling as her nails bite into my forearms while she stares up at me.

I love our height difference. I love that I can throw her around like a rag doll or hold things out of her reach just to irritate her, to get her to press her chest against mine while she jumps around. I love that she's this tiny woman with a huge attitude that some-times seems too big for her body, and I fucking *love* wrapping all of her up in all of me.

But right now, I feel so much bigger than her, and I don't want to be. I want to be on the same level; that's where we belong. So I take a seat on the edge of the bed and guide her down beside me.

"This self-sabotaging, not-trusting-each-other bullshit won't work, Ollie. Not for us. We both have fears, and the only way we're going to get through them is if we face them together. Because you're not alone in this, and I think that might be the biggest factor here, you thinking you have to do this alone. So you're going to admit that you're scared and tell me why while I hold your hand, and then I'm going to tell you why I'm scared, and we're going to start to work through it together." I hold my hand out to hers. "Got it?"

Her chest heaves as she stares down at my hand. Carefully, she slips hers into mine. She stares up at me, brown eyes drowning in apprehension, and I know this isn't easy for her. When her mouth opens, a quiet, broken cry steals her words, and I watch as her walls start falling down like waterfalls.

The process of Olivia's tears is slow and painful, but somehow beautiful. That full bottom lip does an almost imperceptible quiver and her eyes change, melting to a softer hue with bits of mossy greens and shimmery golds as they fill. She holds on as long as she can, and I watch as those tears tip over the edge and come tumbling silently down her rosy cheeks. There's this strange, sadistic part of me that likes them, only because I recognize what they mean: that Olivia cares deeply for me, that the thought of us going our separate ways all over again is as painful an idea to her as it is to me.

But mostly, I hate these tears. I don't want to be the dark cloud that hangs over her. I want to be the light that glows in the dark and eases all her fears.

"Don't cry, beautiful."

"I'm so sorry," she gasps, swiping at her cheeks, turning her face away.

"Hey." Hooking a finger under her chin, I force her gaze to mine. "Your tears are not a weakness, so stop trying to hide them. Don't be sorry for showing me how you feel. Being vulnerable with each other is how we learn to be the best versions of ourselves as partners. When you show me the type of love you need, I learn how to give it to you."

Her watery gaze flickers at the four-letter word that leaves my mouth without warning, and my chest tightens like a squeezing fist. It's part confusion, part familiarity, four letters that came out of nowhere but settle around me with an ease I never expected.

"I don't know how to ask for help," Olivia admits. "I've been pretending that everything is fine, trying to be your brand of perfect, because you're so perfect with me. If I'm not, if some things still scare me . . ." She squeezes her eyes shut. "Why would you stay when it's so exhausting?"

"It's been one week, Olivia. Your fears aren't going to magically get up and walk away. I know now that it doesn't work like that. It's something for us to work on, a way for us to grow together." I brush her hair back, tucking it behind her ear. "Go easy on yourself."

"I'm scared, Carter. I'm scared that I'm your test run. You've spent your entire NHL career doing this, and I'm expected to believe that I'm the woman that's come out of nowhere and made you want something you've never wanted before?" She shakes her head. "I'm not sure I've ever had that level of confidence. I can't even let go of that article. The words replay in my head, wondering if I'm enough, and then I see all the women who want you, some of the ones who've already had you, and I hate . . ." Her shoulders curl, shaking as she cries, hands fisting in her lap. "I hate that I look at them and feel like I'm not enough, that I can't stack up."

I pull her onto my lap and she clings to me as she cries, face tucked into the crook of my neck. My hand moves over her back as my chest aches with a pain I've rarely felt, one that leaves me feeling helpless.

"You're enough, Ollie. So enough you leave me overflowing. And I don't think a good measure of confidence is whether you compare yourself to others. It's only natural. I think it's about showing each other what we mean to the other and being confident in what we have together. That's where that feeling of enough comes from."

Gently shifting her back, I cup her face, thumbs brushing beneath her eyes, catching her tears. "My heart chooses you because you're feisty and fierce. You're sarcastic and you know how to clap back at me, and I love those bits of confidence. But I love when you show me your sensitive side, too, and I love that you think you hide it so well but actually wear it on your sleeve."

She giggles and hiccups, wiping the back of her wrist across her eyes, smearing her mascara, and sweet fuck, she somehow manages to find a way to rock the raccoon look.

"You might've been hesitant to let me in here"—I tap on her heart—"but you let me into your life when I asked nicely enough, because you thought I deserved a chance, even if only to prove there was more to me than what the media shows. You took my friends in without hesitation, made them your friends, too, and that means the world to me. I smile all the time when I think about you, and the way your nose scrunches when you laugh at me is tattooed in my mind. You came back to me even though you were scared, and here you are right now, communicating with me, even if it's hard."

I press a tender kiss to her lips. "You have a big heart, Ollie, and with a big heart comes big emotions. Some of those are fears, insecurities, and that's okay."

"But you're not afraid of anything," she whispers.

A quiet chuckle bubbles. "You think I'm not scared too? I'm scared. Christ, I'm fucking terrified."

"What are you scared of?"

"I'm scared this is it, that you're it for me. And while that thought is scary enough, nothing is scarier than the thought that I might not get to keep you, that you might one day walk away and I'll have to let you because all I want is for you to be happy."

Her warm palm cups my jaw. "You make me happy, Carter."

"That's good, 'cause I'm kinda obsessed with you."

Her nose wrinkles with her laugh, one of my favorite sights. It's kinda snorty, because she's still half crying. She tips forward, her forehead smacking off my chest, and I smile as I bury my face in her hair.

"You're laughing but I'm not fucking joking."

Olivia's beautiful tear-streaked face comes into view. "I'm kinda obsessed with you too."

"I can't change my past, but if you give me the chance, I can change my future. But I need all of you, Ollie. Not half of you." I watch the scrape of my thumb along her lower lip. "I know I flip your world upside down. You fucking demolish mine. Please, let me in. Let me see you. Let me have you. All of you."

"I don't want to hide anymore," she whispers. "I'm tired."

"If you want obsession, fierce appreciation, wild, unrestrained passion . . . If you want fucking magic, Ollie, then it's me. Let it be me."

The soft brush of our lips sends a thrill down my spine.

"Let's be scared together."

33

TRUST EXERCISES

Carter

"Cutest fucking raccoon I've ever seen."

"I don't wanna be a racoon," Olivia pouts, and I chuckle, wiping away the remnants of her mascara.

"There. No more raccoon, just my beautiful girl."

"Thank you," she whispers. "For being patient with me. For helping me work through this."

She slips her hands around my neck and presses her lips to mine, coaxing my mouth open. The sweep of her tongue is tentative, like she's testing the waters, so I grab her hips, rocking them against mine. I want her now, the same way I've always wanted her, so I take the control I crave, giving her what she needs until we're nothing but lashing tongues, rough hands, and searing touches.

I lift her shirt over her head and slip one lacy bra strap off her shoulder, littering the skin there with kisses, dotting it with tiny, purple marks as I suck on her and ditch the bra altogether. Setting her on her feet, I drop to my knees and shimmy her jeans off her hips, down her smooth legs. My thumb teases the edge of her panties, and she sinks her fingers into my hair, her back hitting the wall when I shift the satin and my lips meet the pool of warmth between her thighs. Her exhale is a breath of raw desire and need that fuels my tongue as it dips inside her, and I groan as the sweet taste of her fills my mouth.

"Carter," Olivia whimpers, wrapping my tie around her fist, guiding me up to her.

I slide my fingers into the hair at the nape of her neck, opening her up to me as I devour her mouth. Her fingers tighten around my tie, hauling me closer, and our chests heave together as I bracket her jaw in my hand, our lips a breath apart.

"Want to have some fun?" she asks on a raspy breath.

My gaze dips to the midnight blue tie in her fist then flips back up. *Fuck me*, what is going through her mind right now? Surely it can't be what I'm thinking, watching her wind that thing around her knuckles like she wants to . . . *use* it.

"Trust exercises?" I ask, breathless.

Her teeth tug on her bottom lip, lashes batting, and I'm already pulling the tie free, watching the silk slip between her fingers.

"How do you want to trust me tonight?"

Something mischievous dances in her dark eyes. "Blindly."

Fucking shit, I'm dead. Gone, deceased, six feet under. What the fucking fuck? Is this the result of her reading smutty books? Because o-fucking-kay, I'll buy her the whole damn romance section and turn a room into a library for her.

"Are you sure?" *Because I'm kinda freaking out.*

Olivia takes my hand and leads me to the bed. Like the obsessed puppy I am, I follow. Her lips touch mine, tender and sweet, and when she pulls my tie from around my neck, my cock pitches an entire four-person tent in my goddamn pants.

"I've never done anything like this before," I blurt.

"Me neither." She kisses the dimple in my right cheek when I smile. "I love your dimples."

"I love—" My jaw slams shut. My throat's itchy; I bring my hand to it. "Um. I love, um . . . your butt." *Shut up.* "And, um . . . everything . . . about you?" *Shut up, shut up, shut up.*

Before I can embarrass myself further, I lift her onto the bed. She leans back on her heels and reaches for me. Smiling, I shake my head.

"I'm in charge, remember?" I run the tip of my tie across her collarbone, around one beautiful nipple, watching as it hardens to a stiff peak. Her stomach clenches as the silk swirls around her belly button and dips lower, trailing up the inside of her thighs, ghosting over her glistening pussy. "Isn't that how this will work tonight? I lead, and you trust me?"

Olivia nods, eyes widening as she watches me undress. She licks her ruby lips, shifting, thighs rubbing together. She wants me to touch her, and I will. I won't be able to take my hands off her once I start.

Naked, I join her on the bed, settling behind her. The tip of my nose trails her neck until my lips meet her ear. "I need you to know that I'd never hurt you. Hurting you would break my heart, and you own that thing. You're my Ollie girl."

Her hands quiver on her thighs, gripping that tie like her life depends on it.

"Tell me. Tell me you know I won't hurt you."

Her inhale is sharp, words a whisper. "You won't hurt me."

"Tell me you're perfect."

She tenses, fingernails digging into her creamy thighs. "I'm so far from perfect."

"But you're perfect for me." My lips meet hers before she can object again, and I drag the tie from her hands. "Close your eyes, gorgeous."

I lay the silk over her eyes and loop it together behind her head. The ends drape down her back, the midnight blue a stark contrast to her milky skin.

"Does that feel okay?"

"Yes." Her voice crackles, and I link our fingers together, kissing her lips. She turns her face, seeking more, but I move off the bed. "Carter," she whispers, reaching instinctively for me, chest rising rapidly.

"It's okay, baby." I scrub a hand over my mouth, because sweet fucking *fuck*, she's a vision. On her knees in the center of my bed, my tie stealing her vision, leaving her vulnerable and open to me. "I'm right here. Listen to my voice."

Her hands fall to her knees, flexing. She takes a deep breath, nodding.

"You're stunning. Fucking breathtaking. I can't believe you're mine. I want to take a picture of you like this, burn this moment into my memory forever."

Olivia trembles when the tip of my pointer finger lands between her shoulder blades, falling down her spine. "Okay."

Okay? Okay what? I wasn't asking, I was just—"I can take your picture?" It comes out a shitload breathy, earning me a giggle from my pretty lady.

"If you want."

"If I—if I fucking want? Are you fucking with me right now, Ollie?"

A cheeky smile blooms. "Soon, hopefully."

I huff a chuckle. "Listen to you. Spending too much time with me." I open my mouth on her shoulder, teeth pressing into her delicate skin, and she moans. "For my eyes only. Promise."

"I trust you."

She doesn't, but she will. I'll make sure of it, and when I have that trust, I'll never, ever break it. I'll know how lucky I'll be to have earned it.

I'm glad she can't see the way I scramble for my phone, how it falls from my hands, the way I dive for it before it can hit the floor.

I've got fucking butterfingers right now because I can't believe any of this is happening.

I get my shit together before I climb behind her on the bed, inhaling enough air to submerse myself between her legs without needing to come up for air for at least five minutes, which is basically what I plan to do.

But first, I wind her hair around my fist and tug, tipping her head to the side to grant my lips access to that neck. Her shoulder erupts with goose bumps as my mouth moves over her, licking a slow path across her delicious skin, and I snap the first picture. When her head lolls and her mouth opens with a moan, my fingers tweaking one nipple, I take the second picture.

"Carter," Olivia whimpers, palm closing around my aching cock. "I want to taste you."

There's no holding in that groan. It rumbles out as I squeeze her tits, slamming her against me. "You can't say things like that, Ollie girl."

"Please, Carter."

I rocket to my feet, standing in front of her and fisting my cock. It would be rude of me to decline her when she asks so nicely.

Olivia wets her lips in anticipation. "Will you take a picture?"

My body stills. "Of-of—"

"Yes." She reaches for me, and goddammit, she manages to find my cock on the first try without seeing. Must be some soul-mate shit. And also the size of my sword of thunder.

She squeezes gently, so fucking *tiny* against me, and when she starts stroking my hard length, I snap the picture, one that's definitely going to send me over the edge every time I look at it, which will be fifteen hundred times a day, give or take.

She tilts her face up, waiting for instruction.

I brush my thumb over the sweep of her rosy cheek. "Open your mouth, baby."

I haul her forward the moment her lips part, and the second her tongue flicks out, tasting that drop of cum before she takes me in her mouth, I fucking whimper. My hips jerk forward and my cock hits the back of her throat. Her fingernails bite into my hips as she slides her mouth over me, and my eyes blaze as I take a picture.

I stroke her cheek. "My wild girl."

Something heavy and feral claws up my chest, begging me to lose control, to take everything I want and more. I can't lose control though, not tonight, not when I'm trying to show her all the ways she can trust me. But Jesus Christ, all I want to do right now is fuck her pretty mouth and watch her fucking gag.

Her hand works the base of my cock where her mouth can't reach, and when she hums around me, a sound of desire that makes me vibrate, I hiss, ripping my cock free.

"Lie back and open your legs. Let me see your pretty pussy."

She does as she's asked, dark curls a wild mess against my white pillows, ruby red lips glistening, every inch of her flushed. She's a fucking angel, and when she parts her thighs, I swear I die a little inside. I take another picture, but it'll never do her justice.

"Look at you, baby." I crawl between her legs, inhaling her scent. Like sweet maple syrup, I wanna lick every inch of her up. "So wet. Can you feel it?"

My tongue glides up her slit, and her back lifts off the bed with her cry. Guiding her hand down her body, I stop just below her belly button.

"Touch yourself, baby. Feel how wet you are, how excited this makes you."

The color in her cheeks deepens, and I stop her argument before it can leave her lips with my mouth on hers.

"You're beautiful, Ollie. Every single inch of you flawless, including those soft, gooey insides you try so damn hard to hide. I don't want you to ever be embarrassed with me."

"It's never, ever been like this before," Olivia whispers, trembling fingers gripping mine tightly. "I don't know why it's so different with you, Carter."

I know why. Pretty sure she does too. It's part of what scares us both, I think. Forever is a long time.

Instead, I press my mouth to her ear and tell her, "You're my favorite kind of different."

Her body heats as I kiss my way down it, like my lips blaze a trail of fire in their wake. I guide her fingers up the inside of her thigh, through her wet slit.

"Jesus," I mutter, fisting my cock as I watch her tentative strokes, her breath staggered as she makes herself feel good. "Fucking gorgeous. That's my girl. Make yourself come."

"Are you . . . are you watching?"

"Can't take my eyes off you, but I've never been able to."

Her pace quickens, hips rolling. Somehow—shaky hands and all—I succeed in taking one last picture before I toss my phone, barely registering the sound of it clattering to the floor.

"Fuck the pictures," I growl, impaling her with two fingers and without warning.

Olivia shoots forward with a cry, thrusting herself into my hand. "Carter, please. I want you to fuck me."

"I want that too. And I promise you'll get it, but you have to be patient."

She wags her head back and forth with a whine. "I'm not patient."

"I know," I chuckle. "But you're going to have to trust me."

I flick my tongue over her clit, sucking her into my mouth. Her fingers tug at my hair, and she comes undone on my tongue while she cries my name, begs me not to stop.

So I don't. I devour her over and over until she's a writhing mess, boneless and pliable, and when I finally pull away, I'm still not sated.

I never will be. Not with her.

I flip her onto her hands and knees, her head moving as she searches for me over her shoulder. "What do you need, baby?"

"You. A kiss. Please."

My palm slides along her jaw, and I take her mouth without hesitation. Each sweep of my tongue is a deep plunge, an unhurried exploration I don't want to end as I push my cock inside her warm, slick pussy. I devour her sharp gasp with another brain-melting kiss before I rest my forehead against her temple and begin an achingly slow plunge.

Every time with Olivia is a dance between frantic and savoring, savage and tender. She makes me feel wild, but all I want to do is slow down and make each moment last forever.

I find her clit, circling and teasing while I drive myself forward. The sheets ball in her tight grasp as she starts falling apart around me, whispering my name over and over as she comes.

And then: "*Harder.*"

"Harder?" I grip her throat, nuzzling her hair. "You want me to *fuck* you?"

"Yes."

"Then I'm gonna fuck you like I own you. Tell me you're mine, Olivia."

"I'm yours, Carter."

I pull back until I'm barely inside her, slipping the blindfold off. With her curls wrapped around my fist, deep brown eyes on mine, I tell her, "You're gonna look me in the eyes while I own you."

I slam inside her, and when Olivia screams out my name, a dark smile tugs on my mouth. Every last bit of my control unravels as I piston inside her, driving myself deeper, faster, *harder*. Through it all, Olivia chants my name, begs for *More, please, Carter, more*, and *Don't stop, God, don't stop*.

My tongue glides over her scorching skin, stoking that fire. Holding her head taut, I coax every throaty noise out of her as my hips slap against her ass with each punishing plow. I pull out of her soaked, tight pussy, drop down to my ass, flip her onto my lap, and crush her down on me with a hiss.

"Fucking . . . beautiful," I grunt, bouncing her on my cock. "Tell me. Tell me you're perfect for me." She starts to shake her head, and I cut her off with a snarl. "Don't you fucking dare."

"I'm . . ."

"Perfect."

"For you. Perfect for you."

"You're damn right you are." Wrapping her legs around my waist, I sear her with a kiss that crushes my chest, squeezes my heart. "Come with me. Come, Ollie."

And she does. We do. Together, our bodies quaking as I bury my face in her neck, her nails raking down my back. My sweaty body sticks to hers, which is cool; I think I'd like to be stuck to her forever. The hug I crush her in is nearly suffocating as I roll us to our sides, trying to catch my breath in between the pepper of a thousand kisses on her stunning face.

"I'm sorry about tonight," Olivia whispers after a moment, cheek pressed to my chest while she plays with the smattering of hair there. "For saying things I didn't mean and hurting your feelings. I got hung up on your past and was too afraid to give you my trust. I'm sorry."

"It's okay, baby." I twirl a lock of her hair around my finger. "I need to know when you're feeling scared. And we got through it, didn't we?"

"We fought already."

"It's called passion, Ollie. Wild and unrestrained. Eruptive. I don't want a love that's anything other than crazy, and crazy about you is the only way I know to describe how I feel."

My heart smiles at the way her face lights, and I stroke my thumb over the flush of her high cheekbone, the perfect bow of her top lip.

"I see the fire in your eyes and all I wanna do is fuel it. Light me up, set my soul on fire. I'm yours."

TWO HOURS, THREE MORE ORGASMS, and a snack break later, I'm lying awake in bed, Olivia tucked into my side while she sleeps. I'm staring down at my phone, watching a replay of my fight for the third time, or more specifically, Olivia's face when the camera pans there.

The second I drop my gloves, she leaps up. When I land the first punch, she grips her chest. When Daley and I go tumbling to the ice, her hands fly to her mouth, and the terrified look on her face is one I never want to be responsible for again.

Olivia stirs softly, hand sliding across my torso. "Mmm. Carter?"

"Come here, baby." I hoist her up to me, tucking the blankets around us and burying her in my chest. "Having you in my arms is the best feeling in the whole world."

She exhales a happy sigh. "Like you so much."

"Like you so much too."

Other words want to leave my mouth, words that scare and thrill me simultaneously. Words that come with a meaning so deep, a connection that screams forever. It feels too soon and yet, it's as if they knocked on my door and I let them in without hesitation.

Is this what it feels like? Wanting to share all your pieces, the good ones and the not-so-good ones? Wanting to take her hand in yours and hold tight as you take each step forward? Steps into the unknown, the dark and the light, where we tackle fears together and come out stronger each time.

I trace the soft lines of Olivia's face beneath the fragments of moonlight that stream across her, and I know.

I brush my knuckles across her cheekbone, and when her lashes don't flutter, I whisper the words against her skin.

"I think I love you, Ollie."

34

HELLO, MR. INCREDIBLE

Olivia

EVER LET SOMEONE BLINDFOLD YOU and fuck you into oblivion?

If it's not on your bucket list, add it right now. *Trust me.*

I feel wrecked beyond belief, my muscles groaning with a dull ache as I stretch. And this mattress? A-fucking-plus. Add an obsessed hulk of a man to the mix, and I'm sure I transcended.

Music floats up the stairs along with the clang of dishes, the smell of something both sweet and savory.

And singing. Carter is singing.

I flop over with a happy sigh, not even taking up a quarter of the giant bed when I starfish in the center of it.

I might, uh . . . somehow be in love already. Except I don't think I simply fell. I tripped over my own two feet and face-planted in it.

Heavy footsteps thud up the stairs, Carter's voice coming closer, singing a familiar tune.

"My girl! *Do-do-do-do-do!*"

He pops his head in the room with a grin so saucy and charming, and I bury my face in my hands and curl over my legs as hopeless, embarrassing giggles burst from my belly.

"Quit your laughing," he orders, strolling across the room.

Naked. *Stark* naked. Holding a tray of food.

Also, he's naked.

"You're naked." I'm gaping.

He points to the ridiculous chef's hat on his head that I nearly missed due to his flawless nakedness. "Nuh-uh. Got a hat on."

"Uh-huh . . ." I'm not staring at the hat.

"I see you're staring at Mr. Incredible."

"You're so vain it's incredible."

He sets the tray on my lap, leaning in for a slow, soft kiss.

"What's this?" My heart warms at the sight before me. "You made me breakfast?"

He runs a palm over his proud chest, nodding. "Uh-huh." He swipes a piece of bacon off one plate that appears to hold at least an entire pound of it, placing the tip in my mouth before he devours the rest of it. "Bacon because you love it. Fruit and yogurt because they're sweet like you. Blueberry bagel with cinnamon spread because Cara said it's your favorite. And tea because coffee makes your stomach hurt."

"I l-l-l . . . —" Oh my. Oh my shit. Balls. Oh my shit balls. I almost said it. Out loud.

Carter lifts an amused brow, looking smugger than he ever has. "You l-l-l?"

"I—" flail a hand around, apparently—"*love this!*" *That's* the best I can come up with? "I'm just overwhelmed by the thoughtful breakfast, and you're . . ." I gesture at his body. "Naked."

Carter plants his hands on his hips, swiveling. He sure likes to swing that thing around. "Is my nakedness distracting you?"

"I couldn't spell the word if you asked me to while looking at that."

"Mmm." He swipes a smear of cinnamon spread off the plate and brushes it over my lips, eyes glazing as I lick it off. "I like when I render you speechless."

"Don't get used to it."

Carter collapses next to me, munching bacon while he watches me eat, head propped up in his hand, elbow on the mattress. The cinnamon spread is warm and melty on my bagel, and when I bite into it, it dribbles down my chin, dripping over the swell of my left breast.

His eyes hood, and when I go to wipe it off me, he snatches my wrist. "Don't you dare," he whisper-growls. "Mine."

He rolls to his feet, plucks the tray off my lap, sets it on the floor, dive-bombs the bed, and devours every inch of me three times over. When we finally make it back to breakfast, the food is cold, my bagel is hard, and there's not a single part of me that cares. In fact, by the time he drops me off at the arena for my girls' hockey game, I've had three orgasms, earned a McDonald's breakfast, and a *pat-pat* on my ass when I get out of the car.

"Was that Carter Beckett?" Alannah whispers when I meet her at the front door, eyes wide with wonder as she stares at Carter's SUV pulling out of the parking space. He smiles and waves and Alannah jumps up and down, arms flailing as she waves back. "It's him, it's him, it's him!" she shrieks at her dad, giving him a violent shake.

Jeremy rolls his eyes. "It's him, it's him. Woo-hoo."

"Please do try to contain your enthusiasm, Jeremy." I pull a gift from my bag and hand it to Alannah. "This is for you, from Carter."

She unravels the small jersey. "To Alannah. Hustle hard, hip check harder. Carter Beckett." She clutches it to her chest. "Omigod, omigod!"

Jeremy's still unimpressed, but holds one expectant hand out to me.

I arch a brow. "Can I help you?"

"Where's mine?"

"Your what?"

"My . . . my jersey." He gapes. "You . . . didn't you . . . you didn't—"

I grin, shoving his jersey at his chest.

He holds it in front of his face as he reads, which sucks, because now I can't see his expression. "To Jeremy. Don't be an asshole to your sister. Carter Beckett." He drops the shirt across his hips, giving me a clear view of his face, which is . . . ecstatic. "Oh my God. He signed my jersey. *Carter Beckett signed my jersey!*"

Oh for fuck's sake.

I'M AT LEAST FIVE POUNDS heavier than when I walked in here. Which was approximately seven minutes ago. Seem impossible? Nothing's impossible with Cara.

"Do we need *all* these snacks?" The box of Milk Duds shoved in my coat pocket wiggles free, and I trap it against my side with my elbow, waddling down our row. I've got a can of beer in my other pocket, Twizzlers in my back pocket, another beer in my right hand, and one arm wrapped around a bag of popcorn. "It seems a little excessive."

"What a ridiculous question." Cara scoffs. "Yes, *Olivia*, we need *all* these snacks. Don't ruin my life."

"My apologies, queen."

"Apology accepted." She sinks to her seat and promptly downs half a vodka cooler. "Did Carter tell Adam what happened last night?"

I nod. Carter had a chance to talk with Adam about Courtney while I was at my game earlier today. He said Adam was devastated, not for himself, but for us. "Courtney said she was drunk and didn't remember, and when he kept pushing her, she told him to lighten up and learn how to take a joke."

Cara makes a low, scary sound in the back of her throat. "Liv, you know I don't say things like this lightly, but that woman deserves to have an entire hive of angry bees released on her."

I snicker, and Garrett comes to a stop in front of the bench, sending up a spray of snow as his eyes glide over our snacks. He squirts water into his mouth and lifts his brows.

"You gonna eat all that, Ollie?"

"All I wanted was popcorn," I say, slanted eyes on Cara.

"Well, whatever you don't eat, I'm your man."

Carter crashes into him from behind. "*I'm* her man."

Garrett cross-checks Carter in the chest. "I want her food!"

Carter shoves him back. "Nobody gets her food but me!"

"What am I looking at here?" I ask, watching what appears to be a game of slapsies between two grown men who are supposed to be warming up for their professional hockey game.

"You're looking at what I have to deal with on a regular basis." Adam stops in front of the bench for a drink of water. "Children."

"The food is mine!" Carter shouts out as he wraps his arms around Garrett's head.

Garrett wriggles free. "I won't let you down, Ollie!"

It's at this moment I realize Emmett's leaning over the bench, winking, and Cara's aggressively poking the inside of her cheek with her tongue.

"Oh my God. You two are—" My heart leaps to my throat when Carter's body slams into the plexiglass right in front of me. "Carter, for fuck's sake. You scared me."

He whips his gloves off, cups his hands around his mouth, and breathes on the glass. The tip of his finger etches a heart into the fog, and when he writes *C + O* my weak heart takes flight, as embarrassing as this is. The wink he hits me with holds all the promise of the night we plan to spend alone together after this late afternoon game.

Cara tosses a mixed handful of Skittles and M&M's into her mouth. "That man is head over heels in love with you."

My nose wrinkles, and I send a pointed look at the hand she's dumping both treats into. "That is disgusting and evil. You do not mix the two. And he's not in love with me." But, like, maybe one day. That'd be nice. Or whatever.

Cara snorts. "Liv. Look at that man. I've never seen such a lovesick loser."

My gaze sweeps the ice, and I find Carter in an instant, his eyes locked on me as he plays with a puck, chatting with a few other players. His grin is electric as he lifts one gloved hand and waves.

"*Hi, pumpkin!*" he hollers before firing off a shot on Adam.

My cheeks flame. "Did he just call me pumpkin in front of fifteen thousand people?"

Cara shovels a handful of popcorn into her mouth. "Capacity is nineteen thousand."

Seems Carter's dead set on keeping up with the embarrassment schtick, because when he scores six minutes into the first period, he skates by the bench and yells, "*That was for you, pumpkin!*" When he scores in the third period and dedicates it to his princess, he points up at my red face lighting the jumbotron, places his gloved hands over his heart, and pretends to faint.

I genuinely didn't realize they made people this ostentatious, and yet when he strolls right by the reporters after his game and lifts me into his arms, butterflies still erupt in my stomach.

By the time we get home, the sinking sun paints the sky in stunning hues of pink and orange, splashes of lavender, the dark pines and towering mountains a striking contrast to the beautiful backdrop.

Carter leads me to the kitchen island and sets a small tray of cheese, cured meats, cashews, and grapes in front of me. "Dinner will be late tonight, so munch on this for now." He kisses my forehead. "I'll be back in a few minutes."

When he returns ten minutes later, he's wearing the most adorable, bashful smile, and he's swapped his suit for track pants and a T-shirt.

His fingers thread through mine, tugging me upstairs and toward his bedroom. The bathroom is dimly lit by the warm flame of the candles decorating the edge of the bath, the glow of the stars pouring through the skylight. John Mayer plays softly through the speakers, the book I'm currently reading sitting on the stool next to the large soaker tub. The water is sparkling, a beautiful hue of magenta, littered with rose petals, and Carter's quite literally bouncing on his toes.

"There's a bath bomb in there. That's why the water's pink. Jennie picked it." He scratches his head. "Um, it's got, um . . ."

I inhale deeply as the scent hits my nose. "Lavender?"

His face lights. "Yeah! Lavender. It's for relaxing and all that shit."

I stifle a giggle. This is utterly adorable.

"But the rose petals were all me. And the candles." He couldn't look prouder.

"For me?"

"For you." He touches his lips to mine before wiggling my jeans over my hips, bringing my panties and socks with them. He pulls my shirt over my head, removes my bra much more gently than he ever has, and helps me step into the steamy water. "I want you to relax while I get us some dinner and get set up downstairs, okay? You have to stay in here for forty-five minutes."

"Forty-five minutes? That's awfully specific. What if I miss you?"

"Then you can touch yourself thinking about me." He snickers, then his gaze hardens. "If you do, I need it on video. Add it to the holy bible of jerk-off material hiding in my phone."

With a smile and a sigh, I sink into heaven, hands floating over the water, skimming the petals. I don't last long after he leaves, forgoing the book and humming along to the music as my eyes drift closed. Before I know it, Carter's warm hands are on my face, coaxing me awake.

"Sleepy Ollie girl," he whispers. "Knew I had to come get you when I hit the forty-sixth minute."

He wraps me in a thick towel and ushers me into the bathroom, pointing to one of his T-shirts and a clean pair of underwear from my bag, all while draining the tub, scooping up the petals, and blowing out the candles. He does so much for me, his dedication and compassion unmatched. When he returns, I wind my arms around him, snuggling close.

"Thank you, Carter. I'm so happy with you, and I can't wait to grow together."

"We're gonna have the biggest glow-up." His brows furrow. "Emotional glow-up. 'Cause we're both already hot as fuck." He smooshes his lips to my forehead, pulling back with a loud *muah*. "Come on. I can't wait to show you what I did."

He lifts me into his arms and carts me down the stairs, stopping at the edge of the living room, and my heart implodes. His strums steadily next to my ear on his chest, and I press my palm there, as if I might be able to touch it, feel the way it races.

I slide down his body, fingers at my mouth as I move into the room.

The TV is on, open to Disney+ and showcasing all the classics. The couch is . . . destroyed. The cushions are gone, though I have an idea where they might be. I round the white sheets that decorate the room, set up like a tent, and I find the cushions inside, buried under bundles of blankets and more pillows than I've ever seen. Twinkly lights line the inside of the tent, and the coffee table is littered with boxes of Chinese food.

Carter watches me, reaching for me before seeming to second-guess himself, palming the back of his neck. "I thought we could have a movie night. Do you . . . do you like it?"

Do I like it?

I leap across the room, jump into his arms, and crush my lips to his as he laughs.

"I'll take that as a hell yes. Fuck, I'm killin' it at this boyfriend stuff."

Together, we cuddle up in the makeshift tent, settling on *The Lion King* first, and Carter sings every single word while we eat.

When it's over, he disappears into the kitchen and returns with brownies.

"*Frozen*?" He licks the frosting off his thumb as he sifts through movies. "Or *Moana*? I can sing both, in case you're wondering."

"*Frozen*. I wanna hear you sing 'Let it Go.'"

Carter looks down at me as I snuggle into his side. "You gonna stay awake long enough to hear it?"

"Pfft. I'm wide awake. Had a cat nap in the tub."

"Mhmm. Well, just in case . . ." He scoops me into his arms, settling me against his chest, resting his chin on my head.

We're only ten minutes in when he runs his palm over my back and whispers my name. When I meet his gaze, it's tender and warm.

"My mom always told me that these things don't come easily, that you have to work for the love and the life you want. The hard parts are challenging, but we get through them, and everything else with you feels natural, and I . . . I want to work with you. I want to build a life we love."

With those words replaying in my mind, I don't make it long enough to hear him sing his song, and I'm not sure what time it is when I feel him lay me down on the cushions, his body molding around mine. The heat of his palm warms my belly when it slips beneath my shirt, and soft lips find my ear.

"You're my favorite everything, Ollie."

35

BALLS DEEP

Carter

I PLAN ON SOAKING UP every single hour I have left with Olivia before my road series. That's why I woke her up at the crack of dawn with my head between her legs. That's also probably why she's passed the fuck out on my lap right now, not even stirring at the way I keep shouting at my TV.

"Did you get shot again?" Garrett screams into my headset. "How are you so bad today?"

"There's a hot chick sleeping between my legs!" I shout back.

"She's always between your legs!" He goes quiet for a moment, and Adam and Emmett chuckle. "Okay, that sounded bad. What I meant was you've had her all weekend. Focus on staying alive. You're bringing the whole team down."

"Yeah, yeah," I mutter, navigating my player up a set of stairs.

"That place was loaded with guys two minutes ago, Carter," Emmett says as Olivia stirs in my lap. "Make sure you—" He lets out a heavy sigh as my screen splatters with blood, my character collapsing after being shot point-blank in the head. "—check. Dude, what the fuck?"

Olivia smiles up at me, blinking her bleary eyes, fluttering those dark lashes.

"Beckett? You there?"

Adam sighs. "Olivia must've woken up."

"I gotta go." I tear off my headset, ignoring the way Garrett shrieks about being in the middle of a mission.

Olivia starts crawling up my body, but I push her down to her back.

"Snack time."

"Again?"

"I'm always hungry, Ollie, and there's nothing I'd love more than eating your pussy one more time, then bending you over the couch and fucking you so hard you feel it in your throat. I'd also settle for cuddling."

It's highly inconvenient that my front door swings open at this exact moment, the voices of two occasionally irritating women filtering into my house. Olivia stiffens, and I collapse on top of her, groaning.

Jumping off the couch, I spread my arms wide when I spy the three people taking off their things in my front hall, the dog who's shifting excitedly on his paws, ready to pounce.

"What the hell are you doing here?" I look at Hank. "I thought Ollie and I were going to pick you up for dinner."

He lifts his palms in an innocent shrug. "Wasn't me."

Jennie rolls her eyes, releasing Dublin from his lead. He bounds over, jumping up with two paws on my belly, and I bury my fingers in his soft fur. "That's BS and you know it, old man." She leads him down the hallway. "Mom and you were on the phone plotting this for nearly an hour this morning."

Mom throws her hands in the air. "It's not fair that he got to meet Olivia and we didn't!"

"You can't just walk in here unannounced!" I shout back, gesturing at the way Olivia's frantically trying to smooth her hair and clothes. "We could've been naked!"

"Carter!" Olivia calls in horror, at the exact moment my mom plants two fists on her hips and growls out, "Carter Beckett!"

Jennie gags. "Ugh. Gross. Not an image I want burned into my retinas."

"Then you should've knocked, because I was almost balls d—"

"*Carter!*" Olivia shrieks again, slapping a hand over my mouth. "For the love of God, please stop."

I smile against her palm. "Sorry, pumpkin."

Hank snickers, reaching toward us. I take his hands, but he frowns, slapping them away. "I don't want *you*. I want Olivia."

She shoves me out of the way with one hip and embraces Hank. "This is so much better than what we had planned."

Mom approaches Olivia with her arms wide, wearing the most wondrous smile, like she's discovered life on Mars. "I never thought this day would come," she cries. "My little boy, all grown up, with a *girlfriend*!"

"Only took him twenty-seven years," Jennie mutters, then high-fives Hank.

"Hi, pumpkin pie," Mom croons, folding Olivia into her embrace.

"*Mom!*"

"What? That's what you call her, isn't it?"

Jennie snorts. Once. Twice. She keels over, slapping her knee. "*Pumpkin pie?* You-you-you"—*Another snort*—"you call your girlfriend pumpkin pie?" *Is she crying?* "So much for that big, bad fuckboy rep you've been rocking all these years." *She's fucking crying.* "I mean, we get it. You love your girlfriend."

I would talk if I could. Instead I scratch at my nape, my face burning. When my mom releases her from her talons, Olivia gives me a soft, warm smile that makes me feel like she's lit me from the inside out.

Mom swats Jennie's shoulder. "Don't tease your brother."

"He teases me all the time!"

"He teases you because he loves you; you know that."

"Yeah, Jen." Out come the grabby hands. "Just let me love you."

"Get away from me!" Her gaze slides over Olivia, nose scrunching. "You're too small to make a decent human shield." She considers it for all of a split second before she says, "Ah, fuck it," grips Olivia's biceps, and ducks behind her.

That might work, except my arms are long as hell, so I wrap them around both of them and crush them to my chest. "Group hug," I sing out.

They may have cockblocked me, but right now, I've got my all-time favorite people in one room, and nothing makes me happier than watching the way Olivia so effortlessly fits in, like she was always meant to be here. I don't even mind when she tells everyone about the time she shaved her brother's brows off in his sleep because he broke her hockey stick and carved it into a walking stick, eliciting an evil gleam in Jennie's eyes as they touch mine, like she's plotting.

Two hours later when she's standing next to me grating cheese for homemade pizza, I'm still guarding my eyebrows.

"You fell hard and fast, little brother. Did you hit every branch on the way down too?"

"Huh?" I smile as Olivia throws her head back with a laugh at whatever Hank's saying. Something dirty, judging by the way my mom smacks his arm. I turn to Jennie. "I'm almost five years older than you."

"But your mind is so, *so* small, fuckboy."

I flick her ear. "Do your job."

She does, with as much flourish as I do most things, one foot popped as she sprinkles the cheese over the sauce. "Does she know you wanna marry her?"

"What?" My gaze ricochets between my annoying sister and Olivia.

"I said does she know you're in love with her."

I slap a hand over her mouth, wrapping her in a headlock. "Shut up or she'll hear you."

She bites the flesh of my palm until I release her, cradling my hand against my chest, and when Olivia joins us, I can barely breathe.

"What are you two fighting about?"

"*Nothing!*" I kinda-sorta shriek. The look I pin Jennie with says she'll be the one with no eyebrows if she says anything.

"Well, it was supposed to be a surprise, but Carter was telling me he's finalized the details on horse-riding lessons for us this spring. He thought you'd like to come with me."

Olivia's eyes light up. "Horseback riding lessons?"

I can't believe she's buying this shit. I give it exactly one month until Jennie tells her the entire thing was a ploy to: A) get what she wanted, which at this moment, are the lessons she's been dropping hints about since her birthday passed; and B) distract from the fact that I'm in love with Olivia and don't want her to know yet. Only one month, because I'm impulsive and bad at keeping secrets, so I can't imagine holding out much longer than that.

Case in point, forty-five minutes later when we're at the dinner table, I've got her foot tucked between my legs, because apparently I can't not be touching her.

"We went skating on Capilano Lake last weekend and I beat Carter in a race," she proudly tells my family.

"You *cheated* in a race."

She hums thoughtfully, chewing her pizza. "That doesn't seem like something I'd do."

"It's something I'd do just to knock him down a few pegs," Jennie says. "Carter said you coach your niece's hockey team and teach high school fitness. That's so cool! Did you ever dance?"

"Only when I've been drinking. I'm not overly rhythmic. I did figure skate for a few years though."

"She coaches the girls' volleyball team at school," I add.

"Did you play too?" Jennie asks, amused.

Olivia nods. "From sixth grade to my final year in university."

Jennie folds her lips into her mouth. Her shoulders start quivering, and a tiny snort leaves her nose. I hide my smile behind my palm, staring down at my plate as I try not to laugh.

Olivia's gaze bounces between us. "What?"

"It's just . . ." Jennie jerks forward as a small laugh escapes. "I mean"—*snicker*—"can you even"—she covers her mouth—"reach the net?" She bursts out laughing at the exact moment I do, both of us folding over the table.

Olivia's eyes narrow as she pins her arms across her chest. "Oh, I see. You two Beckett children are one and the same."

"Assholes?" Mom guesses. "Yeah, blame their father, not me."

"Be nice to your girlfriend, Carter," Hank calls from across the table as he slips a piece of pepperoni to Dublin. "Or she won't let you try any of the fun stuff from the book we're reading."

It takes me a solid five seconds to fully register the weight of his words, and by then, Olivia's already choking on her food.

"*Hank!*" I scream, rubbing Olivia's back.

"Uh-oh," he murmurs. "Dublin, I've fucked up again."

I'VE LOST MY MIND. THAT'S the only logical explanation as to why I'm currently listening to Olivia's principal go on about how much he loves when Cara visits.

I saw Olivia three hours ago when she kissed me good-bye from her bed, where we slept last night so she could get up early for work. I promptly passed out for another hour and a half, woke up, devoured most of her kitchen, then ordered groceries because I felt bad.

I'm still not ready to say good-bye to her for the next five nights.

"I was young once," Ray's busy telling me. He told me to call him Ray. "You two seem quite close based on the pictures over the last two weekends." He wags his brows, which is kinda weird; he's Olivia's boss. Also, I'm slightly concerned about that last comment.

"Is that a problem? The pictures of us? Kissing?" Fuck, I never thought of that.

He waves me off as we stop outside the gym doors. I can see Olivia in there, surrounded by a bunch of boys that tower over her, even on a day she's chosen to wear heels.

"Olivia's personal life is her own. She's perfectly entitled to have intimate relationships; it just so happens that hers is photographed. She won't be punished for that, so long as everything stays legal and respectful."

"Legal and respectful; got it." Sounds easy enough, but I'm maybe a wee bit feral when it comes to loving on Olivia. I'll have to make a conscious effort to keep it PG when we're out and about.

"The kids around here love her, and it's no secret she hasn't exactly had it easy, being relatively close in age to them. Many of them see her as a friend, someone they can confide in. I'd say she's gotten a bit more flack since you two took your relationship public, but Miss Parker knows how to handle those kids."

I stifle a laugh. Handle them she does; see the kid she threatened to put in the ground for calling her a puck bunny.

"Thank you for walking me down here. Olivia always talks about how much she loves working for you." Those words have never once left her mouth, but Ray's face lights, so I know I've done my due diligence as a boyfriend.

I slip through the door, leaning against it before it can close as I watch her work. Sometimes I learn the most interesting things about her when she doesn't know I'm watching.

The volleyball net is up, and Olivia's got a ball on her hip, clipboard in her free hand, while a few of the boys fuck around with balls.

"All I'm saying is if you're embarrassed, say so, Miss Parker." A blond kid bounces a volleyball three times before tossing it toward the basketball net, where it bounces off the rim. "If you've been talking yourself up all this time—"

"I have not been talking myself up," Olivia replies with disinterest, setting her ball down and making some notes on her clipboard. "I don't want to embarrass *you*. Wouldn't want to fracture that male ego of yours. I know how sensitive they can be in the teenage years."

"I'm eighteen. I'm a man."

"Right. How could I forget?"

"You always *say* you can play, but you never show us," another boy starts. "It kinda sounds like you're making it up."

"You are not goading me into playing with you."

Mmm, Olivia is 1,000 percent easily provoked, so . . .

"Look, if it's because you're short—"

She smacks her pen down on the clipboard and fixes the boy who's still talking with a look so dark I'm scared from all the way back here. "Seriously? The short comments? Again?"

Uh-oh.

She tears the ball from his grasp and starts stalking toward me, head down while she mutters to herself. "Stupid freaking short jokes. So freaking tired of them. I get it, my legs are tiny. Ha-ha."

I bite back my laugh, slinking farther into the shadow of the doorway, watching my girl kick off her heels and sink three inches closer to the ground.

She spins toward the net and bounces the ball while she speaks. "I'm only doing this once, so make sure you're watching."

I don't think that'll be a problem. These boys are riveted, as am I.

She spins the ball in her hands before bouncing it. On the third bounce, she catches it, tosses it ridiculously high, takes three massive steps forward, leaps into the air, and . . .

Smashes that damn ball straight across the gym, sending it slamming off the opposite wall and rolling right back to her, while the boys lose their fucking minds.

"Hope you got that on camera to remind you why you don't mess with me."

I have to remind myself I'm in a high school, so blatantly adjusting my junk is maybe not the best idea.

"Holy shit. That was unreal." I walk toward them, gesturing at Olivia, registering the look of shock on her face. "That's my fucking girlfriend, gentlemen!"

"Carter!" Olivia drops the ball, running over on her bare feet. "What are you doing here? You saw that?" She wraps her arms around me, stuffing her face into my chest. "Now you can tell everyone to stop with the short jokes."

Given the high she's riding right now, I feel bad telling her that's unlikely, so instead I tell her, "I'm so proud of you, pip-squeak." I drop my lips to hers. "I had to see you one more time. I hope that's okay."

A devious grin ignites across her face as she looks toward her students, every one of them frozen in place, jaws dropped. "You just earned yourself a teaching spot in third period senior boys' fitness."

"That's cool. I'm good at telling people what to do, and I get to spend a little more time with you before we're separated for a hundred and twenty-seven hours. Not that I'm counting or anything." I press my lips to her ear as she slips back into her heels. "You're so sexy in this teacher outfit."

"You saw me this morning in this exact outfit."

"Yeah, but I was half-asleep, and you just rocked this entire gym. Now I wanna peel it off you but make you keep on the shoes."

Before I can make good on that threat, I clap my hands together. "All right, gentlemen, welcome to gym time with Mr. Beckett."

Nabbing Olivia's clipboard off the ground, I flip through the notes, clicking my tongue against the roof of my mouth.

"Ah, here we are. First order of business . . . which one of you called Miss Parker a puck bunny last Monday?"

"I'M BORED. WANNA GO BACK to the room and play Xbox?" I've eaten two pounds of wings and a plate of nachos and crushed a pitcher with Adam. I've been propositioned exactly zero times, because as soon as a woman takes a single step in my direction, I hit her with a scowl so fierce she dashes away. I'm ready to go.

"Come on." Standing, I take out my wallet and throw down a couple bills. Adam and Emmett start to do the same, but Garrett, who's got a petite blonde at his side wearing his jersey and whispering in his ear, looks absolutely horrified. "You can stay, of course, Gare-Bear."

"But I . . . you . . . *ugh*." His head falls backward with a groan, and he whispers what I assume is an apology in the girl's ear before disentangling himself from her limbs.

The bar is a two-minute walk from the hotel, and by the time we reach the elevator, Garrett's adjusting himself for the third time. "You being in a relationship is killing my sex life, you fucking turkey."

"You have bigger problems if your sex life relies on me."

"It doesn't rely on you, I just . . . it . . . Fuck you." He checks me into the wall when we step into the hallway. "You're obsessed with your girlfriend."

"Yes."

"All you wanna do is go back to the room and talk to her on the phone and tell her how much you miss her and how you can't wait to kiss her and fuck her and cuddle her."

"Also yes." In that order. And then on repeat.

Emmett chuckles as he kicks his shoes off inside the room. He tears open a bag of Ruffles All Dressed chips and flings himself across the couch, shaking his head.

"What are you laughing at, dickhole?" I shove my hand in the bag and steal a handful of chips. We had to bring these from Vancouver. They're hard to find in the States and trust me when I tell you if you find them, you'll be sorely disappointed. They're not the same; it's a fucking travesty.

"Do you remember the night before you met Liv?"

"No." I've blocked out my life before her.

"You kicked some girl out of our room in near tears because she wanted to stay the night, and said you'd never settle down."

"She didn't just want to stay the night. She wanted to move to Vancouver and make my home her home." Fucking Lauren. Or was it Lisa? I don't know, but the night's coming back to me, that's for sure. "And I didn't say I'd never settle down."

"Right. You said the day somebody walked into your life and flipped your world upside down would be the day you'd settle down."

"Mmm." *Delicious chips.*

"Look at you now." It's Adam this time, gesturing at the phone I'm checking for the third time. "Can't tear your eyes off your phone when you're forced to spend some time away from your girl."

"It's almost six full days," I mumble.

He chuckles. "It's fine."

"It's *lame*," Garrett corrects.

"We're just saying . . . the day has obviously arrived."

Yeah, no shit. The day arrived in mid-December when I first laid eyes on her, when she rolled her eyes and did that cute snicker-snort thing, then basically told me to go fuck myself.

Regardless, I'm saved from the conversation when my phone vibrates, Olivia's face lighting up my screen. Before I can answer it, Garrett swipes it and throws himself on the bed.

"Hey, Livvie." He kicks his legs, chin in his palm. "What's up, girl?"

I scream, throwing myself on top of him, because what if she's naked? She was last night, but then again, she knew I was alone. Still, I don't want anyone to see her. Ever. Never ever. *Mine.*

Emmett plucks the phone from the middle of our fight and settles back on the couch. "Hey, Ollie."

"Oooh," she marvels. "Are those All Dressed? I haven't had those in years!"

Shoving Garrett off me, I crouch behind Emmett and smile at Olivia. She's not naked, thank fuck. She is, however, wearing my T-shirt, wet hair leaving drips and drops down her neck and on the gray material, and that does things to me, things that make me grab between my legs.

"I used to lick all the seasoning off before I ate them," she goes on.

My gaze hoods. "I'll buy some for Saturday night."

"Ah, for fuck's fake!" Garrett throws his hands in the air. "How do you manage to ruin chips for me?"

I yank my phone away and flop down on the bed. "I miss you, Ollie girl."

She's sitting up in bed, blankets pooled around her waist, and I think she's on her laptop, based on how much of her I can see. Those cheeks tint pink and I wonder if she'll always blush. I hope so. "I miss you, too, Carter."

"Ah-ah," I tsk.

Rolling her eyes, she huffs a sigh. "I miss you, too, sexiest man alive."

"That's better," I say proudly while everyone else groans.

"Care and I had everyone over for dinner and the game," she tells me.

"Everyone?"

"Your mom, sister, and Hank." She snickers. "He was bragging about being the only male invited to girls' night. And Dublin wouldn't get off my lap all night. I accidentally let him lick my ice cream bowl during the third period, so now I'm his favorite."

The hold Olivia has on my family squeezes my heart. "Thank you for inviting them."

"You don't have to thank me. I like spending time with them." She grins, staring down at her phone before she holds it up to me. Carter, what's this?"

"What's—oh. That." I grin, extra proud. "Just me making sure nobody can spin a web of lies. If my hands are in the air, there's no fake gossip about who I might be touching." The title of the article she's scrolling through basically says as much:

"Carter Beckett wants the world to know: he is OFF-LIMITS, ladies!"

I maybe, *potentially*, have been making a conscious effort to throw my hands above my head and smile at whatever camera flashes my way whenever girls have tried to talk to me this week.

Olivia shakes her head, laughing. "Could your grin be any prouder in this picture?"

"What can I say? Letting the world know I'm yours makes me happy."

Garrett chucks a pillow at my head. "Get a fucking room! Nobody cares how balls deep in love you two are."

Adam reaches for my Oreos on the table, but frowns and crosses his arms when I shoot him a look. "Seriously, how long are you two gonna dance around the words we all know you're dying to say?"

"Give them a break." Emmett flops down beside me, smiling at Olivia, and I'm grateful for the distraction.

Until he keeps speaking.

"Carter's still coming to terms with the fact that he loves someone more than himself and Oreos. Ollie's struggling to admit to herself that she's in love with the world's most arrogant, controlling, annoying man. It would be impossible for anybody to wrap their head around such a mind-blowing scenario."

36

LIKE OLIVIA, BUT TALL, AND MINUS THE BOOBS

Carter

IF I WERE TO ADD up all the hours, I'm certain I've spent more of my life in arenas than in any other place, including the home I grew up in. They're not new to me, the smell, the noise, the excitement that races up my spine every time I set foot in one.

But it's *this* I've missed: kids dashing around, the smell of freshly baked cookies at the snack bar, the strong coffees every parent clings to to get them through another morning at the rink.

Being here brings a flood of happy memories, years I spent in rinks like this one, my dad teaching me to skate, my parents cheering me on, helping me become the person I am today by supporting my dreams.

Out of the corner of my eye, I catch someone's blatant stare, the way they nudge the person next to them as I check out the board that tells me which of the four rinks I need to go. Being recognized at a place like this on a Saturday morning is inevitable, but this game isn't about me, so I tug my toque down a little farther and find the rink I'm looking for.

A shiver shakes my spine at the sharp bite of the rink as I step inside and up to the plexiglass, watching the girls zip around the ice. My heart cracks wide open when I spot Olivia in the doorway of the bench, talking to a girl who, on skates, isn't that far off in height from her, regardless of this being the eight-and-under league.

"Well, I'll be fucking damned. Carter Beckett, slumming it at the local rink."

I turn to the man sidled up next to me. With dark brown hair and eyes that match, his smirk tells me he's been waiting for this day, but not in the way most people do. There's a baby strapped to his chest, gnawing on a silicone hockey skate. He's got a glob of drool dangling from his chin, coating his dad's jacket.

"Should you be swearing right now? Doesn't seem like a very good impression to set for little Jem."

Surprise paints his face when he realizes I know exactly who he is, but how could I not? He looks remarkably like Olivia except—

"Damn it, she really does look like me, doesn't she?"

"Except—"

"Except I have a kid strapped to my chest instead of a pair of tits?"

"I was gonna say the height difference, but sure, we'll go with that." Olivia's tits are perfect, but something tells me he wouldn't appreciate that elaboration.

"What are you doing here? Ollie didn't say you were coming."

"She doesn't know. I'm not supposed to come to any games."

"And you came anyway?"

"Mhmm. Caught an early flight back."

Jeremy's brows jump, but his gaze is cautious. "You paid for your own flight back instead of flying with the team? Why would you do that?"

Because I'm obsessed with your sister? "Because I wanted to see Ollie coach and watch Alannah play." I turn back to the ice where Olivia's still talking to that brown-haired girl. Laughing, she grips her cage and gives it a little shake. "Five bucks says that's your daughter."

Jeremy chuckles. "Yeah, Alannah rarely leaves her side."

She throws her arms around Olivia's middle, hugging her tight, before stepping onto the ice. Her eyes roam the stands, and when they settle on Jeremy, her face lights up and she waves.

And then she sees me.

Her stick clatters to the ice, jaw hanging as she stands there, staring. And then shrieking. She's shrieking, and I'm laughing. She jumps up and down on her skates before rushing back to the bench and crushing Olivia in another hug that nearly knocks her on her ass.

"Thank you, thank you, *thank you*, Auntie Ollie," she shouts, and Olivia looks from Alannah, to the stands, to her brother, to . . .

Me.

I wink, wiggling my fingers at her. Her face ignites with the most brilliant, cheek-splitting beam.

"Damn," Jeremy mutters. "Was totally counting on her being pissed at you for showing up unannounced."

Before I can agree, Alannah whips across the ice, leaps into midair, and slams her lanky body against the glass in front of me.

"I'm gonna score a goal for you!" she shrieks.

"What about me?" Jeremy asks. "You gonna score one for your old man?"

Alannah scoffs. "Get lost, Dad. There's a new man in town."

Jeremy swears under his breath before gesturing toward the stands. "Well, come on. My wife refuses to stand, and she's had her panties in a knot since she saw you walk in here."

OLIVIA'S TEAM CRUSHES THE OTHER. Halfway through the second period, she has to tell them to ease up. Alannah scores two goals and gets an assist, and like she's got my DNA, she points at me after both goals before winding up her arm and pretending her hockey stick is a guitar and she's rocking out to a wild solo. Her mom, Kristin, is mortified, burying her face in her hands, and Jeremy and I battle for the loudest adult in the stands.

I win, obviously, but Jeremy will try to tell you differently. Maybe that's why when the girls exit the change room together, we elbow each other out of the way, trying to be the first one to get to them. I win again. Obviously.

Olivia's attaches herself to me, and I feel whole again. "You're here, and I'm not even mad about it."

"Does that mean I get to do more stuff I'm not allowed to do?" For example, there's this hole that I—

"No."

Damn it.

Hooking a finger under her chin, I bring her lips to mine for a soft kiss, ignoring the gagging noise her brother makes. "I missed you, pip-squeak."

"Hey." The little girl at Olivia's side gives me a half wave before leaning against the wall, arms and ankles crossed. She flicks her head up in a nod. "Hi. What's up? I'm Alannah. You can call me Lana. Or Lanny. Or Al. Or Allie. Or just . . ." She lifts a lazy shoulder and lets it fall. "Alannah."

I don't have a chance to respond before her small fists are at her mouth, doing nothing to hide the shriek that gurgles in her throat. She launches herself at me, gangly limbs wrapping around my body.

Chuckling, I hold her tight. "You kicked some serious ass out there, Lanny. Oh shit. Am I allowed to say ass? Oh shit. I said shit. Shit, I said it again." *Hey Google, how do I stop swearing?*

"Daddy says bad words all the time." Alannah hops down. "Sometimes Mommy makes him go down to the basement for a time-out, and then he has to put money in the swear jar. Then Mommy uses that money to buy new shoes and the fancy wine."

My gaze slides to Kristin. "How much money do I owe the swear jar?"

"Four swears equals four dollars." She holds out her hand. "Pay up, buddy. Mama needs the fancy wine."

I slap a ten in her hand and tell her to keep the change, because I'll probably owe more by the end of this day.

Alannah rummages through the messenger bag hanging off Olivia's shoulder, coming out with a Sharpie. "Can you sign my stick?"

"Can *I* sign *your* stick?" I shake my head as I scrawl my name over the taped blade. "Dude, I should be asking you to sign mine after the way you played."

"*Dude*." Alannah lets out a puff of giggles as she swoons back onto Olivia. "Carter Beckett just called me dude."

I wink. "What are you guys up to now? Can I take everyone to lunch?"

"*Yes!* I'm having lunch with a superstar, I'm having lunch with a superstar," she sings, doing some sort of weird dance. Flossing, I think it's called?

"Oh, well, we have that thing . . ." Jeremy scratches his head.

Kristin slaps his hand away. "We have no thing. Don't pretend like you aren't fangirling hard right now. You can't wait to text all your friends." She smiles at me. "We'd love to have lunch. Thank you so much, Carter."

"Where are we going?" Alannah asks as I sling my arm around her shoulders and head for the parking lot.

"Well, what's your favorite food?"

"Pizza and chicken wings, dude!"

"*Dude*." I drop my head back with a groan. "We're gonna be best friends."

"Can I ride with you, Carter?"

I shrug. "Doesn't matter to me."

"Please, please, please," she begs her dad, gripping his coat, giving him a shake.

"Fine. But you have to take your booster seat."

"I'm almost eight." Alannah huffs, crossing her arms and popping her hip out, real Attitude-y Judy. "Car seats are for babies."

"And when you're eight, you can ditch the booster." He shoves it into my chest with a grin, as if I have any fucking clue how to install this thing. "But for now, you're still my ittle-wittle baby."

Olivia laughs at the face I'm making, taking the seat and clipping it into my backseat. "You're an angel," she whispers, kissing me on the cheek. "I came with them, so I can ride with you, but my bag for the weekend is still at home."

"Perfect." Because I'm slightly terrified to be alone with a child. Surely I can't be trusted with a little person's life? I'm barely an adult myself.

Forty-five minutes later, I'm six pieces deep in one of the three pizzas at our table, I've lost count of how many wings I've eaten, and I'm highly impressed at the way Alannah tries her damnedest to match me bite for bite.

"Holy cow." She clutches her stomach. "You can really eat."

"I'm a big boy. I need all the food I can get."

"Yeah, you're huge! Auntie Ollie's a little baby pip-squeak compared to you!" She gives Olivia a pitying smile. "No offense. You have to be careful you don't crush her when you hug her, Carter."

Yes, when I hug her . . .

"Can you hold him?" Kristin asks Jeremy, passing baby Jem off as she stands. "I need to use the bathroom."

"Sure," he replies, but the second that baby is in his grasp, he stands, leans over the table, and plops him into my unsuspecting arms.

It's a fucking miracle I don't shriek.

A baby? I don't know what the hell to do with a *baby*.

I hold the little chunker at arm's length. He's still gnawing on that damn hockey skate, drool dripping down his arm. He blinks up at me with these huge blue eyes, gurgles, and giggles.

"Oh shit," I whisper, chuckling. "You're kinda cute, little buddy."

Olivia's elbow hits the table, cheek resting in her palm as she shoots me a wide, dopey grin, so beautiful.

"Do we look cute?" I ask, snuggling Jem into my side. He presses his wet mouth to my cheek in something like a super-sloppy raspberry.

"So cute." It's more sigh than words as her chest deflates.

"Oh. My. *God*." It's Kristin, back from the bathroom. Well, not fully back. She's two tables away, feet glued to the floor while she flaps at the air. She dashes over and whips her phone out. "Can I take a picture?"

She takes about a hundred, just me, Jem, and Alannah before she waves Olivia in, and then Jeremy, who comes begrudgingly, but not really. Then she asks the waiter to take a picture of us all, except she calls us her family and I'm part of it. Olivia blushes and I kiss her warm cheek before smiling once more at the camera.

Because fuck yeah, this girl is my family.

"We should have a sleepover," Alannah says as we head out to the parking lot. "One day, maybe. Like, if you wanted to. I know how to make pancakes. We can crush up Oreos in the batter. Auntie Ollie says they're your favorite cookie, and they're mine too."

"Deal. You make Oreo pancakes and I'll make Oreo brownies. We'll have an Oreo-themed slumber party."

Her face shines like a lighthouse. "Really?"

"Really-really. I'll check my schedule and we'll pick a day."

"You're the best," she tells me, crushing me in a tight hug.

"Seriously, you're a saint," Olivia says to me two minutes later when we're packed into the car, finally alone for the first time in way too long. "You were amazing with her. And don't worry about the slumber party. I'll get you out of that."

"What? Fuck no! Oreo-themed slumber party? That's, like, my dream come true, right after you."

She lifts a brow. "You want to babysit my niece?"

"Fuck yeah. She's fun as hell. We'll take Jem too." I sweep a kiss across her knuckles. "I loved today. I'm glad I got to meet your family. But I can't wait to be alone with you."

"Mmm. Big plans?"

"*Huge* plans. And by huge, I mean my dick."

"Trust me, I knew exactly what you meant."

"Well, as long as you know. You should also know I'm going to destroy you tonight."

She sighs, but it's a happy, pleased sound, so I waste no time getting started the second we walk through the door, throwing Olivia over my shoulder and carting her up the stairs.

"I'm gonna lick every damn inch of this flawless body," I whisper against her lips as I ditch her jeans. My mouth closes over her hip bone, her fingers sinking into my hair as I leave my mark on her.

Her ass hits the bed, and I fall to my knees. With her foot in my hand, I work my way up the inside of her leg nice and slow, driving her wild, until she's wrapping her legs around my head and begging me to lick her.

"Greedy girl." I kiss the wet spot in the center of her panties. "Look; you're already wet."

"Carter." It's a warning, a demand. "Take them off and get to work."

I laugh, inching them down her legs. "I love getting you worked up, bossy girl." My phone rings, but I don't stop. I've been craving this fix for six fucking days, and I'm gonna get it.

"*Carter.*" It's one part desire, two parts irritation, because that phone won't fucking stop, and she starts reaching for it.

"Leave it."

"But what if—"

"*Leave it*," I growl, ripping her panties off.

Her head falls back with a gasp when my tongue flicks out over that swollen bud. "Ohhh, yes."

And my phone rings again.

"For fuck's sake." Tearing myself away from the only place I want to be, I grab my phone, not bothering to check the name first. "*What*?"

"Carter? I . . . I'm sorry."

I sink to the floor, running a hand through my hair at the broken voice on the other end. "Adam? What's wrong, buddy?"

He sniffles. "I just . . . I just got home."

"And?"

"And I . . . Courtney was . . . she was . . ." His voice cracks as he whispers out a barely audible *fuck*. "I'm sorry. I didn't know who to call. I don't know what to do. I don't think I can drive, but I can't stay here. I need to get the hell out." Each word comes out faster than the last until it sounds like he's on the verge of a panic attack.

"Okay, man, take a breath." I wait until I hear that staggered inhale. "Tell me what happened."

"I caught Courtney in bed with someone else."

37

SPOILER ALERT: I DIDN'T LAST A MONTH

Carter

I'VE SEEN ADAM CRY TWICE. Once when his adoptive grandma passed and he couldn't make it home to Colorado in time to say good-bye, and two years ago when we lost in the conference finals. He's someone who puts too much pressure on himself to be better than he is, but he is without a doubt the best, most compassionate guy I've ever met.

And he deserves a thousand times better than this.

His blue eyes are bloodshot and red rimmed, hair a mess when he climbs into the front seat. "Thanks, man." He scrubs his palms over his bouncing knees. "I'm really sorry."

"Do not apologize for this."

"You haven't seen Olivia all week. You flew home early to be with her."

"And now I'm here with you. I'm here whenever you need me, no matter what, Adam. We gotta take care of each other."

"You're right. I'm sorry." He cringes. "Shit. Got it. No more apologizing. Sorry." He sighs. "Fuck."

I clap his shoulder before I back down the driveway. "You want a drink?"

"I want ten."

That's how we wind up at some dive bar tucked away from the hustle of downtown. By some stroke of luck, no Canadian teams are playing tonight, which means it's relatively quiet. The few people here barely spare us a glance as we head to a booth in the back corner.

Adam's two beers deep when he opens his mouth and starts talking.

"I should've known. I *did* know. On some level, at least." Shoving his fingers through his hair, he shakes out his curls. "Things were fine in the off-season, you know? We spent every day together. We got Bear," he says about his pup. "Things started to change as soon as the season started back up." He tosses the rest of his beer back and Garrett immediately refills it for him. "Is it my fault? Is the hockey too much? Maybe I didn't give her enough attention."

"I'm gonna stop you right there." The words are out of my mouth before I know what I'm doing. But Adam's fault? Fuck that. I've known this guy since he stepped off the plane at nineteen, and Courtney came with him. He's been nothing but doting and attentive. "You're the best guy I know. Better than these tools—" I thumb at Garrett and Emmett, their heads bobbing in agreement. "—and definitely better than me. You're nice as hell, funny as shit, and you've always treated that girl like a queen. Whatever happened here isn't your fault."

Courtney's been with him since they were seventeen. She knows this life like the back of her hand, and if anything, the hockey's been what's, unfortunately, kept her hanging on. Adam's got a net worth that would make anyone balk, and it's damn well deserved. He was a first-round draft pick, the goalie everyone wanted, and we were the lucky team that got him.

I don't know when Courtney stopped realizing how lucky she was.

"I'm sorry," he apologizes for the umpteenth time tonight. "What happened last weekend with you and Ollie, I shouldn't have let it go so easily. I just . . . I wanted to believe her. I wanted to believe that whatever happened, she wasn't in her right mind."

"I get it, man. I do. You wanted to hang on to what you had." I can't imagine it's easy to say good-bye to seven years, no matter the circumstances.

"At the same time," Emmett adds, "you need to recognize the reality of what's happening, what's *been* happening, and respect yourself enough to make a decision that's going to benefit *you*. You need to be selfish here. What do you want? What do you need?"

"Oh, I told her to get the fuck out," Adam says with a dark, albeit tired, chuckle, the weathered vinyl cracking as he sinks farther back into the booth. "Told her she needs to be gone by the time I get home. I won't let her walk all over me." His eyes focus on his glass before flicking back up. There's resolve there, resignation. A little sad, but mostly, he seems at peace. "Anymore."

Our quiet night is well on the way to wild within an hour. Half our team shows up, and there are eleven empty pitchers on the giant table we've relocated to. I'm the only sober one at the table, and my thoughts won't slow down.

All I want to do is hold on to everything good I have with Olivia, every bit of heaven I find in her, in us. Because what if one day it's gone? What if one day is the end, though I swear the end will never come? What if she gets tired of the traveling, tired of being alone too often? What if she decides that there's someone who can love her better than I can?

There fucking isn't, I'll tell you that right now. And I guess all I wanna do is get home and show her every reason why she'll never need another man for the rest of her life.

My phone vibrates, and I smile at the picture Olivia's sent me, a response to me asking what she ordered for dinner. Her beautiful, silly face grins up at me from my phone as she drops what looks like pad thai into her mouth, so I'm gonna gobble the fuck out of that when I get home.

If you're wondering if I'm talking about the food or Olivia, the simple and obvious answer is both. C'mon, don't you know me by now?

Adam's chin lands on my shoulder, his breath warm on my cheek, heavy on the beer and whiskey he's been pounding as he checks out the picture. "She's a good one, Beckett. Don't let her go." Then he whirls around, throws one arm in the air, and screams, "Another round of shots!"

The entire bar erupts. Yes, the *entire* bar. Adam's been buying shots for every person in here. Except I've secretly been footing the bill, so that means *I'm* buying another round.

Thankfully, once it's handed out, Adam suggests we take the party back to his house. We're garnering a lot of attention and the bar is now packed. I suspect the video of Adam standing on the bar with a shot glass in hand as he made a toast that roughly—*and much more respectfully*—translated to *bros before hoes* has already gone viral.

I pay the tab, load my SUV up with drunk teammates, stuffing the rest into Ubers. Adam and Garrett are whining nonstop about pizza, so I grab three party sizes on the way.

Adam bursts through his front door with a steaming slice in both hands, singing "Highway to Hell" of all songs as his cute pup comes racing. He manages to scoop him up without letting go of his pizza, even though Bear, a Tibetan Mastiff, has gotta be at least eighty pounds by now at seven months old.

Adam skids to a stop at the edge of his living room. "What the fuck are you doing here?"

"I live here," Courtney responds nonchalantly from where she's sitting on the couch, feet on the coffee table, bowl of popcorn in her lap. She sips her wine without looking up at us and turns the volume up on the TV.

"Not any-fucking-more you don't."

Adam shoves his pizza and dog into my chest, fists on his hips as he steps in front of Courtney. I set everything down, because Bear is simultaneously trying to lick my face and eat the pizza.

"Could you move? You're blocking my view."

There's a pulsing vein in Adam's neck that looks dangerously close to bursting. There's a part of me that wouldn't mind seeing it, if only because Courtney's reaction to being covered in blood would be so fucking worth it. But I'd prefer my friend doesn't die, so I reach over the back of the couch, pluck the remote from her lap, and turn the TV off.

"He asked you to leave."

Courtney ferocious gaze hits mine. "Stay the hell out of this. It's none of your business, *Carter*."

"You hurt my best friend and now you're sitting here, continuing to hurt him, so, yeah, it is my business. Get a bag together and leave. We'll arrange to have the rest of your stuff dropped off."

Maybe I'm overstepping; I don't know. All I know is she needs to go before Adam loses it. Drunk and angry is never a good combination.

Courtney springs to her feet. "Adam, this is fucking ridiculous! Tell Carter to leave me alone!"

"You need to go," he whispers. "Now, Courtney."

"This is no big deal! This is stupid!"

Surely, she can't be for fucking real right now.

"You're never home! What am I supposed to do?"

She's for fucking real right now.

"Get out," Adam repeats. "My house, not yours." Courtney reaches for Bear, and Adam guffaws, stepping in front of her. "*My* dog, not yours. You don't feed him. You don't walk him. You don't do shit. Get. Out."

"Where the hell should I go, asshole?"

He holds both hands in front of his face like he's had the most fantastic revelation. "Oh, here's a thought! How 'bout the guy whose dick you were bouncing on three hours ago in my fucking bed?"

I try to stifle my laugh; I really do. But my body does a little shake, and that chuckle somehow slips past my lips. It's contagious apparently, because the rest of the guys follow suit, and even Adam cracks a smile.

"You're an asshole!" Courtney screeches.

"Well, that's rich. I'm an asshole because I'm not going to house the woman who cheated on me?"

"I fucking hate you!"

"Yeah, likewise." Hurt flashes across his eyes. "We're done, which is what you wanted, clearly. And now you need to leave."

"Adam," she begs. The tears sure look real, I'll give her that. "Please. I'm sorry."

"Too late."

The two of them disappear into the garage, and the guys start digging into the pizza and finding the beer in the fridge, drowning out the shouts. Adam emerges, heading straight upstairs, and comes down a few minutes later with a suitcase that he takes into the garage. Two minutes later, Courtney's tires screech as she peels down the street.

"You good?" I clap a hand to his back as he leans on the kitchen counter. Garrett offers him a beer and Emmett thrusts a plate of pizza in his face.

"I will be. Thanks for being here, guys." He rolls up a slice of pizza, shoves the whole thing in his mouth, and washes it down with an entire beer. "Now let's get fucking toasted."

I plant myself on the couch and watch, draining bottle after bottle of water.

"You're not drinking." Emmett flops down beside me. "You know, you live close enough to walk home."

"I know."

"Don't wanna be drunk when you get home to your girl?"

"Not really."

"Ollie would never do that to you," Emmett assures me quietly, like he knows it's what I need to hear. "Never."

"I know." And truly, I do. She would never cheat or intentionally hurt me. But that doesn't mean she'll always be happy with me, that she'll never leave. "I just don't want to ever lose her."

"Time to drop to your knees and beg her to never leave then." He hits me with a loopy grin and a wink before scooting off the couch.

It's perfect timing, because my phone lights up with a photo of her in the bath, up to her neck in bubbles, a goofy, sleepy smile on her face.

> **Me:** ur so beautiful, baby. now aim
> the camera a wee bit lower.

I get a picture of her feet next, painted toes peeking out of the bubbly water.

> **Me:** cheeky girls get punished.

The next picture has me shooting up where I sit, slamming my phone against my chest in case anyone happens to be looking over my shoulder. Because the swell of Olivia's breasts sit on top of the foamy water, her slender, creamy neck on display as her head tips backward, eyes closed and mouth open in what looks a fuckload like a moan. And I'm sitting here at a fucking sausage fest.

"You can go home, man." Adam slings his arms around my shoulders from behind. "Olivia's waiting for you."

"What? What's that mean? Did you see the picture? Oh fuck." My balls are gonna be gone. Separated from my body. *Gone.*

His face scrunches. "Picture? I didn't see anything. What kinky shit are you two up to?"

"Oh." My shoulders deflate. "Nothing. And I'm good here. I don't need to go anywhere."

"Dude, I promise you, I'm good. Seriously. Go be with your girl. I know you missed her. You've been whining all damn week."

"You sure?"

"Hundred percent." He hoists me up, ushering me toward the front door. "We'll keep you updated on any stupid shit that happens here tonight."

"Nothing too stupid." *Fuck, when did I grow up?*

He holds two fingers up. "Plomise."

"Did you say plomise and not promise?" I laugh at the guilty look on his face. "Be good."

I drive a little faster than necessary, eager to get home. Inside, a warm glow floats down the stairs along with the sound of John Mayer, and I rush up to my bedroom, peeling my clothes off along the way.

In the doorway, I stop at the sight before me. My gorgeous girl is sitting on the floor in front of the fireplace with her back to me, the throw blanket from my bed pooled around her hips. Her wet hair is draped over her back, droplets of water shining on her skin in the warmth of the roaring fire, a book in one hand while she hums along with the music.

Somehow, I manage to snap a picture before I walk in there. And when I do, I sink to my knees behind the body I worship, the soul that lights mine on fire, the woman who possesses every single bit of my heart.

"Carter," Olivia gasps when I press my lips to her neck. Her book clatters to the floor as she reaches back, fingers running through my hair.

"You're so fucking beautiful it hurts."

"And you're naked. When did you get naked?"

"On the way up here."

She leans forward, sealing her mouth to mine. Her tongue sweeps inside, deep and welcome, and I cup her face as my heart thrashes against my sternum.

"Can I show you something, Ollie girl?" I whisper against her lips.

"Of course, Carter. What do you want to show me?"

Leaning my forehead against hers, I lay her wet hair over her shoulder before kissing her lips once more. My next breath rocks me to my core, and yet not as much as my next words do.

"I want to show you how much I love you."

38

A LOVE DEEPER THAN OREOS

Olivia

I'M NOT SURPRISED WHEN THE tears spring, streaming silently down my cheeks before I have the chance to attempt to stop them. It'd be pointless anyway. My every attempts at repressing anything when it comes to this man have always been futile.

"You love me?" I whisper, cupping Carter's face. "For real?"

"Fu-u-uck." His voice cracks with a hint of a chuckle as he sinks to his butt. "I love you so fucking much, Ol, I don't know what the hell to do with myself. Been screaming it at you inside my brain every time I look at you for the last two weeks."

"Two weeks? But—"

"I know it's soon. It's really fast. But *I'm* super fast. At, like, everything, so it only makes sense that I'm super fast at this too. I'm a fast learner, so obviously I would nail this down quickly, but just because I did it fast doesn't mean I did it sloppily. I do things exceptionally well, as you know." He aims a pointed look at my crotch, then his own, and wags his brows. He takes my hands in his, squeezing. "I'm going to be really good at loving you, Ollie. I promise. Nobody will ever do it like I do."

My brain can't seem to formulate a response, because I'm too focused on how adorable he always is when he does this anxious ramble bit of his. Only he could find a way to make falling in love a competition.

He swipes at my tears, gaze a little wobbly as it bounces around mine. "I gotta tell ya, gorgeous, I don't know what kind of response I expected, but you crying wasn't it. Are these good tears or bad tears?"

I slam my face against his shoulder to hide the tears that keep rushing, because, how much more could I embarrass myself here?

Carter's hand moves slowly over my back. "Hey, what's wrong, pumpkin? You don't want me to tell you again, okay; I'll tell you every night after you fall asleep. It's what I did last weekend. I think I could do it again if that's what you really want."

"No." Still crying. Cool. More of a wail, if I'm being honest.

"No?" He sweeps his thumb over my lower lip. "If it's too soon, if you're not ready—"

"I love you, Carter." Throwing my arms around his neck and my body in his lap, I tackle him to the ground—all two hundred and twenty-five pounds of him—and assault him with an onslaught of kisses that I cannot foresee ever ending.

He pushes my hair back, letting my tears drop to his cheeks. "So these tears—"

"Happy tears." I sniffle, licking the saltiness from my lips.

Carter's proud beam lights the whole damn room. "Ohhh-ho-ho. My soft little Ollie bear. Have you always been such a fluffy marshmallow?"

"Shut up. You're the marshmallow."

He laughs softly, gazing up at me with a tender, crooked smile. "Say it again, baby."

"I love you."

"Again."

"I love you."

He growls, fingertips digging into my hips as he pushes off the ground, nipping at my lip. "One more time."

I drop my lips to his, a slow kiss coasting across his mouth. "I love you so much, Carter."

"If I had to choose between you and Oreos for the rest of my life, I'd choose you every day, always."

"Such a loaded statement."

His nose trails my jaw. "You know how much I love Oreos."

"I found six boxes in your pantry tonight." I quiver as his breath tumbles down my neck, and when his lips close over the hollow of my collarbone, my head falls backward, granting him the access we both want.

"I'm gonna make love to you all night, Ollie. All. Damn. Night."

I try to answer, but his tongue is swirling around my nipple, so all that comes out is a whimper.

"What was that? Didn't hear you."

"C-C—" The sound fizzles as his hand slips beneath the blanket, fingers gliding through my sopping warmth, coating my clit, making it throb.

"Mmm, still didn't quite catch you there. Try again, princess."

"P-please," I manage, fingers raking through his hair, grabbing those soft waves by the fistful. "Please, Carter."

"Please what?" The glint in his eyes tells me he knows exactly *what*, he's just being his smug self. I think he mostly likes hearing that special word, so I'll give it to him again.

"Make love to me, Carter."

His grin is explosive. "'Kay. One round of superior lovemaking coming up."

He pulls me up, the blanket pooling at our feet. His throat bobs as he looks me over, like he's drinking me in, memorizing every line, every curve, every detail.

With his hand on my neck, he gently brushes his lips across mine. "I love you, Olivia. Thank you for loving me back."

How could I not? He's a dream I never dared to dream. Flawed only in such a way that makes him wonderfully perfect. Kind and goofy with a massive heart, fiercely loyal, wildly passionate. I had been so afraid to love this man, a man who holds so much love in his heart, because I was too scared to see through his past, to know the real Carter.

Every part of me knows that this moment right here, right now, is where I'm meant to be.

Carter grips my waist, my hips, his lips following the path his hands take until he's kneeling before me, gazing up at me. "I've made so many mistakes in my life. So many. But you, Ollie? You're the first thing I've done right."

I want to tell him how wrong he is, how he's been the man that so many people have needed him to be. Before I have the chance to speak, his mouth closes over my center, eyes locked on mine.

Each lash of his tongue is steady and sure, precise and unhurried, and yet I feel myself unraveling by the second, heating from the tips of my toes right up to the top of my head. My mouth opens with a breathy whimper, and his hold on my hips tightens as he pushes me against the wall and tosses my legs over his shoulders.

He's feral, the plunge of his tongue sinful and punishing, the starved suction of his mouth drawing out every moan, every cry as his name tumbles from my lips over and over. I claw at his shoulders when he thrusts two fingers inside me, and he watches me with a heady, dark look as I fall apart at his hands.

He throws me over his shoulder and devours the distance to the bed, tossing me to my belly. When I start crawling up to the pillows, he tsks, fingers closing around my ankles, pulling me right back to the edge. Ass in the air, my toes hit the floor before his palm comes down on the soft flesh, making me gasp.

"I love every part of you." His gravely whisper dots my shoulder with goose bumps as he presses himself against me.

"Including this fucking ass, and I'm still hungry, so you're not going anywhere yet."

He drops back to the floor, and when his tongue pushes inside me again, my cry turns to a full-blown sob. He laps and laves, dives and pulses, fingers dancing, massaging, thrusting, and I'm just *dying, dying, dying*.

"My girl," he purrs, dragging his tongue through my slit at an achingly slow pace, over that tiny hole, and I tear the blankets right off the bed, dying all over again at the way his husky, dark chuckle vibrates against me.

Carter's a savage, ravishing me in a way that makes me feral.

"Fuck me." I bury the breathy request in the fistful of blankets that smother my screams.

"What's that, gorgeous?" His thumb finds my clit, pressing, rubbing, *slow, slow, slow*, dragging that orgasm out as it steals my entire body, leaving me quaking.

Groaning, I mumble the words again.

He pulls my head taut, forcing my gaze to his. "I'm gonna need you to ask again and a fuckload louder, so I know I heard you correctly."

"Oh my *God*, you're so annoying sometimes."

He laughs against my shoulder, teeth pressing into my skin. The hot lash of his tongue soothes the bite of pain. "Annoying you is my favorite thing to do, right after loving you. So ask again and ask nicely."

My eyes narrow as I briefly consider shoving him to the ground and mounting him. But I know how much he thrives on control and I like to give it to him, so I bite my tongue before I give him what he wants.

"Fuck me, Carter. Please."

"Fuck you . . ." He shoves his hand between my body and the mattress, working me up all over again, biting his lip at the way

I moan his name, grind myself against his palm. "Fuck you how?"

"Fuck me like you love me," I say on a gasp.

He impales me without hesitation, a single, punishing thrust that makes my eyes roll, pummeling into me with everything he has while he tells me how much he loves me.

And when I come undone around him, he turns me around and tosses me on the pillows.

"Not done," he growls, looping his arms around my legs and jerking me down to him as my ass slams against his hips. "If you want me to fuck you like I love you, that's a forever kinda thing."

"I like forevers."

A gentle smile touches his lips, and he holds me close as he slides inside me, hips moving slowly, each thrust deeper than the last until it feels like we're one. Soft lips brush mine, and when my mouth opens on a cry, he swallows his own name.

"One kiss, Olivia. One kiss and I was done. My world obliterated the second my lips touched yours."

A lone tear escapes, and Carter's lips touch my cheek, stopping it in its tracks.

His pelvis rubs against my clit with every roll of his hips, and scorching hot flames lick at my spine as his pace quickens, his breath choppy against my neck.

"Ready?"

I nod, squeezing around him as unbridled pleasure rockets through me, singeing every nerve ending in my body. Carter's mouth latches onto mine, his tongue delving inside as we come together, bodies trembling, my nails leaving a path of a destruction down his back in their wake.

"Fuck me," Carter wheezes as he pulls me into his chest. "I one thousand percent love you more than Oreos."

*

CARTER LEANS ON THE COUNTER across from me in nothing but a pair of boxers, eyes trained on me as he shovels noodles and spring rolls into his mouth.

My legs swing happily from my spot at the kitchen island, and I smile at Carter as I tip my head back and open my mouth, dropping a forkful of noodles inside.

"If all you wore for the rest of your life were my dirty T-shirts, that'd be good with me."

"I like wearing your dirty T-shirts. They smell like you." He's my favorite smell, all smoky woods and lime, and all I want to do is have his scent hug me all day long.

I set my plate down on the counter. "Can I ask you something?"

"Mhmm. Anything."

"How come you've never dated before?"

His face screws up with surprise, followed by disgust, making me giggle.

"You're a natural, Carter. You're incredible at every part of a relationship, and I think you like it. Why did you avoid it for so long?"

He sets his plate down in the sink, skimming his jaw while he thinks. "In high school, I was too focused on training and getting scouted to make time for a relationship. I could've, but it wasn't what was important to me at the time. Hockey was my only passion, my only focus, and I didn't want anyone to get in the way. When I got drafted, my dad warned me not to jump into anything. He told me that it would be difficult to see through everyone, to sort out the people who genuinely cared about me from the ones who only cared about the fame and money. He didn't tell me not to date or anything, just . . . told me to be careful. To take my time getting to know people, to be sure."

Carter scratches his head and laughs quietly. "That scared me more than anything, not being able to tell. Scared me enough that I didn't even want to try it. I mean, I saw it right away. The team took me out before our first game, and this girl . . ." He trails off with a sheepish glance in my direction. "It's not important. I knew from the beginning that's all a lot of women saw me as: a meal ticket."

A frown tips the corners of my mouth. Although he may have reaped the benefits, it mostly sounds like a lonely life.

"Don't be sad for me." He closes the distance between us and lifts me against him, carrying me back up the stairs, settling me in the bed we remade after I tore it apart.

Carter pulls his shirt off my body and tosses his boxers to the floor before he crawls into bed, and I curl into his side.

"After my dad died, I wanted no part in relationships. When he died, my mom . . . She was crushed. Still is, honestly. She couldn't function for nearly two years. I started to think she would never recover, and I don't think she ever fully will. I know she seems fine, and she's the strongest woman I've ever known. She's come such a long way. But there are still those quiet moments, those days where she doesn't speak, where all she does is think, remember. They were so in love, and I know they'll never lose that, but now all she has is the memories of what that felt like."

Those green eyes shine with unshed tears as he looks down at me, and my nose tingles with my own urge to cry. For once, I'd like to be the strong one for both of us, so I kiss his chest and run my fingers up and down his arm.

"I guess I never wanted to be able to have that effect on a person, or vice versa. It's scary to think that losing somebody can absolutely crush your soul like that, that you'll spend the rest of your days living out your life, waiting for the moment you can be together again."

Well, there goes that strength I was holding on to. It slips out of my eyes, falling on his chest, and Carter chuckles quietly.

"I know you think your tears are a weakness, Ollie, but they show me how huge your heart is."

All I want to do is thank him. Thank him for letting me know him, the real him. Thank him for choosing me to be the person he does this with. Thank him for loving me, for opening up to me, for being everything I need and then some.

But "I'm sorry" is what tumbles from my lips. "Sorry I was afraid for so long."

Carter smiles, brushing his thumb over my bottom lip. "Don't be sorry. I've learned that fear isn't a bad thing. It shows you what's important to you and how hard you're willing to work for it. And I've been afraid of a lot of things in my life, Ollie, but never as afraid as I am at the thought of losing you one day."

He tucks my hair behind my ear. "You know what I think? I think we're afraid of the things that have the power to change our lives. My life changed for the better that day I locked eyes with you. So much for the better, Ollie. I'm better when I'm with you."

Carter brings out a different side of me, makes me feel things I never felt before, face the things that scare me. I can spend my time yearning for the small amount of time wasted by me being afraid to love him, to let him love me. Or I can be grateful for where we are now, the love we share and the relationship we've built in such a short time, the love that gets so much stronger, deeper, every single day.

Carter's lips meet mine in a tender kiss that brews a fire in my belly. "Stay with me forever. Please. I'll be everything you need."

I look into the eyes of the man I love and my heart swells with pride at who he's grown to be, the way he's supported the people he loves, and how he's moved past his own hurt. "I want you to be you, Carter. And you already are everything I could possibly ever need and more."

He turns out the light, curling his body around mine, holding me tight as he makes me a promise.

"I'm gonna love you the way you deserve to be loved every single day for the rest of your life and my life. I promise."

39

IS THAT A MARIACHI BAND?

Olivia

THE UNIVERSE WAS LAUGHING WHEN it planted Carter's birthday on Valentine's Day.

I know, because I sure laughed when I found out. Carter was unimpressed. He narrowed his eyes and told me I'd better get ready, because he was about to unleash a lifetime of missed Valentine's and cheesy "love shit" on me, and that he was allowed since it was *his* birthday.

I'd be scared, but the threat was harmless. He's been gone for a week and we still have five days to go.

Twelve days. It's our longest stretch apart and I've hated every second of it.

But today Carter is twenty-eight, and I hate even more that I can't spend it with him.

I check my phone while I brush my teeth, laughing at the text from Emmett from late last night that says *Ur boyfriend is a fucking goof*. The attached picture is of Carter at the bar, grinning from ear to ear, a beer in one hand and two deep-fried pickles in the other, wearing one of those *I HEART NY* shirts, which makes sense, since they played in New York last night.

Except instead of *I HEART NY*, it says *I HEART MY GF*.

My brother's sent me an article that contains several similar pictures from different vantage points. The only word he's attached to his message? *Loser*.

My phone rings as I'm finishing up, and I answer eagerly.

"Morning, birthday boy."

Carter's naked. From the waist up, at least. That's all I can see, his broad chest, the smattering of dark hair he scratches his fingers through while yawning, giving me a sleepy smile. "Happy Valentine's Day, beautiful girl."

"How was your night?" I ask, rifling through my closet. It's pink and red day at school today. I'm not much of a pink girl, so I settle on a red T-shirt dress, propping my phone up on my dresser as I start peeling off my pajamas. Carter likes to watch me dress every morning. It's oddly endearing. I enjoy his facial expressions and the way he stumbles over his words.

"You, uh . . ." He swipes his tongue across his lower lip. "You didn't, um . . . yeah. Oh. That's a nice bra. I love you."

"Hey, Ollie!" I hear someone holler, and then Carter's shrieking "No!" Everything goes black, and I yank on my dress and a pair of tights.

"Cover yourself, Ollie!" Carter yells. "*Incoming! Incoming!*"

The phone lifts to Garrett's amused face. "Dang. Not even a bare shoulder."

There's an *oomph* as Garrett gets tackled, and a moment later, Carter emerges looking victorious.

"Sorry. He was supposed to be sleeping."

"Can't a guy get a little Valentine's action around here?"

"Yeah, her name was Reba, and you disappeared with her for about forty-five minutes last night."

Garrett looks at Carter like he's lost his mind. "*Reba*? Her name wasn't Reba. Her name was . . . it was . . ." He scratches his head with a guilty, gritty grin. "Rachel?"

"You guys are the worst." I laugh, moving into the kitchen, keeping my phone trained away from the package of Oreos on my counter and the recipe lying next to it. I found the most deliciously tempting recipe on Pinterest for an Oreo cake to celebrate Carter's birthday when he gets home. I've also framed a photo of us, got him a T-shirt with one of his self-proclaimed nicknames on it, and bought tickets to a VIP showing of the new live-action Disney movie, because it's all Carter talks about. That's about all I have planned, plus a homemade dinner. What the hell do you get the man that has everything he could ever want or need, especially when your own funds are severely lacking?

Cara told me to take a naked picture of myself, blow it up to life size, and hang it above his bed. I neglected to tell her he has an entire album full of naked pictures of me already, and though I'm sure he'd enjoy it, I would not.

"Jason's gonna pick you up for work today," Carter says as I shovel Corn Pops into my mouth.

"What?" I don't need his driver to pick me up and I certainly don't need to be arriving at school in a limo. "Why?"

"Because you shouldn't drive yourself to work on Valentine's Day."

"People have been doing it for years, Carter."

"Yeah, well, your car sucks in the snow, I know it snowed a fuckton there last night, and I can't be with you today, so humor me."

"Bossy man," I murmur, sighing as I stare at the several different kinds of decaffeinated teas in my pantry. I rub my temples and frown at the sting of pain there. Lack of sleep—and lack of Carter—is exhausting and painful.

"Need a coffee this morning, pumpkin?" Carter sets the phone down and disappears, and all I can hear is the sound of water and tinkling. This man pees on the phone way too often. He groans deeply before I hear the toilet flush and the sound of the faucet.

"I think so. I'm so tired this week." I shut the cupboard, deciding on a Starbucks run. "Big plans for your birthday tonight?" They're flying out to Chicago this morning for their game tomorrow. I assume that means—

"Oh, big plans, all right. *Huge* plans. I'm gonna fuck my hand while you fu—"

"Jesus fucking *Christ*," someone grinds out. "There are three other people in this room right now, Carter!"

"Sorry." The way he says it lets me know he's not sorry at all. "I'm gonna spend the night in the hotel room on the phone with you. That's all I wanna do. Naked or clothed." The fire in his eyes tells me I'll absolutely be naked.

Carter keeps me on the phone until Jason arrives to pick me up. The bouquet of flowers he's holding covers a good third of his body, and whatever he's got in that cup and brown paper bag smells like cinnamon and heaven.

"Carter texted that you needed coffee this morning. It's a cinnamon bun latte and a cinnamon bun to go with it. He suggested you to drink half now and half later so your stomach doesn't hurt too much."

My phone dings, the man himself reminding me how lucky I am.

World's Sexiest Man: happy valentine's day, princess. i love u & miss u.

IF YOU KNOW CARTER, AND I think you do, you know he doesn't stop there.

Oh no, why would he?

The second gift arrives after first period. It's a teddy bear wearing Carter's jersey. *Something to hug when I'm not there to wrap you in my arms*, the card says.

The third comes partway through second period. It's a bouquet of chocolate-covered strawberries, and the message tucked in the tiny envelope tells me he's imagining licking the juices from the strawberries off my body. I shove that note in my pocket real fast and share the strawberries with my junior girls.

The fourth comes right before lunch. It's Jason again, and he's got a bag of food and a box filled with leggings and yoga pants from Lululemon. *Your ass looks too good in these to only have one pair*, this note says. *It's a travesty.*

I pray that's it, but in true Carter fashion, he saves the most embarrassing gift for last.

"Madam." Brad bows as he opens the gym doors.

"Bradley." I eye him suspiciously as he gestures me into the gym. "Thank you."

Him holding the door for me is the first clue something isn't right. The second is that the lights are off.

Heart racing, I scramble to flick them on, stopping short at the sight in front of me.

"No," I whisper, shaking my head. "He didn't."

But oh, he did.

The gym erupts with music, the sound of guitars and violins and trumpets bouncing off the walls, and my jaw drops in horror.

It's a mariachi band. A fucking mariachi band. Carter hired a fucking mariachi band to serenade me at school.

"This can't be real," I mutter out loud, one hand on my cheek, the other over my mouth.

"Isn't this great?" my principal shouts, shaking a maraca—and his hips.

One of the boys takes my hand and starts spinning me around, but I'm stiff as a board and wind up stumbling over my own feet.

When the music ends, the only thing to be heard above the applause is the cackling. The piercing, high-pitched, evil cackling.

Cara falls out of my office with her phone in hand. She keels over, slapping both knees as she howls with laughter. "Oh my God.

That was priceless." She's crying. I might be too. "You shoulda . . . your face . . . *Oh my God!* This video is gold, Livvie, pure gold! Carter's gonna lose it!"

Oh, he's gonna lose it, all right.

I'm exhausted by the time I get home. All I want to do is take off my bra and devour a pizza in the tub before inevitably passing out mid-FaceTime with Carter.

The man has managed to avoid every single one of my text messages today. At first, I suspected he was scared after the mariachi band. Then I realized he's probably getting some sort of sick enjoyment out of it. He likes to get me riled up. Something about hot sex when I'm mad at him. Except we can't benefit from hot, angry sex tonight, and that thought is more depressing than it should be as I step inside.

I'm not surprised by the red and pink foil heart balloons taking up my entryway, or the small gift they're attached to. He got Cara to film the mariachi band debacle, so of course he got her to finish the day with one more gift at home.

Running my finger along the edge of the pink envelope, I pull the card out. There's a picture of a smiling octopus on the front, and it says *I wish I were an octopus so I had eight hands to touch your butt with.*

The inside of the card? Way better than the outside.

Ollie Girl,
I've made a lot of mistakes, lived my life a little too carelessly, in ways that people didn't approve of. But I wouldn't change a thing. Because I was waiting for you. Waiting for a love that would walk into my life and blow my whole world up.

   I want to celebrate every Valentine's Day & birthday with you.
Love, Carter

I'd like to say the tears are unexpected, but they're not. I've come to learn that every time this man opens his mouth, there's a solid chance he's going to make me laugh or cry in the best way. I don't know where he came from, but I do know I never want to let him go.

The tiny package reveals the most beautiful bracelet. Set on a dainty golden chain is a small heart, the letters *C* and *O* hanging next to it. I slip it on, knowing the last thing I'll be doing tonight is falling asleep on Carter.

One step into the hall, and my heart stops when I spy the rose petals scattered on the floor, leading to my bedroom. My pulse races, every nerve ending alive with anticipation as I follow the trail of petals, the soft music that coaxes me there, the gentle flicker of candlelight against the open door.

"Carter," I breathe out before I even see him.

And when I do . . . oh boy, when I do . . .

"Paint me like one of your French girls," he whispers in a deep, husky voice from where he's sprawled out on my bed, totally naked, save for the box of chocolates on top of his crotch.

My face shatters with a grin at the sight of him. It takes everything in me to resist the urge to jump on him, instead planting my hands on my hips and arching a brow. "Is there actually chocolate in that box, or is the present your dick? Did you cut a hole in the box so you could stick your dick through it, Carter?"

His smile falls. "No. Fuck. Why didn't I think of that?" He looks down at the box, contemplating. "And fuck you! This box is way too small to house my dick and you know it!"

I can't hold back anymore, erupting with laughter as I bound over to him, leaping into his arms and crushing my mouth to his. "Happy birthday. Happy Valentine's Day. What the hell are you doing here? You're supposed to be in Chicago. I love you."

"I wanted to spend today with you," he says between kisses. "I fly out at four-thirty tomorrow morning."

I push on his chest, forcing him to his back as I start pulling off my dress. "So we should go to sleep early tonight."

"I'll sleep on the plane," he growls, jerking my tights down my hips.

I swipe the box of chocolates off his crotch, stopping at the gift below.

No, literally. Carter's tied a red ribbon around his dick. I lift an amused brow as I trace the silk, watching that thick muscle jump.

His grin is devilish. "You can unwrap him, but only after you put on your outfit." He gestures toward my closet, where a beautiful piece of crimson lace and silk hangs from the door.

"Oh, Carter." I climb off the bed and finger the lace, the thick silk ribbons that seem to—just barely—hold it together. "It's stunning. I love it."

"I thought you'd like it. That's why I bought two."

"Two?"

"Uh-huh." Those mossy eyes storm over. "Because I'm gonna fucking destroy that one when I rip it off of you."

There's no point in trying to quell the fire that spurs inside me at his words. I'm going to let him destroy this and me like he always does, and then I'll enjoy every second of the way he puts me back together.

I slip into the closet to change, admiring the ribbon I tie into little bows at each of my hips. "You know, when you said outfit, I was scared it might be that *I heart my girlfriend* shirt you were wearing last night."

"No, that's for later."

My fingers halt. "Later?"

"Yeah, I got you a matching boyfriend one. We're wearing them to dinner later. They're in your dryer right now."

"Carter!"

"*Olivia.* Get your sweet ass out here before I come after you."

"You must know that's not a threat."

"I'll get my face printed on your boyfriend shirt."

Yep, that'll do it. That'll get my ass into gear.

Carter's sitting on the edge of the bed when I step out of the closet, and when his gaze comes to me, his jaw drops. "Sweet. Fucking. *Christ*." He twirls his pointer finger in the air. "Imma need you to do a three-sixty for me, nice and slow."

He hums appreciatively while I spin, biting his knuckles. "Get . . . get over here. Now. Right now."

My steps are slow and purposeful, a little nervous. He's everything I could ever ask him to be, and I want to be the same for him.

He reaches for my hands, tugging me between his muscular thighs. Fingertips dance up the lace, along the ribbon. He tugs one end, watching as the middle falls open, letting my breasts drop, before he quickly ties it back together and rests his forehead against my stomach, whimpering.

I repeat, Carter Beckett is whimpering.

His gaze torches my skin. "Now I need you to lay back and be a good girl."

"A good girl?" I absolutely flutter my lashes. For dramatic effect.

"Uh-huh. You know how to do that?"

I trail the tips of my fingers over his thighs. "I'm not sure. What does being a good girl entail?"

"Doing everything I say."

"Everything?"

Carter's smirk is all dangerous, naughty decisions mixed with a heaping side of pure lust and tender love that's been put on the back burner for the last week. "*Everything*. And you can start with sitting that perfect fucking pussy right over my face."

*

THE BIRTHDAY BOY IS HUNGRY tonight. He's currently working on his second entrée, even after feasting on me for two hours straight, and he doesn't look anywhere close to being sated. That's the only logical explanation as to why his hand is beneath the table, where it's been all evening, stroking my leg.

"Can I tell you something, Ollie girl?"

"Of course."

He stirs his pasta around his plate. "I've never been with anyone before for Valentine's Day. Or my birthday." His cheeks tint as he raises his gaze to me, looking me over in the warm glow of the candles. His eyes land on my shirt—yes, he wasn't joking about the *I HEART MY BF* shirt; I'm here, and I'm wearing it— and he smiles. "Valentine's Day means a lot to some people. People don't want to be alone. They want hope for more. But I . . . I never wanted it to mean anything. Not then, at least. And my birthday, it was my day, my time. I didn't want to spend it pretending, not even for one minute."

He looks down at his plate, smiling. "My mom said she was happy I found someone that makes me want to fly all the way home just to be with her on this day. The best part, for me, is that I'm still not pretending. I get to be myself, and there's no one else I want to do this with, today and every day."

My heart squeezes in my chest, and he leans across the table, taking my chin between his fingers and kissing my lips.

He settles back in his spot and clears his throat. "I can't wait to see the new Disney movie with you."

My fork clatters to the table. "What?"

His head bobs as he avoids my gaze. "Yeah, and I owe you a new box of Oreos for my birthday cake. I accidentally ate a row while waiting for you to get home. That recipe looks fantastic, though. Oh, and you know how I washed these shirts? I also washed the one I found in a gift bag, the one that said *Mr. Incredible.*"

"*Carter!*"

He pins me with a sheepish grin that's anything but innocent. "You can't be mad at me. I'm the birthday boy."

40

I WILL SURVIVE

Carter

OLIVIA'S LATE, BUT THAT'S NOTHING new. I don't mind, except I'm terrified her niece and nephew will show up for this sleepover before she gets home. I think I can handle Alannah on my own for a bit, but Jem? He, like . . . requires a responsible adult. I'm a man of many talents, it's true, but responsible rarely makes that list.

I put the finishing touches on the movie fort and check my phone again. No response from Olivia, and the kids are being dropped off in an hour.

Have I mentioned I've never babysat before?

I dial Olivia's number, hand on my hip, foot tapping until I inevitably get her voicemail.

She should've been here an hour ago, and I can't get ahold of her. I try to convince myself it's my controlling streak, but the last time I couldn't get ahold of someone, he was lying dead on the side of the road. Grief does all kinds of fucked-up shit to you, like pushing you past the point of panic when your loved ones are unreachable.

I call two more times in quick succession, and Olivia answers on the last ring, breathless. "Hello?"

The pain in my chest collapses, but my words come out harsher than I mean them to. "Where are you? Why weren't you answering?"

"I . . . I'm sorry, Carter."

The surprise in her tone, the wave of hurt at mine, tells me to take a deep breath and try again. "Are you okay?"

"I'm fine." She sighs, grunts, and I think I hear . . . kicking? Punching? "Stupid . . . fucking . . . snow . . . fucking Canadian winter . . . piece of crap . . . car!"

I swallow my laugh. It's the second day of March. That normally means the arrival of spring, but this winter from hell means we had a snowstorm yesterday. Olivia drives an old Toyota Corolla, and her snow tires are eight years old.

"Where are you, Ol?" It's easier to beat around the bush sometimes than to come right out and ask her what you really want to know, which, right now, is whether she's gotten herself stuck in the snow.

"Down the road from the school," Olivia grumbles.

"Uh-huh. And why's that? School finished at two thirty. It's four."

"I'm stuck," she mumbles.

"You're what?"

"Stuck."

"Say it again, princess. Can't quite hear you over the roar of the fireplace." If I push her buttons right, we can have a quick round of steamy, angry sex with Olivia pushed up against the wall before the kids get here.

Olivia's still swearing at me as I settle into my truck and start backing out of the garage.

"Are you coming to get me?" she asks quietly as my phone connects to my speakers.

"Uh-huh. Which I could've done an hour ago if you'd called me when you first got yourself stuck."

"I didn't—it wasn't—you—*ugh*!" She huffs. "I'll be waiting on the side of the road, halfway in the ditch."

That's pretty much exactly where I find her. There's only a foot, maybe, but it's that heavy, wet snow, the kind that doesn't want to move, which means the way she's trying to kick it away from her tires is futile. Her body sags when she sees me, and when she does this dramatic half sprawl over the hood of her car, I love her more than I ever thought possible.

"Well, well, well. Who could have ever predicted little ol' Red wouldn't make it in all this snow?"

"I have snow tires!"

"Hate to break it to you, sweetheart, but when your snow tires have no tread left on them, they're not gonna do their job."

She huffs but doesn't reply, choosing to pin her arms across her chest and frown. Her toque slips down her forehead, and she couldn't look more bothered about shifting it out of her eyes to keep scowling at me, my fierce girl.

"You can't drive this piece of sh—" I halt, catching the slow rise of her dark brows, waiting for me to finish that word I started. "Ssshhhiny red metal. It's not built for Canadian winters."

Olivia throws both arms in the air. The floppy puppy ear mittens make the gesture more cute than scary. "Well, excuse me for not having seven cars to choose from!"

"Five," I murmur.

"What?"

"I only have five cars."

Mocha eyes do an exasperated roll. "That's still four more than the average human. But, oh wait, I forgot—Carter Beckett is anything but average!" Her arms are in the air again, and my teeth press into my bottom lip to keep my smile from turning into a full-blown, shit-eating grin.

"Snarky girls get put on time-out."

All that frustration evaporates, replaced with laughter. Shuffling slowly through the snow, Olivia reaches me and wraps her arms around my middle, chin on my chest as she smiles up at me. "I'm sorry. All five of your cars are pretty, and I love that you're anything but ordinary."

"Mmm." I rock her side to side, hands on her ass. "Would you say I'm superhuman? Your very own superman, perhaps?"

Gripping the collar of my coat, she hauls me down to her, lips brushing mine. "Keep talking, big man. See where that gets you."

"I know exactly where it'll get me—between your luscious thighs." I kiss her nose. "I'm sorry I was upset on the phone earlier, Ollie. I was worried something happened to you, and I let it get the best of me." My thumb brushes over the crease in her forehead, hoping to smooth it right off. When that doesn't work, I kiss the spot and try for humor. "Guess I'm not as perfect as you always say I am."

Olivia takes my face in her hands. "You're perfectly flawed, and I'm going to love you through all your faults, because you love me through mine."

"I fucking love you." I clap a hand to her ass and give her a gentle shove toward the truck. "All right. Follow behind me. I'm parking this thing in my garage 'til the snow is gone."

"But I—I can't . . . I've never driven a truck."

"She's real gentle. Promise."

Olivia looks up at the daunting task before her: climbing up. "I don't think I can . . . Carter, I don't think I can reach. I have little legs."

"*Powerful* little legs." I scoot behind her, crossing my arms as I gesture to the seat with the flick of my head. "Come on. Let's see you work for it."

It's amusing. *Highly* amusing. I start reaching for my phone in my pocket, because I know a few people who would get a kick out of this.

"Don't even think about it," she growls without looking at me. Damn teachers with their eyes everywhere.

With a grunt, Olivia throws herself at the seat, feet dangling off the ground and ass in the air as she clutches the center console and starts dragging herself up. Chuckling, I put her out of her misery, boosting her the rest of the way. Grabbing the shovel out of the truck bed, I make my way back to her car, digging her tires out. She's gotten herself stuck pretty damn good, and it takes me a few minutes of rocking the car back and forth before it wants to move.

I hit Olivia with two thumbs up, then climb into her car. It's way too small for me and my knees hit the steering wheel.

It takes me all of one minute to realize she's one of those people who are anxious about driving in the snow, so I drive three miles under the speed limit the entire way back to my place just to placate her.

She follows me into the garage and hops down from the front seat with an *oomph*. "That wasn't so bad."

"New snow tires next winter." I slip the truck keys on her ring. "Or an entirely new car." Birthday present? Maybe. I'll have to work her up to a gift that size.

"What are you doing?"

"Adding the truck keys to your key ring?" I arch a brow and hang them up, opening the door to the house. Olivia doesn't budge.

"I can see that. But why?"

"So you can get around safely in the snow." I gesture toward the doorway again.

"Carter, I can't drive your truck every day."

"Sure you can. I have five cars, remember? Don't need this one right now." I tap her nose. "But you do."

"But-but—"

"I do love your butt-butt."

Back go the arms across her chest. "Carter."

"Olivia. We're arguing over something pointless. Your car is giving you trouble and I'd worry less about you if I knew your tires weren't spinning while I'm thousands of miles away. Please, just use it. At least until the snow is gone." Taking her hand, I haul her back to the truck. "And, look!" I press a button on the inside of the door and a side step appears.

Olivia's jaw drops. "There was a step this whole time? And you made me climb in?"

"It was fun to watch. Plus, I got to touch your butt."

Her little fist pummels into my shoulder. "You're a jerk."

"A perfectly flawed, superhuman jerk."

Her nose scrunches as she tries—and fails—not to grin. "I love you."

I wind my arm around her waist and kiss her cheek. "I love you too, pumpkin."

Olivia heads upstairs to get changed, and I start on the Oreo brownies I promised Alannah. My mom invented this recipe for my twelfth birthday. The bottom layer is cookie dough, and I accidentally eat a few spoonfuls while I smoosh it into the pan. Oops.

"*Carter!*"

I smile to myself. I'm 100 percent sure what Olivia's hollering about up there, so I know a little flattery will go a long way. "Yes, my darling?"

"Get up here!"

I head up the stairs, trying to contain myself, and when I enter the bedroom, Olivia's waiting, fists on her hips, foot tapping.

She gestures at the large canvas hanging above the fireplace. "What is that?"

I examine the print, sucking my lower lip into my mouth, gaze following the lines of Olivia's bare shoulders, the droplets of water that cling to her back in the glow of the fire she sits in front of, though I had the picture printed in black and white. "Art."

"Art?"

"Yeah. Art."

Her hands fly around her head. She's so expressive when she talks. "It's not art! It's a picture of me reading! Naked!"

"Correct." I tap her nose for at least the third time in the last half hour, 'cause it's just so cute. "Art. And besides, all you can see is your back."

My gaze coasts down her body, heating on the way. She's in only a T-shirt and panties, so I do what any man would do: push her up against the wall, my hand on her throat.

"I like having you on my wall. I'd print every damn picture of you and cover every inch of this house with your body if it was acceptable, but it's not, and you might rip off my balls, and I like them right where they are."

"Between your legs?" She gasps as I dip my fingers into her panties, admiring how wet she is.

"Yes, but preferably slapping against your ass."

"Carter." Another gasp, this one with a hint of disbelief. The disbelief at my words will wane with time.

"You're always wet for me when you're pretending to be angry."

"I'm . . . not . . . pretending," she chokes out, nails biting into my shoulders as I sink two fingers inside her.

"Is that right?"

Hazel eyes stare up at me as she pants, grinding against my palm. That pink tongue wets her bottom lip before she gives me a curt nod, so I smile and pull my fingers from her sopping warmth.

Her jaw drops. "Carter. No. What are you—"

The doorbell rings and I suck my fingers into my mouth, licking her off me before I clap a hand to her ass. "Come on. The kids are here."

Once I'm washed up and Olivia is fully clothed—and more pissed than ever—I throw open the front door.

"Carter!" Alannah flings her bag to the floor and wraps herself around me.

I barely see Jem before Jeremy is shoving him into my arms.

"Would you quit shoving our son off like you can't wait to get rid of him?" Kristin scolds.

"He wanted to see his uncle Carter." He smirks as he says the name, but the joke's on him; I secretly like it.

Olivia takes Jem, kissing every inch of his face and making me smile.

"Carter." Alannah winks, holding up a bag filled with all the fixings for her pancakes. "I got the stuff."

"Right on, dude. You didn't have to bring it all, though."

"Pfft. It's no big deal, dude."

I sweep my arms up the stairs. "To your room, milady?"

She dashes ahead of me, flopping onto the bed in the room I've directed her to. "Whoa! This thing is *huge*! Oh my God! I have my own bathroom!"

She rushes from room to room, and when she reaches for my bedroom door, Olivia throws herself in front of it with a nervous giggle.

"Um, maybe not this one."

Jeremy's eyes narrow before he brushes past her and into the room. "Whoa." His hands dust over the stone fireplace before he sticks his head in the bathroom, jaw dropping. Crossing the room, he throws open the balcony doors. "Goddamn fireplace on the goddamn balcony."

"Two dollars for the swear jar, Daddy!" Alannah curls her fingers into her palm. "Pay up, buddy!"

He swats her hand away and makes his way back inside, eyes full of wonder. They stop on the picture of Olivia, and she whips open my underwear drawer, busying herself with fluffing my . . . underwear.

"Ollie," Kristin murmurs. "Is this you? It's stunning."

"What? Oh. That. Um . . . no."

Jeremy's eyes screw shut and he gags. "Gross."

Olivia punches him in the arm, tells him to shut up, and storms from the room.

I grin, tucking my hands in my pockets. "Charming, ain't she?"

"WHAT MOVIE NEXT? CAN I stay up past my bedtime?"

Next movie? We've already watched two. This girl is a ball of fucking fire.

I flop my head over my shoulder, pouting at Olivia. "I'm so tired."

She runs her fingers through Jem's fluffy hair as he drools on her shirt. "I warned you."

"You're tired?" Alannah asks. She's got chocolate smeared in the corner of her mouth. *Saving it for later* is what she said when Olivia pointed it out. "You wanna take a dance break? Get our energy back up? Come on, big boy, you're supposed to be fit and healthy."

I thought I was, until kids. Christ, kids are exhausting. Cute, fun, *exhausting*.

Clearing a space for an impromptu dance party, I turn on *Just Dance* and consider that I might actually be too tired to have sex with my girlfriend later tonight. The thought makes me frown, and Olivia's lips find the corner of my mouth.

"She'll be out within twenty minutes of the next movie. Promise."

I spin Alannah around the living room while Olivia twists and dips a giggling Jem, before taking him upstairs to bed.

When Alannah collapses on the floor, I throw her the remote. "Pick the next movie. I'm gonna go check on Auntie Ollie and Jem."

Upstairs, I lean against the door frame, watching as Olivia sings softly to Jem, hips swaying in the moonlight as she holds him, looking out the windows at all the stars. With a soft sigh, she kisses his forehead and lays him down in the playpen.

"I love you, Jemmy," she whispers.

I catch her around the waist, and her breath snags in her throat, nails biting into my biceps.

"Carter," she breathes into the dark. "I didn't see you."

"But I saw you. And I love you, so fucking much."

I hold her close for a minute, reveling the peace having her in my arms brings me, my own slice of heaven.

Downstairs, we find Alannah lounging in the middle of the fort, munching on pizza.

"I picked *Inside Out*. The girl plays hockey! There's never any movies about girls playing hockey." She rests her head on my shoulder with a happy sigh when I lie down beside her, and laces her fingers through Olivia's.

And Olivia's right, as she often is. Alannah's out cold fifteen minutes into the movie. We give her another fifteen, to be sure, before I haul her into my arms and upstairs.

"Carter?" Her bleary eyes flutter slowly when I tuck her in. "This was the best ever slumber party." She hugs me close. "I love you, dude."

My chest tightens. "I love you, too, little dude."

She waves at Olivia across the room. "Night, Auntie Ollie. I love you."

"Love you, too, fierce girl."

My shoulders sag with relief when the door clicks closed behind me. "I did it. I survived my first sleepover."

"Oh, you sweet, naïve fool. It's not over 'til they're gone." She slings her arms around my neck. "You're not too tired to fuck your girlfriend, are you?"

"Well, I—" My words die a gurgle as her palm closes over my cock, and he rockets to attention. I toss Olivia over my shoulder, dashing down the hall.

"The sword of thunder is never too tired."

41

DILF-ING SO HARD

Olivia

I'm alone when I wake up, which isn't how I'm accustomed to waking at Carter's, nor how I prefer to. My personal favorite is with his head between my legs, or his fingers, and both are often, but beggars can't be choosers.

There's a mug of tea waiting for me on the small table beside the bed, so I can't complain.

I'm not shocked to find Alannah's bed empty, but definitely surprised to find no Jem. Carter likes the little guy and enjoys his snuggles, but I'd be lying if I said he didn't always look mildly petrified that Jem might do a baby thing while Carter's holding him, like poop or cry.

The kitchen's a disaster, there's pancake batter everywhere—a surefire sign that Alannah was in charge of breakfast—and there's nobody in sight, which slightly frightens me.

I pause at the top of basement stairs, the sliding barn-style door cracked, music drifting through it. "Carter?"

"Down here, Ol!"

I stroll through the extensive home theater next to the game room—I know, the irony that we prefer to build a fort—and finally find them in the impressive home gym.

Jem is strapped to Carter's chest, gnawing on that silicone

hockey skate he loves so much. The sight has my lady parts doing a little dance, and I shift a little uncomfortably where I stand.

"Hey, pumpkin. You found us."

He and Alannah are sitting side by side, doing bicep curls. Alannah's weights are tiny and pink, and with each curl, she grunts out a *huuu*.

"Hey, Auntie Ollie. Oh yeah, baby. Feel the burn!"

I press a kiss to Jem's hair before Carter lifts his lips to mine. "Aw, darn. Looks like I missed the workout."

The look Carter flashes says he's onto me. He catches me staring more than he catches me doing any actual work. "We thought we'd let you sleep in. And I don't wanna brag, but I'm killing it."

"He even changed Jemmy's stinky bum!" Alannah thumbs proudly at her chest. "I helped Carter get Jem's breakfast ready."

"And *I* fed him." Carter looks just as proud, bouncing him around on his chest.

The three of them are so freaking adorable together it hurts, and I quell the urge in my ovaries to start reproducing.

Not now, babymakers.

"Quit looking at me like that."

"Hmm?" I pretend to be interested in the squat rack. "Like what?"

Carter juts a hip and winks. "I look good, don't I?"

"Meh."

"Meh?" He steps closer, peeking over his shoulder—Alannah's occupied with an incredibly energetic round of jumping jacks—before his lips touch my neck. "I think I look hot. I'd make one helluva *DILF*, wouldn't you say so, Ollie girl?"

My heartbeat settles between my thighs, and before I can pretend the thought hasn't crossed my mind, Alannah pops between us.

"What's a *DILF*?"

"A dad I'd like to fff—" Carter slams his mouth shut, eyes bugged at me for saving. I'm not going to save him. He got himself into this; let's see him get out of it. He smiles at Alannah and pats her head. "Fish with. A dad I'd like to fish with."

Her nose scrunches. "Wouldn't that be a *DILFW*? Because *with* starts with a *W*. So you have to add the *W*, Carter." She tilts her head, gives him an assessing once-over and a patronizing pat on his arm, before she walks away.

Carter guffaws, twisting to call after her. "Hey, sassy pants!"

She grins at him, all devil.

"You ready to go skating?"

Her resounding shriek as she tears her way up the stairs is answer enough, and a half hour later, the four of us are stepping out on the ice at Rogers Centre, which is something I never, ever thought I'd say. But being the captain of the Vancouver Vipers affords you certain luxuries, like convincing them to let you use the ice before they fix it up for the game this afternoon.

With Jem strapped to my chest, all snuggled and cozy, Carter helps me step over the threshold, and I do a slow spin, marveling at the sight.

"I don't wanna wear my helmet."

"You have to wear your helmet."

"But you're not wearing *your* helmet."

I twist in the direction of the bickering, Alannah's fists on her hips as she argues with Carter. He's holding her helmet out to her and she is adamantly looking anywhere but at it.

"I'm an adult. My brain is fully developed. Yours isn't." He knocks on his toque-covered head. "Gotta protect those growing brain cells, Lanny."

"But—"

"No buts. Helmet on or no skating, little miss." He shrugs. "Seems like an easy choice to me."

Oh my. Is it hot in here, or is it just me?

Alannah throws her head back with a groan before letting Carter snap her helmet into place.

He gives her cage a shake. "There. That wasn't so bad, was it?"

I spy her smile from here as she swats his hand away. "You're just like my dad."

"Handsome?"

"*Annoying.*" With a snicker, she hops onto the ice, steals the puck from between his unsuspecting feet, and takes off like a bat out of hell.

Carter's not far behind her, and before she knows it, he's got the puck on the tip of his stick as he twirls around her.

"Aw, man! You're too fast!"

After a while, I take a seat on the bench and take Jem out of the sling, bouncing him on my lap. He babbles along, waving his hands around as Carter and Alannah zip around the ice. I snap a few pictures and smile when Carter starts giving Alannah tips on crossovers and flicking her wrist *just right* in order to get that perfect "top shelf" shot on net.

"See, when you're checking someone into the boards, you wanna go in low and finish high," I hear him saying, shoving her gently with his shoulder.

"Carter! We're not giving her tips on how to land in the penalty box."

Carter whispers something in her ear that makes her snicker before he flashes me an innocent grin. "Yes, Ollie." He flips the puck to Alannah and tells her to go for a spin, making his way over to me. He taps my nose with his stinky gloves. "Want me to take Jemmy for a ride?"

"Sure." I hand him over as Carter ditches his gloves and stick, and he smooches Jem's cheek, snuggling him close. "Be careful."

"Careful's my middle name, Ol."

"Careful is *not* your middle name. Careful's not even in your vocabulary."

He ignores me, naturally, and I watch in awe as he spins around the ice with my nephew in his arms, shrieking with giggles and making Carter laugh. They're a sight to be seen, and I don't think I could be more in love.

Carter skates by me with an irritatingly smug smirk and an even smugger wink. "You look like you wanna have my babies."

"*Psssh*." I scoff, waving him off.

"Is that a *hell-yes* scoff?"

"It's a *your-baby-would-absolutely-destroy-my-vagina* scoff."

"Hm. Sounds like a *hell-fucking-yes* to me."

Hell. Fucking. *Yes*.

Except hours later, after his game has ended and Alannah hops off Cara's shoulders, scrambling over to Carter the moment he steps out of the change room, her face painted with his now-smeared number, it becomes apparent the general consensus is I already have kids, and Carter's stepping in to play the role of stepdad.

He scoops Alannah into his arms, his apprehensive gaze bouncing between me and the reporters. I shrug. Jeremy would love if Alannah was on TV.

"And who's this, Carter?" one of the reporters asks.

"This is my friend Alannah."

"I play hockey, too, ya know," she tells them. "It's not just a boy sport. And I'm really good. I'm fast. Like, super fast. My mom says I'm like lightning."

All eyes slide my way before someone asks, "Is that right? And what team do you play for?"

Alannah smiles proudly, throwing her shoulders back. "I play for the Avalanche. We're the blue team. And I'm a center, like Carter."

"Right on! And are you having fun hanging with Carter?"

Her head bobs. "Me and Jemmy slept at Carter's last night. We had pizza and Oreo brownies, 'cause me and Carter both love Oreos, and we watched movies, and then Carter tucked me into bed, and this morning I showed him how to change a stinky bum, and then we worked out in the gym and he took me skating." She sucks in a deep breath and releases it with a body-sagging sigh. "Carter's the best ever."

Oh, my brother's gonna *hate* that last one.

"Is that so?" The reporter looks my way, as do the rest of them. "And what do you think of Carter dating your, uh . . ."

I resist the overpowering urge to roll my eyes. They're beating around the bush, trying to figure out what they want to know, which is whether I'm a single mom to two kids.

Alannah doesn't give her a chance to finish the question anyway. She throws both arms around Carter's neck and smooshes her cheek to his. "I hope they get married and I'll be the flower girl and they'll have lots and lots of babies."

Oh shit.

42

BE MY BABY-DOGGIE MAMA

Olivia

"Can I help you, grumpy pants?"

Carter pins his arms across his chest, looking anything but relaxed in the La-Z-Boy he's lounging in. In fact, he looks quite grumpy, hence the nickname. "I'm not a grumpy pants."

"You're being a grumpy pants."

"Obviously I'm being a grumpy pants!" He flails a flappy hand through the air. "Every time we're here you ditch me for those two."

"Sharing is caring, Carter," Hank murmurs from beside me, his hand tucked tenderly into mine as I scratch Dublin's head in my lap with my free hand. "Plus, I haven't seen you two since you got back from your spring break escapades." He chuckles to himself. "Well, I've never *seen* you, but you know what I mean."

Carter scrubs a hand over his face. "You're the only blind man I know who makes fun of the fact that he's blind."

"I think I'm the only blind man you know, period. And if I can't poke some fun at myself, then what is life all about?" Hank slings an arm around my shoulders. "You're just mad 'cause I've got your lady. Don't be upset; I've always been somewhat of a ladies' man."

"You met Ireland at fourteen, started dating her at fifteen, married her at eighteen, and have never been with another woman." Carter pats his lap and wags his brows at me, trying to entice me over there. He rolls his eyes when I don't respond. "I'd hardly call that a ladies' man."

"You sound jealous." It's a wonder these two aren't related, because Hank sounds as smug as Carter right now. "Why don't you quit your complaining and come sit on Ollie's other side?"

"'Cause your damn dog is there, all up in her business!"

Dublin lifts his head to look at Carter. It's one of those adorable, head-cocking looks, all sad chocolate eyes and floppy ears.

Carter sighs. "Yeah, yeah. You're cute, everyone loves you; we get it, Dubs."

Laughing, I shift Dublin closer to me and free a space on the couch, patting it with my hand. "Come here, you big baby."

To say Carter doesn't spring to his feet and haul ass over to the free spot would be a lie. Three months together and this man still hates every bit of unnecessary distance between us. I can't say I mind. His love language is physical intimacy and I love to give him what he needs, which is why my fingers curl around his the second he sinks down beside the dog. His lips touch my shoulder, a whispered *I love you* kissing my skin.

"Speaking of babies . . ."

My shoulders tense at Hank's words. It's been well over a month since Alannah dropped the marriage-and-babies bomb on the reporters outside Carter's hockey game, and while we've managed to avoid directly addressing it, Carter's taken to walking around the house calling himself a DILF whenever the opportunity arises. I even caught him trying to change his name in my phone to *World's Sexiest DILF*. I continuously remind myself it's way too early to be thinking of weddings and babies. I want to live in the present, enjoy every moment we spend getting to know each other deeper, rather than wonder about the future.

And yet, when Hank finishes his sentence, it's not at all what I expected.

"When are you gonna get a dog?"

I look to Carter, one hand buried in Dublin's fur, longing gaze set on the dog as his free hand rubs methodically over the back of mine. "Do you want a dog?"

He nods. "We had Max growing up. He passed away when I was fifteen. My parents wouldn't let us get another because my training for hockey and Jennie's dance was getting so intense. We were barely home. They said it wasn't fair to the dog." A sad smile touches his lips as he pushes one of Dublin's silky golden ears back. "I was so mad at my parents. I didn't see it at the time, but I know now they were right. It wouldn't have been fair to be passing him off to family members to watch all the time, and it still wouldn't be."

"I'd watch your dog for you," I blurt.

Carter smiles tenderly and squeezes my hand. "Someday."

"Great," says Hank. "And speaking of dogs, when are you two gonna think about having babies and making me some type of pseudo-grandfather?"

"Speaking of dogs, when are we having babies?" Carter rubs his eyes. "That makes no fucking sense, old man."

"Well, stepdaddy Carter is all the hot gossip lately."

Hank's not wrong, though I wish he was. The articles that have come out since we brought Jem and Alannah to the hockey game back at the beginning of March have been relentless. For people who are everywhere and know everything, sometimes they don't know shit.

"These journalists know everything about his life and mine," I say, "yet they haven't figured out that Alannah and Jem aren't my kids."

"Oh, they know," Carter replies coolly. "It's just way more interesting if you're a struggling single mom and I'm the hot step-DILF swooping in."

"You keep saying that, but you're the only one who calls yourself a DILF."

"Nuh-uh!" He screws around on his phone before flipping me a photo of him with Jem on his shoulders and Alannah's hand in his as we walk through a grocery store with a basket of junk food. He clears his throat, reading off the title of the article with an air of arrogance that could only belong to him. "'*Carter Beckett: reformed playboy, People's Sexiest Man Alive, hockey phenomenon, and now the stepdaddy we'd* all *like to F!*'"

"Sometimes I think you write these articles yourself."

Hank snorts a laugh. "My personal favorite was the pregnancy one. Called Carter to see if I was the last to find out." He gasps suddenly, leaning forward to find his tablet on the coffee table. His shirt comes untucked from the waist of his jeans, riding up his back, showcasing a nasty bruise that has Carter leaping to his feet. "Speaking of getting knocked up—"

"*Hank!* What happened?" Carter gingerly touches his back while Hank swats him away.

"Oh, quit your worrying. I'm fine."

"Fine? You're black and blue! It's the size of my hand!"

"Barely even hurts anymore. Must've been singing and dancing a little too enthusiastically in the shower the other day. Slipped on a puddle on the floor when I stepped out."

"Why didn't you call me?"

"You weren't in town. Look, Carter, I know you're concerned, but I'm okay. I got up, brushed myself off. Dublin stayed by my side." He ruffles Dublin's ears. "Didn't ya, Dubs? Yes you did. You're my good boy."

"You can always call me, Hank, okay?" I squeeze his hand gently. "We don't need Carter to be around for us to hang out."

"Oooh-ho-ho." His grin is electric. "You hear that, Carter? I'm movin' in on your girl." He shakes his tablet. "Anyway, as I was saying, Ollie, I picked our next book. A whole series, actually. *Owned, Claimed, Ruined*. Reviews say it's one hell of a juicy read."

Carter's eyes widen, and when he brackets his face between his hands, I barely hear the way he breathes out, "What the fuuuck."

"YOU SURE YOU WANNA WEAR that? Your legs might get cold."

"Of course I'm sure." Jennie twirls, hands on her lower back as she tries to look at her own ass in her plum miniskirt. "My ass looks fantastic in this."

"You look hot as fuck." Cara gives her ass a pat-pat. "Gonna have all the boys—"

"No." Carter shakes his head, cracks a beer, and drains half of it. "No."

"I think you look pretty," Garrett says. I wonder if he realizes he's halfway to yelling. Probably, because his ears burn red and he dashes away, sinking down to the couch.

"I reserved us a private booth with service," Carter says. "We can stay there. No need to head out to the dance floor."

"We're going to a dance club; we're fucking dancing." Cara flicks Carter between the eyebrows. "You guys just won the first round of the play-offs; we're celebrating! And if Jennie wants to celebrate by shaking her ass and grinding against something hard, then so be it. She's an adult."

"I wouldn't mind dancing," Adam says with a hopeful smile. "Maybe I'll meet someone." He frowns. "No, wait. Maybe I'm not ready." He shakes his head and brings his beer to his lips. "No, I'm not ready. I'll stay at the booth."

I squeeze his arm. "You'll meet someone when you're ready, and she'll be perfect."

"Yeah," Garrett calls over his shoulder. "If Carter can find someone, it'll be easy as pie for you, bud."

"*You're single!*" Carter hollers.

"Yeah, by choice."

"No, because you're annoying!"

"*You're* annoying!" Garrett hooks his foot around Carter's knee, and when he goes tumbling to the living room floor, Carter brings him with him.

"Children," Emmett mutters as the two of them wrestle. "So embarrassing."

Adam nods. "The irony is that I'm the youngest."

"Definitely the most mature though," Emmett replies, sipping his beer.

"Oh, definitely."

I can't tell you how typical this is—the boys bickering, rolling around. The most embarrassing part is that I find it—*ugh, I don't even want to say it*—endearing. This group of men loves each other so much, and watching them be total goofballs is such a stark contrast to the intimidating way they carry themselves on the ice.

"Your boyfriend's a jerk," Garrett mumbles when I take a seat beside him on the couch. He's trying to fix his hair but it's no use, so he stuffs his hat back on his head. "You should run while you still can."

Jennie sinks down between us, slinging one leg over the other, and Garrett's turquoise eyes widen, staring at the strappy black heel bouncing next to his knee.

"Hey. Hi." He drags his palms down his thighs. "Do you have enough . . . Do you want some more . . . Let me give you some space." He rockets to his feet, knocking his hat off his head when he shoves his fingers through his hair. "Anybody want another beer?"

I snicker-snort, nudging Jennie. "Garrett might be scared of you."

"As he should be. I could kick his ass from here all the way back to the east coast."

I don't at all doubt it. Jennie and I have been taking horseback riding lessons since mid-March, courtesy of her blackmailing her brother. Not only have I learned she's almost entirely a female replica of Carter—confident and lacking a filter—she's fierce as hell too. I get to ride a horse every Wednesday after work, but more importantly, I've found an incredible friend in Jennie.

We've still got an hour to go before our ride comes, so the boys lose themselves in a game of beer pong, one I'm not allowed to play because Carter says I cheat, but he's just a sore loser. When he takes a ping-pong ball off the head for the third time, I know something's up. He climbs the stairs, muttering something about checking the plumbing of all things, and I give him two minutes before I follow, locating him on the balcony, leaning over the railing. He's been off all afternoon since we got back from Hank's, and I think I know why.

Leaning beside him, I nudge his shoulder with mine. "Hey, you."

He kisses my forehead. "Hey, princess."

I follow his gaze, looking out at the sea of evergreens, the caps of the mountains that seem nearly blue from here. Carter's not really looking though. I can tell by the way his gaze never wavers, the small crease between his brows.

I slip my hand over his. "You're worried about Hank."

"He's getting older. He doesn't get around on his own the way he used to. And that bruise . . . What if he hadn't been able to get up? Why didn't he call any of us?"

"He likes his independence, Carter. He's fought for it."

He sighs, scrubbing a hand over his face. "I worry one day he'll need me and won't be able to reach the phone. Maybe I should hire a nurse to come in and help him with things a few times a week. Is that a good idea?"

"It's a great idea, but it's a conversation you need to have with Hank."

He kisses my temple. "Can we stay here a few more minutes? I like when it's just me and you."

When I nod, he pulls me against his chest, his chin on my shoulder. The late-April air is warm, especially after the winter from hell we had, but it's nothing compared to the heat of him when he holds me.

"I'm going to miss you."

"I know, pumpkin. Me too. But the nice part about play-offs is it's never more than two nights away from home."

"I think I was getting used to it, the partial loneliness." I regret the words as soon as they leave my mouth. I don't want him to think I'm lonely or unhappy; nothing could be further from the truth. I've learned to treasure what little time we have together, the nights I get to fall asleep in his arms, and we've made the most out of those fleeting moments. But they swept Arizona in four games, which means the boys have been here in Vancouver for a few extra days before their next round. "Sleeping with you so many nights in a row has spoiled me, that's all."

"I hate leaving you, Ollie. I've never been so eager for the off-season. No hockey, no school, just me and you. You're gonna be so sick of me come September."

"Impossible."

Carter's breath dusts over my neck, each inhale more staggered than the last as his fingers methodically brush my arm. He's anxious, but since we've talked about Hank, I'm not sure why.

"When are you going to move in with me?" The request is a gentle, timid whisper against my shoulder, making my entire body tingle and warm, right down to my toes.

I twist in his hold, the golden glow of the spring sun shining on his unexpectedly bashful expression. "Move in with you?"

He runs an anxious hand through his messy mop of hair before twining his fingers with mine.

"I love you," he starts with the phrase he loves to repeat at least a hundred times a day. "I love you so much, and I know it's soon, but fuck, Ollie, I just really love you. When I'm gone, all I can think about is cuddling you on the couch, or falling asleep with you in my arms, or you walking around the house in the morning wearing nothing but my T-shirt with your sleepy smile, your curls trying to escape from your messy bun. When I get off the plane, you're the first person I want to see. And when I'm home . . . I want you to be home too. I want us to be home together."

How did I find this man? How did I get so irrefutably lucky? Carter's the best thing in my life with the way he stormed in, tore down walls I didn't know I had, lit my whole world up like a burst of sunshine. And I can't imagine anything better than being home together.

"What if I want you to move in with me?" I don't. My tiny house feels like it's bursting when Carter's inside. His legs dangle off my bed and my kitchen only has the capacity to hold enough food to last the man two days, at most. More than that, it doesn't quite feel like my home anymore.

But I like to tease him, and when he's nervous like this, a little humor goes a long way in defusing his tension.

Emerald eyes dance when they meet mine. "But where will I park my five cars? We won't be able to fit our doggie on the bed, and we'll have no room for all the babies I'm going to put inside you, ultimately destroying your vagina beyond repair. But worst of all . . ." He drags his mouth across mine, voice low, thick. "No fireplaces."

He cups my face, his thumb brushing my lower lip. "I don't want you to watch my dog while I go away. I want to get a dog *with you*. I want you to be my baby-doggie mama."

"Baby-doggie mama?"

"And eventually real-baby mama. I love you, Ollie, and what I want more than anything is to make a home with you. Say yes."

"Say yes? Is that a demand?"

"Obviously."

I bite back my smile. "Okay."

"Okay?" His eyes bounce between mine. "Is that a yes?"

"I didn't think I had a choice where demands were concerned." I push his unruly waves off his forehead. "There's nothing I'd love more than building a life with you here. So, yes. A thousand times yes. I'll move in with you."

His shaky hands bracket my face, and he closes his eyes, resting his forehead against mine. Then, with a squeal, he hoists me into this arms and dashes down the stairs.

"*She said yes!*"

The volume in the room promptly dies, and I drop my face to my hand as every surprised gaze lifts to us.

"You're getting married?" Garrett finally asks.

Carter's face scrunches. "What? I mean, eventually, yeah, but . . ." He drops me to my feet, spreads his arms wide, and does a spin. "*Olivia's moving in!*"

43

I'M NOT IMMATURE, I'M GOOFY; THERE'S A DIFFERENCE

Carter

"*I GOT ONE!*"

"What? Lemme see." I try to grab Olivia's fishing rod, but she twists away.

"Back off!" She kicks her leg out, splashing water at me. "You're gonna let it get away!"

"No I'm not!" I reach for the rod again, but she dashes down the stream, reeling in her line as she goes. "I know how to reel in a fish, *Olivia*!"

"I'd believe you if I'd seen you do it, *Carter*!" She's got her tongue out, poking the corner of her mouth as she works, grunting, reeling, and when that salmon breaks the water, she *a-ha*'s, an arrogant beam spreading across her face. "What's that now? Four for me, zero for you?"

"Shut up." I slosh water up at her, and she giggles. It's kinda maniacal and a little scary. "It's 'cause I let you use my good rod."

"It's 'cause I'm better." She winks. "At using this rod *and* the one in your pants."

"*Ollie*," I muse, half gasp, half guffaw. "I've never been so attracted to you as I am right now."

"You're always attracted to me," she murmurs, focused on prying the hook from her salmon.

This is true. Always. *Always, always, always.* Though there's definitely something about standing in a stream, water up to her knees, her teensy denim shorts soaked from all the splashing, holding a fish that's, like, a third of her height in length that makes her especially sexy right now.

Olivia grunts, lugging the big fish up, slinging it across her arms. "Can you take a picture? So you can always remember that I don't just kick your ass at beer pong, but at salmon fishing too."

The rumble of protest in my throat quickly dies as I snap her picture over and over, and when Olivia sets the fish free, I wade over to a large rock and take a seat.

She sinks down beside me, sticking her head over my shoulder. "Did you just add that to your secret spank bank folder?"

I tuck my phone into my pocket. "Yeah."

"It's a little . . . *different* than the normal pictures you put in there."

"You look hot as fuck. Your legs are all wet and your smile is as cocky as mine." I graze the tip of her nose with mine. "I mean, if you wanna take off your clothes and let me fuck your throat right now, I can take a picture and add that one, too, pip-squeak. We don't have any outdoor pictures."

"That's not true. I took a picture of you between my thighs on your balcony last week."

"Oh yeah. Fuck. I ate like a king that day." I nudge her shoulder with mine. "And stop calling it *mine*. It's yours too. Not just the balcony, the whole damn house."

"Not yet, not officially."

I roll my eyes. "It's been yours since you first stepped into it."

Her cheeks tint pink. It's adorable she still blushes sometimes.

"You belong there, Ollie girl, and you always have. It's yours, whether or not you're waiting to officially be out of your house and never ever sleep anywhere but *our* bed again."

"Never ever?"

I brush a kiss across her lips. "Never ever *ever*."

For the first time, Olivia stayed at my house last weekend while I wasn't there. She was all nervous about it, but there's something about knowing she's puttering around my kitchen, lounging on my couches, sleeping in my bed while I'm away.

It's been a month since she agreed to move in, and we finally listed her house last week. It sold in thirty-six hours for 25 percent over asking because Vancouver real estate is on fire right now. It doesn't close until end of June, which means I've got another six-ish weeks to go of Olivia pretending like she's only "sleeping over."

I can't wait to build our home together.

"You know," I say, leaning into her. "Cara and Em's wedding is that weekend."

"Mhmm."

"So we'll be too busy to move. And you'll be too busy hiding from Cara for at least two weeks before that."

"This is true."

"So maybe you should move in now."

"Hmm . . ." Olivia's lips purse, and she rubs her chin like she needs to think long and hard about it.

Ha. Long and hard. That's what she—no. No, Carter. Be more mature.

"Well, I don't know. I'm about to spend all summer with you, you know. Feels like I should soak up all this personal space before you invade it."

A growl rumbles in my chest.

"Hmm . . ." She raises her palm in a half shrug. "Plus, you only have seven fireplaces, and I was kinda hoping for an e—" Her words dissolve on my tongue as my mouth takes hers, and I lift her, setting her on my lap, hugging her to me.

"Stay, please."

Olivia takes my face in her hands, warm brown eyes sparkling in the sun. "I don't want to rush the move itself. You're in the middle of play-offs. I want you to focus on that, not getting me moved out of my house. And it's the end of the school year. I've got exams and wrap-up to work on for these kids." She kisses the corner of my mouth, right where it's tugging down. "But I'll stay, Carter. We can worry about moving things later, or a little bit at a time, when time permits. Okay?"

"Compromise?"

"Compromise."

"And I get to keep you forever? Can it start tonight?"

"Do I have a choice?"

"No." I grip her waist, leap to my feet, and spin her in the air. "*Woo-hoo!*"

Olivia giggles, slinging her arms around my neck. "Are you ready to eat?"

My stomach takes its cue, growling. "Always."

I carry her out of the water, where she takes a seat on the blanket we laid out earlier, right on the edge of the shore, and I start to get the fire ready in the pit.

"You know," Olivia starts, "I grew up on a lake, but I've never had a shore lunch before."

"Really? My dad and I had them all the time." It's why we're here after all. My dad's birthday is this week, and he used to take the entire week off work. He'd pull me from school for two days, then my sister, followed by whisking my mom away for a long weekend. We'd finish on Sunday night, all of us, together at his favorite restaurant. He spent his birthday doing the things he loved most with the people he loved most. For him and me, after hockey, it was this. Hiking, fishing, lunches on the shore. I mentioned it to Olivia a week ago, how it was one of my favorite cluster of days each year, how I haven't done it since he passed, and the next morning she called me to tell me she'd taken a couple days off.

I fucking love her so much it hurts.

"I know it's not the same, Carter, but are you . . ." She trails off, fiddling with the edge of the blanket. She clears her throat. "Are you having fun?"

My heart tugs in my chest. "I'm having so much fun here with you today, Ollie. It makes me feel like he's right here with us."

Olivia smiles. "I think he is. Always."

"I think so too."

I get to work on lunch, filleting the salmon Olivia caught earlier this morning. She wanted to pack sandwiches in case we didn't catch anything, but I didn't let her. I was too confident. Turns out she should've been the confident one.

I place the foil packets over the coals and step back, taking a look around. The small campsite is exactly how I remember it, hidden within all the greenery, plush brush and old, towering trees. Sunshine filters through the branches, making the stream sparkle, and birds sing on a continuous loop. It's as pristine as it always was, aside from the odd camping gear left scattered and forgotten on the ground, like the fire extinguisher lying ten feet or so from the pit.

I pick up the narrow, white canister. The label tells me it's one that sprays water, and the gauge says it's still got some life left in it.

"Hey, Ollie, look." I hold the canister between my legs and aim the hose outward. When she meets my gaze, I squeeze the handle, a stream of water spraying out in a fine mist as I swivel my hips. "It looks like I'm jiz—"

"Yes, Carter, I know what it looks like."

I lean against the trunk of a tree, flicking my brows up. "You wanna go back in the bushes? I can empty my load in your—"

"For fuck's sake, Carter. I *know* your dad didn't teach you this on one of your many fishing expeditions."

"No, he didn't." I chuckle, taking a seat beside her on the blanket as years of memories come flooding back, memories I've spent years wanting to forget. I don't have a clue why, not when they're as incredible as these.

I wind an arm around Olivia, and she settles into my side. She's warm beneath the May sun, and she smells like coconut and lime, the sunscreen she made us both wear.

"He taught me how to set up my rod, how to knot my hooks and bait them. He taught me how to skate, how to puck-handle, how to take a slap shot. He taught me how to turn my shoelaces into bunny ears and tie them, how to make my mom's favorite dinner to get her to stop being mad at me when I messed up, how to work hard and save money. He taught me how to be a good son, a brother, and a friend."

"And a partner," Olivia adds.

"He taught me how to love. I know how to love you so well because I watched him love my mom so well, love me and my sister so unconditionally. Does that make me a good partner? How much I love you?"

"Mhmm. But there are so many reasons you're a good partner, Carter. You're fierce and loyal. You're patient and kind and the most passionate person I know. You never give up, and you're so proud of me all the time, and it helps me be proud of myself. I'm a more confident person than I was six months ago because of the love you show me."

"I like that." A heaviness settles on my chest, a weight that's been looming for years, waiting for a vulnerability to jump on. Olivia's my vulnerability. As strong as I am, loving her makes me weak too. Our love opens up pieces of me I didn't know existed, or maybe pieces I'd tucked away. Because I'd do anything for her, give her anything, and right now, I want to give her the truth I've been avoiding. "I'm not sure I've been the best son, though. Not to my dad."

"What do you mean?"

"I haven't visited him since the funeral, the cemetery where he's buried."

Olivia runs her fingers through my hair. "I don't think that makes you a bad son, Carter. Things like that can be challenging. Maybe that's not where you feel him. And that's okay. Do you want to go back?"

"It's always felt too hard, but maybe . . . maybe one day, if you'll come with me. Things always feel easier with you."

Her smile is soft and warm, like her. "Hard things are always easier when we're together."

She's right. And that's exactly how I find myself turning right where I should be turning left two hours later.

That's how I find myself gripping the steering wheel as I stare down the long path that winds through the cemetery, the simple thought of walking through it daunting.

Think that's how I find myself clutching Olivia's hand as she walks alongside me, and still as she stands next to me while I stare down at the words carved in marble before us.

Theodore 'Theo' Beckett
LOVING HUSBAND & DEVOTED FATHER
BEST FRIEND
"Remember me as I lived: full of love, laughter, and passion"

There's a strange ache in my chest. It's tight and a little painful, but it's not heavy. And when Olivia squeezes my hand, when she turns into my side and presses a kiss to my arm, the pain starts to retreat.

I don't know how long we stand there in silence, but when I'm ready to leave, Olivia presses a kiss to my lips.

"Just a second, Carter. There's something I want to do first."

She approaches my dad's grave, and when she kneels in front of it, head bowing, my throat constricts. Her head lifts after a moment, and she lays her hand over his name before she stands and makes her way back to me. I don't know what to say, but she doesn't ask me to talk, so we ride in silence, her hand in mine in the center console.

"Carter," Olivia says as we drive through downtown. "I hate to do this, but would you mind stopping? I need to use the bathroom and I'm not sure I can wait."

"Sure, baby. Where do you want me to stop?"

She points at the building up the street. "Just at your condo."

"We can't go there."

"I'll be quick."

"I sold the condo, Ollie."

"What? When?"

"Uh, you know the first time I came to see you at work? The Monday after I brought you to the condo? I dropped the keys off to my real estate agent that morning and asked her to take care of it. It was gone by the end of the week."

It was a bonus years ago when I re-signed with Vancouver after my initial contract was up. I had no intention of going anywhere else, but everybody who could afford me wanted me, and Vancouver wanted to make sure I stayed, so they threw everything they could at me. I only lived there for one season before I bought my house, and instead of selling it, I kept it. I wanted that part of my life separate from the rest of it, the most personal parts of me. I wasn't lying when I said Olivia was the first woman I'd had in my bed at home, and she'll be the only.

"Carter . . ."

"It was never my home, Ollie. Not without you."

My home is wherever Olivia is. When we're lying on the balcony an hour later, freshly showered and wasting away the rest of the afternoon, the warm breeze tickling our skin, this is where I feel it the most, where I could stay forever, so long as it's with her.

My fingers dance across Olivia's shoulders, kissed pink and sprinkled with tiny freckles from the sun. "You're so beautiful, Ollie."

"You just like my sundresses."

"I fucking *love* your sundresses." Winter lasted for-fucking-ever here, a colossal shitstorm Vancouver hasn't seen in ages and hopefully never sees again, but spring came roaring in like a lion. April was warm and rainy, and May's been every bit an early summer. That means Olivia's traded in her sweaters for these adorable sundresses that show off her legs, her shoulders, and I get to be touching her all the time, feeling how warm her skin is beneath my lips, or my cheek on her shoulder. "We should relocate to San Jose or Tampa, somewhere it's always warm. You'll never have to wear pants again."

"Mmm . . . and you know what comes with no pants, Carter?"

"What?"

She crawls on top of me, straddling my hips, her yellow sundress riding up. She guides my hand up her creamy thigh, and I think I might cry when I meet that pool of heat.

Her lips meet my jaw. "No panties."

No fucking panties.

She tugs on my shorts, shifting them down, and I hiss when her hand wraps around my cock. I fumble for my phone, snapping a picture as she swallows me in her mouth.

I gather her damp curls in my fist. "I fucking love you."

Fuck, you ever seen the most beautiful girl in the world smile at you with her mouth full of your cock? *Jesus Christ*, it's a sight. I take one more picture before I yank her head back.

"I need you to sit on me, baby. Right fucking now."

She presses herself against me, rocking, letting my cock slide through her sopping slit, and before she can take me, I stop her.

"Wait. I just want to say . . . thank you. Thank you for today, Ollie. Spending the day doing something my dad and I used to do together, going with me to see him . . . it means a lot to me. Thank you."

Her smile is tender and a little bit bashful, and she sits back on my thighs. "I was thinking maybe next year we could do a whole week for your dad's birthday, the way he always did, with you and your sister and your mom. Do the things you guys did together. And Hank as well. We could do something he and Ireland loved to do. Maybe it would be a nice way to remember them."

I don't know how I found her, but I'm pretty sure it was fate, the same way I walked into the bar Hank was in that night.

"Can I ask you something, Ollie? What did you say? To my dad? When you knelt down . . ."

"Thank you."

"Thank you?"

"I thanked him for bringing me another family, trusting me with loving them. I thanked him for raising the man I love, and for bringing him to me." Her hand glides along my jaw. "I thanked him for you, Carter."

My chest constricts, my throat squeezing. I look to the sky, and a single tear drips down my cheek. Olivia's lips trap it, stopping it in its track, and when she whispers how much she loves me, I bury myself to the hilt in the best thing that's ever been mine.

"You're going to burn my steak if you don't stop looking at me."

I grin at Olivia, hitting her with a wink. She's lounging on a blanket on the grass, feet in the air as she reads a book, curls piled on top of her head. I don't know how anybody can be expected to take their eyes off her, but she's picky about her steak and I like to please her, so I manage.

Today's been perfect, a glimpse at the summer to come, days on end to spend together, and I don't want it to end. It's been a welcome reprieve from the constant need to be on, always thinking about the next play-off game. Breaks are few and far between, but we're one game away from taking Winnipeg in the conference finals tomorrow night, and I managed to surprise Olivia by flying her parents out for the game we played there two nights ago. It's been a hectic month, and with the finals looming and Olivia's move, June is shaping up to be even more chaotic.

"Is that your phone?" Olivia calls, head cranking in the direction of the patio door.

My ears perk, and when I hear my ringtone, I shut the lid on the barbecue and jog to the door. My phone sits on the kitchen countertop, and the number is one I don't recognize.

"Am I speaking with Carter?" the voice on the other end asks.

"This is Carter."

"Hi, Carter. My name is Dr. Murphy. I'm a doctor at Vancouver General Hospital. You're listed as Hank De Vries's emergency contact."

The barbecue tongs in my hands clatter to the floor, and I barely register Olivia's voice calling out to me.

"There's been an accident."

44

IT'S SO . . . WHITE

Carter

I DON'T LIKE THE WAY it smells in here. Sterile, like bleach. The hint of orange citrus is nice, I guess, refreshing. But it's just too . . . *clean*. Not something to complain about, I suppose, but I've had lots of reminders lately that I'm hard to please. It's cold and stuffy, not warm and homey like Hank's apartment.

"You sure you wanna live here? It's awfully . . ." My gaze sweeps the office. The walls are stark, with quotes about living life to the fullest and only being as old as you act. "White."

"The color of the walls doesn't bother me, Carter. In case you haven't noticed, I'm blind as a damn bat."

I huff a laugh, glancing at my friend. He's enjoying the warm weather and being out of the hospital. He's also enjoying my girlfriend's hand in his, and I stifle a groan at the outfit he's wearing: a pastel plaid short-sleeve button-up, tucked into beige cargo shorts hiked up nearly to his rib cage, with a hat on that says *Carter Beckett's #1 fan*. The socks pulled three quarters of the way up to his knees are the cherry on top, but Hank insists he must look snazzy, and Olivia says that's all that matters.

"You can stay with us a while longer until we find something better," I offer, earning a pointed look from Sherry, the intake manager at Sunset Living.

I mean, Sunset Living? What kind of name is that? Makes it sound like they're all halfway out the door. He took a bad tumble that required a week of bed rest and monitoring at the hospital, and he's been sending me sneaky grins at the way Olivia's been doting on him since we moved him into the house. This guy's gonna outlive us all.

Hank's chin hits his chest with a rumbling sigh that has Dublin leaping up with concern. "Carter, I love you, but you're the pickiest damn man that's ever walked this earth."

Olivia does a piss-poor job of hiding her snicker, and I grumble under my breath. "I'm not picky; I want what's best for you." I flail a hand in Olivia's direction. "And being picky paid off. I've got the hottest girl in the world sleeping in my bed every night."

"I thought you weren't picky?"

"I can assure you, Mr. Beckett," Sherry starts, "Hank will be very well taken care of here. Sunset Living is the highest ranked assisted living facility in Vancouver. He got along well with the staff during his visit last week, even made a few friends with the residents already. Your mother was quite impressed with the facility."

Yeah, yeah. I've heard it all already. I wasn't allowed to come because I didn't let us finish the tour of the first three places. Apparently, I have a nine-minute limit before I say *nope* and steer everyone out of the building. Mom said she was taking over the search, and everyone but me agreed. Naturally, they chose the next place on the list. I think Hank was just tired of searching. He thinks he's a burden, imposing on me and Olivia.

He's not, but how do you stop a person from thinking that? Olivia's the one who's had to take care of him the most as he recovers since I've been in and out of town for the conference finals.

Which we won, by the way. In overtime. In game seven. Game one of the Stanley Cup Finals is tomorrow. I have every intention of bringing home that cup and making Olivia pose naked with it while I take a fuckton of pictures.

"All right, Mr. Beckett." Sherry points with her pen to a list of dates. "This is our payment schedule. Payment is due on the first of every month. We require postdated checks or preauthorization for bank withdrawal. Which would you prefer?"

I notice the slight shake to Hank's hands and the way he starts rubbing his palms over his shorts. This makes him uncomfortable, me paying. But for fuck's sake, the guy gets a whopping seven hundred bucks every month from his pension, and I think the assisted living facilities that were in his price range gave my MacBook a virus when I checked out their websites. The decision was a no-brainer. He's my family and he deserves the world; the least I can do is make sure he's taken care of in a nice place.

I guess Sunset Living is that place.

"Check, please. Can I write one check for the whole year and pay up front?"

Sherry's jaw hangs and she blinks about twenty-five times. "That's . . . unprecedented. Typically, month-by-month payment is our standard because we can never guarantee . . ." She trails off, gaze sliding to Hank, and he grins.

"I might be dead before the year's up is what the nice lady's trying to say, Carter."

"Fucking—" I drop my forehead until it hits the white metal desk. "You are unreal, old man."

When I'm finished signing all the paperwork and handing over six postdated checks for the remainder of the year, because nobody but me is buying that Hank is immortal, Sherry shows us to his private room. It's large and spacious and . . . white.

"Can we paint?"

Olivia shoves her elbow into my waist. I suspect she was aiming for the rib cage, but she can't reach that high.

I pat the wall. "What? I'm envisioning a Vipers-themed wall, all blue and green, maybe a mural of me with the cup overhead."

"You'd have to win the cup first for that to happen." Olivia gives me that tongue-in-cheek smile I love so much.

"Oh, I'm gonna win that fucking cup. And you know how people eat cereal outta it? I'm gonna eat your—"

"*Carter!*" She slaps a hand over my mouth.

I can't tell if Sherry is uncomfortable or amused. Hank's amused; he always is.

"You can paint," Sherry starts slowly, probably scared of what I'm gonna paint. "But we require you to either paint it back to white or pay for us to do so at the end of the stay."

"Tell ya what, son." Hank claps a hand to my back, staring at the wall like he can see what I see. "You win that cup and I'll let ya paint whatever the hell you want on my wall. You could paint a field of daisies and I wouldn't know the damn difference."

I pull open the sliding door off his balcony and step outside. There's a small bistro table and a couple chairs. "Look at this, Hank. West facing. You can sit out here and enjoy the sunset."

"It's quite a *view*, isn't it?"

Olivia rolls her eyes and stalks off, muttering something about us being immature boys who'll never grow up.

When we're done, Sherry walks us downstairs, rubbing Hank's arm. "Well, Hank, we sure are excited to have you join us next week. You seem to be quite the character and have a wonderful family. We think you'll fit right in here."

Okay, maybe she's not so bad.

She fluffs Dublin's ears. "And you, handsome. We can't wait for you to come for visits!"

Hank stiffens for a moment before pulling on Dublin's lead and Olivia's hand, trying to tug them both away. "*Okay-Sherry-thanks-bye!*"

"Visits?" I chase after them, glancing back at Sherry. "What does she mean *visits*? Hank? *Hank!*"

For fuck's sake, for a blind man with an injured knee, the guy sure can move.

"Hank." With my hand on his arm, I stop him from getting in the car. "What is she talking about? Dublin's going to live here with you, isn't he?"

Olivia lightly shoves me with her hip, helping Hank into the back. He thanks her quietly and she pecks his cheek before asking me to get in. I don't want to, but I do, because Olivia takes me by the hand and leads me to the driver's side.

"What's going on?" I ask, this time a little more gently.

"Well." Hank wrings his hands as Dublin nudges his cheek. "Dogs are allowed to visit."

"But . . ."

"But they aren't allowed to stay."

"*What*?" I'm yelling again. I twist in my seat and Olivia's hand finds my thigh. "Why the hell not? You're blind! You need him! They can't do that!"

"Having pets as permanent residents are liabilities for nursing homes," Olivia explains.

"You knew about this?"

"Your mom gave me a heads-up. We were going to talk to you about it tonight." Her expression says she's sorry she didn't tell me right away. "The insurance policy to have pets is astronomical, and there are some people who don't like—"

"Who wouldn't like that face?" Still screaming. Also flailing. Dublin's cocking his head like he can't believe someone wouldn't like him. "Hank, you don't have to live here. We'll find some-where else."

"Carter, it's quite common. Your mom looked into it. And besides"—he scratches Dublin's head—"Dubs has taken a liking to having lots of space and a backyard these past couple weeks." He smiles sadly as Dublin lays his head in his lap. "Truth is, I'll have plenty of help around the home. I can't look after him on my own anymore, not the way he deserves."

"But where will he go?" My chest hurts. I hate it.

Hank clears his throat. "You know I hate asking you for things, and you're already doing so much for me. But Dublin, he means a lot to me. And Olivia's moving in and, well . . ."

My eyes land on my girlfriend. She's got that sad puppy look, one that looks pretty damn similar to what Dublin's sporting. "You want us to take Dublin?"

"If it wouldn't be too much trouble," Hank clarifies. "And if it is, it's no problem. Your mom said she would be happy to. I thought maybe, you've always wanted a dog, and you seem to love him so much."

"I do," I whisper. "I do love him." I look to Olivia. It's going to be her house as much as it is mine, and it's our life. This isn't a decision I can make on my own.

She lifts one shoulder, biting back her smile. "We have a big enough bed for a doggie or two."

"You know . . ." Hank chuckles, ruffling Dublin's fur. "He's a half-assed guide dog, but he sure is a damn good friend."

Reaching into the backseat, I give Hank's hand a squeeze. "Dublin will always have a home with us."

"Looks so homey." Hank's hands are on his hips as he pretends to look around his new room.

Emmett chuckles, clapping him on the shoulder. "You're the best, Hank."

Adam steps away from the TV he's just set on the dresser as Garrett moves around him, Hank's recliner in his arms. "You gonna listen to the game tomorrow night?"

"You kiddin' me?" He plops down in his chair when Garrett leads him over to it. "Game six; wouldn't miss it for the world. I don't even shut the TV off when you guys are losing horribly." His finger sweeps the room. "But you all better win and tie up this series. Bring it home for game seven and win it in your hometown."

"That's the plan. You're gonna sit behind the bench with Ollie and my mom and sister."

His eyes light. "And Cara? I love that feisty woman."

"My feisty woman will be there." Emmett sighs. "Probably be the loudest one in the whole damn arena."

Once the guys head out, Hank, Dublin, and I relax on the balcony. It's a beautiful day in Vancouver, all blue skies and sunshine, and it somehow gets a thousand times more beautiful when Olivia walks through the door with a smile that lights up my insides.

"I brought lunch," she exclaims, unpacking a big Greek salad and a few pita wraps. She digs around in her school bag, producing three bottles. "And iced tea!"

"My favorite," Hank says.

"Back off," I tell him. "I know you're talking about my girl and not the iced tea."

He snickers into the bottle as Olivia places his pita in front of him. "Damn."

"You're an angel." I press my lips to hers. "How much time you got?"

"Only twenty minutes if I want to get back in time for my next class."

"I guess the real question is whether or not you want to." I wag my brows, an invitation to ditch class.

"Only another week and a half."

"Then I get you to myself for the whole summer."

"Hate to tell ya, son," Hank says, "but you gotta share her with the rest of us."

"I don't gotta do shit. I've been sharing her with a fuckload of horny teens all year. I've done my fair share."

Hank smiles, eyes gleaming beneath the sun. "I can't believe you two will officially be living together in a matter of days. I'm so happy you found each other." He lays his hand on top of Olivia's when she gives him a squeeze. "Are you sad to be saying good-bye to your house?"

She thinks for a moment, chewing. Her eyes find mine and she smiles, shaking her head enthusiastically. "Honestly, no. I thought I might be, but the truth is it's never felt like a home. I can't wait to share a home with Carter." She winks at me. "But mostly I can't wait to have seven fireplaces."

"Mhmm." I reach under the table, slipping my hand beneath her skirt, petting her thigh. "Keep talking, Ollie girl." I keep on my path but stop and make a face when I can't get to where I'm going. "What the fuck is this?"

She shifts back, flashing me her toned legs beneath the army green skirt she's sporting. "It's a skort."

"A skort? What the fuck is a skort?"

"A contraption for horny little shits like you." She snickers to herself, smoothing the stretchy fabric. "A skirt with shorts underneath. Perfect for teaching gym class in the summer."

"I don't like it." It's not easily accessible. "Take it off."

"I'm sure the boys would love that." She tests me with an arched brow.

Fuck. "No. Keep it on."

Hank sighs. "I've never felt blinder than I do right now."

Olivia only eats half her pita, so when I'm done with my two, I devour the rest of hers.

She slips her sandals off and wiggles her toes before pressing her bare foot against mine. "Your feet are massive."

"Your feet are baby-sized," I counter.

Her brows pull down, sassy, unimpressed frowny face in full effect.

"You know what they say about giant feet?" I whisper, kissing the corner of her mouth.

"Giant ego."

"Giant dick," Hank and I say together, earning an outraged gasp from my lovely lady.

"Honestly." Olivia stands, gathering the garbage as she shakes her head. "It's a wonder you two aren't actually related."

"Chances are your kids will be just like him," Hank supplies.

"Great. Can't wait." She checks her watch, sighing. "I gotta get going."

"I'll walk you out," I offer. "You up for a walk, Hank? The river's just through the park down the street."

He nods, and Dublin races to his side as he stands.

Outside, Olivia swings herself up into the front seat of the truck with ease. She's mastered it over the past few months.

"You know, for someone who put up such a fight about driving this thing in the first place, you sure seem to love it." I make a show of looking around. "I don't see any snow."

She folds over the steering wheel, hugging it to her body. "I've grown accustomed to the power that comes with being up so high. I love her; don't take her away from me."

I'd never, of course. She let me fuck her in the backseat a few nights ago. I drove fifty minutes to the drive-in theater just for an excuse to do it.

"Wouldn't dream of it." I take her chin between my hands, kissing her perfect lips three times. "See you at home, pumpkin."

Hank is quiet as we walk, which is how I know there's something he wants to say. He proves me right the second his ass hits the bench at the edge of the river.

"You know, I always knew there was someone out there for you, but I couldn't have dreamed up a more perfect match than that girl back there. You're a teddy bear for Ollie."

"I love her." It might be my only excuse, but it's a good one. She helped me become a person I'm certain my dad would be proud of. I'm not sure I would've found that version of myself if she'd never come into my world and tested me.

"I know you do. There's nothing more obvious in this world than how much you two love each other." He runs a hand over his mouth. "So when you gonna ask that girl to marry you?"

I stare out at the crystal-clear water, the way the sun makes it sparkle. The breeze makes it ripple, rushing slowly and quietly down the stream. "It's soon."

Hank clicks his tongue. "True love doesn't wait for anything and it sure as hell doesn't follow a timeline."

My teeth find my bottom lip and I squash the urge to gnaw on it. "I never thought about marriage before Olivia."

"But you think about it now. With her."

Yeah. I do. All the time. "I can't imagine my world without her in it."

"That sounds a whole lot like a *soon* to me, son."

Real soon.

45

FORBIDDEN OREOS, BETRAYAL, AND WINS

Olivia

"YOU THINK THEY'RE GONNA WIN tomorrow, Miss Parker?" Brad leans against the storage room door, watching me load the equipment from class. It'd be lovely if he'd help but standing and watching while he gabs is his MO, so I can't imagine he'd change now at the end of his high school career.

Next week is exams, which means the curriculum is done. For the most part, we've been shooting hoops and sitting on the bleachers while we talk about nothing but hockey.

"I think so." Carter's motivated. It's been all Hank and hockey-talk around the house, with a side of moving my stuff in. I don't know where he finds the time, but on the days he's in town, I come home from work to find Carter's been to my house, brought another box of my things to his place. *Our place.* "I've never seen the boys so serious."

It's eerie, like I'm walking through the twilight zone. On off nights, the team is gathered in the basement, watching videos of their previous games, talking about where they went wrong and how they can be better. There's no alcohol, no junk food, and very little laughing.

It's the lack of junk food that gets me most. Carter hasn't had Oreos since mid-May. We're a week and a half away from July.

He caught me sneaking some into my lunch bag yesterday morning and the look on his face said *utter betrayal*.

"I think they'll win." Brad pushes off the wall, gathering balls from the floor, tossing them in the basket. "Me and the guys are gonna watch the game outside the arena on Friday if they make it to game seven. They're setting up screens. We're gonna sneak alcohol in our shorts."

"Don't tell me that, Brad." *I'd totally do the same if I were eighteen.* "Also, pockets are the first place security will look."

"Thanks, Miss Parker." Brad chuckles, pulling the door closed for me. The kid even gets down on the ground to click the lock into place.

I wipe a nonexistent tear from my eye. "Are you growing up?"

His head rolls with his eyes as he follows me to my office as I grab my bag, and walks alongside me down the hallway. "I'm sorry we kinda gave you a hard time this year."

"All in good fun. Nothing I can't handle."

Brad holds the door to the parking lot open. "Just so you know, you were the best teacher I ever had. You treated us like real people, not a bunch of kids you had to work with every day to take home a paycheck. You made school fun." He gives me a salute. "Thanks, Miss Parker."

If I weren't an overly emotional wreck at times, my nose wouldn't be tingling like I want to cry. Clearing my throat, I load myself into Carter's truck that I've unofficially adopted, smiling for the fourth time at the note he stuffed in the cupholder somewhere between last night and this morning. It's definitely not work-appropriate, so I have to unfold it seventeen times before I get to the good stuff.

I'm gonna eat you like the last slice of pumpkin pie on Thanksgiving when you get home.

That's not why I'm rushing home. That would be because he leaves tonight for tomorrow's game, and I want to squeeze in all the time with him I can. He's been a wreck this week between worrying about getting Hank moved in and the finals. They lost last night on home ice, and he was so hard on himself. They've been in the finals once before, Carter's first year as the captain, and he blames himself for their loss, saying he was too inexperienced to be the leader they needed.

"Babbbyyy," Carter calls from the living room the second I walk through the door, Dublin at my feet, licking my toes as I slip my sandals off.

I find him sprawled out on the couch, arms in the air, making grabby hands for me. "Can I help you?"

"Yes. You can plant yourself right"—he points aggressively at the bulge in his shorts—"here." He gestures at his face. "Here would also be acceptable."

"Dirty boy." I climb on top of him. Regardless of his request, his arms wind around me, tugging me down to my side, tucking my body into his. I run my fingers through his hair and down his back. "Are you nervous?"

He nods, throwing one leg around both of mine, forcing them between his. "I wish you could come. I'll need you if we lose. Will you stay up to talk with me after?"

"I'm always only a phone call away." Pulling his head back, I kiss his lips. He's been needier than usual lately, softer, which almost seems impossible. Though he has a domineering streak a mile wide, he's mostly just a big, cuddly teddy bear. But the stress of everything that's been going on and all his responsibilities are weighing him down, and I can see how badly he needs this upcoming break.

"Adam's picking me up for the airport in an hour and I just wanna snuggle you until then."

"That sounds nice." I slip my hand between us and pat his belly when it chooses this moment to rumble. "But we should probably get some food in here before you get hangry."

I whip up a quick stir-fry while Carter tells me about getting Hank settled into his new place. He cried when he said good-bye to Dublin, which makes me emotional. Even more so when I look down at Dublin, laying at Carter's feet at the kitchen island. But Carter promises that Hank seems happy, and that's all that matters. We're going to do our best to make sure Hank and Dublin still get to spend lots of time together, and I'm glad he's only a ten-minute drive away.

Carter's digging into his second helping when he asks me a question, looking down at his plate. Actually, it's several questions, spilled out in the form of word vomit, which is usually my forte, not his.

"Do you wanna get married? What kinda wedding do you want? Big? Small? Chocolate cake or vanilla?" He makes a noise, like he can't believe he asked that. "That's a stupid question." He twirls his hand, laying his palm face up in the air. "Chocolate, obviously. Maybe decorated with those tiny Oreos. Or big ones. Double stuffed."

He raises his head to peer at me only after silence has stretched between us for a good ten seconds. It's a slow raise, too, tentative, a little nervous, and pink splotches up his neck and pools in his cheeks, which, again, is usually common for me, not him.

The silence is broken when he offers me a crooked, wobbly grin, and I start laughing, folding over the counter, because what the hell is happening right now? Whatever it is, he looks equal parts terrified and adorable.

"Is this your way of asking me to marry you?"

"What?" His head shakes furiously. "No."

"Oh." I catch my breath and come down from my momentary high. "Good." I knew he wasn't. Obviously. It's too soon.

Teeth pressing into his lower lip, Carter flashes me a grin every bit devious and devilish as he slowly pushes to his feet, rounding the island to stop in front of me. He twirls a wayward curl around his pointer finger before tucking it behind my ear, touch blazing a path down my neck and across my collarbone.

"Do you even know me? I need an audience. I need flair. I need to embarrass the fucking *shit* outta you." His fingers dig into my hips as he pushes me against the cold stone counter. "When I propose to you, everyone in the fucking world is gonna know, and you're gonna be standing there with your gorgeous face buried in your little hands, because I sure as shit won't be quiet about it, and you'll be all like, *Carterrr, stop ittt. You're embarrassing meee.*"

"That's not how I sound." It's all I can manage right now.

His lips touch the corner of my mouth, my jaw, my ear. "It's exactly how you sound."

His fingers thread through my hair, pulling my head taut. "One day, I'm gonna ask you to marry me. You're gonna say yes, because that's the only acceptable answer; no isn't an option." He nips my bottom lip, his hand dancing down my arm, leaving goose bumps in its wake. "And then I'm gonna marry the fuck out of you in front of our family and friends, and you'll be Mrs. Beckett, and I'll fuck you so hard that night you'll feel it in your throat for the rest of your life."

"*Jeremy!*"

Cara's shriek startles every single one of us. Alannah throws the bowl of popcorn in her lap, Dublin darts in to clean it up, and Kristin nearly spills her entire glass of wine all over Jem, who's playing at her feet. I've never seen Jeremy look more terrified than he does right now, eyes wide, body still.

"It's a simple forty-five-degree fold! Forty-five degrees! A child could do it!"

"I can do it, Care," Alannah says confidently, puffing her chest out.

"Yes, thank you, Alannah." Cara sweeps her arm out, lifting a brow at Jeremy. "See? Your daughter can do it." Her eyes go wide as Alannah reaches for the cardstock. "Wait! No. You've got buttery popcorn fingers; that won't work."

Cara looks around the room while Alannah frowns at her hands. "Jennie." She snaps her fingers. "You've got dainty, nimble fingers. Lord knows how; your brother's got damn sausage fingers. You'll do."

"Oh, goodie," Jennie mutters, planting herself on the floor around the coffee table, grabbing a stack of cardstock. "Just what I was hoping for."

Cara narrows her eyes and Jennie gives her that signature Beckett grin, all charming and dimply. It works on everyone, even Cara.

Cara's been screaming all night. She thought it *made the most sense* if we worked on her wedding favors while we watched the game. She's the only one who thought it was a good idea, but everyone was too afraid to tell her that to her face. At least we only have to work between periods; she's too busy shrieking at the TV the rest of the time. Alannah, Jem, and Hank are the only ones who got lucky enough to sit this one out. And I guess now Jeremy.

Cara and Emmett's wedding is eleven days away, two Sundays away, the day before Canada Day. Cara's high-strung as it is, and she's reached an entirely new level these past few weeks. She stayed over last night after the boys left for New York and insisted on sleeping with me. She was all too happy to snap a picture of herself in Carter's bed and send it to him.

She also came to work with me today. She says she can't get any work done for the wedding while she's at home, because she needs an emotional support person at her side for her to actually work. So she sat on the gym floor while the kids helped her with table numbers. I'm exhausted.

"Cara, if I were still young and handsome, I'd marry you myself." Hank thinks Cara's the funniest person in the world.

"You're still handsome," Cara points out. "And you laugh at all my inappropriate jokes. We'd make a great couple. But I'd always come second to your Ireland, and therein lies the problem. Cara soon-to-be Brodie never comes second."

Jennie sighs, eyes bulging at the stack of cardstock in front of her. "How many more of these do we have to do?"

"I think it's fun," Holly, Carter's mom, says. "I love doing this type of stuff. Maybe I'll get to do it again in the near future for one of my children." Her eyes do a blatant shift my way, making Jennie and Cara snort.

"I'm not fucking helping with shit when you and Carter get married," Jeremy grumbles, arms pinned across his chest. "It's bad enough I had to do it for my own wedding."

Alannah rockets to her feet, shoving her finger in his face. "Two dollars for the swear jar! Pay up, buddy!" She swipes the money from Jeremy's unwilling hands, then plants herself between Hank and Dublin. "Mommy said I get to keep all the money this week from Daddy's swearing. I'm making a lot because he's extra stressed from the hockey games. What should I buy?"

Hank taps his chin. "How about we go for cheeseburgers and ice cream sundaes?"

Her face lights. "Hot fudge?"

"*Extra* hot fudge."

Wedding prep is forgotten when the third period starts up, and Cara goes from shrieking to silent, which is way scarier. She's sitting on the couch, kind of, one knee on the ground, fingernails in her mouth while she stares at the screen. They're tied at two goals apiece with only three minutes left in the game.

It's when Emmett gets tangled up with two players from the other team and his stick slips between one of their legs that things heat up. The ref raises blows his whistle, indicating Emmett for tripping, though it was clearly unintentional.

"*That's fucking bullshit!*" Cara screams, jumping to her feet. "Bullshit! It was a fucking accident! Go home, ref; you're drunk!" She pulls a twenty out of her back pocket and slaps it in Alannah's waiting hand without looking at her. "Keep the change; you're gonna need it."

I'm too on edge to pay attention to anything other than the game. It's do or die; win and go to game seven, have one more chance at the cup, or lose and go home. And now they have to kill a two-minute penalty with less than two and a half minutes left in the game.

Carter's busy arguing with the ref over the call when his coach calls a time-out. He switches up the lines, sending out a few huge guys who manage to keep the puck away from the net as the opposing team circles our end relentlessly, and with fifty seconds left, Carter and Garrett dive over the boards from the bench.

Carter's screaming out orders, digging his way between a player and the boards, fighting for the puck, and when it springs free, he sends it across the ice to Garrett.

Garrett hammers it off the boards, around another player, and collects it on the other side before passing it back to Carter, who receives it right before he enters the defensive end.

Emmett's penalty ends with sixteen seconds left on the clock. He bursts through the door, shouting for Carter. Carter spins around a defenseman, the puck moving so quickly, so fluidly between the blade of his stick I can barely see it. Without so much as a glance at Emmett, he slips the puck backward and to the left.

Emmett winds up as the puck hurls toward him, and the second it hits his stick, it soars through the air.

Bloodcurdling shrieks drown out everything around me as the buzzer glows red, and the Vancouver Vipers flood the ice, falling to one big blue and green pile.

They won. They're coming home, and they're going for the cup.

46

YOU CAN DO WHATEVER YOU WANT

Olivia

THE SPEED WITH WHICH I race home from work on Thursday to see Carter is embarrassing. I trip over my own two feet as I burst into the house, calling his name.

I drop to my knees to give Dublin pets as he licks my face, and I'm still calling for Carter as I move through the house.

He's not home. His overnight bag on the bed tells me he's been home at some point, and there's a single rose laying over my pillow next to a small package of chocolate-covered Oreos, decorated with mini M&Ms. A scrap of paper lies next to the treats.

Win or lose tomorrow, I don't have to spend a single night away from you for the next three months, and nothing makes me happier.

I fucking love you.

I tuck the note away in the bedside table with all the others he leaves and pull my vibrating phone from my pocket as I make my way downstairs with my rose and cookies.

World's Sexiest Man: hi princess. sorry i'm not home. *sad emoji* coach has us going over some footage. i'll pick up dinner on way home. luv u *kiss emoji* *tongue emoji*

Needing to keep myself preoccupied, I leash up Dublin, taking him for a hike before we curl up on the couch with *The Office* reruns. Dublin's out immediately, exhausted from the trek, and it doesn't take me long to follow.

I wake to someone playing with my fingers, barely registering Dublin jumping down from the couch. Blinking away the blurriness, I find Carter as he rises to his feet. He's grinning down at me, sucking on a damn Ring Pop of all things.

"I thought you were off junk food." The words are groggy as I try to sit up. I want to jump into his arms but my body's not cooperating. Carter and I were on FaceTime well after midnight, as were Cara and Emmett—in another room, for good reason—and then I had to deal with Cara at work again all day today. Tired doesn't begin to describe how I'm feeling. My only solace is that Cara will be sleeping in her own bed tonight.

"It's a celebration. It's the weekend this house officially becomes our family home, and the weekend I bring home the cup." So much joy lives in his expression, endless excitement dancing in his eyes, and it only spurs my own happiness.

"I can't honestly tell what you're more excited about." My arms fly overhead with my yawn, and I note the heaviness to my left hand.

"You being with me. Forever."

I hear the words. I appreciate the hell out of them. But I'm too busy staring down at the red Ring Pop he's stuck on my ring finger. "Why do I have a candy ring on my finger?"

He sucks his own ring into his mouth. "I just wanna pretend you're mine."

"I am yours." *Haven't we covered this?*

"For all eternity, I mean." Carter picks up my hand, tracing over my nails before sliding down to the ring. His brilliant green eyes find mine, alive and radiant. "So this is temporary until I replace it with one you cannot eat."

"W-w-w—" I stop, because I simply cannot. We've talked about marriage, yet this feels like . . . *more*. I can't explain it, and my mouth agrees, which is why my jaw opens and closes several times.

"You're the cutest when I render you speechless." He swoops me into his arms and starts toward the staircase. "Now let's go. I need to show you how much I missed you, and my dick needs to make a home inside you."

CARTER'S ALREADY LEFT FOR HIS morning skate when I wake up. He barely slept last night, his hands spending most of the night anxiously roaming my body. I swore I could hear the wheels turning, his nerves for the game tonight getting the best of him. It wasn't until two when I turned over in his arms, ran my fingers through his hair and down his back, that he finally drifted to sleep.

Though I only got five hours of sleep and usually require eight to function, I'm feeling exceptionally chipper this morning. I had one personal day to use up before the end of the school year, and you bet your ass I took it today. That also means I have no working Fridays left since exams only go until Thursday next week. Four more workdays and I'm home free.

Dublin and I head out back to enjoy the sunshine while I eat my breakfast, and when Carter walks through the door, I'm on the phone with Cara for the second time this morning, discussing what outfit she should wear tonight.

"Part of me wants to be super sexy for Em and just wear one of his jerseys and heels, but then, like, I'm worried it's gonna be cold in the arena. And also, is it inappropriate? It's huge, so it covers my ass."

"Inappropriate," I murmur as Carter comes up behind me, hugging me around the waist and kissing my neck. He pats his chest and when Dublin jumps up, Carter lifts him into his arms, carrying him around like he's a baby instead of a sixty-five-pound dog.

"You're no fun." I can hear Cara's pout through the phone.

"I'm plenty of fun, but I have no desire to accidentally flash any people or cameras my ass or vagina."

Carter's eyes hood as he mouths *only for me*. His face lights like a slot machine when I slip his breakfast on a plate, and he somehow manages to sit at a stool, keep the dog on his lap, and scarf down his meal, all while humming happily.

"I bet Carter would appreciate you wearing nothing but his jersey."

Carter purrs with satisfaction as he munches his toast. "In our house only."

"Listen to you two," Cara gushes. "*Our* house. Adorable. See, Liv, right from the start I said 'That Carter Beckett is good news.' I knew you'd be the perfect couple."

"That's not how I remember that conversation going. In fact, I distinctly remember you putting me in a headlock and scream-ing *no!* at me." I pat Carter's chest when he pouts. "It's okay. Took us a little while but we got where we needed to be, didn't we?"

Carter tugs the phone from my hand. "'Kay, Care, Liv needs to go now. See you toniiight."

"But I have to talk to her about my wedding!" I hear her shriek, but Carter ends the call and sets my phone down.

His arms wind around me, pulling me close. "Do you think she'll be a nightmare for our wedding too?"

"I think I'll just hand over the reins and let her do whatever she wants. It'll be easier than fighting with her."

"Hmm." With his hands in the pockets of my shorts, Carter twists me side to side. "Good idea. We like to keep Cara in her cage."

Sighing, I snuggle into his chest. "Somebody already let her out and it's terrifying."

Carter laughs, a gruff sound that makes my body warm. His hands glide over my hips, dipping under the edge of my shirt, running up my sides. "I love that you took today off so you could give me good luck sex before the game."

"That's not why I took today off, Carter."

"Shh, shh, shh," he whispers, setting me on the counter, dragging my shirt up my belly. I raise my arms to let him slip it off, and his eyes twinkle as he takes me in. "Good luck sex."

And good luck it is, because Carter scores the first goal of the game only four minutes into the first period. Halfway through the third, the Vipers are up 3–2, Cara's losing her ever-loving mind, Hank's repeatedly said he's glad he's blind because he's too nervous to watch, and Holly's nearly ripping out fistfuls of her hair. Words are no longer possible for me. I feel like I'm going to vomit from the nerves, and Jennie's lounging in her chair, chowing down on licorice like she doesn't have a care in the world.

Until someone checks Carter into the boards from behind when he's got his head down, eyes focused on the puck. Thankfully, he shakes it off and climbs back to his feet, but Jennie's not having it.

She leaps to her feet, tossing the licorice at me as she slams her palms on the glass. "Toss that fucker in the penalty box! Go back to New York! We play real hockey here, you fucking douche-waffle!"

Adam drops his head in his net, shoulders shaking with laughter. Emmett slaps the glass and hollers, spurring Jennie on, and Garrett peers up at her with this little half smile as he shuffles down the bench.

Carter gets a quick once-over from their trainer to make sure all is okay. Once he's given the go-ahead, he hits me with a wink, finding a way to make squirting water into his mouth look like the sexiest thing in the world.

"Yeah, you sit your ass in there!" Jennie screams at the offender as he makes his way to the penalty box. "Get nice and cozy in there, dipshit, 'cause that's your home for the next five minutes!"

She drops back to her seat, ripping the licorice out of my hand, hitting me with a dazzling, dimply smile. "I've got a little bit of my older brother buried somewhere deep down."

"Yeah, I can certainly see that."

The Rangers' goalie is all but standing on his head tonight, and he manages to stop every single shot on him over the next five minutes. With the penalty over and only a few minutes left in the game, we're still up by one.

Until we're not. With thirty seconds left, there's a battle for the puck behind the net. Adam's head whips wildly, trying to keep track of it when another player slips in, steals the puck, and slides it right by his foot.

The game is tied. We're going to overtime.

Adam's a wreck as the period comes to an end, and Carter swings an arm around his shoulders as they make their way through the players' tunnel for a quick break and regroup. Fifteen minutes later, with the ice ready to go and the low thud of the music that drives my anxiety through the roof, I hear Carter's booming voice.

Everyone close enough gathers to watch his speech, the team lining the wall as Carter paces the tunnel, pointing his stick, clapping helmets, hyping his boys up.

"We've come way too fucking far to let this slip away. The transformation we've made from day one to here is un-fucking-believable. I've never been prouder of a group before, and let me tell ya something, this is one hell of a fucking group!"

"Oh my," I accidentally murmur out loud. Heat rushes through me, and I barely resist the urge to fan my face.

"I've never been more attracted to Carter in my life," Cara breathes.

"I will literally let him do whatever he wants to me tonight." I'm more meaning to think it, not say it out loud, which is probably why Jennie jabs me in the ribs. "Sorry." I look to Holly; she lifts her shoulders.

"I'm counting down the days until I become a grandma. Bring it on."

All righty then.

Carter's voice gets louder, and I keep getting hotter.

"We can do it! This is it! This is the team! *My* fucking team! *My* boys! I love this fucking team, so get your asses out there and let's bring this fucking cup home! Let's fucking do it, boys!"

The tunnel erupts as Carter ushers them onto the ice, slapping every single one of their asses. The crowd turns feral as their home team takes the ice for overtime in the Stanley Cup.

Carter waves me over before stepping onto the ice. He taps his cheek. "Good luck kiss."

"Oh, baby." I take his face in my hands. "You don't need luck." I kiss his lips, then his cheek. "Now get your sweet ass out there."

His crooked smile is electric, pulling his dimples in. He winks, and before he steps onto the ice, he gives me the words he gave me so many months ago. "I'm gonna score a goal for you."

Carter is an unstoppable force when he's motivated. The man is the most relentless human being I've ever known. *No* isn't an option for him; if he wants it, he'll find a way to make it happen.

Which is why he takes off like lightning on his second shift, racing up the boards after the puck is poked loose. He glances over his shoulder for his linemates as he moves fluidly up the ice, but they're not with him.

"It's you!" Emmett hollers from behind.

The entire arena is on their feet.

Garrett races up his right, trailing him. "Let it fly!"

And the crowd is silent.

My heart's in my throat as I watch Carter slip effortlessly by one defenseman, then twirl around the other. Holly's gripping my hand so hard the tips of my fingers are numb. Cara and Jennie have their faces pressed against the glass, and Hank's got his buried in his hands, for what purpose, I'm not sure.

Carter finishes his spin with flair, lifting one foot off the ground, and takes note of the forward who's flying toward him, ready to send him straight into the boards. But Carter looks oddly calm.

He pops the puck off the ice on the blade of his stick as he dodges left, turns halfway around, and flicks that puck right over the goalie's shoulder.

The arena's a freaking zoo. All of us are crying, even Hank, and Carter gets tackled to the ground as his entire team piles on top of him. Adam whips down the ice, throwing his stick, glove, and blocker to the side as he finishes the dogpile, jumping on top of everyone.

Seriously, I can't stop crying. I regret letting Cara do my makeup. I wipe at my cheeks and my fingers come away smeared with black.

Cara's weeping. *Weeping.* "I'm gonna let that man put a baby in me next weekend," she sobs, slapping the glass. "I love you, Emmy! I love you and your big, magical dick, baby!"

We watch them roll out the carpet as both teams line up. The Stanley Cup is carried out and placed on a table as another hush falls over the arena, only the odd holler and whistle echoing through, bouncing off the high ceilings. In a turn of events, Carter gets to present the trophy for the most valuable player.

"Every single guy in this team is invaluable," he starts, talking into the microphone. "Every single one of them. But we wouldn't be where we are right now if it weren't for this guy right here." He points at Adam, who stumbles backward in shock before the guys push him forward. "Ladies and gentlemen, on your feet for the best fucking goalie in the world!"

"Courtney fucked that one up, huh," Jennie hums.

Cara claps her hands. "She sure as hell did."

When the Vipers are left alone on the ice, the cup is the captain's to hold first. Carter reaches for that huge, shiny trophy, but pauses, his hands hanging in the air.

His gaze finds mine, and he glides across the ice to me. He opens the door to the tunnel, gesturing for me, and my cheeks blaze. This is his accomplishment; I don't want to take anything away from him.

But still, I go to him, because I always will.

"Congratulations, baby," I whisper, grinning down at him and smacking my tears away.

He crooks a finger at me. "Come here." He brackets my chin in his hand. "Thank you."

"For what?"

"For making me feel like everything is within my reach if I work hard enough. This is amazing. Everything I dreamed of as a kid. But it's you who makes my world complete." He touches his lips to mine. "I love you."

With a wink and a smile, Carter steps back onto the ice. My heart bursts in my chest as he lifts that cup above his head, letting out a wild, unrestrained scream that the entire arena echoes back at him.

47

OLIVIA'S DAMN TIE

Carter

"Oh shit. Fuck. Shit, shit, shit."

I crack one sleepy lid and slam it closed the moment the sun tries to burn a hole right through my eyeball. "Baby?"

Sweeping an arm over the mattress, I register the emptiness. It's warm still, like she was here a moment ago, and I can still hear her, but where is she?

"*Babyyy*," I call again, thick and hoarse. "Come back to bed."

Feet slap against tiles, and Olivia's still spitting out all those curse words, which is oddly reminiscent of the way I woke up on New Year's Day.

"Stop it," I whine, burying my face in the pillow. "I don't like it. It reminds me of the morning you left me."

"Carter," she cries, and I hear the toilet seat slam. "I'm not—" Her words die with her heave, but I don't hear anything actually come out, and when I laugh, she starts screaming. "Are you seriously fucking"—*heave*—"laughing at me"—*double heave*—"right now?"

I flop onto my back, running a hand through my hair. My mouth is dry, my head is pounding, and while I feel like shit, I don't think I've ever been so happy. "You gotta learn how to handle your alcohol better, Ollie girl."

"*I'm five foot one!*" she shrieks, then heaves. "I drank as much as you did!"

"Right. You could learn a thing or two from me."

"I hate you," she sobs into the toilet.

"You love the fuck out of me, princess."

She doesn't grace me with a response. Instead the toilet seat slams again, and then the water cranks. Steam billows out of the bathroom, and I finally sit up.

Everything hurts. The sunshine is way too fucking bright and there's a twenty-pound rock tumbling around in my head, slamming against my skull with every minuscule movement. According to my phone, it's only 7:37 a.m. We didn't get home until after four, which means we got something like three hours of sleep.

I bury my face in my hands and groan. Olivia and I are having the whole team over for lunch, families and friends too, one shitshow that leads to another when we head downtown later tonight to celebrate.

"*Ollieee.*" I scratch my torso and fist the base of my cock as I pad toward the bathroom. "I'm sore, baby. I might feel better if you sucked my—" I fold my lips into my mouth to stop from laughing when I pull open the foggy shower door in search of my girlfriend.

I find Olivia curled up on the floor, knees pulled to her chest, soaked curls plastered to her face, down her back. I'm pretty sure she's crying, based on the redness of her eyes, but it's difficult to be sure due to the water cascading from the showerhead.

"Oh, pumpkin. What's wrong?"

Her wide brown eyes meet mine, and her mouth opens on a wail as I climb into the shower and take her in my arms.

"*I need chicken nuggets!*"

"Oh fuck. Yeah, right there, baby. Harder."

"What the shit is going on in there?" I hear Jeremy scream from the front hall. "You heard the front door open, right? You know I'm here?"

I lift my face off the living room rug. "Maybe you should knock instead of just walking in!"

Olivia snickers, little heels digging into the muscles below my shoulder blades. I bury my face in the soft rug and let out a guttural groan.

"I'm leaving! We're leaving! Jem, *no*! Come back! *Shield your eyes, little buddy!*"

Little Jem comes toddling in on his chubby legs. He's recently picked up walking, though he mostly moves around like a tiny, drunk adult. It's hilarious and cute as hell. His face lights up when he spots his aunt perched on my back and he breaks into a super-wobbly run, diving straight for my ass, which he hugs to his face.

Olivia giggles and hops off, scooping him up. "Hi, Jemmy," she coos, pulling up his Vipers tee and smooching his belly before plopping him on my chest when I roll to my back. He gives me a sloppy kiss before I toss him into the air and catch him in my arms. He smells so good, like fresh baby and coconut sunscreen.

Jeremy cautiously moves into the living room, shielding his eyes, which means he bangs his shin against the coffee table and keels over with a string of curses. Naturally, Alannah bursts through the front door at this moment, declaring he owes her five bucks.

When his gaze finds us, Jeremy sighs. "Oh, thank God. You're dressed."

"I was walking on his back." Olivia flicks his elbow before they hug.

"Why?"

"Oh, I dunno." I climb to my feet with Jem in my arms. "Maybe 'cause I kicked some serious freaking ass last night and won the Stanley Cup." I'm learning how not to swear around kids. I'm sometimes successful.

"Yeah, you did!" Alannah shrieks, dashing into the room. I catch her around the waist with one arm when she leaps at me. I fucking love these kids. "That was the best game ever, Carter. I cried! Really, I did!"

"Really, she did," Jeremy repeats with another long exhale. "She was hysterical."

Alannah scowls as she slides down my body. "You cried like a baby, Daddy."

"Did not." I might believe him if it weren't for the look on his face as his gaze settles on the shiny cup sitting on the kitchen table. His shaky hands fly to his face. "Oh. My. God. It's the . . . it's the . . ." He whimpers, and I absolutely smirk.

I plop Jem in the cup and he giggles, smacking his hands down on it.

"Oh my God!" Kristin enters the living room at a walk, but skids into the kitchen at a run. "Pictures! I need pictures!" She throws one arm around me, pulling me close as she fishes her phone out of her purse. "Congratulations, Carter. You were fantastic. You deserve it." She snaps her fingers at Jem, trying to get his attention. "Look at Mommy, Jemmy! Can you say cup? Cup! Cup, Jemmy!"

He's for damn sure not saying cup, just babbling along, but he looks happy as hell, smiling up at her for all three hundred photos she takes in fifteen seconds.

Jem peers up at me with sparkling blue eyes, reaching his tiny hands out. "Cah-Cah."

Kristin claps a hand to her mouth. "Oh. He said your name."

"He did not," Jeremy grumbles, reaching for Jem.

Jem frowns and grunts, wiggling out of his dad's reach, making grabby hands at me. "*Cah-Cah!*"

I might try to wipe the shit-eating grin off my face if I could, but it doesn't seem that I can. I pick up Jem, smooshing my cheek against his as I stare his dad right in the eyes. "He definitely said my name. Guess that's one more thing I win at in this life, Jeremy, isn't it?"

Jeremy slaps a ten-dollar bill down in Alannah's hand before he opens his mouth and unleashes that famous Parker family fury.

"CARTER." OLIVIA'S HEAD FLOPS ONTO my shoulder as she whimpers. "I'm not sure I can make it through the rest of dinner. I need to go to bed."

Her eyes are doing that dazed, glossy thing, tracking every movement slowly. She's got that drunk perma-grin slapped on her face, and her cheeks have been pink for most of the day. I need to take her home and put her to bed, but I sure as shit can't drive, so I'm trusting my driver to take Olivia and Cara and a few of the other girls home tonight.

We've been drinking since noon, and though we all look fancy as hell, taking up over half of this upscale restaurant, most of us are well on the way to incoherent, some of us somehow thriving on absolutely zero sleep. Olivia is not one of those thriving folks.

I press my lips to her hair. It smells so good, like banana bread, and instead of the fluffy curls that normally hang down her back, it's sleek and pin straight, nearly touching the dip in her back. I wanna take her into the bathroom, wrap that dark hair around my fist, shove her over the sink, and fuck her until everyone in this restaurant knows what she sounds like when she comes around my cock.

"But I gave you nuggets." My lips touch her ear. "And shower orgasms."

Her lower lip slides between her teeth. "*Three* shower orgasms."

Winding my arm around her waist, I yank her closer. In addition to banana bread, she smells like the tequila shots Cara keeps shit-talking her into taking. She's so easily goaded it's not funny.

No, wait. It's funny as fuck.

"You want me to take you home so I can fuck you in every room of our house?"

The lawyer stopped by this morning, post orgasms, to collect Olivia's keys, and tomorrow the new owner moves in. That makes her officially mine, and my house hers. So, our house.

Her fingers walk slowly up my tie. "Too many rooms."

"Sounds like a challenge to me. And you know how I feel about challenges."

Olivia drags her tongue across her bottom lip as she winds the black silk around her fist and lifts one suggestive brow. "I like this tie, Mr. Beckett."

My sword of thunder leaps to attention in my pants. "You do, do you? Let's go home so I can show you what else I like to use it for." I slap my hand over hers when it creeps under the table and lands on my bulge. "Keep it up and I'll tie these grabby hands up too."

"What the fuck are you two doing over there?" Cara slams another tequila shot down in front of Olivia before she sinks to the seat across from her.

Adam sighs, shoving his fingers through his hair. "Making me feel super single."

"Agreed." Garrett gestures to where our hands disappear. "There's a fuckload of hands where we can't see."

"Gare-Bear." Cara pushes his blond hair back. "You won the Stanley Cup last night. When us girls leave, you're probably gonna have six different hands in your lap."

His face floods with heat. "It's a guys' night."

Cara snorts. "Yeah, okay." She lifts her shot glass along. "Come on, Livvie."

Olivia raises hers to her mouth, takes a whiff, and does a whole-body shudder. "Nope. Not gonna happen. I'm officially done."

Done with alcohol, at least, because her entire face lights up when the waitress drops a plate of steak and lobster in front of her. "Oh, baby. Come to mama."

When dinner's done, I escape to the bathroom before the girls head out. It's one of those new bathrooms for all genders. I like that they did that. They're so much nicer now, with soft hand towels and foaming soap that smells like fresh cookies and makes my skin feel like silk.

My phone dings in my pocket. It's my sister with a picture of Dublin sleeping on his back, paws in the air, tongue out. Next to him is my mom, also passed out. They're on the living room floor at my mom's, which seems reasonable. Who needs a couch when you have a perfectly good floor?

Chuckling, I click the screen off and set it down on the counter before I move to the toilet and relieve myself with a sigh. I'm washing my hands for the second time 'cause the soap smells so good when the door handle jiggles.

"Just a sec," I call, drying my hands.

"All the bathrooms are full," a voice cries out. "Please, it's an emergency."

I open the door and a blonde falls into me, one hand on my chest. She's got her other fist wrapped tightly around a tampon, so I get the hell out of the way, something my dad taught me when my sister turned thirteen. Thank God, because it's proven to be extremely useful with Olivia. I don't know if you know this, but that girl sometimes has a big attitude, despite her tiny doll-like size.

When I find the girls in the lobby, Cara says Jason's already out front with the limo. She skips out the door, arms looped through a couple of the other girls' like some sort of impenetrable chain. I squeeze Olivia into me, whimpering.

"Carter, you don't have to feel bad about spending a night away from me. We have all summer to get sick of each other."

"The rest of our lives, you mean." I bury my words in her neck. "I have the rest of my life to annoy and love the shit outta you, and you have the rest of your life to put up with me."

"Mmm. You're lucky I tolerate you so well."

"So lucky."

Olivia presses up on her toes, kissing my cheek. "Just gotta run to the bathroom."

I smile at the way she dances off to the bathroom, but outwardly groan at the tall blonde who starts sauntering over to me the second Olivia disappears. It's the same one who burst through the bathroom door a few minutes ago. She looks a hell of a lot more composed than she did then, and I find myself thinking the tampon emergency was maybe a ruse.

"Every fucking time," I mumble to myself. "I swear."

"Pardon?" She stops in front of me, running her tongue along her teeth as she looks me over. Tampon ruse, definitely.

I sigh, shaking my hair out. "I was saying to myself that this always happens every time my girlfriend goes to the bathroom."

"Well, maybe she shouldn't leave a man as handsome as yourself standing here all alone." She steps into me, reaching for my tie, and I hit her with some sort of pseudo–judo chop before I step back.

That's Olivia's damn tie.

"Is she leaving?"

Seriously, why is she still talking to me? And where is Olivia? She's not allowed to go to the bathroom in public places anymore.

"Maybe we can go somewhere private to talk when she's gone."

I'm about to tell her to fuck off when Olivia swings around her and tucks herself into my side.

"He's good, but thanks for the offer." Her smile is all fake sugar. I love it. "If you hope to ever be happy in a relationship, I suggest you start with quitting whatever the hell this is, going after men who are happily taken. It's not working for you, is it?" She looks up at me. "Carter, do you want to go somewhere private to talk with her?"

"Fuck no."

"And why not, baby?"

"Because I've already got the only woman I'll ever need."

She smiles up at me, hand curving around my neck as she brings my mouth to hers. "Does that answer your question?" she asks Blondie, but doesn't give her the chance to reply. Instead, her fingers twine with mine and she tugs me toward the door.

I don't think it's possible to be more shocked than I already am, but then she pushes me up against the bricks of the building on the sidewalk and yanks my face down to hers. Her tongue is commanding, her touch possessive, and I eat up every single second of it.

The window of the waiting limo rolls down and Cara pops her head out. "Let's fucking go, Livvie-pie! Jay-Jay's gonna take us through the McDick's drive-thru! Fries and McFlurries, baby!"

Olivia pulls away, breathless, and swipes her hair off her forehead. "Have fun, be safe, and I love you." She kisses me once more, gives my dick a loving pat-pat through my pants, and then disappears inside the limo.

I'm in a daze by the time I wander back inside the lobby, half-drunk but mostly just happy as a pig in shit. I can't wait to make that woman my fiancée, and then my wife.

"She's annoyingly possessive."

I spin around, finding the blonde leaning against the bar. She picks up her wineglass, swirling the red liquid, and steps forward.

"Can we talk now that we're alone?"

"That's a fuck no. You heard my girlfriend."

"I might be able to change your mind," she purrs quietly.

"You can't, actually. Nobody will change my mind about that girl. I'd never do anything to hurt her."

"Are you sure about that, Carter?" comes a familiar voice from behind me.

Slowly, I twist. My stomach drops when my gaze lands on the redhead smirking at me. "What the fuck are you doing here, Courtney? Adam doesn't want to see you."

"It's a free country. I can go wherever I like." Courtney shrugs, then pulls something from the purse hanging off her shoulder. "Think you misplaced this at some point tonight."

My eyes fall to the sleek black object she spins in her hand before presenting it to me on her palm.

"What kind of a friend would I be if I didn't return something so valuable, Carter?"

48

SLOW DANCING IN A BURNING ROOM

Olivia

It's four a.m., and this is the third time I've woken up. There's a pit of unease inside me that grows bigger each time, though I can't explain why.

I haven't heard from Carter. Yes, he's out with his team, but he's never gone this long without a word. Even when he knows I'm sleeping I often wake up to multiple messages telling me how much he loves me or what he's going to do to me when he gets home.

But tonight? Nothing.

It's an irrational fear, probably. They won the cup. They're celebrating; they deserve to.

But something feels wrong, so I bite the bullet and dial his number. When it goes directly to voicemail, the sinking feeling in my stomach grows exponentially.

Lying back in bed, I hug his pillow to me. It smells like him, fresh citrus with a hint of smoky woods, but it doesn't help me fall back asleep. When anxiety creeps in, I have a difficult time reminding myself how to breathe properly.

When my phone rings twenty minutes later, I scramble over the edge of the bed.

"Liv?" Cara's voice is low, but I hear the slight edge in her tone.

"What is it? Is everything okay?"

"It's . . . yeah. It's fine. Em just got home. He was wondering . . . is Carter there?"

"He's not home yet. Didn't they leave together?"

There are muted ramblings, like Cara's covering the phone. "Emmett said Carter came back to the table after we left, grabbed his suit jacket, and took off without a word. He never . . . he never came back. Em figured he went home to you, but they've been calling him all night, and—"

"His phone's off." I breathe the words that burn like acid. "I can't get ahold of him." Throwing my legs over the edge of the bed, I grip my stomach, keeling forward. There's a vise around my heart, squeezing tight, and I feel like I'm going to vomit. I can't calm my thoughts fast enough to tell myself that Carter's safe, that he's okay. "What if . . . what if he got in an accident? What if he's hurt?" I rub at my chest, trying to ease the pain.

"I'm sure he's fine," Cara insists gently. It's the voices in the background that are anxiously muttering, wondering where their friend is, their captain. "Do you want me to come over and wait with you?"

"No, I'm . . . I'm fine." The lie tastes sour, like it disagrees with my stomach. "He's fine. I'll text you when he gets home."

I spend the next hour pacing the bedroom, sitting on the balcony, scrolling aimlessly through my phone, waiting for a text message, a phone call that never comes.

It's shortly after five in the morning that I'm tagged in the first series of photos from a popular gossip account.

The first is of me and Carter kissing outside the restaurant. The second is Carter from behind. It's dark, but the people hugging each of his arms are unmistakably female, one with long red hair, the other blonde. They're stepping inside a building.

A hotel.

The caption?

Stanley Cup champ Carter Beckett can't resist the bunnies post-win.

Beckett, seen here with girlfriend, high school teacher Olivia Parker, a mere hour before he disappears inside a hotel with two females!

The pictures keep rolling in. Endless photos, all from different angles, and my heart shatters when I catch a glimpse of the faces of the beautiful women on his arms.

The blonde from outside the bathroom in the restaurant.

And Courtney.

The captions, somehow, get worse. There are old pictures of Courtney and Carter, speculation that Carter is the reason Courtney and Adam broke up, that he's been cheating on me with her the entire time. That I'm the young and naïve schoolteacher— and single mother of two, apparently—that fell for his charm, despite the warning signs. That Carter fooled me.

My phone rings, Cara's face on my screen, but she's not who I need right now.

I need Carter. Because this isn't right. It *can't* be right. This isn't Carter, not the man who's so obsessively in love, who treats me like his queen. Not the man that moved me into his home and talks constantly about marriage and babies and forever.

There has to be an explanation, something they're missing. Something we're all missing.

It's 7:16 a.m. when I hear the beep of the keypad on the front door.

I fly out of the bedroom and down the stairs as Carter steps into the house. I note his downcast gaze, the obvious heartache that weighs him down, but I don't stop until my body collides with his. I wrap my arms around him as tight as I can, needing to feel him, to know he's okay.

His broad body stiffens at my touch before he sinks into me, one hand in my hair, the other at my lower back, pressing me closer, holding me tighter.

I try to force his gaze to mine, but it doesn't come. "Are you okay? Are you hurt?"

"I love you." The way he whispers my three favorite words, laced with brokenness, sounds like they're not quite meant for me to hear.

Or maybe they are.

Just one last time.

"Carter." His face, over his rough stubble, the strong line of his rugged jaw. "Look at me, baby."

He doesn't. He doesn't move a muscle, except for the almost imperceptible tic in his jaw, the vein pulsing in the side of his neck.

"*Carter.* Look at me."

"I can't," he whispers, the words weak, shattered. Something wet drops, splattering onto my forearms where I'm reaching between us, holding his face in my hands.

Something inside me stretches past the point of painful. My body makes the decision to move, to step back, putting distance between us that my mind is trying to convince me we need, even though my heart is telling me to hang on.

"Did you get a room with them?"

Silence.

"Carter. Answer me. Did you get a room with them? Did you go upstairs?"

"Yes," he croaks.

My hand flies to my mouth in an attempt to stifle my gasp. It doesn't work. "What happened? What happened, Carter?" I beg him for an answer, but he doesn't give me one. "You didn't cheat on me, Carter. You wouldn't."

Carter's head whips up, and for the first time since he's walked in here, he looks at me. His bloodshot eyes, red rimmed and glossy, swimming with pain, bore into me. He takes a half step forward, reaching for me, but pauses. His gaze drops to his outstretched arm, then back to me, cowering away from him.

"I—I . . . Olivia." My name is a cry on his lips, a plea, or maybe an apology. I'm not sure.

But the next sound from my mouth is a garbled, strangled sob that makes his green eyes wild, and he finally takes that step toward me.

"No," I cry, spinning out of reach. My chest heaves like it's breaking, ripping wide open, and I can't breathe properly. I place my palm over my heart, willing the pain to stop, but it doesn't. I don't know what to do, and when Carter whispers the next words, everything inside me feels like it's broken.

"I'm so sorry."

Tears freefall down both our faces.

"No." I shake my head. "No." This isn't real. This isn't Carter.

"Baby." He moves cautiously toward me.

"*No.*" I rip my hands away. I can barely see through the tears as I stare up at him, the man I gave my everything to, the love that changed my life. "I trusted you."

"I—I . . . I don't . . . Olivia, I just . . ." Carter stops, dropping his face to his hands and muttering out a *fuck* I almost don't hear. "What's wrong with me? I don't know how to . . . it's not . . . It's broken, Ollie."

Racing up the stairs, I grab my bag from the closet and fill it as fast as I can with whatever fits. Moving into the bathroom, I sweep my things off the counter and into the bag, and Carter's behind me, shaking, frantic.

"No, no, no," he chants, following my every move. "No, Ollie, you-you can't. You can't."

He tears down the stairs behind me, looking like he's on the verge of having a heart attack while I slip my sandals on. That's how I'm feeling, anyway. Like this heart is never going to function properly again.

Carter follows me into the garage, and the only word he seems to be able to say is *no* as he watches me slip the key to his truck off my key ring and grab my car keys off the hook. I haven't driven this thing in four months. I'm only sure it'll still run because Carter turns it on once a week to keep the battery from dying. So considerate, always.

So, why? *Why?*

I can't stick around to find out the answer to that question, since he seems intent on not communicating with me right now. I hit the button for the garage door, and Carter turns feral, slamming my car door the second I open it.

"No! I won't let you!"

With two hands on his chest, I shove against him. I'm sobbing now, making my next words weak and broken, even if I'm yelling. "You don't get to tell me what to do! You're not in charge! I put all of my trust in you! All of it, Carter!" I choke on a sob, burying my face in my hands as I cry. "And you don't even have the decency to tell me what happened. You're not answering me! Talk to me!" I beg, gripping his shirt. "Please, Carter!"

His eyes bounce between mine, strong hands gripping my wrists. "I—I—I . . . I can't. I don't know how." He hangs his head in shame, defeated.

The end is supposed to be easier than the start. Because this isn't the way this was supposed to go. Or maybe it's exactly how it was always destined to end.

In this moment, I'm taken back to the night Carter convinced me to dance with him, the night I realized I was falling for a man I had no business falling for.

And I think the exact same thing I thought back then: we were slow dancing in a burning room.

That's all we've been doing. Pretending the inevitable wouldn't happen. That this all wouldn't go up in flames.

But it is. This life we've built together, the future I put so much stock in, the forever I was so sure about it. It's been doused in gasoline, torched.

My heart will never be the same after Carter Beckett.

He steps away from the car, allowing me to open the door. I throw my bag inside before I climb in.

"I love you." His words are shattered, lifeless. "I love you, Ollie."

"You know, I never doubted that until now." Truth be told, there's still some desperate, sadistic part of me that believes him, or wants to, at least. Because I don't think there's a person alive who loves the way he does, unwavering, wholesome, passionate, and obsessive.

And yet here we are. This is what kept me afraid and at a distance for too long, but he's spent the last six months grinding all those preconceived notions to dust.

I look up at him through blurred eyes. "I'll never stop loving you, even if you've broken me beyond repair." I don't know if that makes me weak or brave. I just know that even though I back out of the driveway, it's the last thing I want to do.

I watch Carter fall to pieces in the garage while I fall to pieces on the inside, and everything feels so utterly wrong, so devastatingly broken.

I don't know where I'm going. I don't have a home, and the person I need more than anything, the only one who can take all of this away, the pain, the heartache, is the one who's brought it all in the first place.

Visiting hours don't start until eight, so I sit in the parking lot and fall apart some more, until I'm sure I can't be put back together.

When I burst through the door of the suite, I find the man I'm looking for sitting on his balcony, looking nearly as defeated as I feel.

He lifts his head from his fist, weathered blue eyes searching for his visitor.

Whatever's left of my heart crumbles to pieces as I cry out his name. "Hank."

"Olivia." He stands, spreading his arms wide. "Come here, sweetheart."

49

FOREVER DOWN THE DRIVEWAY

Carter

FOREVER IS A FUNNY CONCEPT.

People talk about it all the time. It's the only thing they want, a forever spent living the life they've always dreamed of, with the people they can't imagine ever losing.

But nothing lasts forever, does it? We spend our days waiting for it to come, that moment we want to last, that person we never want to let go of, and when we have it, we grab hold. We grip it so tight, say *this is it, my forever, and I'm never, ever giving it up.*

The thing is, it's not always up to us. Moments are fleeting, and people are too. Sometimes these things run their course; they get up and leave willingly. And sometimes they're stolen from you, torn from your grasp as you hold on for dear life.

Twelve hours ago, I had my forever. I had every single thing I'd always dreamed of. Fuck, I'd even convinced myself I'd still had my dad, right there inside me where Olivia told me he'd always be.

And now, I have nothing.

The Stanley Cup sits on my table, taking up space. A reminder of something I don't deserve, something meaningless. I spent my whole life working toward it, telling myself it was all I wanted. But I was wrong, wasn't I?

Because Olivia's my dream, and it all means nothing without her.

I don't need to see the articles. I was there when the cameras were in our faces, lighting up the night around us. I know what it looks like, what it was *meant* to look like. And I know I just stood there in front of the woman I love and didn't put her fears to rest. Didn't give her the truth she begged for, which is that I'd smash my reputation into the ground before I'd hurt her that way. The words wouldn't come, stuck on my tongue, caught in my throat, because the last thing I ever wanted to be was the person who disappointed her, hurt her.

But I don't know how to solve this, this clusterfuck of a shit-storm, and therein lies the problem. How can I open my mouth and be honest with her when I don't have all the answers?

Something's not working inside me, a connection that's been severed at the mere thought of a life without my best friend. My hands won't stop shaking, my heart racing. With every moment spent staring down at my phone, the influx of messages, phone calls from everyone except the only person I want to hear from, it gets worse.

Because this phone. *This fucking phone* is the bane of my damn existence right now, and I hate it.

I stare at my screen, at Olivia's smiling face, the Oreo in her hand. She's everything, my girl, and there isn't a way I could love her more than I do. My thumb hovers over the folder affection-ately labeled *My Pumpkin*, but I can't do it.

How could I have been so careless?

When Emmett messages me to let me know Olivia is safe, my phone goes flying across the room. The shattered screen shines in the refracted rays of sun that shine through the break in the curtains, and I wonder if I'll ever feel it again, the sunshine Olivia brought.

It hasn't always been perfect, but it's always been worth it. We've grown so much together, learned what the other needed, so maybe we weren't perfect, but the way she's loved me has always been perfect. And that's how I've always known.

My forever is a person. It's wide chocolate eyes that peer up at mine, and dark, silky curls that slip through my fingers. It's a small hand in mine that warms my entire body, a smile that gets my heart thudding a little bit harder, a little bit faster. It's the ears that hear all my dreams and the arms that hold me up when I'm tired, when I forget how to stand. It's the lips on my jaw, my cheek, my hand, the ones that whisper my favorite *I love you*, that promise me a lifetime against my skin.

I don't know everything. All I know is I just chased my forever down the driveway.

I'm not surprised that Olivia ran to the same place I did after leaving home. I don't have a doubt that she's been here. I can smell her hair, that intrinsic scent that reminds me of home and Sunday mornings cuddled together on the couch while the coffee brews and the muffins bake.

"Carter," Hank calls from his spot, staring out his balcony door. How he knows it's me standing silently in his doorway is beyond me. "You gonna come in or just stand there?"

I don't say a word as I take a seat beside him. He unfolds his hands, tapping a single finger for a moment of silence that stretches too long. When he sighs, shame makes my neck damp as I wait for him to tell him how disappointed he is in me.

But he doesn't.

He sits in silence, a deep crease set between his brows as he keeps his gaze trained ahead, for ten minutes, and then twenty. It's not until the first half hour comes to a close that he finally opens his mouth.

"I'm gonna tell you the same thing I told Olivia. You are not a man who would intentionally betray someone's trust, someone who loves him, who he loves without a shadow of a doubt. You wouldn't hurt that girl if your life depended on it. She's your whole world. Not hockey. Not that cup sitting pretty in your house right now, the one you've been working toward your whole life. *Olivia. That girl.* She's your world and she has been right from the beginning. If you took your last breath right now, your final words would be—"

"A declaration of how much I love her." I don't need to think about it. Olivia's my first thought when my eyes open in the morning and the last one before I fall asleep. She occupies about 99 percent of the space in between too.

"Exactly." Hank points toward the Nespresso machine Olivia and I bought him when he moved in. "So, you're gonna make me a damn cappuccino, strap on your boots, and tell me what actually happened so we can figure out how the hell you can make this right."

He waves a hand around my face. "I don't need to be able to see to know you look like a damn mess, son, and I won't sit by and let you throw your happiness away because you didn't know how best to keep her safe without breaking her heart."

MY DRIVEWAY IS HALF FULL when I get home, a blessing and a curse. I want to be alone, but I probably shouldn't be. My mind is a dangerous place to be right now.

I note the pile of shoes in the doorway and my naïve heart is desperate enough to think Olivia might be here too.

Emmett, Garrett, and Adam poke their heads into the hallway. Garrett's got a bag of chips out of the cupboard. He stops when he sees me, midcrunch, and slowly drops the bag.

My head swivels, following the movement I hear upstairs.

"Carter," Emmett cautions, but it's too late; I'm already halfway up the staircase.

"Olivia?" Heart racing, I halt in the bedroom doorway, watching Cara pack Olivia's clothes in a suitcase. I tear the clothes from her hands, ripping them from the suitcase. "No. No. It's not—she's not—you can't! She's coming back! She's coming back, Cara. She has to."

I don't know what I expect from Cara. To yell at me, shake me, maybe detach my balls from my body like she's so often threatened if I ever break her best friend. What I don't expect is the tears pooling in her eyes, the grief reflected in her gaze, the sympathy.

"She's coming back," I whisper, but the words are fractured, broken, just like me. When I blink, when a single tear rolls down my cheek, she flings herself into my arms.

"You have to fix this," she cries. "Carter, fix this!"

"I—I—I . . . I don't know how!" Hank told me how. He told me what I need to do. It feels pointless, but then again, I don't have many other options. "Help me," I beg softly.

The floor creaks behind us and the boys trickle into the room, quiet and careful, like they aren't sure what to do or say.

"I would never cheat on her." My eyes fall on Adam, though he's looking at the ground. He may be done with Courtney but that doesn't mean what's happened, or what everyone thinks happened, hasn't hurt him. "Adam, I promise, I didn't—"

His arms come around me, a hug I didn't know I needed. "I know, Carter. I know."

"We all know." Cara sinks to the edge of the bed, a small velvet box in her hand. She pops the lid, examining the sparkly diamond inside, the ring she helped me design for Olivia back in May. I picked it up last week, and I spent hours hiding it while Olivia was at work, choosing one spot then changing my mind five minutes later, picking another I thought might be better. That Cara's somehow managed to find it isn't surprising, and I don't have it in me to be mad that she went snooping.

She brushes Olivia's clothes aside and pats the spot next to her. When I take it, she squeezes my hand. "We're going to help you figure this out, but you have to tell us what happened."

"I don't know where to start," I admit. I'm in way over my head and I knew that from the second Courtney approached me last night.

"Start from the beginning."

I breathe deeply, searching for strength. "Ollie, she . . . she let me take pictures." Too many pictures. Months and months of pictures of my favorite girl in my favorite positions.

"What kind of pictures?"

My throat squeezes as I keep my gaze trained on my hands in my lap. This was our secret and I thought it'd always remain that way. "Pictures of her. Of . . . us . . ."

"Oh fuck." Emmett drops his face to his hands.

"Tell me you didn't keep them on your phone," Adam pleads with me.

My defeated expression tells them everything they need to know.

I kept the photos on my phone. The password I chose to lock the folder was fucking mindless. *1022*. Olivia's birthday. Too predictable, and a simple Google search tells you that answer. It wouldn't be for the average person, but being with me put her in the limelight, which meant the world knew more about her than they needed to. *My fault.*

These are all the things Courtney reminded me of when she dangled my phone in front of my face, a picture of my beautiful girlfriend peering up at me from the screen, when I knew I'd do whatever it took to protect Olivia.

I MAKE IT ONE HOUR on Monday.

One hour until I know she's alone in that house after she gets home from work.

One hour longer than my body tells me it can wait, but it does, somehow.

One hour until my feet are pounding up that staircase, opening every spare bedroom, stopping when I get to the last door on the left.

I don't know what the fuck I'm doing here. I don't have the words, and I sure as fuck still don't have the answers. All I know is I have nothing without her, not a damn thing, and I won't survive this without her.

The bag she packed sits on the floor, the bed a rumpled mess, littered with tissues. The adjoining bathroom door is cracked, the shower running.

My heart tries to leap up my throat when the water stops, engulfing the room in silence.

For only the briefest moment.

Olivia's soft, quiet cries pierce the air, and all logic leaves me as I move toward her. I can't remember what I came here to say, only that I love her, so fucking much, that I'm sorry, that I can't be without her.

That I need her to come home.

My heart shatters at the sight before me: Olivia, wrapped in a towel, her hair drenched and splattered across her shoulders as she sits on the bathroom floor with her face in her hands and cries.

I sink to my knees in front of her, my fingers wrapping around her forearms, and her head whips up with a choked gasp. She leaps to her feet, clutching her towel to her chest, and slaps furiously at the tears streaming down her cheeks. It's no use; she sobs harder, louder, and I think I'm dying.

In fact, when she dashes into the bedroom, cowering in the corner, like she's afraid of me, I'm certain of it.

"Ollie," I plead. "Come here, baby."

She covers her face, head whipping back and forth, and when I whisper her name once more, her eyes flip open. There's no anger there, and fuck, what I wouldn't kill for that. There's just brokenness. Shattered pieces of her heart reflected right there in her gaze.

Her trembling arm lifts as she points at the door. "You need to . . . you need to go." Her eyes squeeze shut as tears drench her face. "Please, Carter."

Another fissure in my heart at the way she tries to smoosh herself into the corner when I approach her, like she's damn near trying to disappear right into the wall. I've earned this, the fear that comes with being too close to me, like I might break her further, but I step forward anyway, taking her face in my hands. I'm not fucking perfect, that much is clear. I make mistakes all the time and she always loves me through them. I'm going to be better, for me and for her. I'm going to fix this, even if it's not right this moment.

"Listen to me. Please."

Her lower lip trembles and her teeth descend, a weak attempt at quelling the quiver as her gaze swims with heartache. Her chest rises and falls in rhythm with mine, both of us battling for air, trying and failing to fill our lungs.

"I'm sorry, Olivia."

Her eyes fall shut, and I swipe at her delicate, raw skin, coaxing her gaze back open.

"I'm sorry that I can't see through this right now. I'm sorry that I couldn't talk, that I still can't find the words to explain this all to you. I'm sorry that my silence spoke words that weren't and aren't true."

"Aren't they?" she whispers. "Because your silence made me feel like I wasn't enough, Carter. It perpetuated a feeling that we worked so hard to get rid of, but one that came roaring back with those pictures, those articles." Her eyes rise to the ceiling before floating back down to me, and the pain that swims behind them twists in my stomach like a knife. "You know what they're saying, don't you? They're saying the verdict is out. Olivia Parker is not enough for Carter Beckett. They're saying I should've known, the way they knew all along."

She shifts my hands off her face, making to move by me. My hand shoots out, wrapping around her arm, bringing her back to me. Mocha eyes widen as they peer up at me, and when I push her against the wall, her breath catches in her throat. I'm as gentle as I can be with her right now but something inside me flips like a switch at her words.

"You have always been enough. *Always*. You're so fucking enough, it's ridiculous."

"That's not at all how I feel right now. I feel worthless, Carter. Worthless and so fucking empty. Shattered. You built me up, but you're also the person who tore me down."

Her lips part as tears tip over the edge of my eyes, clinging to my lower lashes. I blink, and they fall without permission. With them, Olivia's tears fall harder, faster.

"I will build you back up, Olivia. I promise you."

"How?" The whispered word is strangled with a strange mix of hope and disbelief.

"With the truth. With answers. With love. I know everything is broken right now. I know it all hurts. But I would never cheat on you. There's nobody else for me, not for one night, and not for a lifetime."

She wants to believe me; I can see it in her eyes. They say she would've believed me, trusted me without a single doubt if I had only talked to her when she asked. But the pain there says she doesn't know anymore.

"Please don't give up on me. Please, Ollie, because I'm trying so fucking hard not to give up on myself right now. I know it feels like I am, like I'm giving up on us. I don't have the words you need right now, the answers you deserve, but that doesn't mean I'm not trying to find them. None of this makes sense right now and I fucking hate myself because I'm hurting you. But I'm asking you to trust me. I'm asking you to give me a little bit of time to figure this out, to fix it. I will, Olivia. I will fix this."

Her gaze wavers but never drops. "What if it can't be fixed?"

"That's not possible." I rest my forehead against hers, my eyes shutting as I brush my thumbs over her cheekbones, feeling her warm, damp skin. "There is no me without you, and I won't stop until it's fixed." I gather her wet curls in my hand and stroke my fingers down her face. "Do you still love me?"

She places her hand on top of mine. "I'll always love you, Carter."

"Then please. Please, hang on. Wait for me. Give me a chance. I promise, Olivia, I won't let you down. Not again."

Hesitancy flickers in her eyes, and before it can steal her, I press my lips to hers. She opens for me without a second thought, sinking into my touch, and I wind my arms around her, pulling her close, until there's nowhere left for us to go. I memorize the feel of her body against mine, the way I can swallow her whole, the way her skin lights mine ablaze, and I cling to that feeling, the never-ending love, *my forever*.

"I love you, Olivia. So fucking much."

She pulls back, my face in her hands as her heartbreaking gaze holds mine. "I love you, too, Carter, but for right now, you need to leave." Pressing up on her toes, she touches her lips once more to mine, letting them linger before she slips out of my hold.

I don't want that to be my answer, not her walking away.

Just as the last of my heart shatters, she pauses in the doorway of the bathroom. "I'm not going anywhere, Carter. If you come back to me, I'll be here, but I need you to come back with answers."

*

I SIT AROUND ALL NIGHT. Sit at the kitchen island with my head in my hand. Sit on the bench in the shower while the water beats down on me. Sit on the balcony where I fell in love with Olivia, where she looked at the view while I looked at her. And I sit at my dad's grave. I sit there and ask for guidance, for a way out, for a strength I didn't know I'd ever need.

Until finally I find myself standing for the first time in hours, looking up at a building that's much quieter now the sun has gone down.

A police officer looks up from behind the front desk, smiling as I stand in the doorway with my hands in my pockets.

"Can I help you?"

"I need to file a police report."

50

RECLAIMING MY FOREVER

Olivia

I'M GOING ON SIX HOURS of sleep. Six hours split between three nights. Pair that with my shitty sleep Saturday night and the near all-nighter from Friday? It's Wednesday morning and I'm sitting at a grand total of thirteen hours over the last five nights.

Let me be clear: I am not functioning properly. My brain is a foggy, dark mess that I so desperately want out of but can't find the ladder to crawl up. I've been living off iced lattes and Big Macs. My stomach hurts, I feel like shit, look like hell, and don't care.

Frankly, it's a miracle I'm dragging myself to work, but it's the only normalcy I have left, and no one's dared say a word to me.

I roll over, pulling the blankets tighter around my shoulders. The soft orange glow of the rising sun peeks through the tiniest crack in the curtains, and all I want it to do is rain. I've spent months feeling like sunshine, even during the bleakest, snowiest winter, and the grayest spring. Now that the sun's here, all I want it to do is go away.

I still have two hours until I have to be up, but any chance of sleep has left.

There's an irrational, fucked-up part of me that frowns at the notifications on my phone. I have tons, but none are from Carter. The logical part of my brain tries to tell me the space is good. It's what I asked for, after all. The rest of me begs me to call him, to make sure he's okay. Because he promised he'd be back, and he's not. I'm here and he's there, and with each passing minute, the distance feels farther, the hole in my heart gaping wider.

He promised me answers, and the longer he's away, the more I worry there isn't any.

I swipe at my screen, over and over, pictures of us smiling up at me, until I settle on one of my favorites. I'm laughing, looking into the camera, and Carter's got his arms around me from behind, his chin on my shoulder with his biggest, goofiest grin. But he's not looking at the camera.

He's looking at me.

Never in my life has somebody looked at me the way that man looks at me, like I'm the only thing he sees, like someone seeing in color for the first time. He holds so much love in his gaze, fierce appreciation, devotion, and that right there is why my heart keeps urging me that something doesn't add up. It's why I promised him the time he begged for right here in this room, the time to figure it out.

The door to my room creaks open, and I hug my phone against my chest, swiping at my tears as Cara pops her head inside.

She smiles and pads toward the bed, slipping beneath the covers and snuggling into me. "I knew you'd be up. It's like I can hear the wheels in your head turning."

"What are you doing up?" *Besides the obvious, which is checking on me.*

Cara and Emmett are getting married this weekend, and I'm all she can focus on. She insists it's a welcome distraction from wedding worries. I don't know if I believe her, but she sure makes me feel like I belong here.

"Couldn't sleep. You wouldn't talk to me last night and you know I don't deal well with the word *no*." Her hand brushes over my phone, and she gives it a tug. "What's this?"

I hug it closer to my chest. "Nothing."

Cara pins me to the mattress, wrestling my phone from my grasp, because like she said, she doesn't deal well with *no*'s. She doesn't say anything when she finds the picture, nor when she drops the phone on the bed, slamming her body into mine from behind in a hold that has the power to cut off my oxygen supply if she were to squeeze a touch harder.

I can tell she's crying by the slight quiver in her body, the tiny sniffles. She thinks I don't hear her cry to Emmett at night, but I do. My best friend loves me ferociously, and for that, I'm truly blessed.

"Where is he?" My body shakes with a sob, and Cara buries her face in my hair, shaking right along with me. "He said he'd be back. He said he'd fix it, that he'd find the answer and explain everything. He promised, Cara, but it's been two days and he's not here."

"He'll be here," she whispers. It's a promise she sounds so certain making, no matter how heavy the words are. When I roll out of her arms and sit up, she sits up, too, wiping her cheeks.

"My heart hurts so much," I admit, wiping at a tear that gathers in the corner of my eye. "This doesn't feel like Carter. Not at all. He was talking about our wedding and babies. He was calling it our home long before I moved in. He wanted to share everything, his whole life. And I only wanted to be a part of it."

"Oh, honey. You're the biggest part. You know that."

"Why can't he just talk to me? What's stopping him? What doesn't he want me to know?"

There's a part of me that's sure Cara knows what's going on in some capacity, that she's dying to tell me, and if I'd come right out and ask her to, she would. But it puts her and Emmett in a position they shouldn't have to be in, between their best friends. I don't want them to have to choose sides, because I don't want there to *be* sides. I have to believe there's a perfectly logical reason for all of this, even if it's a little misguided.

"If this were reversed, if it were me trying to find my way through this, Carter wouldn't take no for an answer. He'd demand we do this together. He wouldn't let me go through this on my own, no matter how much I'd try to push him away."

Cara's blue eyes hold mine. "You're right."

"I don't want him to do this, to try to be strong on his own."

"What *do* you want?"

I want to be next to my person instead of feeling so lost without him. I want us, together and forever. I want the answers I deserve, and if he's having trouble finding them, then I want to help him look.

"I want to show him what he's been showing me all along. That we're stronger together."

That's why I call him three times on my lunch break. When I get his voicemail a fourth time after work, I wind up out front of the house that was supposed to be my home, the one that's *been* my home all these months, simply because of the person inside it, the memories made within the walls.

His truck sits in the driveway though it was last tucked in the garage. He barely drives this thing anymore; he says it's my baby now, and I'm his.

So if he's home, why isn't he answering the door?

I knock again, over and over, and my phone keeps buzzing, the video doorbell telling me there's someone at the front door. I know there's someone at the front door; the someone is me.

My knocks go from timid and gentle to frantic and hard, my palm slapping the wood as I beg for Carter to come, to open the door, to let me in. I call his phone once, then twice, and when I finally give in, punching in the code to the front door, when it beeps three times and tells me it's wrong, that the code's not the one it was just days ago, the tears come.

I sink down to the porch steps as the floodgates open, and with my knees pulled to my chest, I bury my face in my arms and sob.

Everything leaves me, the hope I was clinging to, and now all I have is the fear I've been trying to ignore, the one that creeps up my stomach and tries to make a home in my chest. I don't want to let it.

Something warm and wet touches my elbow, then my fingers. It laps at my ear, and I sniffle, peeking through the crack in my arms at the two golden paws that rest between my feet.

"Ollie."

My chest cracks wide open at my name, all the love it's whispered with, the shock at finding me here. That fear that's been trying so hard to take root claws its way out, escaping as two warm hands capture my face.

Glossy emerald eyes peer down at me, and when I cry out his name, Carter wraps his arms around me and yanks me into his embrace.

"You didn't answer your phone," I cry. "And the code. I tried the code, and it's not working. You locked me out."

"Oh, baby." His palm skates over my back, his touch rough as I cling to him. "I would never try to keep you out. I changed it to keep everyone else out. Everything's been so overwhelming, and without you here, I needed some time to myself, time to think without people in my ear."

"You said you were coming back, Carter. You said that. But you . . ." I pry my face from his neck, swiping at my sopping cheeks as he holds me. "Why haven't you come back to me?"

Shame tints his cheekbones. Carter takes a seat on the step, setting me on his lap, and smooths my hair back from my damp face as Dublin lies beside us.

"It's still broken, Ollie. I have to fix it before I deserve to come back to you."

"No," I say firmly, fisting his shirt in my hands. "That's not what you taught me. You taught me to communicate. You taught me to lean on you when I need strength, and you're supposed to lean on me too. Because we're supposed to do these things together, aren't we? Work through the hard stuff, the fears?"

His eyes cloud, an uncertainty that takes over, steals the brilliance of his evergreen forest and replaces it with a bleak and hazy fog. He rests his forehead against mine, a tremor in his voice as he whispers, "I'm so scared, Olivia."

"I don't want you to be scared alone. That's not how we do things in this relationship."

My tongue touches my top lip, tasting the saltiness of my tears, and before I can think twice, I cover his mouth with mine. Carter's fingers crawl up my back, diving into my hair, clutching me to him as I kiss him.

When I pull back, I trap the single tear tracking its way down his cheek. "Please talk to me, Carter. Give me the truth, and together we'll find the answers."

His inhale is staggered, his exhale every bit as anxious. But he presses his lips to mine once more, and finally, he talks.

"I did go upstairs with them. Courtney and her friend, I still don't know her name. I only did because Courtney had . . . she had my phone. Her friend found it in the bathroom at the restaurant. I was so careless, and I must have forgotten it, and when Courtney showed it to me . . ." He swallows. "She had one of your private pictures up."

Something strange claws up my throat, a mixture of anger and fear. Anger that somebody could be so callous, fear for what that means for me, for us.

There's something else there, the nagging reminder in the back of my head that I'm not perfect. That there have been so many women before me with smaller waists, rounder breasts. Shame curdles in my stomach, but for only a moment. Because then I remember that I'm perfect for Carter, that he thinks I'm beautiful, and what anyone else thinks doesn't matter in the slightest.

"I'm so sorry, Olivia. I should've been more careful. I never should've kept them on my phone."

I place my palm on his cheek, calming him. "What happened next?"

"She told me she'd already sent all the pictures to herself, that if I didn't want them to get out I needed to come with her."

"What did she want? Money? Did she blackmail you?"

A bitter chuckle leaves his lips. "If she'd wanted money, we wouldn't be in this mess. I tried, trust me. I threw it all at her, but she didn't want it." He runs an agitated hand through his hair, mussing his waves. "She said we ruined her life, that Adam didn't trust her anymore because of what happened that one weekend at the bar, that he would've been able to forgive her cheating otherwise. She said it wasn't fair that I was getting another chance after my past, that she couldn't stand seeing me portrayed as such a perfect boyfriend. She wanted to remind everyone of who I really am."

"But that's not who you are, Carter. You aren't your past, and it doesn't define you. There is such a beautiful, incredible person behind every decision you've ever made."

He looks down, nodding. "She wanted to hurt us, and I think I let her."

"Why didn't you tell me all that?"

"Because she wanted me to break up with you. She wouldn't get rid of the pictures until she knew we were done. I can't ever be done, Ollie, not with you. But I can't let your pictures get out either. You'll lose your job, and I won't let you be exposed that way. I need to keep you safe, and I've already failed by letting someone get their hands on your pictures."

"I love my job, Carter, but nothing in this life is worth risking you. I would trade all of it for a happily ever after with you."

"I've never been so disappointed with myself. I was so scared, and I freaked the fuck out. I didn't have a clue what to do. I was worried if it looked like everything was fine between us, Courtney would leak the pictures. I stayed up all night trying to come up with a plan, but came up with nothing. I wanted to beg you to stay, stop you from leaving. But in the moment I finally gave in, let you get in that damn car, I knew the best thing for you was space. Space until I could solve it, until I could make sure you were safe." He shakes his head, unable to meet my gaze. "I'll never forgive myself if I fail you any more than this."

"Failing is part of life. And we pick back up and start again. We can do that, Carter. As long as you're by my side, I can always start again. Can't you?"

Anguish swims in his eyes as he watches me closely, like he's afraid the words aren't real, that I'll get up and leave at any moment. Doesn't he know my heart belongs to him? As long as he's willing to keep trying, I'll be here.

Before he can answer, the quiet purr of an engine sounds nearby, and a police cruiser pulls up the long driveway. Carter shifts me off his lap, taking my hand in his as we stand, the car coming to a stop next to his truck.

Two officers step out, looking from me to Carter. "Can we talk, Mr. Beckett?"

Carter nods, and the officers smile at me.

"Good evening, Miss Parker. I'm Officer Perry, and this is my partner, Officer Wolters."

I look to Carter in question, and he squeezes my hand.

Officer Wolters steps forward, offering something to Carter as he chuckles. "Well, your screen is still shattered; we couldn't do anything about that. But you can have your phone back."

Carter takes his phone, turning it in his hand, and the hot sun glints off the fragments of the broken screen before he tucks it in his pocket. "What does this mean?"

Officer Wolters smiles. It's warm and broad and makes me feel something I haven't felt in days.

Hope.

"It means we've got both women in custody. This is over."

I CAN'T SLEEP, AND I expected as much. The problem right now is that the solution to my sleepless nights feels obvious.

But Carter didn't want to push me. He was worried it was all too much, too fast, too soon.

We spent hours at the police station, my hand tucked in his while they explained the charges we were well within our rights to press: intent of nonconsensual distribution of intimate images.

Carter filed a police report on Monday night after he promised to come back with answers. I think he made the right decision, and he finally does too.

The problem was they couldn't locate Courtney since her last known address was with Adam, and since Carter didn't know the name of her accomplice, the police were stuck. Until a woman named Raegan showed up this afternoon, ridden with guilt over the part she'd played. She turned her phone in, loaded with messages from Courtney, details of her intent to distribute the photos one at a time, whether or not Carter and I ended our relationship.

And then Carter brought me back here to Cara and Emmett's. He held me in their driveway and told me to take the time I needed to come to terms with this. He told me it was okay to be angry with him, and he'd understand if I was.

The problem is that he's there, and I'm here.

The phone rings once before he answers, eager, as if he were hoping I'd call.

"Ollie? Are you okay?"

The tears that haven't stopped these past four days overflow again, cool trails tracking down my cheeks. "I don't want to sleep without you."

He stays on the phone the entire drive over, for every step he takes up the stairs, and I hear Emmett's soft chuckle both in the phone and through the door as he pokes his head out to see who's here. The bedroom door opens and Dublin dashes inside, leaping up on the bed, covering my face with his tongue. Only when Carter's gaze lands on me does he finally hang up.

I peel back the covers and he wastes no time climbing in, pulling my body against his, his hands gripping my hair, my face, my hips as his mouth covers every inch of my face with kisses.

"I haven't lost you?"

"Carter, you will never, *ever* lose me."

51

REHEARSALS & SPEECHES & BATHS & SHIT

Carter

THE SUN IS WARM ON my face, the breeze ruffling my hair. A chipmunk darts out from behind a tree and stands on its hind legs, tilting its head as it looks at me. This is the third time he's done this, like he wants something from me.

"I don't have any food for you. I'm sorry, little buddy."

I watch him climb a headstone only to slide down the other side of it, squeaking all the while like he's having the time of his life. Dublin lifts his head off my lap, looking from me to the chipmunk then back again, like he wants to join in on the fun.

It's quiet here today but I'd guess most people spend their Saturday mornings in bed, not with the dead.

Until a month ago, I'd been here once, seven and a half years ago, the only day I had to be. For the most part, this isn't where I feel my dad, and Olivia says that's okay.

Yet here I am, sitting on a bench directly across from his grave, the same place I've been every day this week. Ironically, it's the only place I've found a sense of peace this week, other than in Olivia's arms. Being at the house has been hard because it feels less like a home than it ever has. Everything is a reminder of the person missing that makes it a home.

When I woke with her cheek pressed to my chest on Thursday morning, I knew everything would be okay, but it was still hard to say good-bye, to watch her walk into that school for her last day before Cara whisked her away to the resort for some pampering. Which means the house is still empty, and Dublin and I are equally as grumpy about her absence.

So I spend my days here and at Hank's. Hank is quiet, in the way I need rather than the way I hate. He lets me just be, lets me feel what I need to feel.

That I would have never met Hank if my dad didn't die isn't lost on me. I don't know where I'd be without him; he's consistently been there every step of the way in whatever capacity I've needed. He says he reads me like an instruction manual, which is exactly right. He knows what I need by the air I carry when I'm with him. Sometimes it's not what I want, but always what I need.

The time on my watch tells me I need to get home, so I stand and place my hand on the marble stone.

"I promise I'm going to make you proud, and myself. I love you."

Dublin woofs in agreement before we head back to the car, and I load him in the back. I don't know why I bother; he hops up front the second I climb behind the wheel.

Adam's truck is in the driveway when I get home, and he, his dog Bear, and Garrett are lounging on the front porch.

I had to change the lock code on my door. I get that people want to check up on me, and I appreciate it, but the constant visitors became too much. I've needed some space, a break from the voices constantly in my ear. I've needed to feel what I've needed to feel, and I can't do that when I'm always surrounded by people who want to make sure I'm not feeling *too much*.

There was also the one photographer who followed me up the driveway postwalk with Dublin. Two hours later, there were pictures of me punching in three out of four numbers, followed by a photo of me screaming at him to get off my property. Talk about an invasion of privacy.

"When do we get lock code privileges back?" Garrett asks, following me inside.

"When you stop eating my chips when I'm not home."

Dublin and Bear immediately engage in a wrestling match, right there in the middle of the hallway, and I make a mental note to ask Olivia if she feels like getting a second dog.

"It could be worse." Garrett opens my pantry, pulls out a loaf of bread, and pops two slices in the toaster. "I could be eating your Oreos."

"And then we'd be short a right-winger for next season." I flail a hand toward him as he pulls out the peanut butter and jam. "Do you not have food at home?"

"Hung-wy again," he mumbles around a spoonful of peanut butter.

Adam's watching me, grinning.

"What?"

"Nothing." He lifts a shoulder. "I'm just happy for you. And proud of you."

"I didn't do anything," I mumble. "It was Olivia."

"That's not true. You made the report. You put her first and you swallowed your pride and begged her to hold on while you figured it out."

"Yeah, buddy." Garrett smooshes his bread together and takes a massive bite, devouring half his sandwich as he slings an arm around my shoulders. "We're proud of ya. Plus, Adam was so mad when *she-who-must-not-be-named* called him from jail, he told her to go fuck herself and move back to Denver. Angry Adam is so rare, I cherish every moment I get with him."

Adam rubs the back of his neck, but before he ducks his head, I catch sight of that smile, and fuck me, I smile too.

By the time the pups are with the sitter for the weekend, I've watched Garrett eat so much of my food that now I'm hungry too.

I beg Adam to make a pit stop at McDonald's, making sure to add something special for Hank, who's already sitting on a bench out front of the nursing home, luggage by his feet, oversized Vipers Stanley Cup Champs hat on his head, beaming grin on his face.

"All right, fellas. I've got my snazziest suit ready to go, so if Cara decides to ditch Mr. Brodie at the last second, no worries; I can jump in to take his place."

I'm fairly certain dealing with Cara on her wedding day would be enough to give my old friend a coronary. I'm worried about Emmett's health and he's an all-star athlete.

The wedding is at the Four Seasons in Whistler, about ninety minutes away. Cara booked the venue last summer even though they only got engaged six months ago. They've been planning their wedding since the day they met, though.

It sounds like I'm exaggerating. I'm not. I was there the night they met. Emmett called her Mrs. Brodie. *To her face*. Cara ate that shit right up and they've been inseparable since.

The hotel is bustling when we arrive. They've got something like 80 percent of the rooms rented to wedding guests. Though the rehearsal dinner tonight is only for the wedding party and imme-diate family, most of the guests are here for the weekend or longer.

I'm not sure if it's off to a good or bad start when we find our way down to the reception space where Emmett said he is. He's there, hiding in the corner with Olivia, and Cara's walking around in a robe, slippers on, hair wrapped in a towel, screaming about fork placement and how the sunlight shining through the wall of windows is going to cause a glare on her face at the head table.

"But, Care." Olivia takes a cautious step in her direction, but when Cara whirls around, Emmett yanks my tiny girl back to the corner with him. "It's just that, um, it's not even noon yet. It'll be dinnertime tomorrow when you're sitting here. The glare won't be the same." She pulls Emmett's hand from her shoulder and steps up to the window, gesturing at the sky. "The sun will be over there, low enough in the sky that it should be a pretty shade of orange and pink by then."

Cara blinks at Olivia. Six times. She approaches the window, gazing out, like she's seeing what Olivia sees. Then she throws her arms around her bestie. "Oh, you're right! Thank God." She giggles like a hyena. "Kinda lost my head there for a minute."

"Yeah, a minute," Emmett mumbles, and immediately cowers back into the wall at the glare Cara shoots him. His gaze lands on the three of us, partially hidden by the door, and he dashes toward us. "Oh fuck. Thank fucking *God*."

Olivia's entire face flushes red. She sweeps an arm out, knocking a napkin and several pieces of cutlery on the floor in a move that looks entirely intentional despite the way she claps a hand to her forehead. "Oh no. Would you look at that? So clumsy." She drops to her knees, busying herself for way too long with picking everything up as Cara flutters across the room to us.

I had a feeling this would happen. We haven't had much time to talk, to decide what our next step is since she's been cooped up here with Cara for two nights already. I know what our next step is. Pretty sure she knows too. But I'd still like to get her alone so we can put this tension to rest.

"Oh goody! You're here!" Cara kisses our cheeks before linking her arm through mine. "I've got big jobs for you boys. Big jobs." She winks at me. "Nothing too big for you. You've got the most important job of all this weekend. Can't have you being overworked."

I highly doubt she's going to cut me any slack where work is concerned, and I'm proven right when she leads us to a room filled with chairs.

She points to the stacks of chairs with white covers next to them. "I need these in the cocktail room for dinner tonight, covers on." She points at the wooden chairs. "These you can do tomorrow morning. They're going outside to the ceremony area." She beckons us closer like she has a secret to tell. "Six inches between each chair. No more, no less. Got it?"

"Are you not paying somebody to do this for you?" Adam asks the question we all want answered.

"Yes, but I don't trust them."

Garrett's eyes bug. "And you trust *us*?" He rubs his neck, tugs on his T-shirt. "I don't wanna be on the receiving end of your wrath if we fuck something up on your wedding day."

"Do I trust you?" Drumming her fingers on her chin, Cara hums. "No, not really. But I'll still love you after my wedding, so it's best it's you guys." She grins, but it's one of the scary ones, the kind that has us inching backward. "Plus, how hard can it be to set the chairs up perfectly? Just make me happy, that's all I ask." She pats our shoulders and dances away, giggling.

"I want to go home," Adam whispers. "I'm scared."

I clap a hand to his back. "We all are, buddy."

Cara's gorgeous in her white lace. She's glowing, happy and cheerful, and when she walked in here, she looked at the chairs and said "Good job, boys."

I repeat, *Cara* said *good job, boys*. We high-fived the *shit* out of each other.

But it's the stunning woman dressed in midnight blue satin with her dark hair draped down her back in big waves I can't take my eyes off. They follow her everywhere she goes, counting each glass of wine she brings to her lips, watching as she retrieves a piece of paper from her purse, lips moving as she reads, and then crumples it up and stuffs it away. This time though, she sighs, tosses her wine back, eyes squeezed shut, then stalks off to the bar.

To my surprise, she orders a glass of water.

I stick my chin over her shoulder as she reads her speech for the seventh time. "Just picture me naked."

Olivia gasps, sloshing water over the bar when she jumps. "Jesus, Carter."

"That's the kind of reaction the sword of thunder aims to elicit when being pictured." I lean closer, watching her cheeks flush as my voice drops. "A hint of surprise, a little bit of fear, and a fuckload of excitement."

The corner of her mouth quirks, and before she can overthink, I pull out my phone.

"Hey," she says softly, holding my forearm as she peeks over. "You got a new phone."

"Uh-huh. Couldn't see your gorgeous face through all the shattered glass."

She smiles at the background, one I haven't used before. She's drowning in the bed, the blankets trying to swallow her whole. Her curls are a rumpled mess but her smile is as breathtaking as it's always been.

I swipe through my photos, finding the one I took early this morning. "Dublin made you this picture."

His head is on her pillow, resting next to a drawing of a dog and a stick figure woman. Out of the dog's mouth comes a speech bubble that says *I miss u, Mommy. Woof!*

Olivia's entire face detonates with her bright smile, the laugh that bubbles in her throat nothing short of fucking magical. "Dublin drew this, huh?"

I lift a shoulder and let it fall. "He's a Beckett now. It only makes sense he'd be an overachiever."

Another laugh, and just as I consider stealing it right from her mouth, she wraps her arms around me. I hold her to me, reveling in the feeling of being so complete once again. Olivia rests her chin on my chest, gracing me with that goofy smile, and I brush my thumb over the corner of her mouth.

Adam's voice comes over the microphone, requesting Olivia's presence at the stand for her speech, and her face pales.

"Pretty sure my dinner's about to make a reappearance."

I press my lips to her nose. "You've got this."

"Woo-hoo!" Cara pumps a fist through the air as Olivia takes the stage. "That's my bestie! Go, girl!"

I see the apprehension from here, the nerves that eat at her, and when our eyes meet, I wink, and she smiles.

"They say there comes a time in everybody's life when you meet your soul mate, the person who will love and cherish you for the rest of your life, hold you close and never let you go."

The women in the crowd all *aww* and Emmett grins at Cara.

"For Cara, that day happened at seventeen when she met me."

Emmett's jaw drops and Cara smacks the table, hollering, "Hell yeah it did, baby!"

"I don't know how in the world I got so lucky to land Cara as my roommate, but all five foot ten of her took one look at me, declared I was the perfect size for her to boss around, and then promptly shoved a shot of tequila into my hands. It was ten in the morning, and as terrified as I was, I knew I'd found my best friend.

"When Cara met Emmett, she came home in the middle of the night, jumped on top of me, and told me I needed to teach her everything I knew about hockey because she'd found her husband and apparently he was 'really into hockey or something.'" Her air quotes are perfectly placed, impression of Cara spot-on. "Emmett, you asked Cara to go skating with you a total of four times before she finally agreed. That's because I first spent three weeks teaching her to skate. She spent at least half of that time lying on the ice, complaining that she was too pretty to have to work so hard to impress a man."

Cara shrugs. "It's true."

"Emmett, Cara took one look at you and knew you were the one that was going to change her world." Olivia's eyes flicker to me before she licks her lips and looks down at the paper in her hands. "When you met, it was like two worlds colliding, an explosion of color. You met her wild with your calm, and you've drowned her in love every step of the way. The love you share has always been an inspiration to never settle for anything other than unrestrained passion, fierce obsession, a love that knows no bounds and only gets stronger every day."

She sniffles, swiping at her downcast eyes. When she looks up, her gaze meets mine. She blinks, a single tear rolling down her cheek before she smiles at Cara and Emmett.

"A man who loves her as ferociously as you do is all I could ever ask for, for my best friend." She raises her glass. "I know you two will live a long and happy life together, mainly because you didn't kill each other throughout the wedding process, which is incredibly impressive considering who the bride is. I love you both endlessly."

I watch two of my favorite people embrace my most favorite, and for the next hour I pretend like I'm not green with envy at the way Garrett and Adam and one of Emmett's brothers keep spinning Olivia around the dance floor.

She's sipping a glass of sparkling wine when I step up beside her.

"You look like you could use a bath."

One dark brow lifts. "Do I? Because I was thinking I've gotten less than twenty hours of sleep in the last week and I desperately need to go upstairs and pass out."

"You definitely need a bath first."

She hides her smile behind the rim of her glass, finishing her wine before setting it down. I lace my fingers through hers and tug her down the hallway, ushering her into the first elevator that opens. We ride in silence, Olivia trying to bite back her grin while I wink at her in the reflection of the mirrored walls.

"How do you know which room is mine?" she asks as I lead her there.

"I have connections."

"Is your connection named Cara?"

"Hmm . . ." I pluck her key card from her hand, swiping it through the door. "Rings a bell, but I can't be sure."

Another giggle. I swear I'm living for these tonight.

"Go take your dress off," I tell her, urging her into the room before I step into the bathroom. "I'll run you the Carter Beckett specialty bath. Extra relaxing and all that shit."

I crank the faucet on the bath, keeping my hand in the water until it's nearly scalding, the way she likes it, then toss in her favorite bath bomb, which I may or may not have requested the hotel put in her room. When I'm done, I find Olivia in the doorway, still fully dressed, watching me.

"Naughty girl," I tsk, crouching at her feet. I take her ankle in my hand, removing her strappy black heels one by one. I smile to myself at the way she sinks three inches, gripping my shoulders to keep steady. "You remember what happens to naughty girls, don't you?"

"They get punished." A cheeky smile crawls up her face as her eyes dance. "Over your lap or on their knees."

I chuckle, though the truth is I'm not in the punishing mood. I don't think Olivia is, either, but it's fun to pretend, to be ourselves again. When I have Olivia next, I'm going to take my time. I'll spend the entire night loving on her, worshipping her, and in the morning, well, she'll still have trouble walking, but I'll feed her breakfast in bed.

So instead, I twirl her around to find that dainty zipper.

"Can I?"

Her skin warms. "Yes."

The zipper slides with ease, blue satin falling away and reveal-ing the milky skin I've kissed every inch of, marked with love, and when it reaches the swell of her ass, I suck in a sharp breath.

I don't mean to take it any further than this, but then I spy the mark I left on her skin with my mouth the last time we made love, right there, curving around her waist. Before I know it, I'm pulling the straps of her dress down her arms, satin slipping over her hips, pooling at her feet.

Dropping to my knees, I slide my hands into the lace on either side of her hips and press my lips to that little bruise. Olivia gasps, creamy skin erupting in goose bumps as her hands find mine, holding on for dear life.

"Let go, sweetheart," I murmur, and she does, letting me slip her underwear down her legs.

I want to stand before her and drink her in, all of her, appreci-ate every inch of the body I love. But this is about so much more than that, and I won't rush her into this.

So I take her hand and lead her over to the tub. She steps inside, sinking into the bubbly water, and I disappear into the living room. I return a few minutes later, setting down a steaming mug of tea on the edge of the tub as my knees hit the plush bath mat.

"I wish you could stay, Carter."

"So do I." But we both know I can't. I'm responsible for the groom tonight, and there's a request for help from Adam waiting on my phone, an attached picture of Cara standing on a chair, and Emmett looks like he's about to catch her.

I sweep her hair over her shoulder, trailing my fingers along her skin on the way, touching the tiny freckles that decorate it. She's beautiful, my perfect companion, like we were made at the same time, two halves of a whole meant to find and complete each other one day.

I drop my head, trying to ease the pain that's already well-buried itself in my chest this past week. When I look up at Olivia, it's everything I can do not to cry. "I know what it's like to live without you. That's something I never wanted to experience."

And I'll be damned if I ever put either of us in that position again.

"Carter," Olivia whispers, fingers fluttering over my cheekbone, threading through my hair. "I want to come home."

My heart stutters. "Yeah?"

She smiles. "Yeah."

She leans forward, pressing her mouth to mine. It's tentative at first, slow as she tests the waters, and when my fingers sink into her hair, her mouth opens on a whimper.

It takes everything in me to pull apart, to press my lips to her forehead and stand.

"I'll see you at the altar," I tell her with a smile, and my heart swells at the way her face bursts like sunshine.

"Carter." Olivia's timid voice turns me around at the doorway. "I love you."

"I love you, too, Ollie girl."

52

WHAT IS HE DOING?

Olivia

I WAS HOPING TO INTERCEPT the server in the hallway, for obvious reasons.

The obvious reason is the way Cara's head snaps like lightning at the knock on the door before it creaks open. When the server pops his head in, he looks about as terrified as most of us have been all day. It's only noon.

"*What*?" Cara barks out.

"I think it's for me." My chuckle is *not* anxious. Also, it's *definitely* for me. I can smell it.

I take the tray with a smile and a quiet thank-you, then sneak into the bathroom and pry the lid off.

Oh, baby, yes. Come to mama. I might whimper, and I definitely bite my knuckles.

The second my teeth sink into that seven-ounce all-beef patty with American cheese, bacon, and grilled onions, my taste buds explode. My lids flutter closed, a moan rumbling through my entire body.

And then the bathroom door whips open.

"Are you kidding me right now, Liv?"

"I'm so sorry."

The beautiful bride pins her arms across her chest. "You are not."

"I can't live off grapefruit slices and water. I need substance." A cinnamon bun would also be nice, as would a mimosa.

Cara throws her arms in the air, nearly knocking my burger out of my hands. "But *I* have to eat grapefruit and drink water so I can fit into my dress! You're supposed to be supporting me!"

"I do support you. But it's your wedding, not mine. Plus, you look banging in your dress and you've got room to spare." I've gone to every fitting with her; I know this. I hold out my burger and wag my brows. Beyond the annoyance is the temptation twinkling in her eyes. "I can't last until cocktail hour to get some real food into me."

Cara laughs. It's the humoring, exasperated kind, and I don't feel good about it. "Oh, sweet, naïve Olivia. You think you'll get to eat at cocktail hour? No, no, no. You'll be getting your picture taken. No, you won't be eating 'til dinnertime, babe."

My entire face falls with this devastating news, and Cara lunges forward, gripping my wrist as she takes a bite half the size of my burger.

"Oh. Fuck. *Yes*. So good."

"Don't you dare ruin your makeup!" The makeup artist rushes into the bathroom, sighing when she spies me. "Your lipstick is all smeared."

"*Sowwy*," I lie, shoving the rest in my mouth.

Cara nudges me in the side. "You're glowing. I'm not buying that you didn't get laid last night."

"I didn't," I insist for at least the fifteenth time.

Cara woke me up at midnight to ask me how good I got dicked. Her words, not mine. The answer was *no dick at all*, but twenty-five minutes later, with the lights out, our door opened, and Carter appeared at the foot of my bed. He didn't say a word and neither did I, just enjoyed the way he snuggled up behind me, his lips pressed against my neck. Cara mumbled something about at least having the decency to make the sex silent so she could get her beauty sleep, but I was out minutes later with Carter wrapped around me, and when I woke this morning he was already gone.

So while I didn't get dicked, what I did get was a decent night's sleep for the first time in a week. I feel refreshed and mildly hopeful, and that right there does wonderful things for a woman.

Two hours later, my lipstick is fixed, I'm draped in shimmery champagne, and am several more inches off the ground than I'm comfortable with. I watch Cara's mom fasten the final button on her dress before she stands back, flapping at her eyes.

I fold my hands together beneath my chin. "You look absolutely beautiful, Care."

Forget glowing, she's fucking luminous, shining from the inside out. She runs her fingers down the delicate satin and inhales a shaky breath. "You think so?"

"I know so." I adjust the diamond on her finger and smile. "I'm so happy for you."

"Oh, fuckers." She dabs at the corner of her eyes. "I'm getting a little teary eyed over here." She shakes her hands out. "And nervous. I'm nervous. What's wrong with me?"

I still her frantic hands, squeezing. "You have nothing to be nervous about. It's you and Emmett. You've been planning this day since you met. Literally."

"What if he gets cold feet? What if he backs out?" Her ocean-blue eyes bounce between mine. At my disapproving look, she giggles, dismissing her worries with the flick of her wrist. Her hands flutter over her curves and she pops a hip. "Yeah, you're right. Who could resist all this?"

"There's my girl. Now let's go catch you a husband."

"Ow." I WHIRL AROUND, GLOWERING at Cara. "Would you quit pushing me?"

"I'm sorry. So sorry. I'm nervous. What are they doing? Why aren't they ready?" She cranes her head like she's trying to sneak a peek.

"Stop it. Calm down. They're just standing around, talking. Emmett probably figured you'd be a half hour late like you are to everything else."

He's currently bent over a row of people, laughing without a care in the world, polar opposite of his bride. I scan the scenery, the trees and mountains a stunning backdrop to this gorgeous blue-sky day. Adam and Garrett are talking to a handful of their teammates, but I don't spy Carter anywhere. Not that I'm looking or whatever.

"Will you go tell him we're ready to start?" Cara shoves me toward the glass doors.

"Only to get you to stop pushing me." I open the door and she gives me one last push, shoving me out into the garden, and I bounce off a brick wall.

Not a brick wall. My boyfriend. My . . . Carter.

"Oh. Shit. Sorry." My fingers curl around his biceps as his find my waist, steadying me on my ridiculous heels.

Carter's eyes dance, dipping down my body, that half smirk all parts arrogant. "Did you grow overnight?"

My knees wobble at the sight of him in his black suit, his usually unruly waves tamed and combed neatly to the side, face freshly shaven, showing off those heart-stopping dimples.

"Four and a half," tumbles aimlessly from my mouth.

His brows quirk. "What's that?"

"Uh, the, my . . ." I hike up my dress, giving my foot a wiggle. "Four and a half. Heels. Tall." *Well, folks, it's been grand. I'm heading home.*

Carter's face detonates with a cheek-splitting grin. "You are absolutely stunning, Miss Parker."

"Thank you. Thanks. You too." *Why am I like this?* "Your hair is . . . your face . . . Cara wants Emmett to know she's ready."

He chuckles, bending and pressing his lips to my cheek. "I'll tell him."

Cara's arm whips out, pulling me back inside. "I heard more than I'd like to admit. Have I not taught you anything about playing it cool? You are a lost fucking cause, woman."

I can't say I disagree, so I line myself up behind the rest of the bridesmaids as the music starts. When it's my turn to head down the aisle, I find the only person I want to see.

Carter's wearing a goofy smile as he watches me try to keep count with the steps in my head—the coordinator said I walk too fast, which I find ironic, because, you know, I'm short as hell. He stacks his shoulders, standing taller, and his grin grows wider as I step below the archway and take my place. He gives me a wink as the music changes, and everybody turns to the glass doors as Cara steps through them with her dad at her side.

She floats down the aisle like the queen she is, beaming, nose wrinkling while she tries to fight off tears. Emmett is losing his battle, silent tears streaming down his handsome face, and Carter hands him the pocket square from his jacket.

I'm lost in their heartfelt vows, the promises they make to love and support each other for always, and Carter's eyes remain locked on me while I swat at my tears.

The crowd of nearly five hundred people jump to their feet and go wild as Cara and Emmett kiss for the first time as husband and wife before she leaps onto his back and he tows her down the aisle and out of sight.

Carter steps up to me, offering me his arm. "Shall we, princess?"

I grin at him through my tears. "We shall."

*

"You gonna finish that?"

I glance at Carter pointing at the remainder of my prime rib with his knife, eyes wide with question. The moment I sigh, he grins, stabbing my beef and shifting it to his plate.

"I'm starting to think you only requested to sit beside me so you could clean my plate."

"Nah. I requested to sit beside you because I'm fucking obsessed with you." His hand lands on my thigh, slipping below the slit, warming my skin, luring that heartbeat down, down, down. Bracketing my chin between his fingers, he angles his mouth above mine. "And so I can do this whenever I want."

He kisses one corner of my mouth first, then the other. My bottom lip next, followed by the bow in the top. And when his mouth finally covers mine, my lips part, eager for him, to feel him, taste him, give him every single part of me he desires.

Every bit of this day has been perfection, and I'm only mildly horrified when I return from a trip to the bathroom after dinner to find Carter talking to my brother in one corner of the ballroom.

And then the oddest thing happens. Jeremy laughs, they shake hands, and then they . . . hug.

What. The. Fuck.

Alannah tears across the room, flinging her arms around Carter's legs, and he hugs her tightly before taking her out on the dance floor for a spin.

Jeremy sidles up next to me, tugging on my earlobe. "What, did you think I was gonna kill him or something?"

I slap his hand away. "It crossed my mind, yes."

"Nah, Carter's a good guy."

My brows rocket up my forehead. "Never have those words ever left your mouth."

He shrugs. "I can admit when I was wrong."

"You literally can't. Ever. Never in my life have you ever admitted such a thing."

"Ah, shut up."

The music changes, and I smile at that familiar tune, the one Carter's been singing to me since we met, as he ambles across the dance floor, smiling sheepishly at me.

"Did you request this song?" I ask him for the second time in my life.

"Uh-huh." He holds his hand out. "Dance with me?"

I shove my wineglass into Jeremy's chest and slip my hand into Carter's warm one, watching it swallow mine up as he spins me into him. He's the same as always, his smell, his touch, the way he holds me close, his lips at my ear as he sings along to his favorite song.

My body quivers as his breath rolls down my neck, and butterflies erupt in my stomach when he dots my skin with millions of tiny, tender kisses in between lyrics.

"Carter." I squeeze my eyes shut. "I—"

"I love you," he tells me, bringing his face in front of mine. "I love you, Olivia."

His lips, soft and gentle, touch mine as the music drifts to an end, fingertips on my lower back pressing me closer. When his name is called, he leans his forehead on mine, and smiles.

"Gotta go make my speech, Ollie girl." He kisses me once more before heading to the podium. The simple act of clearing his throat and tapping the microphone earns him a holler from the entire hockey team, and his electric smile lights the room. "How's everyone doing tonight?" He grins through the roar of the crowd. "I'm so happy to have control of the only five minutes Cara couldn't plan tonight. She tried, obviously. I was given a very specific set of rules that detailed what I was and wasn't allowed to say. But I accidentally lost that list."

Cara pins her arms across her chest; that list was 100 percent real.

"For those of you who don't know me, I'm Emmett's best friend and teammate, Carter. I'm honored to stand beside him today as his best man, but it's also very honorable of him, as he's finally admitting to himself and everyone else that I truly am the best." He pauses for the laughter that rolls through the room. "Cara, you're absolutely fucking stunning tonight, a picture of perfection as you always are. Emmett is one lucky fucking man."

"*Carter!*" Cara screams, slamming her fists down on the table.

"Oh, right. Oops." He chuckles, looking mildly sheepish. "I'm supposed to limit myself to only five curses. Guess I'm down one already."

Cara holds up her pointer and middle fingers. "*Two!*"

Carter's eyes bulge as he runs his fingers through his hair, messing up that perfectly coifed mop. "*Two*? Fuck me. I mean, shit. No. Fuck. Ah, fuck it. Cara, you know I can't!" He flashes everyone his perfect grin, and Cara groans, dropping her face to her hands. "I can't be perfect at everything. But anyway, enough about that. I was talking about how lucky Emmett is. He'll leave here tonight with a beautiful wife who's feisty, hilarious, and has one hell of a huge heart. And Cara, well . . . you'll leave here tonight with a lovely new dress."

Cara stands, holding the skirt of her dress as she does a little spin.

"It's been an emotional day for all of us." Carter points at the four-tiered cake. "Even the cake is in tiers."

I drop my forehead to my hand as the room explodes with laughter. "Oh sweet Lord."

"I met Emmett when I was eighteen when we were drafted to Vancouver. If you can believe it, we didn't click right away. There was a sense of competition between us, like we both wanted to be the best. Emmett was serious and focused, and I was goofy and easygoing. He was quiet and driven, and I was and still am exceptionally good-looking.

"Emmett, I wormed my way into your heart, breaking your shell one inappropriate joke at a time until you let me see the big teddy bear you really are. You've always inspired and pushed me to do better when you knew I could, and I'm proud to say I am the man I am today because I had a friend like you.

"And Cara. I knew. I knew the second I met you that you were going to steal my best bud. You walked into that room and his jaw hit the floor. All he wanted to do was spend all his free time with you, hide in the hotel room and talk to you on the phone all night instead of going out with us. I didn't understand how he felt until I met . . ." His eyes move, finding me, and he smiles. "Until I met her. And then it all made sense."

Carter pauses, running a hand over his chest. "Watching you two create a life together has been incredible, and I know it's only going to get better. How lucky you are to be sharing it with your very best friend. To the bride and groom." He raises his glass, but holds up one finger. "Oh, and one more thing. Cara, this is from the guys on the team. Best of luck with Emmett. We found him to be useless in most positions, but we're confident your experience with him later tonight will be satisfactory."

I don't have time to tell Carter how beautiful his speech was, even the tiers bit, because the DJ announces it's time for the bouquet toss, and Jennie starts dragging me to the center of the dance floor with her and the rest of the women.

"I don't want to," I whine.

"I didn't ask." Jennie starts stretching out. "If I have to do it, so do you. But fair warning: Watch your back. We Becketts are competitive as fuck."

"You can have it. This tradition is ridiculous."

Cara gasps, spinning to me. "I know you didn't just call *anything* at my wedding ridiculous, Parker."

I press my lips together, shaking my head.

"You're damn right. Now get into goddamn position."

With a sigh, I stand next to Jennie, Alannah bouncing up and down in front of me, and I seriously hope one doesn't pummel the other to the ground in a bid to get this fucking bouquet. I roll my neck over my shoulders, close my eyes, and wait for this to be over as the crowd counts down.

"*Five! Four! Three! Two! One!*"

I wait.

And I wait.

Finally, I crack my eyes open. My heart does a backflip at Cara standing in front of me, tears in her eyes as she smiles so brightly, holding out her bouquet.

To me.

She wraps my fingers around the ribbons of silk and velvet that keep the stems together, then spins me around to where Carter stands before me, waiting, smiling.

"Rest assured the beautiful bride gave me her full support to do this here tonight."

Cara's chin lands on my shoulder. "We'll reflect on my selfless-ness later."

Full support to do this? Do what? Selflessness? Why am I so hot, and more importantly, why is Emmett pointing his phone at me?

"Have I told you today why I love you?" Carter takes a step toward me, then another, his smile growing with each inch he eliminates. "I love you because you're funny and snarky, sarcastic as all hell, and the night we met, you told me to go fuck myself." He ignores the way Cara shrieks his name. "You're also kind and soft, sensitive and sweet, the best auntie, and a teacher I would've died to have in high school. You're not just my girlfriend; you're my biggest cheerleader and my best friend."

He takes my face in his hands, thumbs wiping at the over-flowing tears dripping down my cheeks. I don't even know where they came from.

"Why are you crying, Ollie girl? I haven't even gotten to the good stuff yet."

"I don't know what's going on, but you called me your best friend and your girlfriend," I sob, folding toward his chest as I grip the loosened collar of his shirt.

His soft chuckle is warm against my lips as he tips my chin up to kiss me. He takes a step back, dipping his hand in his pocket, pulling out a small velvet box, and he sinks to one knee.

"I'm hoping to call you something else when I'm done doing what I need to do here."

53

FLIPPY-FLOPPIES

Olivia

"Are you embarrassed?"

The bob of my head is barely perceptible, but it's there. My gaze drifts over the room, the unrelenting stares, the hands clasped under chins or pressed over hearts. Finally, it lands back on the man kneeling before me. "So embarrassed."

"I told you I'd embarrass you," Carter reminds me. "Would you like me to stop?"

"Please don't," I whisper.

"You know, I originally wanted to do this at the Stanley Cup Finals. But Cara said you'd be mortified, in front of twenty thousand people and another seven million on TV. I wouldn't have minded, all those people seeing. But I only wanted to embarrass you a little, not mortify you. Cara suggested this might be a better option."

"I appreciate the consideration. I'd like to live to see the day, not die of embarrassment."

Carter chuckles, rising to his feet. Stepping into me, he cups my cheek. "I know we've had our struggles. This relationship didn't start as smoothly as I imagine most do. We've had to learn a lot along the way, but I personally think we fucking nailed it."

I giggle, and he smiles.

"Until you, there was only hockey. I didn't think it was possible to want anything more, to love someone . . ." He trails off, closing his eyes, and when they open again, his stare is unwavering, blatant need and desire running rampant, making those eyes shine like the emeralds they are.

"The way I love you is inexplicable. It's so much more than just wanting to be with you but needing to more than anything. I need you, because without you, something will always be missing in this life, just out of reach. Because you make everything better, and everything makes sense. You're all the best parts, the cozy snuggles, the quiet conversations while we're lying in bed, the sleepy mornings. The way my whole body comes alive when I see you for the first time after coming home, the way your face lights up and you jump into my arms and hold me like you need me as much as I need you."

"I do need you," I tell him quietly. "Everything fell into place the moment I gave in to what my heart was telling me I needed. I love you, Carter, even if I was afraid to in the beginning."

"Before, nothing scared me more than the idea that I might fall in love. But nothing has ever scared me more than the thought that I might lose you. I know you like to say that I'm ostentatious, that I like to flaunt what I have, that I do everything with flair. And you're right. Because why wouldn't I? I'm proud of every damn thing I have, and at the forefront of things I'm smug as hell about having earned is you and your love."

He looks down, turning the small box in his hand. When his eyes come to mine, they're sure and steady. He drops back to his knee, gently prying the top off the box in his hands. "Are you still embarrassed about all the people?"

"What people?"

"That's my girl." He chuckles, slipping my left hand into his. "I fucking love you. So fucking much it's terrifying."

My hand shakes in his, and he squeezes, stilling the tremble.

"All I'm doing when I'm away from you is counting down the minutes until we can be together again. There is no other option for me than a life with you. I know it's soon, but I don't need time to tell me what I already know, that a forever with you can't come soon enough. Be my forever. Officially, because forever is all you've ever been to me. So . . . marry me, Ollie girl. Say yes."

"Are you asking? It sounds more like you're—"

"Demanding? That's because I am. I refuse to be without you. Absolutely refuse, because that's the last place either of us belongs. You're mine. My best friend and my lover, my only version of forever, and I don't intend on ever letting you go. My only intention is to legally bind you to me for the rest of our lives."

"So romantic." Dropping to my knees, I wrap my arms around his neck as he winds one arm around my waist. The crowd is buzzing. This conversation has been going on for quite some time now, but I don't care. "Are you sure you want to be tethered to me forever?"

There's that grin I love, lopsided and arrogant, a man who's never been surer of himself. "For-fucking-ever, Ol. Lock me up and throw away the key. I'm yours, baby. Always have been, always will be. And I'll romance the shit outta you when we get home."

My nose wrinkles, trying to quell the tears that keep rolling as I study his face, the fire in his eyes that never dims, the hope, the promise. "I love you so much, Carter."

"Then why am I still waiting for an answer here?"

"I thought demands didn't require answers?" I brush my thumb over the heartbreakingly beautiful smile that decorates his handsome face. "I love you, Carter. There's nothing I want more in this life than to spend it with you."

His throat bobs with a hard swallow, eyes dancing in the golden glow of the ballroom. When he blinks, a single tear rolls down his right cheek.

"Why are you crying?" I ask, catching the tear with my lips.

He doesn't answer. Not me, anyway.

"*She said yes!*" Carter scoops me up, clutching me to his chest as he springs to his feet and spins me around. "She's gonna be my wife!"

He sets me back on the ground, slips the most stunning diamond on my finger, tips me backward, and claims my mouth with a kiss that's nothing but possessive and wild, frantic, filled with all the love we've been missing this past week.

And I know without a doubt in the world that we'll never have to go without again.

CARTER WASN'T JOKING ABOUT NOT taking no for an answer. The limo was waiting out front of the hotel, my luggage stowed inside. The second Cara and Emmett took off, we followed.

He's looking awful cute and shy as he punches in the new code to the front door: *1215*.

"December fifteenth," he says, pink creeping up to the tips of his ears under the porch light. "The day we met."

I take two steps inside and stop, mouth falling open as I look around. My heels drop from my hand, clattering to the ground. I trail my fingers over the frames littering the hallway wall, filled with photos of us and all the amazing people in our life. I turn back to this incredible man, catching him staring at the word scrawled in wood hanging overtop of the photos: *family*.

"When did you do this?"

"Friday." He takes my hand, tugging me toward the stairs. "Come on. There's more."

He brings me to the first spare room, revealing a small office with a desk and a leather chair, a loveseat and a floor lamp with one of those pod coffeemakers and a canister full of tea bags and decaf coffee pods. My workbag leans up against the legs of the table, and my laptop sits on top.

Carter rubs at the back of his neck. "You're always sitting on the floor around the coffee table, planning and marking. I thought maybe you'd like—"

I cut him off with my lips on his. "I absolutely love it. I'm not going to ask how you got my things, but I'll assume Cara was involved."

His chest puffs with pride. "I was in your room as soon as you two left for Whistler."

That explains literally everything. Cara was waiting for me when I finished work on Thursday. The car was already packed, and off to Whistler we went so we could be up at the butt crack of dawn on Friday for a spa day. No complaints here, though. The bags under my eyes were puffy as hell, as Cara so kindly reminded me several times via prodding fingertips.

Carter leads me down the hall to the bedroom, his hand tightening around mine as he opens the door. It's always been a beautiful room, but now . . .

By the fireplace I love to curl up beside and read on cool nights are three large pillows, a basket with blankets, and a side table with a stack of my books. A dresser that matches Carter's, though this one is shorter and wider with a large antique mirror on top, rests against a wall that was previously empty, and inside are my clothes.

Carter gestures to a beautiful glass vase filled with sunflowers, pink roses, and orange daisies. "The florist called it 'Hello Sunshine.'" He scratches at his temple, eyes bouncing between the flowers, me, and the floor.

"You're not playing shy right now, are you? Not Carter Beckett. Not possible."

He grins, pulling me into him. "I wanted you to feel like you were home."

"I've always felt like I'm home with you, Carter. It doesn't matter where we are or what we have."

"I want to give you everything." The words are quiet and sincere as his hands trail up my back, fluttering over my zipper. "Absolutely everything."

"You're all I've ever needed, I promise you."

His breath catches in his throat as I push him gently against the wall, my fingers working the buttons of his shirt while my tongue finds his. I run my hands over his torso, feeling the way the muscles flex beneath my touch, and I sweep over his shoulders, down his arms, until his shirt falls to the floor.

Carter flips me over, pressing my chest to the wall as he slowly tugs my zipper down, his warm breath kissing my spine. Strong hands grip my waist, my hips, as my dress falls to the floor, taking my panties with it. He sets me on the edge of the bed, and I pull at his belt buckle, guiding his pants and boxers over his thick thighs. When he ditches them behind him, he falls to his knees at my feet.

Carter drops his face to the space between my legs, and I feel the cool dampness of his tears on the inside of my thigh. My heart breaks when his gaze lifts to meet mine.

"I was so afraid, Olivia. Terrified. Watching you walk away from me and not being strong enough to stop you in that moment, to be honest with you, to ask you to be patient with me so we could work through it together . . . I didn't feel like I deserved you. You deserved more than me. And I'm sorry I couldn't be the person you deserved." His eyes fall, followed by his face, as if he still thinks himself unworthy, as if he doesn't forgive himself for a situation that was beyond his control in the first place.

And that won't do.

I stroke his cheek, tipping his face up to mine. "I love you through the perfect moments, and there are so many, but I will always love you through the imperfect ones too."

His eyes shine with appreciation, overflowing with love. "I thought I lost you forever and I . . . I . . ." Fear steals his words, and he shakes his head ever so slightly. He blinks, and a tear rolls down his cheek. "I won't ever lose you, Ollie. You make me better than I was before."

I don't believe that, not for one second. This man on his knees before me was always the man I know now, the one I love so endlessly. I think he was just cautious about who he shared all these special parts with. I'm so lucky and grateful to be the person he chose, the one who gets to see him, know him, all of him.

"I was lost before you, Ollie, and I'd be lost without you. You're my best friend."

"And you're mine." Curving my palm around Carter's neck, I guide him up my body. "Now come here and love me, Mr. Beckett."

"Yes, Mrs. Beckett. One round of sweet, sweet lovin', coming right up."

"Only one?"

"Oh, baby. You're not going to sleep 'til the sun comes up."

I expect hard and rough, a symbol of his need, the ferocity with which he's missed this. But tonight, he's soft and tender, savoring each moment as his fingertips dance over every inch of my body. His lips move with gentle precision down my neck, across my collarbone, over my belly and the curve of my hips, igniting my skin and leaving a trail of need so raw it makes me tremble with lust.

I lace my fingers through his silky, rumpled waves, and pull his face from between my legs where it feels like he's been lapping for hours instead of only minutes. Wonderful, amazing, toe-curling minutes.

He licks me off his lips, and I whimper out my next words. "I need you. Please. Now. I need you, Carter."

"You have me," he whispers, the weight of his body settling over mine.

He parts my legs, hiking one around his hip as his cock pushes at my entrance, and my nails bite into his shoulders as I cling to him. Carter brings his mouth to mine, searing me with a mind-blowing kiss, swallowing my gasp as he thrusts slowly inside me.

"I love you." He kisses the tears that fall freely from my eyes. "And I'm gonna love you for the rest of my life, and after that too."

"Liv, Liv, Liv, Liv."

Poke, poke, poke, poke.

"Ollie, Ollie, Ollie, Ollie."

Poke, poke, poke, poke.

I make a rough, grumbly sound, and slap at the finger currently poking at my cheek.

"C'mon, sleepy bear. Wake up, Ollie girl."

"I just fell asleep," I mutter, cracking one sleepy lid, squinting at the sun pouring through the glass doors over Carter's shoulder. He shifts until his smiling face is the only thing I see.

"You've been sleeping for four hours."

"Four hours?" I flop onto my back, arms wide. "Well, if I've been sleeping for four hours, surely it must be time to wake up."

Carter's morning chuckle is one of my favorite sounds, deep and rumbly, raspy with sleep, although he's clearly been awake much longer than me. His attitude is remarkably chipper.

He rolls on top of me, spreading my thighs, smearing the wetness between them. He hums appreciatively, dipping his fingers, making me bury my head in the pillows as I moan. "Hmm. Seems like you were waiting for me to wake you."

Then he rolls off me, tugging me up, too, and *what the fuck?*

"Come on. Up you get. We've got a busy day ahead of us."

I grab a pillow and smack him in the side of the head. "It's rude to start something you're not going to finish."

"Oh, I'm gonna finish. About ten times over, and then you'll really need to sleep." His grin is all devil, but then he tugs on my hand again, towing me toward the balcony. "I wanna show you something."

"Show me what? And why do we have to do it on the balcony? Can't we stay in bed? And why do we have a busy day? It's a holiday."

Carter shoves me down to the lounger, in front of an impressive breakfast spread and his laptop. I go willingly, because there's bacon, and also, I love him.

"We have to do it on the balcony because this is where the food is. But more than that?" His gaze coasts over me, shining with adoration. "I fell in love with you on this balcony. I fell in love with the way you slept peacefully next to the fire. I fell in love with the way you gazed with wonder at the sky, the millions of stars. I fell in love with the way you opened up to me, let me see you and let me show you me too. I fell in love with the way we laid here, your body wrapped in mine, all the times we've made love here, and when I asked you to make this house yours. I fell in love with you over and over again, and I keep doing it every single day, right here on this balcony."

My heartbeat skips, and I lift his arm, snuggling into his side. "Okay, you got me. I love this balcony. In fact, those are all excellent reasons for us to stay right here all day long and never leave. Don't you think?"

Carter props his feet on the coffee table and sets his laptop in his lap. When I spy the screen, I sit up so fast I knock it off his lap, lunging across him to catch it before it can fall to the ground.

"How do you feel about a fall wedding?" He sips his coffee, then offers it to me, ignoring the way my jaw hangs.

"A fall wedding? Like, this fall?"

"Mhmm. This fall."

"But that's so—"

"Soon." His brows rise. "You got a problem with that?"

"I just . . . I . . . no. Are you sure that's what you want? You'll be so busy with hockey. And we don't have to rush. If you want—"

"I don't want. I don't want to wait because I don't want a life where you're not in it. My world only spins so beautifully because of the way you've opened my heart and made me feel like myself again. I didn't know who I was anymore after my dad left. All I was was tied into being a hockey player, a leader. That's all I knew how to be. Until you showed up and reminded me I was capable of so much more, that I had so much to offer. So, fuck me, I wanna marry you right now, but that seems unrealistic and definitely impulsive—we should probably invite our family and friends— and there's a week in November where we don't play for four days, so fall seems like a good time, if you're open to that."

"I'm-I'm—" *Oh my fuck.* "I can do that. If we can find a venue and everything on such short notice."

He spins his laptop back my way. "We've got four appointments today to look at venues that all have that weekend open."

My jaw drops. Again. I'm not sure it's ever actually closed since this conversation started. "But it's Canada Day. It's a holiday."

"Listen, you know I don't like to boast—" He does a courtesy pause for my snort. "—but being rich and famous affords me certain privileges, like looking at wedding venues on a holiday Monday." He pokes my cheek. "And also, Cara's been low-key planning our wedding since I took her with me to design your ring back in May, and you have three dress appointments booked before they leave on their honeymoon."

"But they leave on Saturday."

His expression tells me he's sorry; nobody wants to spend three days with Cara trying on dresses. I've just finished doing so, except it was a month-and-a-half-long endeavor to choose her dress, and the scars are still fresh.

"Listen, it was hard to reel her in once it all started. And honestly, I got kinda scared, so I let her run with it." He gestures at the screen. "She set up all these appointments and we just have to choose which one we like best. Then she said, and I quote, 'leave the rest to me.' She kinda cackled while she said it and did that creepy thing where she drums her fingers together." Carter shudders, then shrugs. "So I agreed and got the hell outta there."

"Okay." I snuggle into him, laying my head over his chest. "Show me where we're going today."

He smiles so brightly that I smile too. "Yeah?"

"Yeah."

Every venue is gorgeous, of course, but my favorite thing is the way his face lights up as he talks about each one, what he likes best about them and which one he thinks I'm going to like most, his hands moving wildly while he speaks. When he's done, he closes the laptop, sliding it onto the table and pulling me into his arms.

"First appointment's in two hours," he hums against my neck.

"Ah. So we can put forever on hold for another round of fun?"

"Forever started the second you said *yes* on midnight all those months ago, the second my lips met yours for the first time. I have every intention of spending the rest of my life the way the year started, with me loving on every bit of your sassy little body. Everything begins and ends with you and me and the way you make my heart pump wildly and my stomach do flippy-floppies."

"Flippy-floppies?"

"Fucking flippy-floppies, Ol."

Carter pushes me to my back and climbs on top of me, straddling my hips. With my wrists in his hands, he pins my arms above my head. His face dips, the tip of his nose ghosting up my neck until his lips find mine.

"I don't think I have slow and gentle in me today, Ollie."

"Is that right?" I gasp as his teeth bite down on the delicate spot on my neck, just below my ear.

"No. I'm gonna love you hard today, and I'll only know I've done my job right if I have to carry you down to the car when we're done. That all right with you, princess?"

"Every way you love me is perfect."

He chuckles softly against my skin before he sinks inside me. "That's good, 'cause I love you in a million different ways, and I can't wait to spend the rest of my life showing you how."

I brush the waves off his forehead and press a tender kiss to his lips, drawing out the soft side of this man a little longer before he becomes the feral animal I love just as much. "I love you, Carter."

His crooked smile pulls those dimples in, lighting my soul. He sits back on his heels, pulling me onto his lap, never severing that connection as his fingers sink into the hair at the nape of my neck and his tongue takes my mouth.

"Thank you for choosing me, Ollie girl. I couldn't have imagined a better life."

Epilogue

OOPS

Carter

November

"ARE YOU NERVOUS?"

"Yes. No. Yes. Fuck. No. I don't know." That right there is probably answer enough. I tug at my tie and adjust the sleeves of my jacket for what must be the twentieth time. It's not hot outside, but it's fucking hot in here. Why is it so hot? "It's overdue."

Someone chuckles, and I glare at the five men standing at my side. Hank, Emmett, Adam, Garrett, or Jeremy—it could be any of them. They're all assholes.

Dublin whines at my feet. He's not an asshole. He's a good boy wearing a pup-tux.

"You've known each other all of eleven months, and it's overdue?" Garrett shakes his head. "Fuck me, if I ever become as pussy-whipped as you . . ."

I give Adam a look and he does exactly what I need him to: elbows Garrett in the ribs. I hide my smile at the way he keels over, gripping his side, but then the music starts, and I might be having some sort of panic attack as the procession of beautiful women starts making its way down the aisle.

"Calm the fuck down," Jennie mutters to me as she passes by, and Garrett chuckles way louder than necessary, earning an eyebrow from both me and my sister. He clears his throat, and Jennie gestures at her neck, bugging her eyes out at him.

What? he mouths to her.

She keeps tugging at some imaginary tie, eyes wide as she throws pointed looks at his neck.

I don't know what you're saying, he yell-mouths back to her, gesturing around with his hands in some sort of show of how much he really doesn't get it.

"Oh for fuck's—" Jennie buries her face behind her bouquet for a moment. "Your tie! Fix your tie!"

"What? Oh." Garrett looks down, face bright red when he spots his crooked tie.

This day is off to a fantastic start, which only further spikes my anxiety. I at least manage a smile at the way Alannah dances down the aisle, throwing flower petals in unsuspecting faces. Jem makes it halfway before he decides to lie down and start munching on one of the petals.

"Jemmy! No! Jemmy, up!" Alannah tries to tempt him with more petals, backing slowly toward the altar. "C'mon, Jemmy. C'mon. I got lotsa petals for you right here, little guy."

Olivia told me this would happen. In fact, she bet me. Now I owe her a foot rub and brownies.

"Kid's got his mom's attention span," Jeremy mutters.

I snort a laugh, 'cause yeah right. The way Kristin scowls at him from my right tells me she agrees.

Alannah eventually ends up hoisting her brother into her arms, carting him down the aisle. "Give Uncle Carter the rings, Jemmy."

By some stroke of luck, the little guy grins up at me, holding up the small box in his pudgy fist.

"Thanks, buddy," I tell him before I plant a kiss on both their cheeks. My fingers curl tightly around the box, and I pull in a staggered inhale as the music fades out. "Holy fuuuck," I breathe out when the next song starts.

"Millionaire" by Chris Stapleton. Olivia thinks I picked it because I'm a millionaire. I picked it because if all I had was her and her love, I'd still feel like the richest damn man in the world.

Every single shred of anxiety dissipates the second that stunning woman steps through the doors, all five foot one of her draped in lace and satin, and every bit of oxygen is sucked from the room.

"Describe her to me," Hank whispers.

"She's . . . she . . ." I squeeze my eyes shut for the briefest moment, because I don't wanna miss a second of this. "I can't. I'm sorry." There are no words. She's like . . . waking up on Christmas morning when you're three years old and you finally understand what it's all about. She's the moment the rain stops and the sun comes out, lighting up the sky with color, and everything smells new and fresh. She's the first skate on a frozen lake, surrounded by snowy mountains and pine trees and the freshest breath of air. She's rolling over in the middle of the night, pulling that warm body into yours and curling around it, and everything's just *right*. "She's just . . . she's just . . ."

"Perfection," Hank finishes quietly.

Utter fucking perfection. *And she's all mine.*

That's probably why I only let her get three quarters of the way down the aisle before I take off, running toward her while our guests gasp with surprise.

But Olivia? She doesn't look surprised. Not in the slightest.

"Impulsive and impatient," she murmurs, right before her dad releases her and I lift her into my arms, spinning her, crushing her to my chest as I kiss her with everything I have.

"That's why you're marrying me."

"Mmm." She tilts her head, nose scrunching as she pretends to think. "Among other reasons, yes."

"You're so fucking beautiful." I want to sink my fingers into her hair, but she'll likely kill me. It looks so pretty.

"*Hey!*" Cara snaps her fingers from her spot at the altar. "Quit making out and get your butts up here and get married!"

Olivia giggles and I hold my hand out to her. I'm sure I've never smiled so wide when I ask, "Ready to get married?"

She slips her hand into mine, our fingers tangling, and hits me with that tender smile I love so much. "Ready."

"You are absolutely spectacular tonight, Mrs. Beckett."

Her dress is a gorgeous, intricate lace, draped over satin, delicate beading over her perfect ass, leading up to her back, fully exposed and creamy perfection. *Blushing maple*, the shade is called. I don't care what the fuck it's called; my wife is a goddamn masterpiece tonight.

I spin my stunning bride around the ballroom like my sister taught us, and catch sight of her in the corner, hands at her face like she's nervous we're going to mess up at any second, mouthing the counts to each step.

"You say that every night."

"That's because you are. Naked, dressed up, wearing sweats and a messy bun, or nothing but my T-shirt, you're the most beautiful thing these eyes have ever seen. But tonight . . ." I trail my finger down her side and wrap my hand around her hip.

"My dress is too tight."

I pull back to look at her pout, and grin. "It is not."

This dress fits her perfectly. I don't need to inspect it; I've been staring at her in it all damn night. She also caught me red-handed trying to sneak a peek a couple weeks ago in one of the spare bedroom closets. She judo-chopped me so hard I iced my wrist after just to make her feel bad about it. That worked, until she caught me laughing to myself. She slept in pajamas that night and made me keep my hands above the waist.

"I can barely breathe, Carter, and I definitely can't bend over."

"Oh, no." Placating her gets me pretty far these days. "Well then, we should probably get you out of it, ASAP." I make a show of looking around for an exit, or maybe a bathroom. The more I look, the less of a show it is. I'll take her somewhere private right the hell now. "Let's go somewhere I can rip it off you."

"This dress cost an obscene amount of money. You're not ripping it off me. Ever."

"Mmm." We'll see about that. I'll pay to have it sewn back together if I need to. "Planning on wearing it again, are you?"

She flashes me a cheeky grin. "Yes. When I marry my second husband."

"Naughty girl." I slip a palm down her back, letting it curve over the gentle swell of her ass, giving it a little squeeze.

"You realize all two-hundred-plus guests can see your hand on my ass right now, right, Mr. Beckett?"

"Mhmm. I like it, Mrs. Beckett. Let's them know you're mine."

Olivia snorts my favorite giggle. "Think that was the point of the wedding vows they witnessed earlier today."

"My hands all over your luscious body is better. More *in your face*. You know my motto: go big or go home."

Olivia's head drops backward, smoky lids falling shut as she shakes with laughter. "I can't believe how much I love you," she tells me with a soft sigh before touching her lips to mine.

"I think I can't possibly love you more than I do right now, but tomorrow you'll prove me wrong, like you do every day."

I hold her close as I whisper the last few words of our song in her ear and cop one last feel before we take our seats at the head table, and Olivia dabs at her eyes throughout every course as we listen to speeches from our friends and family. It's when

Hank's halfway through his speech that she really starts to lose her shit.

"Carter, son, I know the day we met . . . well, I know it was probably the worst day of your life. And gosh, how I wish we could've met under better circumstances. But, well, meeting you was one of the best things that ever happened to me. I truly believe that Ireland set us on a path to meet, and your dad, too, and I'm grateful every damn day for that. Ireland and I couldn't have kids, and I may not have met you until I was halfway out the door, but the second you walked into my life I knew you were special. You filled a hole in my heart that nobody else could, and I know for damn sure that my Ireland would've loved you, and that your dad is looking down on you today, proud as all hell of the man you've become. Olivia . . . my God. I'm glad I can't see. I can hear you sobbing, and seeing that would break my old heart."

Olivia curls forward with a gurgle of laughter, and I drop my hand to her back, rubbing her smooth, warm skin.

"I knew the second I heard the news that Carter asked a lady to dance at a bar that he'd found the one. Knew right away. The two eyes on my face might not work so well, but the third eye right here"—he taps the space between his brows—"works mighty fine. That boy's been enthralled with you ever since you walked into his life. I've never known a pair more perfectly suited to each other. The way you work so hard to make yourselves better, to be better together, a true team, it's inspiring. I don't have to wish you all the happiness in the world, because I know you've already found it." Hank lifts his glass. "To a love that only grows stronger with age and never ends."

Olivia's out of her seat before I can push back from the table, crashing into Hank with enough force that I'm momentarily concerned the two of them might go tumbling to the ground. But I steady them, joining them and enjoying every second of this group hug.

As the dinner plates get cleared and the chatter is at an all-time high, I lean into my wife's ear. "It's almost time for our speech. Wanna get outta here for a quick five minutes?"

She lifts one knowing brow. "A quick five minutes, or a *quick five minutes*?"

"I'd prefer a long two hours, but a quick five minutes will do."

"You're never quick, and you're certainly never five minutes." And yet she stands anyway, folding her napkin by her plate and pulling me from my chair.

The second I've got her behind a locked door, I pounce, backing her up against the vanity. "I love when you cry."

"What an odd thing to say."

"You're fucking beautiful when you cry. Your eyes turn soft and melty, and they get the prettiest flecks of green and gold in them." I hike her dress up as delicately as I can, shimmy her white lace panties down her legs, and hoist her up on the counter. "Plus, you're such a softie, and I find great pleasure in that. Such a stark contrast from the tough girl you pretend to be."

"I am tough." Her head lolls to the side, tongue dancing across her top lip as she watches me pull out my cock, fisting it at the base, dragging it through her pussy and over her clit. Wet, so wet.

"So tough." I pull her into me, pressing my lips against her collarbone as I sink inside her. "You sat through an entire Sarah McLachlan SPCA commercial the night we met just so you didn't have to make eye contact with me."

"It was torture," she says on a moan, rocking her hips into me. She starts yanking at my tie, fumbling with my buttons. "Off. I want this off."

"Ah-ah," I tsk. "Quick," I remind her. "Five minutes."

My God, nobody pouts like Olivia, all frowny, pushing that bottom lip out as far as it'll go. Laughing, I kiss it right off her face.

"I'm trying so hard not to ruin your hair right now," I grunt out as I pick up speed. "But all I wanna do is stick my hand in there, pull out all those damn pins and tiny little flowers, and fucking . . . *fuck you*. I wanna fuck you so hard and long you can't remember what it feels like to not have me inside of you. I wanna lay you down on our bed, rip this fucking dress off you, and worship every inch of this body until you know what it's like to have every piece of you loved beyond measure."

Olivia whimpers, gripping my shirt in her fist as I rub her clit. "I already know . . . already know what that's like."

"Yeah?" I rest my forehead against hers and watch as she falls apart around me, her body trembling as I thrust once, twice more, and then I fall apart with her.

She touches her lips to mine. "If your love was all I had for the rest of my life, that would be more than enough."

I like that answer a hell of a lot, and by the time we're presentable enough, we make our way back into the ballroom.

My sister looks us over with pure disgust. "Oh, yuck. You two totally just had sex."

"We did not," Olivia insists at the exact same time I exclaim, "Sure as shit did."

Jennie rolls her eyes and gags, stalking off to her seat.

"We're ready for the champagne toast, Mr. Beckett," our hostess tells me as we find our way back to our table. "Would you like us to serve it now, or hold off 'til after dessert?"

"Now is perfect. Thank you."

Once the champagne is distributed and I have the microphone in my hand—Olivia says I don't need one because I'm loud enough, but, pfft—we take our place in front of our friends and family. A server comes by with one last tray, offering a glass of champagne to Olivia.

"Oh, no. No alcohol for her." I place a protective hand over her belly. "Isn't that right, little mama?"

"*Carter!*" Olivia gasps, and the dangerous slant of her eyes and pursed, cherry red lips tell me—wedding night and all—this girl might murder me, right here, right now.

"What?" I ask as innocently as I can manage, because I don't want to die tonight, but I've obviously made a huge mistake I'm not aware of.

My eyes fall over her face, the expression that only seems to grow more outraged by the second, to my hand on the tiny swell of her little belly that you can only really see when she's naked, the one I can never seem to take my eyes off of at home, and finally, out to the crowd, our family and friends, their shocked but happy faces.

Because I just told all two hundred and fifty of our guests that my wife can't drink alcohol.

Somehow, my lovely lady manages to narrow her eyes way past the point of what seems possible. Is she even seeing me still?

"*One rule,*" she scolds me in that whisper-yell teacher voice of hers that has the power to make all six foot four of me cower. "You had one rule tonight."

I did. One rule.

Don't tell anyone about the baby I accidentally put in my wife over the summer.

And I thought I could do it. Really, I did.

Cara and Jennie are cackling because they knew I couldn't. I catch Adam sigh, slipping a bill to both Garrett and Emmett, who look about as smug as I normally do.

Well. I fucked up.

I dig deep, as deep as I can, and conjure up my most charming grin, extra dimply, the one that's been known to get me out of trouble. I watch the anger dissipate, melting off Olivia's gorgeous face.

And I lift my shoulders in a shrug that's anything but innocent. "Oops."

Acknowledgments

To my husband, for gracefully accepting his place as number two, because Carter Beckett doesn't know how to share the stage. Thank you for your love and support.

To my girl gang—Erin, Hannah, and Ki—thank you for being with me every step of the way, and for always keeping me laughing.

Paisley, there aren't enough words in the English language to convey how grateful I am for your expertise and hard work in helping me tell Carter and Olivia's story. How did we get here from passing notes back in sixth grade and endless sleepovers? So lucky to have you.

Louise, thank you for holding my hand through this very fun—but also scary—process, and for your hard work and dedication.

Anthea and Sarah, thank you for seeing what I see in my little Vipers family, and for helping me spread the love. So lucky to work with you two.

Miss Bizzarro, thank you for being the kind of teacher who inspires and encourages her students to go after their dreams, who makes them feel capable and confident. One day, years ago, you told me I could, so I did.

To you, my readers, thank you. I may not do it perfectly, but I pour my heart and soul into my stories, and I hope you can feel that. Thank you, from the bottom of my heart, for being here with me.

And finally, to my big brother. I hope you know I chased my dream because of you. I love you, and I miss you.

The Consider Me Playlist

1. "Something Like Olivia" – John Mayer
2. "Good For You" – Josh Gracin
3. "Consider Me" – Allen Stone
4. "I'm With You" – Vance Joy
5. "Can I Kiss You?" – Dahl
6. "Shape of You" – Ed Sheeran
7. "Yours in the Morning" – Patrick Droney
8. "Saturday Sun" – Vance Joy
9. "You & Me" – James TW
10. "Cross Me" – Ed Sheeran, ft. Chance the Rappe & PnB Rock
11. "Half of My Heart" – John Mayer
12. "Conversations in the Dark" – John Legend
13. "Let's Stay Home Tonight" – Needtobreathe
14. "Coulda Loved You Longer" – Adam Dollar
15. "If It Weren't For You" – Finmar
16. "Slow Dancing in a Burning Room" – John Mayer
17. "Try Losing One" – Tyler Braden
18. "Please Keep Loving Me" – James TW
19. "Speechless" – Dan + Shay
20. "Until You" – Ahi
21. "Millionaire" – Chris Stapleton
22. "Yours (Wedding Edition)" – Russell Dickerson

About the Author

BECKA MACK IS AN AVID romance reader, writer, and kindergarten teacher. Growing up, Becka's ambition was to be able to create a dream world for readers to slip into, a place to escape and fall in love, much like the ones she enjoyed getting lost in herself. It wasn't until the unexpected loss of her brother that Becka finally decided to put pen to paper and pursue her dream, because she knew life was too short to live it any other way. Becka enjoys writing swoon-worthy romance with lovable and relatable characters, loads of humor, and a healthy dose of drama on the way to a happily ever after. She lives with her husband, children, and four-legged babies in Ontario, Canada. For more, visit beckamack.com.